Miller's Rules

Grateful recognition is given to Jack Radcliffe, creator of the Frontispiece artwork.

1-7-2001

Buck,
Thanks for all the advice & direction you gave me during those first years — you've no idea how much it helped. My very best to you & yours and I look forward to seeing you in the islands.
— Wade

Miller's Rules
A Novel

Wade Tabor

Writers Club Press
San Jose New York Lincoln Shanghai

Miller's Rules

All Rights Reserved © 2000 by Wade Tabor

No part of this book may be reproduced or transmitted in any form or by any means, graphic, electronic, or mechanical, including photocopying, recording, taping, or by any information storage or retrieval system, without the permission in writing from the publisher.

Published by Writers Club Press
an imprint of iUniverse.com, Inc.

For information address:
iUniverse.com, Inc.
620 North 48th Street
Suite 201
Lincoln, NE 68504-3467
www.iuniverse.com

This novel is a work of fiction. All characters and events portrayed herein are fictitious, and any resemblance to any actual persons living or dead is purely coincidental.

ISBN: 0-595-09399-X

Printed in the United States of America

Dedication

For Shannon, whose beauty makes my knees weak.
You are my world, little butterfly.

Epigraph

Adapt yourself to the environment in which your lot has been cast.
           Marcus Aurelius, *Meditations*

There's rules.
     Scott Alalof, December 31, 1994

Acknowledgments

I owe a debt of gratitude to a number of people, and want to take a moment to thank them here: My incredible wife and best friend, Shannon, supports me in all I do. Professors Fox, Matalene, and Rhu read and edited various versions of the book and provided me with helpful insight and criticism. Dr. Patrick Nolan, of The University of South Carolina, went through it with a red pencil, slashing and burning, making it a better book along the way. Jack Radcliffe did a terrific job on the frontispiece, and he did so at a moment's notice. Dr. Michael Tabor, Dad to me, kept the medical stuff straight, though I still bent the rules a little.

Scott Alalof, for the past thirteen years of trust, friendship, and support, for his contagious faith in serendipity, and most of all for being there when it counted. This writer will never find words worthy of those years; a thank you and a hug will have to do.

Pat Villegas, who turned coffee into beer, and whose prophetic words in '92 kept me going through years when little else did; Will Andrew and Mark Ellis, and all the Southern summer nights spent popping tops in a Pee Dee breeze, where there is no gray in the color gray; Patti and Tom Allman, who did for me a greater service than they could ever know; Sonny and Joye Peagler, who entrusted me with the most precious of treasures; Grannie and Pop, who make our world a brighter place; Weezy, who will always be for me a toothless five year old with blonde pigtails and chubby thighs; Mama T. and Grandaddy, whose blood I am so proud to call my own; Clyde Taylor, who indulged me and listened, even though it didn't turn my way; and Officer Craven of Augusta, Georgia, who isn't likely to have a clue why he's mentioned here. On a cold January night he showed me something and made a promise, and the amazing thing is he had it on the nail; My friend and mentor Scott Kaple, who eased my way into the Fort (though he let me sweat a bit along the way) and who, along with Buck Creighton and Keith Guess, continue to help me keep it straight now that I'm inside; Ben Greer deserves a particular note of thanks for opening this dark chest of wonders so many years ago, and encouraging me to take a peak inside. You had it right all along, old friend.

And none of this could have happened without the encouragement and the support, from day one, of my mother and father, who have always left the light on. I realize every day how much you've done—and continue to do—for me. I hope to one day figure out a way to properly tell you how grateful I am, and how much I love you.

...Oh, yes. A special mention for my muse and little buddy, Roma, who sat with me through all the nights silent save the singing of the keys.

One final note...thanks to Carsten Stroud, who had the good sense to write *Sniper's Moon*, Miller's—and my—favorite novel. If I'm ever in Thunder Beach, the Beck's is on me.

Chapter 1

29 Days Before   (November 7)

He'd heard that all crimes, whether against man, nature, God, or state, have at their most base level a defining moment, a time of clarity when the players involved are able to remove themselves from the events, even as they assemble and assimilate with hurricane-like ferocity. It was here, he believed—this time of clarity—that the die of character was cast.

English Mason, 22, a senior majoring in finance at the University of Chicago, decided this on November 7, and after that, everything changed.

A man had died and he had played a hand in it. The extent to which he was responsible was, he knew, arguable, but resting quietly within the rational part of his mind was the realization that had he never been born, others would today still be alive.

As it all progressed—the discovery of the body, the uncovering of the cover-up, the convening of the grand jury, and ultimately the trial—the guilt began to take its toll. He thought he could deal with it, that with Amanda's help he might be able to work his way around it, or through it, or whichever way it took to avoid the brunt of it and somehow go about the business of leading a normal life, if it wasn't for Miller. Miller Dispenberg, his friend of almost a decade. Miller Dispenberg, double-murderer.

If it had been for money, English would have understood. Money wasn't noble, wasn't worth dying for, and was even less worth killing for, but at least there would have been some logic to it all if there was cash involved. And English supposed there may have been for anyone else; the total purse for Wallace's death was, if Miller's calculations were near, somewhere around the two million dollar mark, enough money, English imagined, for any number of people in the world to cheerfully kill any number of others. There would have been some sense there, or, at the very least, some reason for the senselessness. That Miller seemed wholly uninterested in the money simply served to compound the problem for English. There was reason to fear one who is motivated by an impalpable incentive, one who acts without remorse.

If it had been done for jealousy, hatred, or revenge—that eldest of malignant motives—English thought he could have gotten behind it to an extent. Miller was, after all, his best friend.

He'd saved English's life once, six or seven years back. It was a car wreck, the memory of which still made English's stomach roil with nausea. English had been switching CDs somewhere in the city over the Thanksgiving holiday when he was broadsided by a minivan carrying a family of six over the river and through the woods to grandmother's house in Gary, Indiana. The driver of the minivan—a wealthy lawyer in life, something less in death—his wife, and one of the three children—a newborn, as it turned out, on her first trip to grandma's—were killed in the crash. One of the other children lived three days at the hospital before slipping softly into a coma and finally dying, but not before the remainder of her family, Gary, Indiana's grandmother among them, had the opportunity to eat hospital turkey and dressing and cranberry sauce with plastic forks as they sat sleepless in her room, watching the machines beep and blink and wondering how one little girl could have so many tubes and wires running through her.

English had been lucky. The van had clipped the front end of his Mustang, sending the car pinwheeling through the intersection and into a parked city bus. Two of the ribs on his left side had been fractured; his spleen was ruptured. All of the fingers on his right hand were broken against the steering wheel, but that wasn't the problem. His femur had been severed through, the thick, meaty arteries running its length torn in two, pumping heart's blood into his thigh in blue-red spurts. That was the problem. He lost over half his blood in the ambulance, and was given seventy units of donor blood during the course of the night. Amanda, his parents, professors, relatives, friends, and others came to the hospital to donate. Miller would have as well, had he not been in need of transfusions himself. He had been in the car with English when the van had struck—his sternum cracked, his nose a pulpy mass, his eyes burning as they filled with blood—but had remained conscious long enough to reach into the warm muscle of English's thigh and hold the two ends of bone in place with one hand. He'd heard the echoes of sirens wailing somewhere in the distance, and the buzzing chatter of people talking nearby, yelling something to him—*hold on, hold on, help's coming, don't move*—before he passed out.

The EMTs said there wasn't much doubt that Miller had saved his friend's life that afternoon. What they didn't say, what no one would know for another six or seven years, was that others would die because of it.

So if someone had wronged Miller in some way, it would have been incumbent upon English to help Miller do whatever Miller thought he had to do to set things straight. Revenge was a dangerous business, but it was something English could, if not completely respect, at least understand. Besides, they were friends, and Miller would have done it for him. He had already proven that.

But revenge had nothing to do with Wallace's death.

As near as English could tell, there was nothing in Miller's life, despite how thinly you cared to stretch things, how far you wanted to reach, that had anything to do with Wallace, his life or death.

What did you gain, Miller? English found himself wondering countless times throughout those days. What good—what *anything*—came of it, besides pain?

And it was this, more than anything else, which bothered English Mason about the whole ordeal. The sheer pointlessness of it all.

This, and fear.

And now, on November 7, sitting on the same dock they had fished from since middle school, English stumbled—fell into, he would later tell Amanda, much the way one falls into an unseen hole in the ground—upon the defining moment of their crime, saw for the first time with clarity the path down which he would have to venture before all this was over, and he knew he had never really had a choice to begin with; you are what you are, and when all is said and done all you really have is a list of things you won't do. Everything else you make up as you go.

He was sitting next to Miller, holding his fishing rod, thinking this when Miller said, "you talking today, or do we just do this silent treatment thing?"

English shrugged.

"What's on your mind?" Miller pressed.

English sat in silence a while longer before saying, "The weight of the world, Mill."

Miller's brown hair was blown back away from his head by the breeze.

"Ah. So it's the trial." He said. "Palto, perhaps."

English tugged the line and wiped a film of sweat from his brow. He shoved his thoughts aside and nodded. "The trial, Palto, the rest of it. How do you find the strength to think of anything else?"

He could see Miller next to him out of the corner of his eye, could see him staring off across the lake into the sky.

"I'm terrified," English said.

Miller exhaled and watched the water ripple. He had heard somewhere that water ripples went on forever, expanding indefinitely, free of boundaries or constraints, right into the side of the bank. He liked the way that sounded.

"Amanda's pissed at me all the time now," English continued. "She's worrying herself to death over this Wallace business. The lawyers this, the police that. The goddam news media's everywhere. I'm going crazy listening to her. She cries if I look at her wrong these days."

Miller cleared his throat and spit into the water. "That's what happens when you stay with the same girl too long. They get used to things being a certain way, to the rhythm and rhyme of day-in, day-out. When something comes along and upsets their peace and order they fall apart. Amanda's worse about it than most. You have to juggle things around a bit. Keep it all fresh."

English let that go; ordinarily he would have had a hell of a lot to say about that. He didn't care much for anyone—and particularly Miller—telling him what Amanda did and didn't like, but he didn't have the energy today. His moment of clarity had cost him.

So instead he sighed and slumped his shoulders and said nothing. He pulled on his reel a bit and wondered if he had the stuff to see this whole thing through. He thought he might, but he didn't know what the price would be, only that if it involved Amanda he'd never be able to pay it.

But despite all of this he felt familiar warmth building inside. If he pushed the reality of their situation back into the black spaces of his mind he could almost enjoy being out here with Miller like this, fishing and drinking Beck's beneath the sun, the November air cold and thin against their skin, the wind pulling a pink shade to their cheeks and feathering through their hair. They didn't do this much anymore, not since it all went down at Grand Beach. Each of them had gotten caught up in their individual lives, which lately were taking roads traveling in any direction but the same. Even without the impending trial, they were both occupied with final exams and job interviews and all the rest of it. Miller was applying to Yale Law, and would get it if everything cleared up in time. He'd been preparing since middle school for it.

English was less sure of what he would be doing this time next year. He was considering a Master's in marketing, maybe an M.B.A, or perhaps an end to the school scene for a while in lieu of gainful employment. Take some time to make a little money, pay down his student loans a bit. He tried to picture himself in that crowd, suiting up every morning in a Botany 500 or a Brooks Bros., riding the subway into the city with the other four million nine to fivers while he rubbed elbows and wingtips with a bunch of wooden lawyers and accountants that smelled of new leather and Old Spice. Whatever it was, he'd be doing it here in Chicago; Amanda was a junior in a five year nursing program, and neither of them were enamoured with the prospect of a long-distance relationship. Aside from the trial—which was taking its toll on their relationship on an almost daily basis, a growing and omnipresent irritant that refused to go away, refused to be ignored—things were going too well for them lately. They had entered that smooth, comfortable phase of the relationship that came after years—almost seven—of being inseparable, where she didn't hold back in bed and he didn't worry about closing the door to take a piss. He had spent the summer kicking around the idea of asking her to marry him, and had decided to give her a ring sometime around the new year before whoever was in charge upstairs pulled off their celestial britches and decided to take a shit on his life.

"These next few weeks won't be fun,"—Miller, gazing across the hammered-copper surface of the lake, spitting into it and watching the ripples—"my lawyer says we should pray Palto pushes for the death penalty. Says it won't happen, but pray anyway. No Illinois jury has convicted someone like me in a capital case since the turn of the century." Miller looked out over the water and spit again.

"Someone like you?"

Miller nodded. "Young. White. Educated. Good family, clean record, the whole deal."

"They'll be going for life, Mill. As in forever. You might want to consider your options while you can. While there's still time. I don't know…maybe disappear or something. Hope they get tired of looking for you."

Miller didn't say anything to that, and English found that strange at first.

As the weeks passed and things began moving at what would in retrospect seem twice their normal speed, pushing each day into the next until it was all just a steady blur, English would wonder if Miller knew something he wasn't telling him, if he had some sort of plan resting in the wrinkles and folds of his mind, waiting for the lights to dim before making its entrance. He would decide later—too late, perhaps, depending with whom your loyalties lie—that yes, he probably did. Miller always had an angle.

It wasn't in Miller's nature to sit back and let others decide his fate. English's parents, particularly his father, had pushed from the beginning for English to testify, advice to which English had summarily turned a deaf ear, saying something about how of the multitude of options he may or may not have had, betrayal wasn't one of them.

But then Amanda began suggesting it, and English had begun listening to her. It was nothing outright in the beginning, Amanda having always moved more subtly, more quietly, like a whisper of silence or a gesture in the dark, for as long as he'd known her. A hint there, a gentle nudge in this direction or that. English didn't like that Amanda wanted him to testify, didn't want to accept that she felt the way she felt, primarily because he knew that if Amanda thought it was the right way to go, it probably was. He believed, though he had never told her, that she was smarter than he, and he knew, as much as he knew anything in life, that she was good and pure and decent to the core.

English had to assume Miller would expect Amanda to have some influence over him, and he would certainly know which side of the line she would fall when it came to her decision. The papers were billing English's testimony as the coup de grace, the piece of evidence likely to put the prosecution over the top. Miller's charm would go a long way with the jury—he could work emotions out of people as well as any actor English had ever seen—but it wouldn't get past the story English would be telling them. English expected Miller knew that, as well. Wondering what Miller intended to do about it—and you could be sure he'd do something—kept English up at night.

He had only to look in Nicole's direction if he doubted Miller's willingness to encourage silence, or his adeptness at succeeding.

He tried to keep it shut out—the idea of testifying against Miller. He tried not to think about Miller's reaction. He told himself Miller wouldn't try to prevent it, and it took more than he was able to give to make himself believe it. So he gave up on the lie and concentrated on just keeping it shut out.

The one time English had asked Miller what had gone through his mind the moment he pulled the trigger and sent the bullets into the cop's face and stomach, Miller's look had turned to stone and his eyes had gone some place inward and he had said in a voice completely void of regret, "not missing."

When English had pressed him, Miller had explained further.

"I didn't want to do it, but things had gotten out of hand. I hadn't much of a choice. We were in the center of what was turning out to be a very nasty shitstorm, and I was looking at it from the cop's point of view. All he knows is there's a robbery in progress at the Wallace place and he and his partner are in the middle of the woods without any backup. So he's got his gun out, and he's about as keyed up and on edge as a man can get. If I'd given him the chance, he would've popped me and saved the wonder-why's for the paperwork afterwards. So I got him first. I took no pleasure in it. I had no choice. It was a clear case of him or me, and I did what I had to do to make sure it wasn't me."

There, English thought, feeling the blood drain from his face. There's the rub.

(It was a clear case of him or me)

Miller was a lot of things, but he wasn't the kind of person to let someone—best friend or no—testifying against him slide.

(I did what I had to do to make sure it wasn't me)

English pushed those thoughts away again. He told himself he didn't have time for that kind of thing. He had job applications to fill out, recommendations to gather. He had a future to plan. These were the things he needed to keep his mind focused on. It was the only way he'd keep his sanity. The system had Miller now, and all he had to do was stand back and let the system work.

Right.

Miller reached across and tassled his friend's hair.

"Don't worry so much," he said for the fiftieth time since it all broke open. "Just sit back and watch the show with the rest of them. Nobody's after you. It's me they want." Miller's face went hard. "Everybody wants a shot at the title."

There was nothing to say so English said it. That was the one part of it all that he didn't want to discuss, not with anybody, and certainly not with Miller. It was true. They didn't want him, not directly. Although he hadn't said as much, English knew Michael Palto, the District Attorney, wanted to use him as a tool, a connection to Miller Dispenberg. Miller knew it, too. Palto and his band of legal-eagles wanted to use English as their doorway into the dark and convoluted mind of Miller Dispenberg, the Chicago-native who had, quite rapidly, risen from relative obscurity in the halls of academia into the spotlight of statewide media attention.

No, English thought, trying to refocus his mind on simpler days, days when all that mattered were Friday afternoons in the city, Saturday mornings at the dock, and Amanda on Saturday nights. Days when nothing much really counted except the size skirt Nicole Henderson wore to the party that weekend, or the number of beers he and Miller could drink standing on their heads. Days before Palto, before the District Attorney's office, before "Grand Beach" and "Kenilworth" became household words, taking Miller and English with them. No, his mind repeated again and again and again, as though it found some form of twisted solace in the fact, they weren't after him.

No, not me, English thought, forcing himself to not glance across at Miller. As Palto himself had put it on the evening news—back when it became clear to English that they weren't going to get away with what happened at Wallace's place in Kenilworth that day, that their secrets were no longer safe—speaking slowly and deliberately into the camera like a candidate for higher office, his face shining with intensity and confidence, Palto was going after the big dog.

The following morning a haircut for Channel 9 News caught Miller on the Chicago campus as he was walking to his car, and had asked him what he thought about that, about an aggressive prosecutor like Michael Palto referring to him as the big dog, and pledging to come after him with everything he had. Miller had glanced at the reporter like he was something slithering across his back porch on a warm night and managed a terse "no comment."

"Do you have a plan?" English asked, not looking at his friend.

Miller shrugged.

"Have you thought of—" English interrupted himself. It was a stupid question. Miller thought of everything. There wasn't much he missed. It was what made him Miller.

Miller chuckled. "I think Palto's thought of enough, don't you?"

English nodded. There was a solid minute of uncomfortable silence between the two. "What I meant was—"

"I know what you meant. And yes. I've thought of everything."

English waited in the center of the miserable silence, wanting to let it go but needing to know just as much.

"And?" He ventured.

Miller said, "well I'm sure as hell not going to make it easy for them."

He rolled back on his buttocks and slid his feet beneath, standing, brushing his jeans off with his hands.

He stood there, staring at English beneath the bone-yellow sunlight.

"They want to waltz into my life with their pious rules and their rhetoric and do all they can to run it through a shredder like so much shit…" he stopped, stared far across the lake, seeming to consider something for a moment, then said, his voice a whisper, "I've got something for them if they push too hard."

"What?" English asked, already knowing.

Miller looked at him, his eyes stone, and it was that look—the hardness of it, the sheer will festering behind it—that English would carry with him through the days that lay ahead.

"Me," he said.

* * *

Friday night, a little before midnight and over seven hours after English and Miller returned from the dock, twenty-one year old Amanda Peterson sat before her vanity mirror in the bedroom she had grown up in and did her best to hold the tears at bay once more. As with the night before, and the night before that, and every night since Kenilworth and Grand Beach, she failed.

A thin girl, with long blond hair that was at the moment pulled back into a tight pony-tail and tied with a white ribbon, she sat at the far end of her large, pink bedroom and hoped she had locked her door. Her textbooks and notepads and pens and anatomical charts were scattered around the room like toys in a nursery. There were occasionally times during college when she wished she hadn't decided to stay at home, that she had done what English had pressed for and gotten her own place, but never had she wanted more to be anywhere but here than lately, now, when all of this, whatever this was, was crumbling down around her. She checked her door again, made sure it was locked. Things were bad enough lately; she didn't think she could stomach her mother's endless questions, no matter how honest her intentions. She wasn't sure which was worse, her mother's nagging, almost meddling concern for her or her father's blatant indifference to the whole affair. He had never cared for English, not since the beginning, and had never cared enough to give Amanda a reasonable explanation why. To him the investigation and trial was just more news, another headline in his evening paper. From somewhere buried deeply within her festered the realization that she would, when all of this was over, have to learn to forgive him for that.

With a gentle defiance she framed her face with her hands and squeezed her eyes closed until it hurt, as if forbidding the tears to fall. But worse than the tears, worse, even, than the looming possibility of the days to come, was the relentless onslaught of memories—memories of her and English together before the Wallace thing, a time that seemed now an eternity ago. Amanda Peterson would come to learn in the following weeks that remembrance was a dangerous, painful draught, and she would discipline herself to shy from all but the smallest drop.

But now there was no such knowledge, no such discipline, and she did remember, and what memories came and could be separated and deciphered from one another she held to fast—fractured glimpses of what might have been. She and English had been an item almost from the beginning, and it seemed she had loved him even longer. It would be seven years this Christmas.

She glanced over at her calendar and saw the small box outlined in red. Twenty nine days. That's all he had left. That's all *they* had left. The totality of their relationship, a relationship Amanda had for as long as she could remember wanted to mold into a permanent fixture in her life, was coming to a dramatic and indelible end as she knew it.

Twenty-nine more days.

Less than a month.

She cried herself to sleep that night as she had all the others since Kenilworth, and slept restlessly until English's call woke her.

*　　*　　*

When he had gotten off the phone with Amanda, English Mason walked down the middle of the dirt road until he came to the eleventh telephone pole. He checked his watch and noted the time. Two-twenty-two in the a.m. A casual glance over a shoulder suggested that he was alone and had sufficient time to do what he had come out here to do and get back home.

He began digging with the small fold-away shovel, stopping several moments later when the hard metal nose of the tool struck solid wood. He removed his gloves and blew into his hands, rubbing them together. He bent over and began scraping the remains of the dirt with his hands, wet slivers of it imbedding themselves beneath his nails as he scooped it away, flinging it over his shoulder. Crumbs of it slid down the back of his jacket.

Once the top of the small wooden box had been exposed—roughly a foot and a half beneath the earth's surface—he removed from his coat pocket a bag, opened the box, dumped the contents of the bag into the box, and recovered the box with dirt.

There.

His prints were on it now.

He began to walk away, unwilling to consider the implications—the permanence—of what he had just done.

Now, he thought, his insides burning and his throat tight with bile, now it's for real, and now we'll see who wants it more.

* * *

Miller Dispenberg, twenty-two years old and days away from being handed an indictment from the grandest of grand-juries, lay eight miles away in his bed in the two bedroom apartment he and English had shared for the past three years, and tried for another night to find sleep. He had begun going to bed earlier and earlier as the insomnia progressed. Tonight he had turned off the light and buried himself beneath the covers at a quarter after nine, swallowing two halcyon with Gatorade to help things along. He had over fifty pages of Beowulf that there would in all probability be a quiz on in lit tomorrow, plus an oral presentation on the evolving role of the Secretary of State in a post-cold war democratic government, but he didn't have the energy to make himself sit down and look over any of it. He was tired. The events of the past few weeks were taking their toll. Miller had begun to believe that of all the players in the Wallace thing, the most fortunate by far was Wallace himself. At least it was over for him.

Miller turned and rubbed his temples with the heels of his hands. His neck and lower back had begun hurting from the stress; his head throbbed more often than not lately. There were times when the pain was so bad he wouldn't make it to the bathroom before the vomit came. The doctors said it was—all of it—from worrying and fear. Whether it was or it wasn't Miller didn't know or care much; he just wanted it to go away.

Last week, when the pieces he had been struggling to find began to resemble something he could fit together and work with, the headaches had begun to subside a bit.

That was good. That meant there was a chance.

He understood that it was going to be difficult to pull off, and that to think of it as anything other than a long shot was to indulge in the optimism of fools, but still there was a possibility, and no matter how slim it was it was more than he had a week ago.

But he would need help.

This kind of thing wasn't done without cooperation.

He heard English come in from his night with Amanda a little after ten, heard him leave again to who knew where sometime after two, and heard him come back at three-thirty. He debated getting out of bed and talking to him a bit, try to set him at ease a little. For as long as Miller had known him, English had been the type to let things eat at him until he worked himself sick. And that silly girlfriend of his, she didn't help things along much, the way she was about every little thing in the world. Miller didn't think Amanda would be happy if she didn't have something to worry herself with.

He laughed in the darkness. Poor Amanda. This must be one extended orgasm for her. She and English should be having a regular ball, worrying each other to death with talk of lost futures and stolen youth and such.

Miller listened to the sounds of English's routine through the wall that separated their rooms. Run the tap, brush the teeth, rinse and spit, tap the water off the toothbrush against the sink (always two taps), take a piss, flush, set the clock on the bureau then the one on the nightstand, cough once or twice, then shut out the light. The same thing, every night. Order and harmony, English's staple.

Listening to English he realized he had forgotten to brush his teeth again. He was doing that sort of thing more and more often lately, forgetting the little things. He wondered if this was a bad sign, or merely a symptom of his perennial distraction. He thought about getting up to do it but decided against it, figuring English would feel like he had to come in and talk to him, and figuring that that wouldn't be good for either of them right now. They had gone out beneath the bridge earlier this afternoon after they had finished fishing, passing a bottle of whiskey between them and chewing on cigars, and the misery and almost tangible fear of the upcoming trial had been like an undercurrent running through their conversation, a steady hum of electricity laced through the silence between their words. Both of them had felt it and both of them had grown more and more uncomfortable with it. It seemed that was all there was to talk about anymore.

* * *

Nine miles to the west of Miller and English's apartment, beneath a black and white bed of stars that shone down upon Chicago and the rest of Illinois, rested the Our Lady of Perpetual Peace Cemetery.

J. Fullard Wallace lies dead out here, a man who died, many would tell you, years before his time in a way men of his stature shouldn't die. A man worth millions in life, he lies face up, like all the other eternal residents of Perpetual Peace, hands folded across his chest, eyelids pulled down till they meet their mates, face drawn into a mask of contentment and peaceful resignation, aided by the skills of several talented morticians. They had earned their pay with Wallace's corpse. Nearly sixty percent of his skin surface had been gone when they brought him in, the majority of his gut rotted out. His face had been minus the fleshy cheek pads, but they had touched that up nicely with cotton balls and putty.

But of this Wallace is unaware. His problems are over, and perhaps no one—not wife, child, friend, nor coworker—wishes that he were alive more than do Miller Dispenberg and English Mason, for he left behind a legacy with which they've found themselves forced to deal.

If it is possible to be happy in death, then Wallace is, for he died doing what he loved best, and doing it with vigor with someone he had, since first seeing her several weeks earlier, wanted very badly to do it with.

J. Fullard Wallace had not previously known Miller Dispenberg, nor English Mason, nor Nicole Henderson, nor any of the rest of that crowd and this is, ultimately, what did him in. He had spent the first fifty-seven years of his life wholly ignorant of their existence. He had a wife, two sons, and three daughters. There was some speculation throughout parts of Illinois that the congenial Mr. Wallace had sired his share of bastards across the Midwest, but such was only rumor, and generally not taken seriously. All things told, Wallace was a good man, a kind man, a caring man. He was a faithful member of First Methodist, sat on several corporate and civic organizations, and had loved his wife dearly.

Had he been stopped one fine afternoon on his way to the office, sitting comfortably, perhaps enviably to some, behind the wheel of his mint green BMW, and presented with the simple question, *how do you like this perfect life you've made,* he would have most likely smiled and said he liked it fine. It would have been the truth; J. Fullard Wallace was a happy man throughout those fifty-seven years.

On his fifty-eighth birthday his wife threw an extraordinary party for him, a preview of the extravaganza to be given in his honor upon retirement on his fifty-ninth. He and his wife had planned it like that from the start. Even before law school, before the day Mrs. Wallace often referred to as the happiest of her life—her marriage to Fullard—that had been the plan. Graduation from law, a cushy job making God's own fortune, and retirement on birthday number fifty-nine. They had a small cabin near the water at Grand Beach, Michigan, in which they were going to live as they left prime-time and entered late-night together.

On the fifth day of his fifty-eighth year, his path had crossed, quite blamelessly, that of Miller Dispenberg. Neither had been searching for the other. Wallace had not known it at the time, and, in truth, it wasn't until much later that he recalled the exact moment when he and the

Dispenberg boy met. The absurdity of the encounter bothered him until the end—he was not tormented for long, however; by this point the end was only minutes away.

On the tenth day of his fifty-eighth year, he did something that would alter the course of his life forever, though once again Wallace did not come to recognize, or regret, this fact until it was too late.

On day twenty, three hundred and forty five days before retirement, he became aware of what it was that was occurring around him, realized that he was more than just a key player in the awesome actions and events that were assimilating like mad—that he had, in fact, set them in motion himself. On the heels of this came the understanding that it was too late. His epiphany occurred in a moment of utter and exquisite pain, when he was posed with that same question, *how do you like this perfect life you've made?*

Of course, by this time, he hadn't been able to say much at all.

J. Fullard Wallace had been fifty-eight years old for twenty days when he died, and it is solely because of this fact—that he was dead—that he had no interest in the proceedings of the trial that was to commence in twenty-nine days, on December 6th.

It could be argued, however, that had Wallace been alive—or had a few others been dead—there would be no trial. There wasn't much Miller could do about Wallace not being alive. There was a lot he wanted to do about others not being dead. But that, much like the sequence of events that led to District Attorney Palto successfully indicting and arraigning Miller Thadius Dispenberg on charges of first-degree murder, is the subject of this story.

CHAPTER 2

(Two and a half months earlier)
105 Days Before   (August 23)

Nicole Henderson checked herself in the mirror one final time when the doorbell rang, then crossed the living room of her townhouse and opened the door. She was wearing a tight blue denim mini-skirt, black flats, and a tight-fitting aqua shirt tucked into the skirt.

"Hello, Miller," she said, opening the door, smiling. "I was beginning to wonder if you'd changed your mind."

"Wow," said Miller, wiping his shoes on the mat and stepping inside, leaning over to kiss her on the mouth as he passed. "Don't you look the part?"

"Thank you," she said, closing the door after him and watching his butt as he walked. "I suppose."

She noticed the bag in his hands. "My, my. Is this the new you, bearing gifts and such?"

Miller set the case of Zima Gold on the dining room table and laid the single rose beside it. A few tiny droplets of water fell from the leaves to the table's surface.

"I was in a weak mood when you called. Who says chivalry's dead, hhmmm?" Nicole glanced at the Zimas. "And Malt liquor at that? This must have set you back at least a ten-spot."

"Eleven-fifty."

"And they say Jews are cheap. New shirt?"

"I guess," Miller shrugged. "Tracie bought it for me a while back. Figured I needed to wear it."

"How is darling Tracie these days? Still sexy as ever?"

Miller shrugged. "She's a doll," he said. "Entirely too sweet to be with me."

"We are all entirely too sweet to be with you," Nicole said, then opened the case of drinks and handed Miller one. She opened one for herself, downing half of it in a single elegant swallow as she left the living room for the kitchen. "Help yourself to a chair. The remote's on the coffee table."

She disappeared into the kitchen and Miller settled back into a lazyboy. It was a nice place, Nicole's new condo. She had moved here from her apartment a couple of months ago. Miller had been to a few parties here since then, but this was the first time he'd come alone. Tracie thought he was out with Laney and English, which was fine. She didn't need to know too much of what went on at Nicole's. No one did, far as that was concerned.

"You don't mind living alone?" Miller called from the lazyboy, flicking through the channels, settling finally on Headline News.

"No," Nicole said, reappearing from the kitchen with a vase half-filled with water. She slid the rose into the vase and brought the vase over to the coffee table. "I did the roommate thing for four years of undergrad and one of law. It's time I had a little space to myself, don't you think?"

Miller shrugged. "The old man didn't mind?"

"I'm not sure," she said, sitting on the couch opposite Miller. "Doesn't matter much, really, so long as he signs the checks."

Nicole's father was David Henderson, an exceedingly successful corporate lawyer in a city overrun with them, a narrow-shouldered man with a pinched face and a head for numbers who was rumored throughout the circles where rumors matter to have made somewhere around the million and a half dollar mark last year. Nicole liked the money, liked what it could do for her, but she had always been thankful that she had gotten the one thing her father's money couldn't buy—though, she mused, with the wonders of suction and saline, even this was changing—from her mother. With short, auburn hair that fell just above her shoulders, full, naturally red lips, legs forever and all of it covered with skin that glowed like ivory glazed in gold, Nicole had never had to work for the attention of others. Until she started law school a year ago she had been one of the top two or three gymnasts in the state, as well as captain of the girls diving team at Chicago for four years, setting the NCAA record for the ten meter platform her senior year. When she walked the muscles in her thighs and calves rippled, and, Miller had discovered years back, occasionally returning to reaffirm the truth of the experience, you could count her stomach muscles with your tongue on the way down.

Miller and Nicole had had an on again, off again thing of sorts for a number of years, through college, all the way back to high-school. Each of them was often involved with someone else, as they were now, but theirs was a relationship that was quietly understood, if not openly acknowledged. She had been his first over six years ago, his sophomore year of high-school, her senior. He had been her third, but was still, six and a half years later—every orifice having been visited a myriad of times by a multitude of men since then, mornings following drunken nights where she'd awaken, hair and skin sticky, all apertures drying and covered with white stuff of varying consistency having become, if not the norm, not quite the exception, either—the only one that had ever mattered to her. She had fancied herself in love with him a few years ago, but Miller had, as Miller did, kept her at a distance, for reasons he would never share.

Nicole was about a year into a weekend and holiday relationship with a football player at Notre Dame named Rock or Fist or something similar, and Miller was seeing a cute little number named Tracie he had met over beers at a downtown club a couple months back. She was a senior at the University, majoring in Elementary Ed., a future teacher working on her Mrs. degree. By a stroke of luck that made Miller feel like he ought to sacrifice a small animal to Shiva or Zeus or someone, tonight was Tracie's mother's birthday and they were celebrating it at a Japanese steakhouse—one of those places where Asian-Americans with questionable commitments to personal hygiene threw food and knives alike into the air between hungry watchers, sneaking sips of Saki here and there—"just the family." So Miller was free for the evening, which so far was working out fine.

"You ready to be a 2L?" Miller asked. He entertained himself between swallows of Zima by tossing peep shots her way, smiling if she caught him, enjoying a comfortable semi-erection in either case. He thought her breasts looked especially firm tonight, resting prominently beneath her shirt like that. Kind of pushing against the fabric, not really trying to get out but not content to sit by unnoticed, either.

"I guess. It's the same thing as the first year. Just different courses. I'm trying to get out of having to clerk with my father next summer, but who's to say? They're not exactly giving clerkships away in Chicago these days. Lately he's been pushing the idea fairly aggressively. I've had to start screening my calls."

Miller finished his drink and set the empty bottle on the glass coffee table. He stood and retrieved the other twenty-two from the dining nook and set them on the coffee-table between them.

"Don't feel like we have to drink them all tonight," Miller said. "That's a shit-pile of alcohol."

Nicole laughed and got herself another. Her legs were folded elegantly over one another, like a dancer's, the meat of her calves slightly flexed, flowing beneath her skin like cream, tapering downward into her tiny ankle joint. She leaned back and kicked off her flats, raised her legs and set her feet on the table, crossing them at the ankle. Miller noticed she was wearing the gold anklet he had given her a few birthdays back. He and his family had vacationed down off the Gulf a couple years ago, and Miller had found it in a gift shop and thought it looked like her.

"I picked up a few spoonfuls from Laney the other day," she said, opening the bottle and taking a swallow. "If you're interested…"

"He still selling? He told me he wasn't."

"I think he's a little more selective these days, now that he's in med. school. Said one of his friends in the pharmacy department was bounced out for helping himself to the Viagra. Supposedly they're filing charges against him."

"There's a fall from grace. And all for a better boner." He nodded at the coke. "What'd it cost you?"

"Six hundred."

Miller whistled. "Pretty steep."

"It's good stuff. He tried to push a quarter bag of grass on me, of all things. Surprised me a little, someone like Laney selling such a passe drug. I mean, it's fine to smoke, but who really buys it anymore?"

"You shouldn't be smoking dope anyway. It kills motivation. Brain cells, too."

Nicole raised her bottle and tapped it with one of her nails. "Enough of this will do the trick, too. I've fairly well damaged an entire lobe this summer alone, I imagine."

"You come those out, you know." Miller said. "Brain cells."

"Only the dead ones," Nicole replied. "Thank God. Otherwise I wouldn't be able to read."

They sat and talked for several hours, about their summer, about their futures, about Tracie and Buck and anything else that came to mind. As the hours passed they talked and they drank and flipped back and forth from presidential politics on CNN to music videos on M.T.V. They stacked the empty bottles on the coffee table, Miller toying with the idea of building a pyramid but figuring that if they fell the whole coffee table was liable to shatter, so he satisfied himself with lining them up in rows of three, peeling their labels one at a time. He stopped drinking after his eighth. He had a pretty hefty buzz but was still in control enough to know what was going on; Nicole, however, was somewhere around number eleven when she decided she wanted to get high. Miller had known it was coming. He had been drinking with her for years now, since high-school, and had discovered long ago that Nicole's urge for stronger stuff usually wasn't far behind drink number ten.

"Are you staying the night?" she asked him, standing, wobbly, balancing herself against the couch. Miller watched her legs as she walked, following the flowing lines of symmetry that ran the length of her thighs and up beneath her skirt.

"Guess I could," Miller said. "Imagine English'll be all right at the apartment alone."

"How is that gorgeous English, anyway?" She asked, walking across the living room, looking for her purse, finding it in the hall closet. "Are he and Amanda still one?"—Bending over, her skirt riding up high on the back of her legs, the muscles taut there, none of this lost on Miller.

"Until the end of time," Miller said. His head was thick and fuzzy; Nicole's words sounded like they were coming through water.

"I can't imagine what in the world he sees in her."

"You've been saying that for years," Miller said. "I assume you're looking for a response more sophisticated than her attractive looks, bubbly personality, and downright worship of him."

Nicole sat back down on the couch, setting a small vial the size of a wine cork on the table next to a razor. "You don't really find her that attractive, do you?"

Miller sat up, leaned over the table to watch Nicole cut the lines, and shrugged. "Not my type, really. Too domestic. I like my women a wee wilder." He winked at her. "Don't make them too fat," he said, nodding at the lines. "It's been a while."

Nicole wiped the surface of the table with a rag, then poured out a small pile of the white powder and began chopping it with the razor. She motioned towards the television. "Be a dear and hit mute, won't you? I think the C.D. player has a disc in it."

Miller silenced the television with one remote, dug around beneath his seat cushion until he found another, and turned the disc player on. Marc Cohn's "Wait for the Miracle" began playing softly.

Nicole was still separating the coke. "Does she go down on him? She was probably the first, and the poor angel thinks he's found heaven." She shook her head. "That's criminal, if you'd like my opinion."

Miller sat and watched her work, having forgotten what they were talking about. "Does who go down on what?—Amanda? Imagine she does. How the hell should I know?"

"You're his best friend and his roommate as well," Nicole said, setting the razor down on the table and taking a fairly impressive pull off her Zima.

Miller was always amazed at the amount of alcohol Nicole could put away. He'd won bets at parties because of it.

"You can't tell me the two of you don't discuss that sort of thing."

Miller shrugged. "Sooner or later, Nicole, they all go down."

Nicole shook her head. "You'd be surprised. I've spoiled you. Lots don't." She shaped the coke into six lines, each about an inch and a half long.

"Even if she does," she said, leaning over the table and snorting three of the lines, wiping at her nose with her hand, licking her fingers, "no way she swallows."

Miller was disgusted enough with that to leave it alone. He stood and circled the table, sat down next to Nicole.

"Just do two of them," Nicole said, sniffing.

"Why two?"

She reached down and moved one of the lines to the side. "Trust me," she said. Miller snorted the remaining two, misjudging, thanks to the Zima Gold, the distance to the table, bumping his nose on the glass, and wiped his face. He leaned back in the couch and stared at the light hanging overhead, sniffing his nostrils clear. The drug numbed his mind like ice.

Nicole got up and turned the lights off, washing the room in black. Miller listened to her make her way, carefully, knocking into the lazyboy, then the table, back to the couch. He heard a crackle and a hiss, then saw a flame in front of him as Nicole lit two candles. The remaining line of coke shimmered and glowed in the flickering yellow of the candlelight.

Shadows danced in silence across the walls and around the room as Nicole pulled her shirt over her head as casually as she might alone, undressing for bed or a shower; her bra fell to the floor without a sound. Miller felt himself smiling, felt the cocaine doing its thing. The stereo's lone red light shone in the darkness like an eye in the night.

"Undo"—sipping the last from her eleventh Zima, swallowing in exaggerated motions—"your belt."

Miller didn't say anything. He pulled the belt from around his waist and tossed it to the floor in front of the couch. Nicole kicked it out of the way with her foot. Her breasts, perfectly shaped, each a mirror image of the other, their nipples small and the color of blood, sat firm and high on her chest.

"The pants, too," Nicole said. "Come on, Miller. You're acting like a frosh at summer camp. You've been here before. You know the drill."

Miller laughed and slid himself out of the jeans, kicking off his topsiders as he did. As he pulled his shirt over his head he found himself, only briefly, thinking of Tracie, wondering if she in all her sweet naivete had ever thought the shirt she'd bought him would find its way to the floor of Nicole Henderson's living room, next to his belt, shoes, and pants, the first night it was worn.

Miller sat on her couch in his boxers, as high Orion and climbing still, watching Nicole try to balance herself as she stepped out of her skirt, then, with a whisper of her thumb, unsnap her tiny white panties at the hips and let them fall, drift, almost sail to the carpet below like an autumn leaf. He watched as she licked the forefinger on her right hand, saw her turn and roll it across the sixth line as delicately as a surgeon, then kneel down in front of him.

"God you're beautiful," he said, unaware that he was speaking, removing his own underwear, balling them up and tossing them onto the lazyboy across the room.

"My mother always told me," Nicole said, taking him in her hand, squeezing, releasing, squeezing again, "there are two times in a man's life when you can never believe a word he says: Before you fuck him, and after you don't."

Miller tried to focus on that but he lost it all in a numbing spread of fog.

"If you say so," he managed. "God in Heaven I shouldn't have rushed into that coke. Fucking insides feel like they're on fire—"

"—Shhhh," Nicole said. "You always were too talkative during this."

So Miller quit talking.

Chapter 3
104 Days Before   (August 24)

English, decked in a white dress shirt, black slacks, and a burgundy tie, sat in the church pew beside Amanda and her mother and listened as the preacher spoke about love and forgiveness and a host of other things that sounded to English like the same things he had talked about last Sunday, or the one before, or the one before that. Who the hell knew. At any rate, it was a re-run so he grabbed the bulletin from beside him on the pew and scribbled across the top of it with one of the tiny pencils, *your tits look great today.* He passed it over to Amanda, who read it and wrote back, *How sweet. And quite the place for such charming compliments.* He looked for a smile but didn't get one.

Well, he thought, flicking the pencil stub into the rack with the bibles dejectedly, so be it. It was the truth, anyhow. They did look great. They always looked great, but today they looked especially perky. She was wearing the light blue dress he had bought her last Christmas, the one with the lace collar and the tiny white flowers all over it, and though she had tried it on for him that morning, he hadn't quite remembered her boobs sitting as high or sticking out as far as they were today. Just sitting there he could smell her, her scent like flowers and summer rain radiating off of her like heat.

English casually leaned forward and sneaked a peak at Mrs. Peterson, who met his eyes and smiled pleasantly, approvingly.

Such a fine young man, with such proper priorities.

It was the usual scene after church, English changed into sweats and a Chicago T-shirt, Amanda the same, English's head in Amanda's lap, lying on the couch, alternating between sleep and the game on television while Amanda twirled his hair between her fingers and glanced through a magazine. Classes resumed tomorrow and she was taking an overload of hours, which meant that all the reading she did for the next fifteen weeks would be from textbooks and lab manuals. Moments like this where they could just sit and vegetate a bit would be few.

English stayed for dinner that evening—boiled chicken, peas and carrots, baked potato, Pepsi to drink—as he did many evenings, and left around nine. Before Amanda walked him out, he took care to tell Mrs. Peterson how very delicious the meal was, which wasn't quite the truth but sounded better in any case. She smiled as usual, and advised him, quite motherly, to get to bed early; classes started back tomorrow.

"Are you and Miller staying at the same apartment?"

English nodded. "Fourth year."

"Fourth and final," Amanda added.

"Oh?" Mrs. Peterson said, a wry smile emerging across her face. "Something in the works I should know about?"

English didn't feel the need to explain anything to Amanda's mother, who was a touch meddlesome for his taste. He preferred that he and Amanda simply make their plans and inform the others as the need arose, but that just wasn't the way Amanda was put together. She and her mother talked about everything. Years ago, when he and Amanda had first slept together, he'd been reduced to begging her not to tell her mother; to this day he still wondered if she had or not.

English kissed his girlfriend goodbye that evening on the front porch. He left relatively early—a little after ten—intent on going to bed shortly after getting back to the apartment. He was tired, and had an early class tomorrow.

It would not be amiss to say that the following few days were a turning point in the life of English Mason, and, in that respect, in the lives of many others as well. There are times in our lives when we come to crossroads, and must make decisions that, ultimately, alter the course of every day thereafter. The first week of English's senior year—which should have been his easiest academically and most likely his final as a bachelor—was one of those times for English Mason, and it is indeed somewhat of a shame, for he was wholly without the advantage of knowing it.

Chapter 4
103 Days Before   (August 25)

English's first class was Small Business Management at 8:00 A.M. He had AdvancedAccounting at 1:00, which left him with a four hour gap in between classes during which he figured he'd meet Amanda at the Nursing building.

After Small Business English chatted with a couple of people he hadn't seen since last May. Kevin Fullner, and old pal from high school, made a big show out of checking English's left hand for a wedding ring and asked when he was marrying Amanda, said if English didn't propose to her soon he was apt to give it a go. English said soon, soon, not too soon but soon. Kevin shook his head and laughed, told him a woman like Amanda, beautiful and intelligent and good as gold, you got your hands on one of those, you needed to scoop her up quick.

There's time, English said. We're young yet.

Always plenty of time.

English crossed the campus at a brisk walk, his black bookbag slung over his right shoulder, the muscle there hurting from not carrying it for the past three months. He was wearing the standard college attire: jeans, a button down red and green flannel, unbuttoned and untucked, the t-shirt he had slept in underneath.

Amanda was waiting in the lobby, sitting with a book opened on her lap as usual. She'd been valedictorian of her senior class three years ago, a nice little perk of which was a full ride to virtually any school she wanted.

She chose Chicago because English was there, and would probably finish up in the top four or five of her nursing class in another two years.

Their eyes met as English entered the building. She flashed him the smile that had made him fall for her so hard almost seven years ago, in a high school history class.

"Hey," he said.

"Hey yourself," she said, kissing him quickly on the mouth. English held her at arms length and looked at her. She was wearing white shorts and a pale blue short-sleeve shirt. Her hair was pulled back into a ponytail. Around her neck was a golden locket her mother had bought her a few Christmases back, in which she kept a picture of the two of them.

"You look great," English said. "Don't smell half-bad, either. What is that? Navy?"

"Moroc. And thank you. How's your schedule?"

"I've got two on Monday, Wednesday and Friday, and two on Tuesday-Thursdays. How about you?"

"Four classes? Please, English. Why wasn't I a business major? Four classes and no labs. Twelve credits. Know how many I have?"

"More than twelve, apparently."

"Seventeen. Five classes and two labs."

"Any chance your Friday morning's are clear? You could leave the house early and come snuggle for a few."

"I'd like to, but it wasn't meant to be this semester. On Fridays I'm here from nine till six. Tuesdays and Thursdays I have to be here at 7:30 in the morning."

"Great scheduling, doll."

"I should have been a liberal arts major. I could teach. I'd like teaching. Summer's off. No late nights."

"Naaah. Just think of all the money you'll make in nursing. I can retire early."

"You'd better marry rich. I've got my sights set on a doctor."

"I've heard they make great husbands. Ninety hour weeks and always on call. They have their buddies beep them when they want to go out carousing. Hey, you know what the head nurse's job is?"

"Of course I do. They—"

"They keep the doctors happy. Know how you can tell which one she is?"

Amanda sighed. English had a laundry list of nurse jokes. "She's the one with the dirty knees. You used that one years ago."

"I did? I'll get some new ones. What time's your next class?"

"Eleven. P-Chem."

English looked at her funny.

"Physical Chemistry. The one I've been putting off for two years."

He nodded. "Wanna grab a bite?" English led her out the building toward a burger-shack down the road, his arm wrapped around her shoulders. The weather outside was nice, in the mid-eighties with low humidity. It would stay this way for another month or so, and then around late September or early October autumn would turn nasty and the snow would come and stay for almost half a year.

"I've got some money," Amanda said, reaching for her purse.

"I think I can spring for a burger. Push for fries though and you're on your own."

Amanda laughed and kissed his cheek. "Is Miller meeting us?"

English shook his head. "His first class isn't until noon today. I swear, honey, those liberal arts majors. You think I've got it easy. At least I *do* something in class. They've got it made from square one. Read a few books, write a few papers. Small wonder he has a four-point."

"I heard he was going to law school next year. Any chance he'll pick one far away? The University of Alaska, maybe?"

"Now, now, love. Let's be nice."

They reached the restaurant and English held the door open as Amanda went inside. The cool inside air—smelling of cooked meat, grease, ketchup—whooshed past them out the door.

"I can be nice," she shrugged. "I don't mind nice. I just want to spend a little time with my boyfriend now and again during his senior year. Is there anything wrong with that?"

English kissed the top of her head and pointed to the menu. "Anything a buck'll buy, honey. Don't hold back."

* * *

Miller hung up the phone in his bedroom and felt himself smiling. He checked the clock on his nightstand: a quarter after eleven. His first class started in another forty five minutes, and he was still in bed, still naked.

Nicole had been quick; the first thing she said after "good morning" had been "is Tracie over?" to which Miller had responded with a "morning, mom. Yeah, slept fine."

The phone call lasted about a minute. Miller—his hand on the sleeping Tracie's left bare buttock, predictable prick behaving predictably—said little, simply listening and grunting in the affirmative or negative at the proper places, then hanging up with a detached "goodbye."

He sat up and rubbed crust from his eyes, smiling still, the forest green sheet falling off his shoulders and over his erection, poking up absurdly, pushing the sheet into roughly the shape of a pyramid, and pictured the way she had looked two nights ago, on her knees, between his, small but strong fingers spread wide across his thighs, a single gold ring on her left hand leaving an imprint in his skin, her auburn head moving back and forth, up and down. They had moved from the couch to the floor and eventually her bed where Miller—his arteries and veins laced in coke, his senses sharp and acute and his nerve endings on fire—had passed out in the middle of things, the room spinning in wild colors and the air hanging heavy with the smells of sweat and flesh.

Nicole.

Chicago Law didn't start back for another week; Nicole had called to complain that she was all alone over there at her townhouse, had recorded

The River's Edge—one of Miller's favorites—the night before, and was looking for some company. Miller was generally happy to oblige Nicole when it came to that sort of thing—no real effort in it; waken Tracie, rush her through a shower, kiss her out the door and promise to call later—but there was something else Nicole had mentioned that had piqued his interest. It seemed her old man was attending a fundraiser in the city for a Senatorial candidate, and Nicole had come upon a couple of extra tickets.

Miller wasn't particularly interested in the Senate race, but Nicole had said the Governor was scheduled to speak there, as well as a number of other heavy-hitters. Showing up and shaking a few hands, making a few acquaintances, picking up a few names and dropping his own, could only help him down the line. After all, if the Governor was speaking at an election-year fundraiser, then every influential lawyer in Chicago—a group to which Miller had every intention of belonging in the near future—was apt to be in attendance.

He nudged Tracie to see if she was awake. She moaned gently, her eyes closed, and he kissed her neck, waited for a response. When he didn't get one he pulled the sheet down a bit and kissed her upper back once, twice, dragging his tongue down her spine and over the small of her back, and considered turning her over and climbing atop, but his conversation with Nicole had distracted him. So he rolled out of bed and got in the shower, thinking about the possibilities of it all—the fundraiser tickets and all the rest.

He decided—turning on the water, adjusting the temperature, urinating a bright yellow stream into the drain while obliquely imagining what a treat it would be to have Nicole and Tracie at the same time, their bodies pink and slippery from spit and sweat, their arms and legs hot with friction, entwined, their breasts (Tracie's slightly bigger, Nicole's more experienced) pressing into one another, a writhing mass of skin atop his bed, beneath a strobe perhaps—that he'd skip classes today.

Chapter 5
99 Days Before   (August 29)

"Don't go. We both know what's going on over there, and there's no need for you to be involved with it. Nicole has no respect for boundaries of any kind. She never has."

Amanda was noticeably upset; a distinct air of adamancy had overtaken her tone. English, the role of consummate diplomat one he was used to, was engaged in the frustrating task of trying to calm her down. He wasn't having much luck with it, and found himself glad he wasn't face to face with her, the act of disappointing her much easier over the phone.

"I *don't* know what he wants, that's the thing. He called me here at the apartment and said he couldn't talk about it on the phone." A meager excuse, offered in the hopes that it would be enough to avoid a fight with her, knowing that it wouldn't.

"How James Bond. Miller thrives off that kind of covert, back-alley silliness, you know that. He always has. Nicole and one of her slutty friends are probably both as high as kites and doing strange things with each other's bodies while he films it all. There's probably a midget in the middle somewhere."

"Amanda. Please. Let's be realistic here."

"He's probably got them playing naked *Twister* or something. Did he ask you to bring baby oil?"

"Honey…"

"Well," she said, easing up a little, not entirely ready to let it go, "she's notorious, English." There wasn't, she knew, any reason to distrust him.

There never had been. She was aware of that. But the thought of him descending into that place—and that was how Amanda Peterson viewed Nicole's lair, as though one had to descend beneath the fabric of decency to enter it—without her made her a touch uncomfortable. Miller was his best friend—his best *male* friend, she amended—and the two of them got off on such silly games as this. She supposed it was probably normal and even healthy in a way, boys at play and all of that, especially this year, which was probably, if things worked out the way she hoped and he popped the question sometime soon, his final year of being able to keep all hours of the night and run around with his friends. But still, it bothered her. Miller bothered her. She was constantly worried that one day Miller's idea of fun was going to surpass the parameters of game and enter a more dangerous realm, and that English would be there when it did. For all his docile outward appearances, Amanda was aware that Miller had a wild streak in him, a deeply buried hunger that wasn't easily sated. He had for as long as she'd known him. Amanda believed, in a way she had trouble articulating with words but felt nonetheless, that Miller was dangerous.

"Look," English was saying. "I'm gonna go see what he wants, and I'll be at your house in a couple of hours. I promise."

"What time is it?"

"It's a quarter after three. I shouldn't be over there more than an hour or two." And then, in hopes of injecting a touch of play into their disagreement, "I'll be a good little boy, honest engine."

"I believe you, English. Just..."

English listened as her voice trailed off, and remained silent until she finished.

"Just be careful." She said.

"I will," he promised. And he was.

And none of it counted for anything in the end.

* * *

"I don't care what you look at," Nicole was saying, leading Miller and English up the steps of her parents' home, her parents off for the week at one of their condos, the one at Seabrook Island, Nicole thought, "but put it all back the way you found it. It's my ass if he thinks something's missing."

"And such a nice ass, too." Miller said.

Nicole giggled, shaking her behind a little more for effect, English noticed, as they walked down the hall and into the Henderson's bedroom. English felt his shoes sink into the thick white carpet and wondered if he should take them off.

"He's so neurotic about this garbage," Nicole said, flinging open her parents' walk-in closet. "Won't even let the maid back there to clean it."

They—English, Miller, and Nicole—had met at Nicole's townhouse. When English had gotten there Miller and Nicole were well into a pitcher of Long Island Iced Tea, and there was talk of maybe firing up a bowl or two, but English had been able to squelch that idea using something as radical as honesty, telling both Miller and Nicole, but primarily Miller, that he had promised Amanda he'd meet her at her house for dinner, and that Amanda didn't have the first clue that he had ever seen marijuana, much less smoked it. Miller said he understood and apparently did, because he didn't put up much of a fuss and they left Nicole's place soon after, riding 94 to her parents' house in The Edens. English still wasn't sure as to the reasons for the trip, Miller and Nicole, the both of them, having always been into secrets and secrecy.

Now Miller stepped around Nicole, who had stopped at the mouth of the closet door and was just standing there, as though she were waiting for something important to happen inside. The closet was long, narrow, lined with dresses and blouses on one side and stiff business suits on the other.

"We're going through the man's clothes?" English said.

Miller nodded towards the back wall.

"A safe, right? You've discovered a secret safe. The land of Narnia awaits us...lions and tigers and bears and such."

"That's *The Wizard of Oz,* moron," Miller said.

"You should know. You probably have it on your syllabus this semester."

Nicole had retreated into the center of the large master bedroom and sat down on the bed, her legs crossed, flipping through the pages of a magazine. Clashing violently with the overall leitmotif of the Henderson bedroom, which was washed over in white and pale greens, she was wearing navy blue athletic shorts and a gray tee-shirt that read ARMY and fell several inches shy of the tops of her shorts, leaving a stripe of pink skin revealed between. That had been the first thing English had noticed when he arrived at her townhouse. Her hair had also been done slightly different than English was used to seeing it. It was pulled back into a ponytail from the top of her head, and bobbed playfully when she walked. Just like Amanda's did, English noticed. It made her look strangely younger.

"Don't mess anything up," Nicole called from behind them. "I'm going down the hall to my father's study to make a tiny withdrawal from petty cash."

Miller and English had squatted down on their haunches. Miller produced from behind a large shoe tree a small, leather briefcase. He flicked it open with a twist of the brass lock.

"How fortuitous," Miller said.

"He probably didn't count on his daughter's friends poking through his shit while he was on vacation."

English was watching him without much interest, debating whether or not he should stop off at a grocery store and pick up a few flowers for Amanda. It hadn't been hard to see she had been disappointed with his decision to come here. She wouldn't say anything about it later, but it'd be there still. Flowers wouldn't be a bad idea.

English remembered a story he heard about Nicole once, nothing he could document but one he thought could be just as easily true as not. Word was Nicole had lost her virginity in this very closet, up against that wall there, her bare back as smooth as snow and pressed up hard against one of her father's blue pin-stripes. Nicole had been a sophomore in high school at the time, dating a fellow a couple years her senior named Lance

Saxon. The two of them had been rolling around her parents' bed one afternoon, her father presumably at work, her mother out shopping or having an affair of her own, when they had heard the front door open and shut, followed by the sound of footsteps across the marble floor of the foyer. The story went that Lance was fairly close to a critical moment at the time, and that the two of them, naked and shiny with each other's juices, had disjoined momentarily, snaking back to the end of the closet, huddled in the farthest corner in a mass of naked arms and legs, Lance getting religious in a hurry and Nicole finding the danger of the whole ordeal wonderfully arousing. Turned out it had only been the maid downstairs, and Lance Saxon, internal pressures building, had decided that here was as good as anywhere. Whether David Henderson ever figured out where the rust-colored stain on his suit came from English wasn't sure.

"Found it," Miller said, passing a manila envelope to English. "Have a look."

English opened it slowly and began reading, more to humor Miller than anything else. It didn't look like much, a bunch of facts and figures and names. Across the page from each name, in an adjacent column, ran a separate column of what English supposed to be phone numbers.

"So?" English said.

"Notice anything odd, there?" Miller asked.

"Did you see Nicole's tits underneath that shirt?" English said, disregarding the whole thing. "Her nipples look hard to you?"

"Like erasers. You know she digs you, buddy. You ought to slip over there sometime, do her a favor."

"I'll run that by Amanda, she what she thinks," English said, glancing down at the pages in front of them, looking at them the way he would look at a Swahilian textbook, just groupings of random, useless letters and lines on a page.

Miller chuckled and pointed to the sheets in English's lap—"look at the third name on the list there."

English read. "Walter P. Michel. Why does that name sound familiar to me?"

"The evening news."

"The news...? Our state senator?"

Miller nodded.

"And a couple names down." Miller said.

"Gregory M. Simpson. Senator Simpson? From Colorado? *The* Senator Simpson?"

"Yep," Miller said. "You remember he was the first Democrat to cross lines and come out in favor of impeachment. Word is he's going to change parties right after the election. He's probably the only honest bastard in the bunch. Check out the next name."

But English was already ahead of him. "Barney Thomason. The Rep. from Michigan. The one that got into all that trouble for sexual harassment a few years back."

"He was copping a feel off a male page in an elevator. Keep reading."

But English already was. The list grew more impressive on the way down. There were two more Senators, one from Iowa and one from Michigan. A former Representative from their own district, and a Supreme Court Nominee who had been narrowly rejected by the Senate last year and now taught law at Northwestern.

He read the last name on the list without recognition. "J. Fullard Wallace."

"Filthy rich attorney from Kenilworth. Has a house and a practice down here. Has houses scattered everywhere, like litter across the state. He's the one that put Jimmy Jameson on trial."

English knew the name. Jimmy Jameson had been, many years ago, Illinois's answer to the Boston Strangler, raping and killing by his own admission at least sixteen girls in a bloody three year spree. Wallace had gotten him convicted on nine counts of forcible abduction and three of murder, and had sent him to the chair.

"Big cheese," he said. "Mr. Henderson's got some pull, huh? Is this a client list of some sort?"

Miller handed English a small blue and gold envelope. "Now read this," he said,

English did. 'The friends and supporters of Brian Doyle Timmons, Clerk of Deeds, request your presence at the first post-primary fundraiser for the general election.' I didn't know Mr. Henderson was a Democrat." English said. "Thought the shit-rich were always Republican."

"Never mind that. See the date at the bottom. It's two weeks from today. Downtown Chicago. Everyone who is anyone on the political scene will be there. It's an incredible opportunity, English."

"An opportunity to do what?"

Miller replaced the list of names in the manila folder and slid the folder back into the briefcase. He shrugged. "Just to see," he said.

"You forgot this," English said, extending the invitation to Miller, who shook his head.

"We're keeping that," Miller said.

"We can't keep his invitation, Miller. The man's going to need it in two weeks. He'll notice it's missing."

"He can get a new one. We can't. We need it more."

"Miller, there's no way we can get into this sort of thing. It's like a thousand dollars a plate. Do you realize how much jack that is? For one meal?"

"There are ways around that."

"Oh, hell," English said, "here we go. Listen, Mill. This is a fund-raiser for a Clerk of Deeds, for crying out loud. The Clerk of Deeds in Illinois. The Clerk of Deeds doesn't do jack shit. It's a zero position. Even I know that. He's an absolute nobody. He'll be lucky if his own mother supports him, much less any of the names on that list. These guys all just say they'll be there to attract other idiots who have a spare grand or so to drop, and then they call and say they couldn't attend, sorry, please vote for me next year. Same old story. This is politics, man. Nothing's real in politics. It's all just appearances. That's why people hate it so much." He shook his head. "It'll be a waste of time."

"Maybe, maybe not. But it can't hurt to go and check things out, can it? Just to see. It's at the Sears Tower. That alone should be enough reason to go. My dad went to a conference there last year. Said the view was the tits."

"The view may well be a big deal, but the Clerk of Deeds is anything but. This is a zero event, Miller."

"Listen, number-cruncher. I don't tell you how to work a spreadsheet. Don't talk to me about politics. The Governor's up for re-elect this year, so you can bet your left nut he'll be there. And if the Governor's going to be there, a whole slew of people that *want* to be Governor one day are going to be there as well, not to mention the media. When I worked for Congressman Richie a couple of years back, he had a few dinners like this, and I'm telling you my friend it's a cathouse with a dress-code. Women coming out of the walls and almost all of them hot. And everyone there is someone it's good to know. It's like one big networking party. We're going."

"It's on a Friday night," English protested.

"And what? You had a big date planned? See a movie? Eat a hamburger at Hardees? Come on, English. This is a chance to rub shoulders with some of the most influential men and women in the state. You've seen the news. This race is attracting national attention. Look at this list of names. This is supposed to be the year the Dems route Gambon. The people on this list could do a lot for you if they wanted to, but they're sure as hell not going to come knocking on your door. If it sucks, we'll turn around and come home. No loss. We get a free meal out of it."

"Find anything interesting?" Nicole, suddenly next to them, asked. Her skin smelled like lotion, and something lighter under that. "I see you found the ticket, Miller. I can't believe you'd want to go to something like that. How hopelessly boring."

"We better get going." English suggested to Miller. They were all standing now, walking out of the closet, Nicole in front. She turned her parents' bedroom light off and shut the door as they left, followed the other two down the steps into the foyer.

"I'd invite you to stay," Nicole said, "but my parents will be home sometime tonight, and I'd hate to run into them."

"You're not too close with your folks, are you Nicole?"

"Close enough to call for money and not have to pay long-distance rates,"—Nicole, opening the front door, waiting for English and Miller, the invitation to the Timmons thing sticking half-way out Miller's back pocket, closing the door behind them, locking it, searching for her keys in her purse—"which is as close as anyone really needs to be to their parents, don't you think?"

* * *

"Well," Nicole said into the phone, "it's official, Dana. The poor dear is utterly clueless. I've all but thrown myself at him and he hasn't caught on. I suggested we do a little grass before going over to my folks' place but he would have none of it. Said he had to meet her for dinner."

Nicole was lying on her bed, on her back, staring at the ceiling as she twirled the purple phone cord around her fingers.

"This isn't news to you," Dana said. "He's completely devoted to Amanda. Has been since high school. You can't blame him, really. She really is pretty. And she dotes on him like crazy. She once told me she thought he was the sexiest thing she'd ever laid eyes on."

"How quaint. Miller said she goes down on him. Can you believe that?" Nicole asked tiredly. "How Monica of her. She's so innocent looking. I just can't imagine her getting into something like that. She'd have to mess up her hair."

"Forget about him, Nicole. I'll give you Bobby after tonight. I'm only going out with him tonight because we're going on the Odyssey dinner cruise and I've wanted to do that forever."

"A guy springs for a dinner cruise on the first date, he's going to want you to go to bed with him. They always do."

Dana laughed through the phone. "Cheer up, Nic."

"I want English. I refuse to accept the notion that he's totally impervious to my advances."

"I think it turns you on, him being so faithful. You're an iconoclast, Nicole." There was a brief pause.

"Maybe it does," Nicole said. "And maybe I am."

Chapter 6

97 Days Before   (August 31)

"We'll do it." English conceded. He took another bite of stuffed pizza and sipped his Coke. It was two-thirty, and he was going to Amanda's after he and Miller were through here. They were at Giordano's downtown, which was a bit of a drive from their apartment, but the waitress, a pretty redhead named Melanie Pine, was one of Miller's ex-girlfriends and usually brought their orders no charge.

"You won't regret it, English. I've got a great feeling about this one." Miller said, shoveling half a slice into his mouth, dripping sauce all over the table.

"Oh, there's no doubt I'll regret it. I always end up regretting it. And you've always got a great feeling about this kind of stuff. Last time you had a great feeling we almost got nailed for trespassing."

Miller chewed on a piece of crust and smiled across the table at English. "It's different this time, English."

"Oh, yeah. Different. Now I feel better. How's it different?"

"This time we have an invitation."

*   *   *

Hours later and minutes shy of midnight, English stood in the Peterson foyer and kissed Amanda on the lips again before gathering his keys and wallet from atop the piano. He had a habit of tossing them there as soon as he walked through the front door, and had discovered years ago that it bothered Mr. Peterson immensely, for reasons the man either couldn't or wouldn't articulate. Just something else about his daughter's boyfriend that irritated him with reliable frequency.

When English found that out, he decided that if it wasn't already a habit he would have made it one, just to keep the old guy on his toes. Remind him some new blood was moving in.

"I love you," he whispered into her ear, and Amanda, who had never in her life heard anything as sweet and wonderful and promising as her boyfriend say those three little syllables in that particular order, melted in his arms and pulled him tight. Chills ran up her arms and legs. She pressed into English's body, which was a full foot taller than her own, and grinned.

"That's quite a compliment," she giggled, glancing downward. "Almost seven years and a hug still does it for you."

English smiled. "What are you going to do about it?"

"Here?" She asked, blushing, glancing away.

English nodded.

"English, my parents are upstairs. I've got class tomorrow, and so do you."

"So?"

"What if they come down?"

"They have to know by now. You're twenty-one. We've been dating seven years."

"Six and a half. And there's a big difference between knowing something and catching your daughter in the middle of it. Absolutely not. My father would shoot you, English. He really would."

"You know," English said, nibbling on her ear, "you really are beautiful when you're denying me. You pick up a certain glow."

"I'm not denying you, English. I'm just using common sense. One of us has to."

"I think it can kill a guy if he goes too long," English confided. "I read that somewhere. I swear I did. You don't want me to die, do you?"

"Oh, please, English. You tried that in the tenth grade. It didn't work then, either. Besides, it's been less than a week. I hardly think you're terminal."

English lowered his mouth down the side of her neck and kissed it gently. He felt her press in closer to him, and kissed the hollow of her throat.

"English…you're not making this easy on me."

"Go tell them we're going to get some donuts."

"Donuts? At midnight on a Sunday? That's ridiculous."

He ran his hands down her sides and spread them lightly across her narrow hips.

"Tell them we'll bring them some if they want." He said. "We can go down by the pier for an hour or so."

"English…"

"The moon's out tonight, honey. You like the moon, remember. We can open the sunroof." He continued kissing her neck and throat, occasionally rising to touch his lips to hers, holding her small body against his own. "The water trickling up beneath the docks. Crickets, bullfrogs, the whole bit. Think about it."

"Mosquitoes, police…besides, the pier's too far."

"Then that new development down the street. It's deserted. No streetlights, nothing."

"I can't just go up there and tell them we're going out for donuts. They're going to know something is going on. Can't you think of anything more original?"

"They always go for the donut story."

She shook her head. "They never go for it. My mother shakes her head and my father peers over whatever book he's reading and looks at me like I just told him I was going into the city to have a sex-change. Think about it, English. Donuts? At this hour?"

Before they left, Mrs. Peterson said she wouldn't mind a jelly donut, since they were going anyway.

Chapter 7
87 Days Before   (September 10)

Jenny Palto picked up her red dress with the sequins from the cleaners at half past two that afternoon. Michael would be coming home from work in about an hour, and she needed to be ready by five. The dinner started at six, and the elbow-rubbing and name-dropping session afterwards would probably last well past midnight.

By five, Jenny and her husband, a relatively obscure district attorney with a savvy legal mind and an almost overwhelming desire to make a name for himself, were in their brown station wagon on I-90, headed for the Sears Tower downtown.

On the way, Michael Palto entertained his wife by filling her in, for perhaps the hundredth time since their marriage, on the details of the career of his all-time hero—*the reason I went to law school,* he would often say—and possibly the best prosecutor of his time, J. Fullard Wallace.

A man who would, in fact, be present at tonight's event.

*   *   *

At a quarter after three English left the apartment carrying his tux by the hanger. He told Miller he was going over to Amanda's for a while and would meet him at the Tower. Miller had looked up from the book he was reading, *Crapshoot: the Selection of America's Vice-Presidents,* and nodded okay, fine, whatever, just don't be late.

"You may even enjoy yourself, English," Miller called after him from his book. "Decide you want to try your hand at politics."

"I doubt it," English replied, punctuating his response with the shutting of the door.

Now, two hours later, Miller stood in the center of his room in the tuxedo he'd bought the day before at Tessuti. It had set him back four bills and he'd bled handing over each one, but Miller figured it was the kind of investment a man had to make for his career here and again.

And now he stands in the center of his bedroom and buffs his shoes with an old t-shirt. He had spent the last hour showering and shaving and getting his hair just so. Once he could see his face in his shoes he stood in front of the mirror and practiced his delivery. He'd start back up against the far wall of his room and approach his mirror, face smiling slightly, hand moving out to shake and be shook, until he thought it looked confident enough.

"Good evening, Mr. Timmons. I'm honored to be able to be a part of this exciting campaign." Miller backed away from the mirror and smiled. Fuck Timmons. Timmons would probably be the least important person there, a nobody Clerk of Deeds who would win a state-wide election when the White Sox won the series. If he wasn't up against Senator Gambon none of these people would even be showing up tonight, free booze or no. But the omniscient Poll-Gods had declared this a weak year for the Senator and his Party, so everyone on the other side of the fence was scurrying around like a bunch of hungry alley-cats looking for food.

But that was the way these things went. There were times when Miller very nearly decided he had enough of an interest in politics to know that he didn't want to get any more interested.

Still, regardless of Timmons being an idiot without a prayer, he had been right when he told English there would be a plethora of influential people at this gala tonight. The Governor, Illinois's other Senator, and more likely than not an impressive array of congressmen. Miller could do worse than to press palms with some of that crew for an evening. Probably nothing would come of it, but you never knew about these things. A room full of politicians, all trying to impress each other.

Things happened in places like that.

*   *   *

Nicole stepped out in front of her full-length mirror and decided that even she was impressed. She had on her most expensive dress, a solid black number that stopped above the knees and wrapped around her body like mist. It was a strapless, showing the slightest hint of cleavage in front, and virtually all of her smooth, brown back. Beneath the dress she had put on a pair of black hose which clung to her legs like skin. She was wearing a new pair of heels she had picked up on the way home from class today and her short auburn hair was brushed back behind her ears, exposing her neck. Nicole had learned years ago that men absolutely adored bare necks, the way a veteran skier adores fresh snow. They saw it as an invitation.

Her full, red lips looked even more red against the shiny black of the dress. She slipped two gold rings onto the fingers of her right hand, one onto her left. A gold anklet—the one Miller had given her years back—went around her left ankle, then a touch of perfume—L'Envoi, her personal favorite—along her neck. She had already applied a little to her stomach and her inner thighs. One never knew.

She grabbed her miniature purse, also a new acquisition for the evening, checked herself one last time, popped a mint into her mouth and smiled as she left her townhouse and drove across town in her Miata to meet her father.

On the way, she decided that tonight would positively be her last attempt at enticing English. If things didn't fall her way this evening, she'd let it go and move on.

Most likely.

*   *   *

Mr. Henderson, looking a lot like a very tall and very thin penguin in one of his six tuxedos, drove himself and his only daughter off forty-five minutes later in his Mercedes convertible, at five after five. They would be late, but that was okay. David Henderson's firm was a major party contributor, and dinner wasn't apt to begin without him.

As the valet was taking the Mercedes, David mumbled something about having misplaced his invitation, then dismissed it. Major contributors didn't need invitations.

They would arrive at the ballroom at a quarter before six, where Mr. Henderson and his daughter would navigate their way through various circles of the upper echelon of Chicago's society, explaining, truthfully, that his wife was ill and was regrettably unable to attend. Nicole would smile and accept their lavish compliments graciously, all the while keeping an eye on her watch, waiting for Miller to appear. Having only a single invitation, Miller was to use it for himself, then, once inside, locate Nicole, who would politely excuse herself from whomever at that moment would be trying to take her home for the night, then return on the arm of English Mason. The theory was that David Henderson's daughter would not be questioned as to the validity of her guest's attendance.

It is worth noting that more than one of the older and richer male members of the political upper crust propositioned Nicole in one fashion or another throughout the course of the evening, with one man—no doubt aided by large volumes of expensive alcohol—going so far as to offer in exchange for an immediate encounter in the men's room a thousand dollars in cash, an article of agreement that held little interest for Nicole, daughter of the wealthy and indulgent David Henderson. Nicole had simply smiled when she told him she'd do it for two thousand, and only if the gentleman's wife could be included in the fun, a comment that sent the intoxicated gentlemen (intoxicated congressman, Nicole learned later that evening) abruptly in the other direction, whether permanently or simply long enough to run the idea by his wife, Nicole wasn't sure.

At a little after seven, dinner still not served, Miller walked up behind Nicole, who was engaged in a terribly boring conversation about securities with one of the partners at her father's firm, and kissed the back of her neck. She forgot her conversation and spun around, greeting Miller with a hug somewhere between friendly and suggestive, as all of Nicole's hugs were.

"What took you so long?" She asked. "I'm about to go mad. Do you know how draining it is to have to concentrate on such utter drivel to the extent that you know when to nod and say, "oh, really?" at all the right places? This man behind me could have been telling me it was him atop the grassy knoll for all I know, confessing his dark secret after however many years of carrying it in silent shame, and there I stood and nodded "oh, really?" I think I'm the only one here without some form of incurable halitosis. Do you think there's anywhere else in the entire universe where so many lawyers congregate in one place, other than Hell, perhaps?"

Miller was scanning the monstrous room, eyes bouncing from tux to evening gown to tux again, searching for faces he recognized from the news.

"Nice tux." Nicole said. "Is it yours?"

Miller nodded. "Same one I wore to that ball with you last year."

Nicole smiled. "Did you ever get that tear in the armpit repaired?"

"Yes, I did as a matter of fact. Quite kind of you to care."

"The least I can do," she said. "It was, after all, somewhat my fault. I was in a hurry to get you out of it, as I recall."

Miller suppressed a smile. "Something like that, yes."

"Where's English?" Nicole said. "I'm eager to speak to someone born after The New Deal."

"I saw him out in the lobby, by the piano bar. Don't go get him just yet."

"Problems?" Nicole asked.

Miller nodded. "He's having trouble with his cummerbund. It's pink of all things."

Miller and Nicole migrated through the varying groups of people until they reached the buffet table. Miller found the punch bowl and poured them both glasses. Fine china, he noticed.

"Careful," Nicole teased. "It's more bite than bark. Want me to get you a chaser?"

Miller sipped the punch slowly. "I think I can handle it, thanks. How much have you had?" He asked, examining the hoards of well-dressed, well-groomed, well-mannered people around him.

"Not too much," she said, sipping her drink, "I want to be sober for tonight."

"Listen, Nic. About that. I never promised anything, remember. You two will walk in together, and probably that's all."

Nicole, producing a compact from her purse and checking her make-up, said, "you're going to do fine in law school, Miller. You're the only person I know who prefaces every statement with a disclaimer."

"I just don't want you to get your hopes up for nothing. English doesn't often cross the lines on his own."

"He won't be alone, darling. I'll be there to guide him each step of the way." She snapped her compact shut. "I've made preparations."

Miller held up a hand. "This is don't ask, don't tell material here. I'm not asking, so don't you start telling. I do have to live with the guy when all is said and done."

"Oh settle down. You worry too much. How do I look?"

"Stunning," Miller said, his eyes surveying her familiar body. "Simply stunning. I'm hard as enamel right now."

"Did you know," Nicole said, waving across the room to a middle-aged man with glasses and greasy hair whom she thought she remembered being introduced to earlier, "that one or two of these men actually thought I was my father's girlfriend? As if simply because it's all the rage these days for twenty-something women to take up with men in their fifties that I would be so desperate as to sleep with such an unfortunate looking man as my father."

"Yeah," Miller said, "this is a real family-values crowd." He sipped at his punch. "Imagine English is done by now. He's down the hall, down the staircase, near the grand piano next to the lounge."

Nicole finished the rest of her punch and smiled. She removed a mint from her purse and slipped it beneath her tongue. "Don't wait up," she said.

"Try not to expect too much, huh, Nic?" Miller said. "The kid's practically married."

Nicole blew him a kiss. "Mum's the word on this, cutie," she said, and headed for the door.

Miller, having spotted several faces he'd seen in the papers and on the news, left the punch table and began mingling, unaccompanied and without the benefit of being known by anyone within the magnificent room, relying entirely upon his charm and his wits, and feeling completely at home throughout it all.

* * *

It was about this time that Amanda's father, John Peterson, was finishing up another late but productive night at the office with his secretary, Patricia Simylton. He was dabbing at his sweaty forehead with a monogrammed silk handkerchief as Patricia gathered her clothes from various corners of the room. At the moment, she was on her knees, naked from the waist down, searching for her panties beneath the leather couch.

"I think they're somewhere over there," John said, gesturing towards the other side of the office. He was almost dressed himself, and set the handkerchief on his desk long enough to fasten his belt and gather his tie.

"They flew quite a ways, as I remember." He smiled as she scurried around nervously, like a child on prom night. They'd been carrying on with one another for years now, and she was as uninhibited as any woman he'd met, but the afterwards always left her nervous. The tops of her breasts were still red, and her bush was matted with come. It dripped down and streaked her inner-thighs like tears. The sight of that was enough to make John consider another round. He would have suggested it, but he was already late for the Timmons affair, and he was a full twenty minutes from the Radisson.

Patricia smiled and blew him a kiss across the room. At twenty-eight, she was substantially younger than her fifty-two year old boss, but she had discovered sometime ago that John was a healthy fifty-two, back when he was a healthy forty-nine, in fact. This evening, which had started on the desk and eventually progressed to the leather sofa and finally the floor, had lasted almost two hours, not bad at any age, Patricia felt, having fucked many men of many ages.

"Do you need a ride home?" John asked as he sipped a glass of water.

She emerged from the open closet with her white lace panties and stepped into them. "If it's not too much trouble."

"None whatsoever," John replied. "I'll drop you on the way to the gala. I'd ask you to accompany me, but I've learned from my daughter that her boyfriend is supposed to be there for whatever reason, and I'd hate to risk giving him leverage. You understand.

*   *   *

Nicole found English sitting in the lounge, sipping a coke, tapping his foot softly in time with the piano man. He had apparently solved the cummerbund problem.

"Well look at you," she said smiling, sitting next to him, elegantly folding her legs. "Didn't you polish up nicely?"

"Hey, Nicole," English said, trying not to look at her legs. "Am I going to need boots for this shindig tonight?"

"Of course. For the price of these tickets, everyone here would be disappointed if there wasn't a steady supply of bullshit."

"You know," English said, "I told Miller just to come alone. It's not like he's going to need me here tonight. He'll have twenty names and numbers before the night's over, and be exchanging Christmas cards with them come December."

"Well," Nicole said, running her gaze up and down English's long body, "I'm glad you came. It'll give me someone to talk to while he hobnobs."

They stood, English extending his arm, Nicole snaking hers within it readily, aligning her hip next to his leg. He offered her a nice smile—"full of possibility"—she would later tell Dana, then said, "you look really nice."

"Thank you, English. And you quite handsome."

English nodded, smiled again, and the two strode down the richly decorated hallway towards the ballroom. The maitre-d did had remembered Nicole, had remembered the glow of her skin and her good, hard ankles, and had not bothered to ask either her or her escort for their invitations.

* * *

Inside, English spotted Miller almost immediately, drinking punch as though it were a daily ritual of his, flipping the glass to his mouth in refined arcs of the wrist, engaged in conversation with three distinguished looking gentlemen and at least as many urbane ladies. English shook his head. Nicole was standing next to him, holding his hand.

"Look at him go," English said.

"Like a pro," Nicole replied, gathering both she and English a glass of punch. English, who had not eaten anything since lunch because Miller had said it was important to eat hearty at these things, was starving, and consumed the drink in one gulp. "Strong stuff," he remarked, as Nicole handed him another.

"When's dinner? I was afraid we'd miss it." English said.

"They always allow a couple of extra hours so everybody can work each other for votes and funds. We'll eat soon."

And they did. Twenty minutes later, with English and Nicole both having graduated from the punch table to the open bar, where it was rum and cokes, an elderly black man wearing an impeccable white dinner jacket entered from the far end of the room and announced with the ringing of a silver bell that dinner was now served. Nicole led English through a large archway into an even larger diningroom, where they were seated at one of many octagonal tables. A gigantic chandelier hung from the center of the room, refracting light and sending it into all corners of the room like brilliant stars. Miller, English noticed, had managed to get himself seated at one of the smaller tables and was listening intently as an older, balding gentleman spoke to the table of seven. He had the air of a college professor lecturing his class, and he seemed to be speaking to Miller as much as any of them, as though he had known him for twenty years.

"How do you like that?" English nudged Nicole. "He's not even out of college yet and they're priming him like he was the owner of *The USA Today*."

Nicole, sitting to English's right, folded her napkin into her lap and told the circling waiter that she and the gentlemen would like wine with their meals, then glanced across the room at Miller. "I used to watch him do that with instructors when I was in undergrad."

English nodded. "He plays golf with half his profs. The ones that don't play golf he drinks scotch with. Son of a bitch knows how to get what he wants,"—English's vision doubling slightly from the punch and rum, his head starting to float a bit, numb and feeling full of gauze—"I told Amanda I thought he could be president if he wanted to."

Nicole agreed. "A scary thought, but probably true."

The red wine arrived shortly after, and continued to arrive every five minutes. Before the appetizers—stuffed crabs and sautéed mushrooms—, were served, English had polished off two glasses, Nicole three.

The main course was a choice of veal or pork. English and Nicole both chose the pork. Several more glasses of wine were finished throughout the course of the meal, and by the time desert was served—a scoop of something lime green they were calling sorbet but which looked and felt more like toothpaste—English had caught a fairly respectable buzz.

He began noticing some of the stares he was getting from the surrounding gentlemen, unsure at first as to why, then realizing that they were probably wondering what his connection was with the gorgeous woman by his side. English, who was not a politician and had no plans of ever becoming a politician, had no political viability and decided to have a little fun with this crew. He began glancing as obviously as he could manage at the women accompanying these wondering individuals, smirking and shaking his head. He threw one old man a condescending wink after the aged pervert had craned his head around the others for the fifth or sixth time, cutting at his veal and chuckling with a couple other self-important whatevers about the did-you-knows and had-you-heards.

But the effects of the alcohol were beginning to assuage his anxieties and apprehensions about this evening, and he casually draped his arm over Nicole's naked shoulders, massaging them gently. That's right, folks. She's with me tonight. Eat your mushrooms and get over it.

He took another swallow of the wine, felt his lips numb a bit and his head lighten, and leaned over and whispered into her ear, "everybody is watching you."

"Really?"—wiping her mouth with her napkin, whispering back, "I hadn't noticed." She caught her father's eye from a table near Miller's and smiled her good-girl smile. He returned it with his proud-daddy smile. Both were lies, and both of them knew it, which, she thought, made it an appropriate exchange for a political event.

English heard, through a foggy haze of red wine and rum, the ringing of another bell off to his right. He looked up, and Nicole was nodding towards a grotesquely overweight man standing at the center of the room.

"Speech time," Nicole whispered.

He nodded, his head floating, wondering, distantly, why Nicole wasn't drunk at all, then remembering that she was an alcoholic. An alcoholic, a coke-head, a nympho, every goddam thing they had an anonymous support group for, all wrapped up into five and a half feet of straight A law student addicted to fun and games.

English leaned over towards Nicole's ear again, holding on to the table to keep from falling over, and asked: "How long do these things usually last?"

"Speeches? Anywhere between twenty minutes to an hour, depending. So and so will introduce someone, who'll in turn thank half a dozen people before introducing himself, and so it goes. Eventually you get to the candidate, who generally speaks for a length roughly twice as great as the collective attention span of the room." Her breath, English dimly noticed, smelled of roses—light and sweet. He wondered how that could be. She had just eaten pork, same as him.

They sat there for another ten minutes, English finishing off another glass of wine, before Nicole leaned over and whispered in her breathy voice, "we can leave if you'd like. I can have a car take us home."

From somewhere in the more remote corners of his mind, English recognized the lasciviousness underlying this polite offer and identified it as something he was supposed to try to avoid, unless it was coming from a certain little blond with cotton hands and sky-blue eyes, though he could not quite remember, now, at any rate, exactly *why* that tone, being delivered in that soft, raspy voice, was supposed to instill him with alarm. He imagined part of his sluggish brain functioning was due to the enormous volume of alcohol he had consumed in the last two hours, but couldn't really find anything wrong with that, either. It wasn't like he drank a lot or anything. He and Miller rarely drank when they went out, there was never any booze in the apartment, and the last time he himself had anything at all was weeks ago.

Before he realized it, he and Nicole were standing, his arm around her shoulder once gain, heading in the direction of Miller and his bunch.

"Howdy, Mill," English said upon reaching them. Miller was laughing too hard at something one of the others had said, his Cohiba cigar bobbing in his mouth. When he saw English he excused himself for a moment. He stood English up straight and escorted him through the ballroom and out the door into the hallway. Nicole lingered behind long enough to explain to her father that she had a ride, and that maybe she would see him in a couple of weeks, if her studies permitted. Mr. Henderson, the outwardly proud and clearly drunk father, acknowledged the lie and simply smiled as he kissed his daughter on the cheek.

They took the elevator to the hotel lobby, and Miller sat English down on one of the couches. "You're bombed, English."

English, hiccuping, nodded in the affirmative. "Sorry. It's your fault I came here on an empty stomach. I wanted McDonalds on the way."

Miller wrapped his arm around his friend's waist and held him up. "Nicole's going to take you home."

"Yeah," English said. "Like I don't know the fucking deal with that one." He tried to focus on Miller's face and couldn't. The world whirled. "She's been hitting on me all damned night." English giggled, concentrated on left after right after left.

"That's just Nicole," Miller said. "Just have her drop you off at the apartment. You have your keys?"

"Got 'em."

And then Nicole was there, slipping her arm around his waist, signaling the valet with a wave of her hand. Miller walked with them.

As they climbed into the cab—Miller and Nicole feeding English's long frame into the door and onto the seat, Nicole kissing Miller goodbye before situating herself next to English's now supine frame—Miller wondered if old Nicole might actually get her way this time.

She turned around once as the cab pulled off, Nicole did. To wave through the back window, perhaps, or maybe just to see if Miller was still standing there, still watching. He was, and both Miller and Nicole were thinking the same thing then.

When the evening was over, she would owe him.

* * *

When they arrived at her townhouse forty-five minutes later, Nicole left English, half-asleep, in the back of the taxi, and went inside to get the fare. She grabbed three twenties from her dresser, stopped briefly to check herself in the mirror, and went out to collect English.

Once inside, she sat him in the living room on the couch and took off his shoes. She helped him get through two cups of black coffee before leading him down the hall into her bedroom. There she laid him down atop the blankets and loosened his jacket. With a little coaxing he sat up, and she pulled his arms free of it.

"How do you feel?" she asked him, removing her rings and setting them on the nightstand next to the phone.

"Like dancing," he said. "And I don't dance. You can ask Amanda." He collapsed back down on the bed, and began to laugh. "Where are we?"

"The end of the rainbow," she said, removing her watch and sliding out of her heels. "And let's forget about Amanda for a while, shall we?"

"Yes," English thought, everything within and without spinning in opposite directions, "let's."

To be completely fair, it should be stated for those who would stand in judgment that English Mason was more than fashionably intoxicated after the fundraiser. He had treated himself to three glasses of punch, two rum and cokes, and seven glasses of wine, all within a two or three hour period. He understood what was happening as it happened, but he found himself unable to care too much, even while knowing that he should. Perhaps you can relate.

As he lay there on Nicole's bed—which smelled like she did, flowers and fresh linen and sunshine—he became aware that his shoes were gone, and wondered if he'd left them back at the hotel. He heard Nicole whispering from the other end of the room, but was unable to make out exact words. She seemed to be speaking from a great distance, and through water.

His head was spinning rapidly, in time with the room and everything else, and he became faintly aware that she was removing her dress, and then her bra, and then her hose and her underwear, something he dimly realized he had fantasized about before.

Before his mind could assimilate what his eyes were seeing, he saw Nicole's naked body hunched over him, messing with his cummerbund. He remembered how hard it had been to get the damned thing on there right, and there she was, just taking it off like there'd been nothing to it.

He felt himself respond beneath his pants, thought that there should probably be some guilt somewhere because of the fact, but decided it would come tomorrow, during the hang-over. There was no reason, he reasoned, to rush things. He would deal with it—all of it—in the morning.

And then he saw her slide off the bed, moving across the room as deftly as a cat. He caught a good enough look before she flicked the lights off to see that all she had on was a gold anklet dripping like honey off her left ankle, and then it was dark.

* * *

As Nicole was doing her thing, Miller was doing his, making the rounds, introducing himself to anyone that might matter later, small-talking with several prominent attorneys and making it known that he'd be in law school in a matter of months—Yale, probably, or perhaps Harvard or Chicago—and available for clerkships the following summer. He acquired a number of business cards, committing the names and numbers to memory. He worked the room like a seasoned politician, doing the grip 'n grin with the right men, laughing at the right jokes, smiling politely at the right wives.

It wasn't until sometime after midnight that the crowd began to thin, and it was around this time that Miller caught from the corner of his eye a man whom he had hoped he would have the opportunity to meet this evening. J. Fullard Wallace stood next to his wife, towering above her small, gray-haired frame, chewing casually on a large cigar. He stood with a group of five or six other couples, and, from Miller's vantage point halfway across the room, seemed to be, judging from the amused, easy going looks on their faces, talking about such trivialities as sports and stocks.

Miller straightened his tie once more and cleared his throat, then began walking in Mr. J. Fullard Wallace's direction. He remembered reading something in the paper last week about Wallace's monstrous birthday bash—they'd rented out several floors of the downtown Hilton, and had run up a fairly impressive damage bill—and decided that that was as good a conversation starter as any.

It turned out he was right, and lives were forever altered because of it.

And Wallace, for all his money and power and wisdom, Wallace never really had a chance.

Chapter 8

86 Days Before   (September 11)

The telephone ripped through the room hours later, and Nicole pulled the blankets up over her head and tried to pretend it away. It didn't work, which meant it was Miller on the other end, which meant it would ring until the end of time if she didn't answer it.

Nicole fumbled her hand across her nightstand, knocking rings and watches onto the floor, and finally came upon the receiver.

"What?" She said into the phone, lying her head back down on the pillow, her eyes closed. The shade in her room was drawn and the light off, and the room was completely dark. Her head was pulsating in time with her heart. Her skull felt too big for its skin.

"Is he there?" Miller asked neutrally.

"No." She lied, sliding her hand out to her right until it came upon the warm body of English sleeping next to her. "Why would he be here?"

"You tell me. Put him on, Nicole."

"There's no "him" in this house. Really, Miller. What kind of girl do you think I am?" She dropped the receiver into its cradle.

It rang almost instantly.

"Nicole," Miller said, "put him on."

"He's sleeping."

"Well wake him up. Come on, Nicole. This isn't difficult. You got him off, now be a doll and put him on."

Nicole flicked on the small lamp next to her bed and rolled closer to English's warm, prostrate body. His breath smelled of skin and alcohol.

She nudged his shoulder and said, "It's Miller."

English opened his eyes wide and struggled for his bearings.

"I'm afraid to ask where I am." He said, glancing around the room through half-shut eyes.

"Heaven, I've been told. Do you want to speak with Miller?" She asked, extending the phone in his direction.

He rolled over onto his side. "Oh...my—"

Nicole replaced the phone to her ear. "He doesn't want to talk to you, Miller. Sorry.

She hung up and quickly flung herself atop English, who had been pulling himself to a seated position.

"What in the hell have you done, Nicole? My God, what...what have I done?"

"Me, and with a vengeance." She kissed his nose lightly. "You were terrific."

She had probably intended it as a compliment, but it had sounded more like a death sentence, an irreversible condemnation of sin. "No. Oh, no."

"Afraid so, sweetie."

"Oh for...this...this didn't happen. None of this...what happened, Nicole?" He asked, swinging his feet onto the floor and rising, then realizing that he was, save for his left sock which was hanging feebly onto four of his toes, completely nude. "Oh my God," he said again, his head falling into his hands. "I...I can't believe this. I can't fucking...I don't believe this." He sat back down onto the bed, not bothering to cover himself. There was no use now.

"It was the wine. The beshitted wine. Goddam every drop of alcohol I've ever had. Fuck, fuck, fuck, fuck!" He repeated this over and again, laying the blame somewhere else as men will do and finding little to no comfort in it.

Nicole remained on her stomach, on English's side of the bed. "What's the big deal? *I'm* not going to say anything? Are you?"

English turned and looked at her, struggling with the urge to punch her in the mouth. "Are you fucking nuts?"

Nicole shrugged, and the telephone rang again.

"Yes, Miller?" She answered.

"This is no longer amusing, Nic."

"I understand, Miller, but he really is noticeably upset right now, so maybe it'd be best if—"

"No, wait!" English interrupted. "Give me that." He reached for the phone and she hung it up.

"Nicole," English said, his voice rising. He fell back onto the bed, striving desperately to awaken from this nightmare. Nicole took the phone off the hook, turned off the light, and snuggled up closer to English, whose head had begun pounding rhythmically, whether from the hangover or the guilt, he wasn't sure.

"This is horrible," he said. "Oh God in Heaven what in hell have I done?"

Nicole didn't say anything, preferring instead to let him work through it himself.

"Well," English was saying, "I've done it this time. I've finally gone and fucking done it. I've completely destroyed my life. The world is over."

"Nonsense," Nicole replied. "You spent the night in my bed. That's not illegal."

"Tell that to Amanda."

"I'm not entirely sure what purpose that would serve," she said.

English said nothing for a long while. Finally, after several moments of weighing his options, he said, almost pleadingly, "did…did we do it?"

He felt her warm up against his side, her hand draped across his stomach, its fingers whispering across his skin. He was not drunk now; terribly hungover, but not drunk, and knew that she needed to stop, but it seemed that for the moment, until he had sorted everything out, there was no need to act too hastily. It was, on a very shallow level, nice lying there like that.

"Like wild animals," Nicole said.

"Oh my God."

"English, there really isn't any reason for you to torture yourself like this. What happened happened, and that's the end of it. You might try to focus a little more clearly on the bright side of things. You seemed to be rather enjoying yourself at the time, and besides, nobody has to know."

"Miller knows."

"Miller isn't going to tell anyone. He could care less about this kind of thing. Furtive sex is actually rather boring to him. He fancies himself too sophisticated, I imagine."

"Nicole," English said, pleading more than not now, "why did you do this? Why did you let me do this? This…this isn't kosher at all."

"Do what, English? We spent the night together. It's not like we killed anyone. You don't even remember it, which really is a shame, I might add."

"I have a girlfriend, Nicole," he said into the darkness, "in case you didn't know that. A girlfriend. Listen to it. A bona-fide commitment with someone else. And this…" English waved his hands around before him, pointing at himself, the bed, and Nicole now sitting up beside him, her breasts perched out on her chest in plain view, the cherry red flesh of her nipples swollen to the size of half-dollars, "is not the way to go about strengthening it."

"You were drunk. Don't you think she might understand? Maybe not the sex, of course, but staying here? If anything were to leak, which I can't see how it could, we'll simply say you slept on the couch. She'll be grateful I wouldn't let you drive. Friends don't let friends, and all that."

He shook his head. "Somehow I just can't see that washing."

"Honestly, English," she said. "Do you truly think she's never slipped? A few random moments of passion in a Nursing School bathroom? A sudden bout of groping with a stranger in the Macy's dressing room? Fidelity is an endangered species, these days. Look at you."

English looked over at her, wondering how she ever became so pathetic.

"I'm not even going to respond to that nonsense," English said.

"Well," Nicole said, turning the lamp back on and dismissing the entire issue with a wave of her hand, "at any rate it happened, and I guess you'll see that it goes away just fine. These things often do."

She batted her eyes and whispered, "what do you say? Once more for the history books?"

"My God, Nicole, haven't you been listening to me? Have you heard a single goddam word I've said?"

"Of course I have. But there's nothing I can do about it now."

"Well,"—English, once again rising from the bed, this time taking a second to remove the sock clinging stupidly to his foot, "I'm getting out of here. This never happened, all right. Say 'okay'. This never happened."

Nicole nodded her head.

"Say it."

"This never happened," she said.

"Good," English said, pulling on his pants, searching for his shirt. "If someone," finding his shirt stuffed beneath the bed and putting it on, "asks you what you did last night, what are you going to say?"

"That you and I fucked like wildcats."

"This is serious, Nicole."

"Oh, English. Don't be so dramatic all the time. I wish you could have seen yourself last night. You really are a different person altogether when the lights are low. Did you know you came three times, and quite vocally every time? You should have heard yourself. Whose my daddy, indeed? You were quite the caveman. Does Amanda inspire that sort of poetry from you back at the apartment?"

English simply stared at her, unable to speak. Disgust and arousal rose over him in waves.

"You hammered away at me for almost two hours, darling, and if I could have recorded some of the things you said…well English, I must say my eyes were opened." She winked. "Among other things."

"I don't want to hear about it, Nicole. I'm not kidding. I really do not want to fucking hear about it."

"Oh, lighten up," she laughed. "You've been uptight since middle school. You are positively going to have a heart attack one day if you don't learn to relax." She smiled at him. "If anyone asks, I didn't do anything. I stayed home and painted my nails. Highlighted my roots. Whatever."

"Yes. That's good. You painted your nails. Perfect. Excellent. Wonderful."

English began for the door, buttoning his shirt as he walked, and Nicole extended her bare leg in front of him before he could reach the handle.

"I really am terribly in the mood right now, English," she said. "All this talk has me thinking of last night. Do stay." The slightest hint of wet tongue behind full lips, "I'll make it worth your while."

"Fuck that. I've got to get home."

"Why the rush? What's done is done. Why not do it again, if the punishment's the same?"

English plopped down on the bed. "They teach you that bullshit line of rationalization in law school?"

"For Heaven's sake," she said, standing and crossing the room, removing a light green silk robe from the back of a chair and slipping it over her head. It came down to just above her knees. "I'm going to go make some coffee. Would you like some?"

English looked at her the way he might look at a priest in a liquor store. "No," he managed. His head dropped and he covered his face with his hands.

Nicole looked at him like that for a moment, not sure what she thought about this whole scene. She had had such high hopes for English, but this regret routine was a little tiresome. Same modern scenario. Girl gets fucked. Guy gets fucked. Girl gets sticky. Guy gets guilty.

"It'll get better," she finally said, deciding to play the dutiful, comforting woman's role. She reached over and flicked the light-switch off again. English sat in the darkness for some time, feeling his heart chopping like a fan inside his chest, listening to her slow, patterned breathing coming from beside him, and prayed to God he could find some way to keep this quiet. He'd have to lie to Amanda, something he hadn't done more than once or twice since they'd met. But it wasn't something he enjoyed. People had a way of talking, things had a way of spreading. She already suspected Nicole was after him.

He would say he slept at Miller's parents' house. No problem there. Amanda wouldn't call over there late at night, and if he said he slept at the apartment she'd wonder why he didn't answer the phone throughout the night, and when he wouldn't have a suitable answer, she'd assume he had been drinking, and the two of them would probably end up fighting over it. Better to just say Miller needed a few things from his folks' place and that they crashed over there rather than drive back to the apartment so late at night. All he had to do was get in touch with Miller and explain the story to him.

But first he had to get out of here.

"Nicole," he said, his voice low and steady, "why did you ever let me do this? Why did you ever let me get here…in your room? You knew I had too much to drink. You knew I was…"

"You were just too persuasive, I guess." He felt her behind him as he sat on the edge of the bed, her hand on his back, then her lips. He could feel her breasts pressed up against his skin, the softness radiating heat like something alive.

"Why don't you lie back down?" she said. "We'll have breakfast in a little while."

"I can't stay, Nicole," he sighed. "No matter how much I enjoyed last night, I just can't stay."

"I didn't think you remembered last night."

"I remember parts of it."

There was a lengthy pause. Her hands were on his shoulders, her lips on the back of his neck. Her scent was very strong.

"You can stay another hour or two," she whispered, punctuating her words with kisses on his neck and back. "Stay, and I'll make us breakfast, and we'll eat it naked in front of a fire."

English did stay, and she did make them breakfast, but whether they ate it naked or before a fire is immaterial to this story.

* * *

Amanda got out of the shower at precisely eleven the following morning. When English hadn't called at noon, as he always did on Saturdays, she called the apartment and let it ring, leaving a message after the third ring. Then she called his parent's house. His mother said that she hadn't heard from him since earlier yesterday evening, and that if he wasn't at the apartment he was probably over at Miller's house. Amanda thanked her and hung up. He had spent the night at Miller's, probably drunk.

Amanda sighed and sat down before her vanity mirror and began rolling her hair. She thought today she might wear it down. English always liked it better down.

By one, when English still had not called, Amanda began to worry. She called the apartment again. Miller answered on the fourth ring, and assured her in a tone that reeked of trivial complicity that they had both had a little too much to drink, and that English was there at the apartment, safe and sound, in the shower.

"Have him call me when he gets out," Amanda said.

"Are you at home?"

"Of course I'm at home," Amanda said, disgusted. "Where else would I be?" She hung up without saying goodbye.

After a moment she returned to her vanity and pulled her hair back up.

* * *

Nicole answered the telephone on the first ring. She had replaced the receiver after English had fallen back to sleep, hoping Miller might have gotten the message and quit trying for a while, knowing this was a foolish notion, that quitting wasn't something Miller did.

"Is he still there?"

"He's sleeping."

"I'm sure. Wake him up. It's important."

"A life or death emergency, no doubt."

"For someone who got exactly what they wanted last night, you sure are a testy one. I can appreciate your reticence, but I'm afraid I need the boy on the phone. There's a real world out here which doesn't, the more memorable moments of your days and nights not withstanding, function orgasm to orgasm,—"

"—if you think that," Nicole interrupted, "you aren't living in it properly."

Miller sighed, and noticed with a touch of irony that it was only because they were on the phone and not face to face that he was able to hide his deep, almost visceral admiration for Nicole Henderson. She was as dignified and unabashedly self-aware as anyone he'd ever encountered. Her world consisted of her own moral constructs, and no one else's. It was a rare quality, which, Miller decided, was probably a good thing.

"In any case," Miller said, his tone suddenly subdued and relaxed, "he and I have some fairly pressing business to discuss."

"Well now. That wasn't so terribly difficult, was it? You should have tried the more polite manner to begin with."

"My sincerest apologies," Miller said, not surprised at all that he meant it. Whatever else she was, whatever else she might do, Nicole demanded respect.

A moment later and English was on the phone. He listened to Miller for about a minute, then said, "oh, shit."

* * *

It had taken English a little over an hour to fully placate his girlfriend, who had found English's drinking the night before, as she found English's drinking anytime he drank, to be a little much.

"I was just worried," she insisted. "Downtown isn't safe in broad daylight, much less Friday at midnight." English informed her that, aside from drowning in an ever-growing sea of ostentatious posturing and outright bullshit, he had been in no physical danger.

She had, of course, invited him over, adding as a postscript that her parents had taken the day to go visit her grandmother in Springfield, and that the Jacuzzi in their parents' bedroom was bubbling in lonesome solitude. Normally it would have taken more self-restraint than English possessed to keep him from forgetting the world at large and rushing over there with the single-minded fury that a hottub and his girlfriend combined instilled in him, but this morning he didn't think he'd be up to it, or, at least, not up to doing it well. Nicole—and the unnerving moments afterwards—had taken their toll. Besides, he had too much regard for Amanda to debase her in such a way. The idea of facing her just now turned his stomach with guilt.

He had some trouble worming out of it, but in the end satisfied her by saying his father had requested that he come over and help him remove a stump from the backyard. He made a mental note to himself to find a stump somewhere behind the house and pull it up before he took Amanda by his folks' place again.

He had called Amanda from the apartment, approximately half an hour after Nicole had finally let him take Miller's call.

Eighty-eight days later almost to the hour, on December 8th, sitting behind the thick, mahogany beams of the witness stand, English will testify that yes, it was indeed possible to attribute it all to that brief, minute-long telephone conversation he had with Miller.

Palto will push him a little further, ask him to elaborate for the jury, and English will reiterate.

"If there's any one thing I could change about the past several months, and there are many, many things I'd nearly give my soul to change, but if there were one…only one…" a pause, a momentary hitch while he pushes back tears as he pictures Amanda as she'd been before all this, before his entire world imploded, "it would have to be that phone call."

"And why is that, English," Palto will ask him eighty-eight days from now.

But English won't be able to answer. Miller sees to it.

* * *

When he got back to the apartment Miller was waiting, leaning over the kitchen counter, the television on CNN, reading something in *Newsweek* as he ate a bowl of Grapenuts. English walked past him to the freezer, got out a half gallon of chocolate mint ice cream—Breyers, the real shit, not the grocery store brand that was dyed green and tasted like toothpaste—found a spoon in the sink and headed for the couch.

"Fun night?"

"I don't want to talk about it."

"Why not? Some of us had to sleep alone last night. You can give me a little taste, can't you?"

"Tracy didn't stay over?"

"An irrelevant question, compadre. Once you've slept with Nicole, it's all sleeping alone."

"Then you know how it was. And I don't want to talk about it. It was a mistake. I was drunk."

"Don't worry about it," Miller said over his cereal. He finished the article, letting English sit there and dilute his regret with chocolate-mint Breyers.

"Did she do that thing with her teeth? You know, where she—"

"I really don't want to talk about it," English said.

"Fair enough. Just say so, shit." He paused. "What I said on the phone,"—Miller, closing the magazine and tossing it to the card table in the dinette, circling around English and sitting in their only chair, a run down blue-black job they had stolen from a fraternity house several years back—"about that Wallace fellow. It's true. I just spoke to my father on the phone."

"Nothing personal, Mill, but I don't really give a good goddam."

"Hey, English, ease up a bit. Remember what Mamet says about times like this. Fuck little girls—so be it. Cheat on your wife—you did it, live with it."

"Fuck Mamet. He's your idol, not mine."

"He's not my idol. He just has some pretty good insights into life. You're not the first to mess up, or even the first to mess up with Nicole, for that matter. Quit flagellating yourself. Let it go."

English said, "She's going to find out."

"Not if you don't tell her she won't."

English shook his head. "No one ever plans to get caught. Shit like this, it gets out. It always does. She's going to find out, and when she does she'll leave me. And then I'm going to kill that fucking cunt Nicole."

Miller flipped through the channels with the remote while English dabbed at the ice cream. "Remember that chick I was popping a couple summers ago. The redhead with impressive tits? Had everything pierced? Nipples, tongue, little button downstairs?"

"Not really."

"Sure you do. The one I said liked it in public places. Always wanted to be taken to the park."

"Oh yeah—Sylvia something."

"Osterhouse. That's the one. I must have slept with her two, three hundred times. Every day for a while. Three, four times a day. Bam bam bam. And the whole time she's got this fiancé over in Springfield, came to see her on the weekends. Big Dianabol-eating type. Muscles on top of muscles. Stretch marks in places you and I don't even have. So that's bad enough, but when I decided it was time to cool things down a bit, she couldn't let it go. Why? Who knows why. Oscar Wilde said women were made to be loved and not understood, and maybe that's the case. Either way, she threatened to confess everything to her fiancé."

"I remember. You were out of sorts for a while."

"Naturally. Hercules would have killed me. But remember what happened next?"

"No, I don't, and is there a point to this, or are we just rehashing old war stories?"

"She had a nervous breakdown. Ended up in detox, then a nuthouse. Detox for a couple of months, the nuthouse for longer. And when they let her out to visit—"

"You took her flowers. Stupid. Stupid and mean, actually. You've always had a bit of a mean streak in you, Miller. I've been meaning to mention it."

"Well," Miller said, "it was a little crude, I admit, but I was younger then, and more easily swayed by the momentary hormonal-surge. But you're wrong about stupid. She was certifiable. It was the safest snatch in town. They had institutionalized her, given her a number and a little pink jumper to wear, and all of a sudden her credibility was about as existent as her hymen—the land of myth and memory. Didn't much matter what she said after that—who's going to believe a strung out twenty-something shacked up in a padded room in Charter Hospital's East Wing?"

"I still don't see the point."

"The point is, Nicole is safe. Your name is just one of many, my friend, like an entry in the dictionary. Lost amidst the numbers. Nothing to worry about."

"I still feel like shit about it. The fact that she's a fuckmachine doesn't help much."

Miller responded with a shrug. "That'll pass. This is airtight and over years ago. You Protestants, man—this guilt thing with you has got to go. It's pointless. That's the beauty of being a Jew. We just don't give a shit."

English scoffed. "Some Jew. When did you last go to temple?"

"I've been busy."

"Right. Busy banging little psycho-whores, maybe. Have you been even once since your barmitzvah?"

"No, but my mother has."

"Then your mother's Jewish, maybe. You're about as Jewish as the Pope." Miller laughed. "Everybody take a look at the Jewish Studies Scholar."

"My mom's brother-in-law is named Abe," English said.

"Abe is a Jewish name," Miller finished for him, his voice lilting in sing-song fashion. "Ergo, Abe is a Jew."

"Precisely," English said, smiling. "You're not my only connection to the keepers of Kosher."

"I've met your uncle Abe. Nice fellow. And he's only part Jewish."

"Which," English said, finishing the ice cream and setting the empty carton on the floor, "is a part more than you."

Miller was saying something in return, but English was suddenly gripped with a slowly rolling wave of nausea as brief flickers of remembrance danced sporadically in and out of his head—her breath on his face, the smell of new sweat and warm skin.

English breathed in deeply and glanced at his watch. His breath tasted thick and heavy, and he could smell last night's activities on his skin.

"What's this you're saying about the judge?" He asked, ready to get whatever it was Miller had in mind over with so he could shower and take a nap.

"He's not a judge. He's a lawyer. A big-time lawyer. J. Fullard Wallace. He hung the moon as far as the old guard around here are concerned."

English vaguely recalled Miller mentioning him in the Henderson closet. "The Jameson thing. What's that got to do with us?"

"Nothing really, until last night. You know the guy the Democrats are sending to the slaughter?"

English nodded. "Timmons."

"Right," Miller said. "It's a farce."

"What's a farce?"

"His candidacy."

English offered him a quizzical stare.

"I'm convinced of it. I've given this a lot of thought, and I can't find any other explanation."

"Explanation for what?"

Miller sat forward, leaning over his knees the way he did when something had him excited. "Listen," he said, not looking at English, watching instead the television skip from channel to channel, occasionally resting on something he found of interest, then skipping some more. "Gambon is undefeatable. Everybody knows that. He's an institution, for God's sake. Like Santa Claus, or The Fourth of July. Like that old guy down in South Carolina. The people aren't going to let him go. Timmons is a paper tiger."

English, who didn't much care for things political, never understood Miller's infatuation with the stuff. He decided after the first political event Miller dragged him to years ago—an exploratory committee meeting for one of the University professor's run for the local schoolboard—that he'd rather spend his life cleaning shit-tanks than have even the slightest association with a profession that was equally dependent upon an adeptness at lying and the will of the people. At least in the shit-tanks he could see where the odor was coming from.

"I don't know, Mill. Upsets happen all the time. Especially in things like this, where everyone in the state has a say."

"I found a book at my folks' place this morning. I've got it in my room," he said, standing, disappearing around the corner into his room, still talking, "this is going to amaze you."

* * *

Several hours earlier and miles across town, when English had still been in bed with Nicole and Miller had been trying to get through to him, J. Fullard Wallace sat on the edge of his bed and slid his naked, cold feet into the slippers. His wife, Claudia, was still asleep. She would remain that way for several more hours yet; she had been sleeping later and later these past few years. Already it was eight, two hours later than the time she used to rise when their kids had been home. But now, with him working fifty to sixty hours a week with the firm, plus the additional time he had been spending on the Timmons campaign, his wife was spending more and more of her spare time in bed, as though she lacked any reason to rise.

J. Fullard Wallace sighed lightly and laid the paper, folded closed, at the foot of the bed. He would go make them breakfast, then bring it back to bed for the two of them. They didn't eat breakfast together very often anymore. Instead, he spent his breakfasts across expensive tables discussing either law or politics—though he had never seen where one ended and the other began—with men in expensive suits sitting next to women with hourly rates. Today would be a nice day—as would every day, he knew—to show his wife how much he appreciated her patience and understanding. She had remained devoted since the beginning.

He looked at her now, with her hands folded neatly beneath her left cheek. Her thin lips fluttered noiselessly as she drew in breath; he thought he could see a slight movement of her eyes beneath their closed lids. Even now—especially now, he thought—she was beautiful, beautiful in the way that acceptance and familiarity is beautiful.

Smiling, suddenly aware of the warmth of the morning sun shining through the large windows, J. Fullard Wallace rose from the edge of the bed and left to make his wife breakfast.

He was in the middle of scrambling the eggs when the telephone began to ring.

*   *   *

"My father"—Miller, taking his seat next to English on the couch, a large, leather bound volume in his lap—"bought a special edition of encyclopedias a couple years back at a business fair in Virginia. This one," tapping the volume in his hand, "is a supplementary edition, entitled, no less, *Our Country and its Leaders.* Neat, huh?"

"As can be," English replied drolly.

Miller ignored him. "At the fundraiser last night, hours after you had and Nicole left to do your thing, I had the pleasure of talking to one Mr. J. Fullard Wallace about various odds and ends. He was very friendly and seemed overly interested in what I had to say. Whether he was genuine or no I couldn't tell you, but it doesn't matter anyway. By and by we came to the campaign on hand, and I learned that he was working as an unpaid consultant to the Timmons' campaign. He wasn't at all bashful of the fact."

"Why should he be?" English shrugged.

Miller smiled. "Well, I have a theory on that." He handed English the monstrous volume and pointed to a small, four line paragraph in the middle of page four thousand seventeen. English read it aloud. "*Wallace, James Fullard. Prominent criminal defense attorney in the greater Chicago area. Began his career in the district attorney's office. Lead prosecutor in the Jimmy Jameson trial. Frequent political strategist and consultant for the Illinois Democratic Party. Associated in various capacities with dozens of campaigns including Senator Moseley-Braun's maverick Senatorial bid in '92.*"

"I asked my father about him," Miller said, "and he simply said Wallace was a real big-wheel. That's the actual term he used. Big-wheel. Is that Green Hornet or what?"

"So?"

"So I called Wallace. Just to see. I re-introduced myself to him, told him we had spoken at the dinner the night before, and asked if perhaps I could interview him for a paper I have to do about politicians and the men behind them. I think he was a little pissed that I called his house on a Saturday morning, said something about being in the middle of breakfast blah blah blah, but that if I called his secretary at his office Monday morning, he would see what he could do for me. He was about to hang up when I asked him the next question."

English waited patiently.

"Curious?" Miller asked.

"I'm curious as to why you care so much about this crap."

"I'm not sure I do," Miller confessed. "But I do think there's something else to this, though."

Miller closed the book and held it across his knees. English noticed his thumb was still stuck in it, marking a page. "I did some snooping at the library on campus on my way home from my folks' place this morning. Found a couple of things that seemed…interesting. First, I think it's worth noting that with the exception of a few of the smaller ones, every single major campaign that Wallace has ever been tied to in any notable way…" Miller reopened the book, pointed to a small, italicized caption in the upper corner of page 2500, and said, "this guy's been linked to as well. In some form or another, the two of them have been teamed on the same campaign some ten or twelve different times."

English glanced only half-interested at the name. Raymond Patterson. It was an unfamiliar name to English.

Miller was still going. "Most of the campaigns—virtually all of the later ones—Wallace has worked with have Patterson's fingerprints all over them. Maybe just a consultant, or he handled the legal end of things, but he was always there. Kind of like Carville and Begala."

"Who?"

"Twins from the Clinton-Gore years. Never mind. The two have a history. But there's more. Do you know what J. Fullard Wallace does?"

"He's a lawyer."

"Sure he's a lawyer. But for the party."

English shook his head.

"He's acting treasurer. Has been for nine years. He was deputy treasurer for eleven years before that."

English waited to make sure Miller was through before saying, "I know I sound redundant, but so what?"

"That's what I kept thinking. So what? But just consider it for a moment. There's a line of commonality at work here. Wallace has been connected in one way or another to the state party's money supply for twenty-plus years. He's known Patterson for at least ten. And now there's a candidate who cannot win but nevertheless brings in an enormous sum of cash because his opponent is seen as politically vulnerable. And who oversees all that money?"

"The treasurer," English said.

"Give the man a prize. The same treasurer that's been managing the party's money for almost a decade."

English sat quietly for a moment, then said, "o.k. Let me run through this like I'm four years old. One, we've got a Senate race with lots of green pouring in. Two, Wallace, a trusted, seasoned, savvy lawyer is in charge of it. Three, there's this other joe…"

"Patterson."

"Right," English said. "Patterson. He's the…the what?"

Miller shrugged. "Dunno. Consultant. Pollster. Administrative assistant. Limo-driver. No telling, really. But he's there. Again. Like always, he's there. Just like Wallace."

English finished for him. "He's a shadow. A specter. A ghost."

"I called the state election commission and asked for a report of the Timmons campaign fundraising this quarter. If my hunch is right, we're going to see relatively very few corporate and pac dollars, and an ever-loving shitpile of soft money."

"Individual donations."

"That's right. Individual donations. The national party is airing ads on Timmons' behalf in various key states—California, Oregon, New York, Massachusetts, Wisconsin—places where Timmons' pro-environment record and labor-union connections will be well received, not because they give two shits about Timmons, but they want the Senate back, and they think this might be the year Gambon finally falls. That means checks for 10, 20, 50 dollars floating in like candy from all corners of the country, all of it soft money, all of it small enough to slip through compliance laws. The national party's been doing this for over a month now, English, which means its been working."

"Good for them. Why do I care?"

"This is hardly ever done, English. It's a rarity when a national party will take a candidate under its wing like this, and its almost never done during a presidential season. The Republicans did it in 94 with Oliver North and that fuck George Nethercut, and maybe back in 90 with Jesse Helms, and I think the Democrats pretty much targeted Gingrich on a national scale every two years until he self-destructed, but that's basically it. This just isn't done, English, and the fact that it's happening here and happening now has to mean something."

"Look, Miller, it's probably like you said. The Democrats smell blood and they're digging deep. Gambon's one of those guys you either love or hate, and he's been around long enough that anyone who reads the papers knows his name. It's not any big thing that people around the country are pitching in."

"Yeah, but what I'm saying is this: Wallace and this Patterson fellow haven't had this opportunity before. In all the campaigns they've been involved with, they haven't seen the kind of money that this race is bringing in. There's never been a candidate who draws so many *individual*, difficult-to-trace donations. And he's a loser. He's supposed to lose. No one's expecting him bring in the kind of money I think they're probably bringing in."

"So what?"

"So where's the money *going?* The race? I doubt it."

"You think they're stealing," English said matter-of-factly. "Stealing it themselves and setting up slush funds in Switzerland."

Miller nodded. "Damned right. I think they're looting the race, and maybe the whole party. Skimming off the top or scooping from the bottom I don't know, but I'd bet a big toe that's what the hell is going on. They're probably dumping it in some country where the banks don't ask questions—like Switzerland. Been doing it for years, I expect, though never at the level they're able to now."

Miller stopped and looked off to some place far away. "They could have millions by now, English."

"That's crazy."

"What's so crazy about it? It makes perfect sense to me."

"Oh, Miller, for…who cares?—We're not going to get involved with this. We aren't. No way."

"Who said anything about *involved*? Aren't you just a bit curious?"

"No."

"Why not?"

"Because there's no point. It's boring, and its stupid, and it's absolutely without relevance to my life, which is ticking along just fine, right now."

"We're talking about intellectual curiosity, here. Not some life-changing discovery. I just…I don't know, English. Aren't you curious a little? Just a *touch*?"

"It'd be a waste of time. Besides, I've had to give Amanda the short end lately, and if we start in on this it'll be just like that damned Berry thing that took every second of every day and almost got us tossed out of school."

"I was right about Reverend Berry."

"So what? Who cares what the man does in his spare time?"

"Mrs. Berry cared a hell of a lot."

"Miller, we probably spent a total of five hundred hours on that stupid little project of yours. Following him around town, staking out motels at all hours of the night, sneaking into the University photo labs. And for what? A couple of seconds of fun at the student movie theater?"

"You see, English. This is where you lack imagination. Right there. What you're calling a couple of seconds will be an enduring legacy on campus. People still talk about that night. The good Rev. resigned because of it. Everyone who paid to see that vampire shit—which by the way really was an awful film—finally got their money's worth. You didn't see anyone getting up to re-butter their popcorn, did you?"

English thought back to the evening and managed a laugh. "No, I guess not."

"Hell no. And let me tell you, that was one involved audience. The U.C. Program Union owes us a thank you note; they sell the student theater out every fucking night now. One minute its over-priced coke and stale raisinettes and the next Tom Cruise and Brad Pitt yield the screen to the wife of the Dean of the entire Humanities Department as she gets glory-holed by a man of the cloth. A couple of seconds," Miller sneered. "We should have won an award for that. I'm still seriously considering sending a copy to Sundance."

"Well," English said dismissively, "if '*Spanking the Monkey*' and that other piece of shit flick you like so much can fare well there, who knows? You might stand a shot with Redford's bunch."

Miller looked genuinely injured. "What piece of shit flick?"

"The gambling one. The one with all the drinking and the 'money's' and 'babies'."

"'*Swingers?*' You didn't like '*Swingers*'? That settles it, then. I know there's something wrong with you. English, that movie was quite possibly one of the best films—" he stopped himself—"I'm wrong. It wasn't film. It was art. Pure, soul-inspired art."

"Give me a fucking break," English said. "It was horseshit."

"The trailer scene? At the beginning? Where Trent's spinning the "audition story" and he pulls that 'swear to God… swear to'—never mind. We shouldn't even be discussing it. We're not qualified." Convincing dramatic pause here, followed by a subtle sigh. "Never mind," he said again, shaking his head, looking at his friend like he'd just discovered he was dying of a terminal disease, and Miller was trying to find the heart to tell him. "You're embarrassing yourself here," Miller said. "Back to whatever you were saying," he said. "Back to mediocrity."

"We could have gone to jail, Mill."

"When?"

"The Berry thing. We could have ended up in jail. Did you ever seriously consider that?"

He shrugged. "But we didn't. And besides, even if we had been caught, what law did we really break? Trespassing, maybe. Violation of privacy. We're talking a couple hours picking up trash on the interstate and washing down police cars. It would've been worth it."

There was a moment's silence, somewhere in the middle of which Miller said, "we'll just nose around a bit. Lift up a rock or two."

He winked at English.

"Just to see," he said, then left English alone with his regrets of the night before.

English sat there in motionless silence for a long time. He was there again, that distant, craggy, gulf which stood between him and his lifelong friend. Over the years English had more than once been escorted carefully to the edge and encouraged to peer out and over it, just to see what waited on the other side. But that was just it. With Miller, it was never enough just to look. Never enough just to see.

There was always a way down into the canyon, a means of going further, a partially obscured path leading deeper into things.

Sometimes though, English knew, sometimes getting back out could be the problem.

Chapter 9
85 Days Before   (September 12)

The Wallace house is a sprawling brown two story job set back on an acre of some of Kenilworth's most exclusive property. Immaculately trimmed shrubbery stands six feet tall and flanks the sides and front, reaching as high as the bottoms of the upper windows. The front door is a flat black, with a brass kick-plate, brass doorknob, and brass door-knocker with the inscription W. The serpentine driveway leading to the front walk is gravel.

Wallace purchased this house twenty-seven years ago, when his law practice had first begun to generate the large sums of cash it has since become legendary for, and noticed, upon arriving home from work those first weeks, that after the dull, monotonous sounds of the interstate beneath his car, the crunching of the gravel seemed strangely pleasant. It meant—came to mean after some time—that he was home. He told his wife to cancel the cement order, and the driveway has remained gravel since.

On either side of the Wallace home there is a spacious section of healthy lawn, bordered by thick redtips, transplants from the backyard of their previous home. English ivy climbs the Western side; jasmine nearly completely covers the Eastern side, its spidery green and white tentacles stretching their way up the stucco like children reaching for the clouds.

The distance from the road leading to their gravel driveway and the house is approximately fifty feet. From the nearest point in the treeline, two hundred feet. On this peaceful Sunday afternoon, there are four golf balls—two white, two orange—in various positions on the lawn. A bag of clubs lies against the front door. Above the house, the afternoon sun shines down approvingly, warming everything beneath it. To the South, the Hancock building stands as erect as a soldier, a needle-like silver and gray stripe climbing out of the steel and glass city and seemingly piercing the skyline.

And this is how things are on Sunday, September 12, a little after noon as, nineteen miles west of the Wallace place, in the burbs of Chicago, English and Amanda eat Sunday dinner with her family, and here, in Kenilworth, where Miller sits behind the wheel of his car, parked sixty yards down the dirt road and concealed by the foliage, sipping a Pepsi in the can, studying the home of Mr. J. Fullard Wallace, Attorney-at-Law.

* * *

At a little before two that afternoon Miller, lying on his bed, reading a chapter from *The Science and Art of Political Fundraising*, a book he had picked up a couple of days after the Timmons affair, dialed the number to Laney Taylor's apartment. Laney had come up through highschool with Miller and English, and had gone to Brown after graduating. He had returned after graduating Brown to attend Medical School at Chicago. He was a brain, no question, but he was a pliable brain. Miller could work with him.

After the fourth ring, Laney answered, and got started.

Chapter 10

74 Days Before   (September 23)

Thursday afternoon, a little before five. On the way to the apartment after class, Miller stopped off at a convenience store, picked up a six pack of Zima and headed over to the Park, about a half mile outside the city limits. He had called Nicole the night before and asked her if she could meet him there around five tonight; there was something he wanted to discuss with her.

When he got there she was waiting, on a bench beneath a gigantic fir. Her chestnut hair caught the evening sun and shimmered red; her face was bright and cool and without expression, a snowy field beneath the sun. Miller had known her long enough to know that with Nicole, that generally meant she was deep in thought. She was wearing black jeans with a billowy red sweater tucked in, clinging to her small waist. Her legs were crossed at the ankles, and she was wearing the black designer boots Miller had bought her last Christmas. Miller stopped and looked at her before approaching; she looked like a model sitting there, virtually every curve perfect, each facial feature deliberate and poised.

When she saw him she stood and met him with a hug when he got there, and the two sat and started in on the Zimas. Miller didn't waste a lot of time. He needed a favor.

What favor, Nicole asked.

Miller hadn't answered her, not directly, but had instead changed gears a bit and asked her, as if he hadn't known, if her evening with English after the fundraiser had turned out the way she had hoped.

Nicole figured out the deal before she answered, said that yes, it had turned out fine, and sure, she'd be happy to do a favor for Miller. After all, she said, casually pulling her bangs down and examining their ends, they were old friends, and old friends looked out for one another.

Miller capped off a Zima and told her it'd take an entire night. Nicole asked what in the world Miller needed with her for a whole night, and Miller told her. She balked at first, then looked as if she had been overtaken with the chills, then finally said she'd do it, that it might even be fun in a weird, twisted way.

Miller wasn't so sure about that, but he kept that to himself.

"How's Buck?" He asked, after they'd worked out the specifics of the plan.

Nicole finished her first Zima like it was water and opened a second. "He's fine. Still Buck. We're seeing other people now. We kind of always were, but it's official now, I guess." She took a swallow of the drink and lit a cigarette. "Trevor's been calling from Harvard a good bit lately. He wants to get things started again."

"You could do worse, Nic. Harvard M.B.A. Not a bad looking fellow. Why not?"

"That's called settling," she said, shaking her head. "Not my style."

"No," he replied, "I don't suppose so."

"I guess the Harvard bit is impressive," she continued, "if you're an over-achiever who needs that sort of thing." Nicole puffed the cigarette and flicked a length of ashes onto the ground between her feet. Miller watched the wind stir it and carry it off.

"I don't know," she shrugged, continuing, "we're different people. Different lives. Everybody kind of thinks we'll get married eventually—I guess because we dated so long, if you want to call it dating—but I think I'd rather die, or even work as a check-out girl at Wal-Mart. Please,"—a sigh, followed by another sip of drink—"but Trevor's been mentioning it a good bit, lately. Imagine, me and Mr. Harvard Business Man living happily ever after in white-collar suburbia, the big house and the Volvo, the two or three kids, college accounts and coastal vacations. Bores me to tears, Miller. I just don't see it. When he calls we have nothing to talk about, except his favorite subject, which is a toss-up between him or the two of us in bed. And I cannot tell you how boring an hour of discussing either one of those topics can be. And when he's home, I can't wait until he goes back. Doesn't seem like much to get married on, does it?"

"No, it doesn't." Miller agreed.

They sat in silence for several moments, watching couples walking across the grass together. Joggers ran back and forth in front of them on the footpath in a flurry of walkmen and wristbands. Miller watched two women pushing their babies in strollers, following them down the path with his eyes until they were blips on the horizon. Behind them, the slate gray city loomed like a wall.

"You really think this'll take all night?" Nicole finally asked.

"It'd be better if it did."

"He'll want sex, of course."

"You don't have to do anything you don't want to do, Nicole. I just need him occupied for one night."

"A lot can happen in a night," she said.

"Some nights," Miller nodded.

Nicole slid closer to him, gently rubbed her nose against his neck. She saw the gooseflesh rising on his skin and smiled.

"Remember," she asked, "that night we had down in Savannah a couple summers ago?"

"I remember," Miller said, and he did. He did more than he would ever admit to Nicole. After a moment, Nicole said, "I'll have to take my books with me. He isn't going to freak, is he, if I'm toting a Federal Procedure Hornbook around for the night?"

"I doubt he'll have a problem with it. I'm sure he remembers his years at law school. The whole student scene'll probably turn him on, actually."

Miller took a pull on his Zima and listened to the sounds of the park. Children calling to their parents. Voices carried by the wind like music in the rain. Fifty yards in front of them a group of guys were getting up a game of touch football. "Is it as hard as they say?"

Nicole shrugged. "Law school? It's what you make of it, really. I've got classmates that make themselves sick with stress, and I can see where that could happen if you let it, especially in the first year. But it's like anything else. All the answers are in the books so all you have to do is read the books."

"I can't wait to get there."

"The professors'll try to intimidate you. They like to scare you your first year, make you wish you hadn't enrolled. It strokes their egos to see you sweat."

"I can handle it."

Nicole laughed aloud and said, "I'm sure you can, Miller." She took another swallow of Zima and the last drag of her cigarette, blowing the smoke out in a single gray ribbon. "Of that I have no doubt."

Miller averted his eyes from her and turned his attention inward. The city's breeze, cool and thin and smelling of burning leaves and diesel fuel, blew his hair back from his face. He thought of Wallace, of what he was doing. He wondered if Wallace had planned for something like this, if he'd prepared for a contingency of this sort. He wondered if Wallace was smarter than he, then just as quickly took comfort in the knowledge that he wasn't.

He wrapped his arm around the back of the bench, let his hand fall over Nicole's shoulder. He felt her move into it a bit, sliding over towards him on the bench. She rested her head on his shoulder, her hair brushing against his cheek as delicately as lace. To a passer-by they would have looked like a couple in love, enjoying a romantic evening in a city park.

"It all goes by so fast, doesn't it?" Nicole said. "High school, college. I'm going to wake up one morning and realize law school's over, too. The next day I'll be fifty and worrying about wrinkles and gray hair. Everything. Life. It just flies by."

Miller nodded. "Yes. It does."

"We're going to be old soon."

Miller rubbed her shoulder. "Not too soon, Nic. We've got time, still."

There was a lengthy pause before she said, "do you worry about the future much? What you'll be doing in ten years, where you'll live, who you'll be with?"

No, Miller thought. Never. "Some," he said. "Why? Do you?"

She nodded. "I always have a little, but lately it seems I catch myself thinking about it more and more. It worries me. I try to picture myself in ten years—I'll be thirty-four, a lawyer like my father. Only better looking, I hope. I wonder if I'll be married, will I have children. Do I even want those things?"

"Nothing will happen without your wanting it to, Nic. Whatever happens in your life, it has to get past you first. And we own the world. It's not those old guys, the ones with all the money and the power. They're on the way out. It's you, me, our generation, we make all the rules now. Technology, information, communication, finance, all the big fields will be controlled by our peers. By us. Look at the average age on Wall Street; look at the mean age for new millionaires. We're on the cusp, you and I, waiting to walk a couple of stages and earn a couple degrees, and then the world is ours. It'll be our time." Miller pulled Nicole's head close and kissed the top of it. Her scent was light and sweet. "There's a line in a movie I saw once. This guy's worrying himself to death over this and that, and his buddy takes him aside and tells him there're two rules, and only two rules, in life. As long as you follow them both you'll be fine."

Nicole waited for a while, the muscle in Miller's shoulder as hard as rock beneath her head. And comforting. He was a presence, a complex and solid individual she'd loved through the awkward years of his boyhood, loved into a man without metaphor.

"Invest wisely and always wear a condom," Nicole said.

"No, those are my father's rules." He rubbed her neck as he spoke. "You and I, we have to play by the new rules." He rubbed her neck as he spoke. "One, don't sweat the small stuff. And two, everything's the small stuff. You know what that means, Nic? It means things have a way of taking care of themselves sometimes. You're a bright girl with everything in the world going for you. Just keep your eyes open and you'll be fine."

Nicole considered that. "This thing you want me to do, it stays between us, right?"

"Hell, yes," Miller said. "Circumstances mandate it."

She seemed satisfied with that. "Why me? Other than you thought I'd go for it."

Miller stared ahead and called to memory the night of the fundraiser.

"It wasn't because I thought you'd go for it, Nic. To be honest with you, I figured you'd say no."

"Why would I say no?"

"Why would you say yes?"

Nicole didn't have an answer for that and she didn't bother looking for one.

At the fundraiser, Miller's table had been four removed from Wallace's, and Miller hadn't had any special plans to seek the man out. He had made a list the night before of men and women he presumed would be present at the event and whom he wanted to meet, and had memorized it before he left, checking names off in his mind as the evening progressed. Wallace's name had been one of them, but not one of the main ones. There was the Governor, who as it turned out sent a letter in his absence, along with two or three congressmen whose hand he would've liked to shake, plus a smattering of high-profile Chicago attorneys, Wallace among them. But as the night wore on, Miller began to notice something about the gentleman's eyes, about how they would occasionally—and then more than occasionally as the night wore on—glance over in Nicole's direction, skittering across her breasts, around her neck, over her face before returning to his meal or to whomever he had been speaking. Lots of men were doing it, but there was something about the look on Wallace's face. Something Miller couldn't quite put a name to.

Miller glanced down between his feet at the Zimas and thought about having another. One or two more would take the edge off all this planning nicely. Numb things a bit. Put it all in perspective.

Zima. Zomething different, was how the advertisement went. Zomething in common. Zomething bold. He thought about Wallace that night, about the look behind those cold gray eyes, as if they were trying to look past her, through her, as though he might have found there what it was she possessed that wouldn't let him go.

Yeah, Miller thought, but lots of men looked at Nicole that night. Lots of men looked at lots of women that night. That sort of thing was as common at those dinners as wine."

True enough, but there was…well, something different about the way Wallace had stared. Amazement instead of lust; incredulity rather than simple desire.

Miller smiled and thought that if he was right on this, if whatever it was he thought he had seen in Wallace's eyes had in fact been there, then what could be done with Nicole was…

What?

Endless, he thought. Virtually endless.

"I realize it's probably wasted breath," Nicole said, 'but why are you doing this? What's the point?"

Miller shrugged and picked up another couple of Zimas, twisting off the caps with his teeth, spitting them on the ground at his feet.

He handed one to Nicole. She took it and held it on her knee. A thin, silver-gray stream of gas slipped out of the mouth of the bottle, unfolding in the cool Chicago air like a ribbon.

"I mean," she continued, absently watching the ribbon unfurl, "do you have any idea how powerful these people are? What they do for fun?"

"Sure I do," Miller said, his tone as hard as stone, his joviality gone. "They play chess with people's lives. They maneuver and manipulate, pissing on the populace from atop their ivory tower. Like Clinton with his intern, and Gingrich and his aide. They do what they want with people's lives, then wash their hands and rinse their mouths and never consider the consequences." He took a long, extended swallow of the Zima and stared out across the park, through the trees, the city, the stratosphere beyond. "They're untouchables."

"And you want to touch them, don't you?" She looked at him. "I was raised around them, Miller. Power is their motivation, and nothing else—not sex, not drugs, not money—quite does it for them the same. The power is their impetus, because it's the power that provides these things. They are unequivocal."

Miller was rubbing at something on the ground with the toe of his shoe, considering Nicole's admonition, when she interrupted him.

"But then, so are you. Unequivocal. That's the crux of all this, isn't it? You're burning alive inside looking for your match. It's a game, and you've already begun." She shook her head, and Miller thought he could detect a certain sadness there. "You're dying to replace them, aren't you? New blood over old guard. The world is yours and you make the rules."

"Nothing so serious," he said. "I'm just curious, mostly." But he smiled at her then, and in the smile there was the understanding shared between them that not everything in life can be expressed in words. Sometimes one encounters the inexplicable.

"Mostly," he said again.

*   *   *

A couple of hours later, when he and English were on their way to a Taco Bell, Miller laid it all out for English. What he knew, what he suspected, why he suspected it, what he wanted to do about it. English took it about as well as Miller had expected, which was not too well at all. It would be too hard, too difficult, illegal, no point in it and so on and so on.

Just think about it, was all Miller had said.

And so English thought.

On his way home from Amanda's that night he took a detour off the interstate and drove through the city. He hadn't mentioned any of what Miller had said to Amanda because by the time he had gotten to her house he had decided that there was no way under the sun and stars that he was getting involved with this. Several hours of studying with Amanda later and he was certain. Miller could run with this as far as he wanted, but English was not getting involved. Things were going too well lately. He was eight months from graduating with honors from one of the most prestigious universities in the nation; a few months after that and he and Amanda would probably be married. Another year or two after that, knowing Amanda, and they'd have a baby. He'd have a cushy job in a carpeted office downtown somewhere, and he'd come home each evening to Amanda. It was a life for which he'd been preparing since meeting her. And it was, in his opinion, something worth protecting.

But on the way home he continued to think about it, and he continued to wonder what could account for all the inconsistencies that had Miller so excited.

As he rode the Dan Ryan through Greek Town and past Little Italy, the night's skyline ablaze with office lights fifty stories up, English thought about what Miller had said. It was crazy. It was more than crazy, it was ridiculous.

But look at the evidence.

That's what Miller had said, visibly excited as they flipped through the several sheets of paper Miller had put together. Look at the evidence.

And so he had. But evidence or no, the thought of something of this magnitude, of these proportions, actually occurring beneath the noses of all fifteen million citizens of Illinois…it was inconceivable.

Wasn't it?

Look at the evidence, Miller had said.

Just look for yourself.

What you are telling me, English had argued, is too big to have gone on this long. For you to have figured it out, just like that.

Just look at the evidence, Miller had responded, speaking deliberately slow, emphasizing every word, handing the stack of ten or twelve sheets of paper to English.

So English had taken the papers, had fanned through them quickly at first, and had then, after thinking about it some more, read through each line of each one very carefully, sitting on the couch in Amanda's living room, supposedly studying, Amanda sitting next to him.

Now, off the Dan Ryan and driving slowly down Roosevelt to State, through the red light district of Chicago, English realized that those papers had been Miller's case. His neatly arranged argument stating his thesis—Wallace was looting the party—and offering some very persuasive evidence in support of it. Miller was arguing a case before English, determined to convince him. It had all been there, packaged concisely; a succinct synopsis of the situation on hand. He'd even typed it.

English ran his hand through his hair absently and turned left onto a side street. Bums littered the alleyways, crumpled in the gutter like dirty laundry. Whores clustered in groups on the corners, peddling their wares. Hey mister, I go down. Hey you, want some company? Want a date? Fucky fucky. Real cheap. Real good.

Across on the other side of the street, beneath the blue and gold awning of a sidewalk coffee shop, two men were kissing. A French poodle with a pink collar sat at their feet and waited patiently for them to finish.

English concentrated on concentrating. Miller's suggestions had been very real, very plausible in fact. On paper it all seemed perfectly logical. As Miller had said, it was a wonder that nobody else had caught onto it yet.

"There's the rub," English said aloud. To Miller, who was always, always, always on the lookout for these kinds of things, it didn't seem normal that everyone else in the world wasn't doing the same. He was surprised he was the only one interested in them. But for English, who didn't really care what other people did, it seemed completely usual that the vast majority cared so little about the lives and doings of others. But, English wondered, was it possible that Miller had really stumbled onto something?

Just look at the evidence.

It all made sense. English had been reluctant at first to admit that, but it was true. Miller had brought it all together in his little report. First, he had copied from the local library all the available biographical information of Brian Doyle Timmons, would be Illinois Senator. Timmons' rather unimpressive graduation from The Illinois School of Law (one hundred and eleventh in a class of a hundred and twenty-two), followed by every political campaign the man had ever embarked upon. There were four, the last being the low-profile Clerk of Deeds race, in which the persistent Timmons had been victorious. The first three, which included two shots at a state House of Representatives seat and one at a state senate seat, all ended in losses. If the Democrats hoped to oust the six-term Republican, you would think they'd pick someone with a better track record for the job. And, particularly with Timmons, you wouldn't expect to see the money come pouring in from wealthy Democrats across the country the way it was. If history's tales were true, money sent to the Timmons For Senate campaign would have been put to better use as rolling paper.

Next came Ray Patterson's stats. On him there was less available information, though Miller had gone to extremes to dig up as much as possible. He knew from his father's handy little book that Patterson was a third year drop-out from Harvard, and so he had called Harvard's info line and asked for the number to the library. The head librarian there had been friendly and cooperative, but had been unable to turn up anything new about Mr. Patterson. It was the same deal with the Marine Corps, another institution from which Patterson had suddenly dropped from sight.

And finally there was Wallace. Miller felt that Wallace's being involved made perfect sense for a number of reasons. One, he had the political muscle to get things done, like drawing large, affluent crowds to the dinners and fundraisers—and he probably had enough respect throughout his inner circle so that whatever he was doing he could do without someone looking over his shoulder. Wallace was trusted. That he was a senior partner in a law firm that probably handled over a hundred million dollars a year for various clients, and was therefore in an excellent position to funnel any money that may be accidentally mischanneled from Timmon's campaign into other, less public accounts, didn't hurt Miller's case. To Miller, it was a perfect opportunity for Wallace to make an enormous amount of money with very little effort on his part, and nary an eyebrow raised. Timmons' campaign was bringing in more money than anyone could have ever projected, would have ever believed possible, and even English knew that many campaign donations were anonymous, untraceable, without documented origin. Wallace could probably skim ten to fifteen percent off the top of the donations, and still have a war chest big enough to baffle even the most optimistic party faithfuls.

But did that necessarily mean they were doing it, simply because the numbers made it feasible that they could?

Miller thought so. It was, he explained, too perfect. The pieces—a rogue campaign manager, a failed candidate, a party filled with supporters starving for victory and willing to pour tons of money into the war chest, and Wallace, who had the business connections to pull off such an operation—fit together too easily. The obvious motive, money, would be too tempting, Miller maintained, for men of their nature to refuse.

And therein lay perhaps Miller's most important point. It was, in any case, without question the detail that convinced Miller that his suspicions were more than mere suspicion.

Men like Wallace, Miller believed, couldn't operate any other way.

English was reminded of the parable of the scorpion and the frog. The scorpion, wishing to cross the river, asks the frog to carry him across on his back. The frog refuses. When the scorpion asks him why, the frog says that he's afraid the scorpion will sting him, causing him to drown. But the scorpion, wise in the way of words, counters with logic, explaining that if he does sting the frog, both of them will drown, and the scorpion would never intentionally endanger his own life. Satisfied with this, the frog agrees, and the scorpion climbs atop the frog. Halfway across the river the scorpion stings the frog, and as they both slowly sink below the surface of the water, the frog looks up at the scorpion and says, "why did you do that? Now you will drown as well." And the scorpion, sinking into the river atop the frog, simply says, "I had no choice. It is my nature to sting, and no one can go against his nature."

Wallace, Miller explained, was a man of power, of intellect, of privilege and accomplishment, and it is in his nature to want more.

And no one can go against his nature.

For as long as English had known him, Miller had subscribed to the notion that there was a class of individuals who through varying combinations of fortune, family, or fame were able to raise themselves above the rest to a perch from which they governed, controlled, confined, and oppressed the unwashed masses. English had always suspected that Miller harbored a deeply-rooted desire—a need, almost—to stand with them, to be counted amongst their numbers. But lately, with the Berry fiasco and now this, English was beginning to wonder if Miller's motivation wasn't to be one of them at all, but was rather simply to hurt them.

The thought sent a shiver of chills up the length of his spine.

English slowed his Mustang to twenty, lost in thought. He came to a stop at a red light, idling quietly. Gay porno houses lined both sides of the street. Hot neon signs proclaiming "Live Sex Shows Nightly" and "Steamy Sexcapades" flashed through the night. "Chix with Dix" and "Sluts with Nuts" bleeped on and off in liquid blue light off to his right. Men walked hand in hand down the sidewalk. A pack of drag queens stood and smoked clove cigarettes outside a liquor store, their purses hanging from their wrists with dainty femininity. English stared at one as he drove by, and was embarrassed to admit that she was as pretty as a girl.

When he got back to the apartment Miller was perched in front of the television with a book—that same one about political fundraising English had seen him carrying around lately—open on his lap. English dropped two grape pop-tarts into the toaster and took a seat on the ottoman. They talked for a while about this and that, neither of them mentioning the Wallace thing. English knew why. Miller, always planning, always calculating, was giving him time to think about it.

He would decide that evening while lying in bed that yes, Miller was probably right. Wallace and possibly others were more than likely looting the state party's treasury. These days, English knew, getting the money was the hard part. Moving it electronically and making it invisible was the easy part.

On this day, seventy-four days before the trial was to commence, neither English nor Miller understood fully what it was they were getting themselves involved with. They thought it was simple. They thought they had an idea.

And they were wrong.

Chapter 12

73 Days Before   (September 24)

Friday night.

Unlike most Friday nights, when he was either at a party or out with Tracie, Miller was sitting at his desk in the apartment, studying the sketch of the Wallace home. The lights in his room, save for the lamp on his desk, were off, his shade drawn. When his hand moved, making notations here, adjustments there, his shadow danced across the wall before him.

He had told Tracie he needed to catch up on some reading and would give her a call in the morning, that they could go to the mall or something, or maybe catch a flick. Tracie offered to come by and see him, keep him company while he read, but Miller declined.

Miller held his head with his hands and studied the sketch. Above the home, beneath a penciled-in sun, lay the diagram of a compass, indicating the four directions. Thin, hair-like, almost imperceptible lines marked the distance, in feet, from the front door to the driveway, the backdoor to the forest, the front door to the nearest windows, the roof to the ground. A thin sheet of clear plastic, like those used by any high school teacher on an overhead projector, fit perfectly over the Wallace sketch. When lain atop the drawing of the home, the spatially accurate transparency displayed the location of the flood light atop the pole on the northern side, the wires running down to the northern corner of the house. It superimposed the image of the lightening rod atop the roof, as well as the exact placement of the nearby trees. The small metal box in the eastern side of the front yard, which Miller knew connected the Wallaces to city power, was also visible on the transparency.

When he had finished, he replaced these items within an unmarked manila folder. From within that folder he produced another sketch, this one of the interior of the home. Illinois state law requires all homes built above the thousand square feet mark to be registered with the city for property tax purposes. The blueprints of these homes were also required. Miller simply drove to the courthouse and, explaining that he was doing a report on home equity rates for larger than average houses for a real estate class at the university, asked to see the plans to any and all homes above four thousand square feet and within five miles of the lake. As he had suspected, there had been many throughout Kenilworth, and the county clerk had blacked out the names of the owners and residents, but it hadn't taken Miller long to figure out which property belonged to Wallace. The clerk had been foolish enough to leave the longitudinal and latitudinal coordinates on the blueprints, allowing Miller, with the help of a naval atlas, to pinpoint the Wallace property precisely. He had photocopied the blueprint to Wallace's on the library's copier and returned the plans within three minutes.

So now he knew where Wallace slept. In which room he ate his meals. Where he took his morning shit, where the refrigerator was. He saw that there was a sunken basement beneath the front staircase, with only one door and no windows. There were six bedrooms upstairs, one down. There was a large kitchen, connected to an even larger formal dining room. A living room on one end of the home was offset by a family room at the other. Upstairs, situated on the western side of the home, sat a large, sprawling great room. It was this room that faced the road which climbed the hillside and led to the Wallace home. This room, with its single window and floodlight attached above it. This room, which had, Miller noticed during his most recent visit, a large oak growing less than five feet from it.

Chapter 13

66 Days Before   (October 1)

"Yesterday was the third time I followed her, and it's always the same thing," Laney was saying. He, Miller, and English were sitting around a table during happy hour at The Beverage Station, a red meat and ale type place not too far from the University. They were working on their second pitcher of beer and a third pile of ribs.

"The first time, two Thursdays ago, she went into twelve different stores and bought something in every one. From her walking into store number one and leaving store number twelve took exactly two hours and nineteen minutes."

"Pretty fast," Miller said.

"Not where I was sitting, it wasn't. Last Thursday she went into nine stores, but took over three hours. Ten minutes over three hours, I think. I've got it all written down at my apartment."

"How long did it take her to drive home," English asked.

"I'm getting to that," Laney said. "I had to watch this bag for over eight hours total. Don't get impatient with me."

Laney signaled the waitress for another pitcher with a hand covered in rib sauce "Yesterday, which makes Thursday number three if you were keeping count, she took two hours and thirty two minutes to go into eight stores and one restaurant. Old lady feels the need to buy something every goddam time she turns around." He polished off the rest of his beer and let a belch slide out the corner of his mouth. "The drive home," he shot an elbow into English's side as he spoke, "was over forty minutes every time. She didn't stop any of the three times."

"Did she park in the driveway or the garage?" Miller asked.

"The garage. It's electric. She pulled in and shut it before getting out of her Mercedes."

"Did she use the phone in her car at all while driving home?"

"Not that I could see. Hard to tell."

English asked, "is she a fast driver?"

"Average, I guess," Laney said. "Except on the dirt road leading to her driveway, where you have to go less then ten or leave your suspension on the ground behind you."

Miller sat silently a moment before saying, "then we do it next week."

"When?" English asked.

"Thursday. I'll call Nicole tonight and tell her to be ready. If everything goes the way we've planned, Wallace will be thinking of that exquisite body of hers by lunchtime Thursday, and that afternoon the three of us will make our move. Laney, English and I will meet you here around noon. You're the only one with a truck, so don't be late. Not a word of this is breathed to anyone. Not one word. Nicole is going out of her way to help us on this. We couldn't do it without her."

The waitress brought them another pitcher and another plate of ribs, and the conversation changed to other things. Driving to Amanda's that evening, English realized that, despite the nature of what it was they were planning to do, his concerns could generally be boiled down to he and Amanda fighting because he was spending too much time doing what she considered to be ridiculous and potentially dangerous stuff like this with Miller. That what Miller had planned was more than a simple prank, and was instead a high-stakes game with a renowned high-roller, didn't make things any easier for English.

* * *

Nicole left that evening on her date at a little after seven. She was going out with a fellow law-student from her Professional Ethics class, a fellow named Michael Lifter. When he had asked her she had been less than enthused, but had said yes simply because it was easier than saying no. It wasn't that he was a bad looking guy; he was tall, reasonably built, with a head of closely cut sandy blond hair that made him look like a military cadet. She imagined that if she were to be honest she would have to admit that his only evident negative was that he was not English Mason.

Lifter had called her two days ago and asked if she had plans for this Friday, and if not, would she like to go to dinner at *Riva* with him that evening. Nicole suspected that he had mentioned the restaurant by name as a means of enticing her to go. It wasn't a completely irrational move on his part; she had been to *Riva* several times before on dates. It sat on the waterfront on the second floor of Navy Pier, surrounded by refulgent skyscrapers on all sides, the city's watery skyline wrapped and shining around it like a halo. Entrees ran anywhere from twenty-five to seventy-five dollars there.

But Lifter hadn't left much to chance. He had called his friend Miller Dispenberg, whom he knew from college, because he knew Miller was tight with Nicole. Lifter had asked for suggestions as to where to take her, and Miller had said he'd talk to Nicole, see what she liked. Two days later Miller called Lifter and told him Nicole liked lots of places, but simply adored *Riva*.

When Nicole had accepted his invitation, Michael Lifter had immediately called and confirmed their reservations.

When Michael and Nicole arrived at the restaurant that evening, their table was waiting for them, nestled snugly in the corner next to the plate-glass window. Most of the surrounding tables were occupied by ladies and gentlemen who looked noticcably older than they. The maitre'd seated them, and left them with the menus.

There is little to mention about the evening Michael and Nicole spent together. Aside from the price of the meal, which, from appetizer to desert to the bottle of wine he ordered ran poor Lifter—who was living off student-loans and barely, at that—a hefty $205.00 including tip, theirs was an ordinary night. They talked about the law and their college years. They talked about other dates they'd had. Likes and dislikes. Politics and religion. Music, traveling, turn-ons and turn-offs. They both liked Elvis, ice-cream, and cold pizza in the morning. He loved the law slightly more than she. Neither cared for the return of the seventies.

After dinner, they drove by one of the city parks and walked through it slowly for the better part of an hour. Michael then took her home, escorted her to the front door, and extended his hand as he told her good night. He asked if he could see her again, and she had told him to give her a call.

And this is the way the evening was remembered by both Nicole Henderson and Michael Lifter.

The Maitre'd working that night at *Riva* would remember a handsome looking couple arriving shortly after seven, eating an averaged size meal, and leaving without incident. The waiter would remember nothing about the tip, stating for the jury that it must have been average; he never forgot the ridiculously low or exceptionally high tippers.

The registrar would have a Mr. Michael Lifter down for a party of two at seven. In parentheses next to the reservation, a special request for a terrace table was noted.

None of *Riva's* other patrons on the evening of October 1st would remember seeing either Michael or Nicole, although several of the men would recall Nicole upon being shown a picture. Not even Mrs. Wallace noticed them that evening, as, presumably by coincidence, she ate her London Broil two tables over. Her husband, however, spotted her almost immediately when she walked in. He noticed that the room began to glow, that the air became lighter and warmer all at once. He had finished the raw oysters and was well into the quail before he remembered that it had been the Timmons fundraiser where he had seen her before.

J. Fullard Wallace would spend the rest of his meal glancing occasionally but regularly in the direction of Nicole Henderson, making a conscious effort to keep his heart rate down. For her part, Nicole either didn't notice or didn't care about the attention. When she and her date left the restaurant, Wallace had to fight the almost overwhelming urge to follow her simply to look at those good, hard ankles as she walked.

That evening, as he lay in bed next to his sleeping wife, full and tired from the intoxicating effects of the dinner and wine, J. Fullard Wallace would find himself thinking intently, obsessively, about Nicole Henderson, picturing her the way he had seen her at the restaurant...her short auburn hair pulled back behind her ears...he wanted to touch it with his fingertips, pull it to his face and whisk it over his skin and breath its scent deeply into his lungs. Her deep almond-shaped eyes, her thick black lashes, her smooth, naked shoulders—his desire to touch them, kiss them, feel them against his mouth was almost overwhelming. He pictured her breasts, young and fresh and firm, beneath the silky black gown she had been wearing, and imagined the coolness of their skin, the stiffness of the nipples as they touched his own. When she had walked away earlier this evening he had watched her hips, coiled tightly beneath her evening gown, and as she had left the terrace he believed that he could make out the slightest hint of a panty line beneath. His wife had noticed the sweat gathering on his forehead and had asked him if he was feeling all right.

As he lay there in bed on his back that evening, J. Fullard Wallace wondered what she must smell like in the morning after sex, the night's sweat still sticking to her skin, the thin white sheets whispering over her back and between her legs. How she would feel beneath him, with her legs far apart and her smooth hips lifting slowly in rhythm with his own.

He thought about the shape of her toes, their feel in his mouth. He pictured their contour, the brightly painted nails, and imagined her walking across the floor of a wide open room draped in white as she approached his bed, coming towards him, those deep, dark eyes catching the light and her lips parted and moist. He felt her warm breath on his neck, his face, his eyes; he heard the raspiness in her throat as she breathed with effort. He felt the pain of fingernails digging into the flesh of his back and almost cried out from the pleasure.

And J. Fullard Wallace rose from bed and went into his bathroom, where he masturbated feverishly in the concealing darkness.

Chapter 14

60 Days Before   (October 7)

At seven twenty-five A.M., beneath a warm blue sky and surrounded by the pleasant morning calls of sparrows, robins, and jays, Miller Dispenberg pulled up in front of Nicole's townhouse and blew the horn.

A minute later and Miller was watching her approach his car. Her deep auburn hair was pulled back behind her ears, exposing a pool of shadows that shimmered along her neck. A few strands of her hair had fallen free, and danced alongside her face like wisps of tinted smoke.

She was wearing a smart beige suit, and even now, after all the past years and experiences he'd shared with Nicole in one capacity or another, Miller still felt a twinge as he watched her buttocks when she walked.

"Morning, lover," she said as she let herself into the passenger side. The interior of the car filled with the delicate scent of her perfume.

Miller inhaled. "Jessica McClintock."

"Mais, oui."

"I love that stuff."

"I remember," she smiled, smelling like flowers and summer rain, fresh and alive. "Today's the big today. Nervous?"

Miller shook his head. "You're doing all the hard work. I'm just the chauffeur."

Nicole giggled and leaned over to check her make-up in the rearview mirror.

"Don't pull that too hard," Miller said. "It'll fall off."

Nicole checked her teeth and returned the mirror, gently, to its original position.

"Now," Nicole said several moments later, "walk me through this again. Particularly the part about his wife."

"His wife won't be a problem…I expect to be in by four in the afternoon and out by four-thirty, five at the outside. But if something were to happen and it takes us longer than we thought, he could come home from work and we'd be stuck in the house, which is where you come in because that we don't need. I have to be sure he won't be coming home from work at all today. Besides, if he spends the night with you, he'll have to come up with his own alibi in case something should go wrong. If it's just an hour or two at some restaurant, he can say he was at a business meeting, or stuck in traffic. Anything. But if it's overnight, it's a different animal all together. He spends his nights at home, so he'll have to come up with some reason as to why he chose this night not to. And," Miller said, slowing the car, signaling, turning left, "it's a safe bet that whatever reason he chooses will be the one he thinks will be the furthest from the truth."

Nicole thought about that for a moment before saying: "so it's blackmail, then?"

Miller shook his head. "I want him in a position where he'll do whatever it takes to keep his night with you a secret. If that night incriminates him in something as scandalous as an all-nighter with a twenty-four year old law student who just happens to be the daughter of a semi-associate, maybe he'll see that it's kept quiet. Which is what's best for all concerned."

"Daddy would absolutely shit if he knew."

"Let's not test that."

"No worries. You were getting to the part about his wife…"

"That's all taken care of," Miller said.

He steered onto the expressway, and accelerated the car up to the sixty-five mile an hour mark for the twenty mile drive to the city.

"Did you bring your phone," he asked. She smiled and produced a black cellular flip-phone from her purse, no bigger than a credit card.

"What if we end up somewhere other than Grand Beach?"

Miller stared straight out at the road, his thoughts reviewing for the thousandth time the sequence of events as they were planned for this afternoon. "Don't worry. It'll be Grand Beach. There's no question. It's the closest of all his properties, and aside from a condo in Barbados, it's also the most secluded. The two of you could shack up in that place for a year and no one would ever find you."

"How do you know all this?"

"I did some snooping around." He shook his head and dismissed the subject. "And even if I'm wrong," he added, "and the two of you end up somewhere other than the mountains, it won't really matter. You've got the phone. You'll be safe. He's harmless. Like you said," he smiled, "no worries."

They reached the law firm of *Rogers, Stiles, and Wallace* at precisely eight-fifteen.

"Parking lot's already packed," Miller said. "Lawyers start the day early, don't they?"

"They screw more people before eight a.m. than most sororities do all day," Nicole said.

Miller pulled the car around to the side of the modest four-story building and parked. "This is it," he said. "You're sure you're all right? You can pull this off?"

Nicole gave him a look full of condescension. "Really, Miller. Please. With my eyes closed."

Miller switched off the key and started to get out when he stopped himself, turning to regard Nicole once more. He placed his hand on her bare thigh and suddenly became very sincere. "You be careful. This man isn't dangerous. If he was, I wouldn't have asked you to do this. But be careful all the same."

Nicole didn't know if she believed that or not, but she nodded anyway.

"I don't think there's anything to worry about, but if something should happen, call me at the apartment. You know the number." She nodded.

"I'll be sitting by the phone all day and night. I'm ditching classes today. If I go to sleep it'll be by my head. Don't hesitate to call if you need to." He leaned over and kissed her on the cheek. "I won't forget this, Nicole. I owe you one. I mean it."

"Let's just call it even after this. These debts with you are often difficult on both sides of the equation."

"Fair enough," Miller said, and escorted her to the door. When they were inside the waiting room, Miller handed her a small piece of paper with a number typed across it. "I'll be at this number for the next three hours. If it works out and the two of you are going to leave together, call me there and let me know. If not, call me and I'll come pick you up."

"Yes, daddy," Nicole said.

Miller hesitated for a moment, looking her up and down, then said, "you look great."

Nicole smiled. "Of course I do. That's the idea. Once we pull this off you and I can take a night out and celebrate. Dutch, of course."

"Of course," Miller said, and left. He did not turn back, but continued out the door and into his car, where he drove directly to a pay phone in a gas station parking lot four miles away. There he sat. And there he waited.

* * *

As Miller stood inside the phone booth, re-reading Delillo's *Libra*, the receptionist of *Rogers, Stiles, and Wallace* noticed Nicole sitting in the waiting area, flicking through a fashion magazine, and asked if she might be able to help her.

"I'm waiting to see Mr. Wallace," Nicole said.

"Do you have an appointment?" The woman, a pretty, nicely made-up blond, inquired.

"No, but I believe he's expecting me."

"One moment then," the woman said, picking up the phone and dialing Wallace's office. Nicole stood on the other side of the desk and noticed that the receptionist had dark roots, as well as dark eyebrows. A bottled blonde. Her face and neck and hands were all the same tone of deep, golden tan.

Nicole smiled. Even at this level, it was all an image thing.

The young woman said, "one moment, sir," into the phone, then asked Nicole, "what was your name?"

"It was, and is, Nicole. He and I met at the Timmons fundraiser."

* * *

A half hour later when the telephone rang, Miller dog-eared his page and answered it. He listened to Nicole for a moment, then breathed a sigh of relief that he had been unaware of holding.

"Perfect," he said.

Pause. More listening.

"Have fun, and Nic... thanks again."

And then he hung up.

* * *

Mrs. Wallace hadn't worked a day outside the home since putting her husband through law school, and never really saw the value of sitting around inside the house watching soaps and eating chocolates, particularly once the children were married and gone. There was always something to do: an errand J. needed run, bridge club, a sale at Macy's, tennis lessons, golf with Sue Ellen or Maureen. Not much sense in being bored all the time, in any case.

So often was the day, such as this one, when Claudia Wallace could be found strolling from shop to shop—expensively dressed, bag matching her shoes—and her blood-colored Mercedes 190E could be seen, if you were looking, parked in one of the many parking garages outside the various shops, plazas, and malls scattered throughout the city.

It was not an often occurrence, however, to see that blood-colored Mercedes 190E with both its back tires slashed, as was the case this day, as it sat on the fifth floor of a city parking garage on 5th Avenue.

But this was the city, and strange things happened in the city.

* * *

By a quarter after three that afternoon Miller, Laney, and English were sitting twenty yards away from the front door of the Wallace home, Laney at the wheel, English between the two of them.

English whistled beneath his breath. "That is some house."

Laney said, "bet there's an ever-loving shit-pile of art and jewelry inside."

Miller ignored him and pointed to the uppermost window on the westernmost side.

"There's our door. Hurry, Laney. We don't want to make a day of it."

Laney threw the truck in reverse and turned it around. He drove back down the single-lane road that led to the Wallace place and parked the truck ten yards into the woods off the road, about a half-mile from the house. As Miller stood behind the truck and directed, Laney positioned it between two large oaks and behind a thick bunch of shrubs. As an added precaution, the night before Laney had stashed a camouflaged net in the truck bed, the kind used for shielding mosquitoes on camp-outs, and the three of them draped it over the truck. From the road, it was difficult to find even when looking for it.

"We'll be lucky if *we* can find it," Laney said, the three of them walking back up the path towards the Wallace place. "Hope to hell we don't have to leave in a hurry."

"Me, too,"—English, fidgeting with his hands, nervous, anxious, agitated. "Long as Nicole can keep the old man busy, we should be golden." Laney said.

"She will." Miller replied.

"I'd like to trade places with Mr. Wallace," Laney said. "Imagine getting to boff Nicole Henderson all day and night in some enchanted cabin while a couple of guys download a few of your files. Not a bad price, if you ask me."

Laney shook his head. "It's on my things to do list, fucking Nicole. Her and Amanda."

"Yeah," English said. "It'd be the last thing you did too, bitch."

Laney was opening his mouth to respond when Miller said: "There it is."

And there it was.

The three boys stood fifty yards out from the west end of the house, at the tree-line. For the first time, they became aware of the silence of the forest behind them, as though the creatures within it recognized the presence of intruders and had grown still. English especially felt unnerved by it, and he turned around, wrestling with a nagging feeling that they had been followed. Laney looked over his shoulder as well.

Miller pulled three sets of surgical gloves out of his front jeans pocket and passed them out.

"Suit up, gentlemen. No need to leave our mark. Remember, we don't know what kind of recording devices he might have lying around the house, but power's twin is paranoia. So we have to be careful not to use our names. English, you'll be Larry. Laney, you're Curly. I'm Moe."

"Why am I Curly? Curly was a bald fat fuck."

Miller sighed. "Laney, this isn't *Reservoir Dogs*. We're not going to argue over who's Mr. Black. Just remember the fucking names and don't take any chances."

"It would make more sense for me to be Larry. Larry and Laney are similar. Moe and Miller is fine. Let English be Curly. Amanda said he had a curly little cock, anyway."

Miller waved his hands. "Never mind the stooges. Laney, you're Rocky, English, you're Paulie, and I'm Adrian. Everyone happy with that?"

"Rocky's cool," Laney said.

"I swear to God, Laney," Miller said. "You're such a damned dipshit sometimes."

"Talk like that to me again Adrian and I'll bitch-slap you like I did that Russian."

English tried to laugh but it came out hollow. He could feel his heart rate increase, felt the pressure build beneath his temples. His mouth tasted coppery; the image of Amanda's face forced itself upon him and he fought it back.

"We shouldn't do this," he whispered.

"What?" Laney said.

English shook his head. He spun and faced the house with Miller. "This," he motioned towards the house, the lawn, the woods behind them, "we shouldn't do any of this."

"Fuck you talking about,"—Laney, no longer whispering.

"What do you mean, English?" Miller asked. "This is what we talked about."

"I've got a bad feeling about this, Mill. Something's wrong here. Something could go wrong. This seems...I don't know, this just seems like it might be too big for us. I mean, what do we really know about this guy, anyway?"

"It's a fucking empty house, English," Laney said. "Strap on a pair. All those times growing up I told you you were a pussy? This is what I was talking about."

"Shut up, Laney," Miller, perhaps seeing weeks of preparation unraveling at the hands of English's jitters. "English, you're just getting a little case of wedding night worries. It shows your intelligence. It's a reaction thing. But really, this isn't a colossal deal at all."

English shook his head. "It just feels wrong. There are too many people involved. Too many chances for something to go awry, for something to get out. What if you're right? What if Wallace is stealing from the party's treasury? You think he's just going to let someone waltz in take his shit and not ask questions? What would someone like that do to cover something like that up? This is a powerful man we're trifling with here."

"English, we're in and out like the wind. No one will ever suspect us. Besides, we've got Nicole, just in case. She's our insurance policy."

"You're a pussy, English," Laney, again. "A big, wet, sloppy, worn-out—"

Miller interrupted him. "There's only you, me, Laney and Nicole. That's all. The three of us are going to be done here in about an hour, and then we're through with the hard part. Nicole will be done by tomorrow morning, and then its over."

English nodded. "I know. But there are too many what if's. Too many loose ends."

"No, there aren't. I've thought through all the possibilities. The only what if's are the ones surrounding Wallace's files. And that's what we're here for," Miller answered. "To answer those questions. If it turns out there's nothing worth pursuing, we back off. No blood no foul. Mr. Wallace gets a free night with Nicole, and we go about our business."

Laney tapped his watch. "It isn't getting any earlier, fellas."

Miller ignored him, keeping his eyes focused on English. "We don't do this solo. We're not going in half-ass."

Laney threw up his hands and spat in disgust. "Oh for…English, I tell you what. You can hold my hand and daddy'll make sure no monsters get you, okay?"

English ignored him, looking at the house before them, then turning to look back out into the woods. If he sat there long enough, he could almost convince himself that the trees were moving, shifting perhaps, to get a better view of what was going on.

He heard something crack off to the right and looked for the sound. There was nothing. No small animal. No falling limb.

"The wind," Miller said. "This is Chicago."

"Miller, are we going or are we not going? I've got a load of studying I need to do and I don't really have time to stand around all day and debate this thing."

English looked at him. "Why should you give a yippety-shit if we do or we don't?"

Laney smiled. "Two words, baby. Cash is king."

English rolled his eyes.

"Hey, you can get pious if you want, but if this dude really is dipping into political donations, then there's more than likely some fairly large green floating around out there. That means something to me."

"English?" Miller said.

English looked once more at the house and then at Laney. Miller was right, it was only going to take an hour or so, and even if Mrs. Wallace came home, which was improbable, the house was big enough that they would be able to climb out of one of the top windows and be back to the truck before she ever knew what was going on. But still...

"English?"

English felt his heart chopping like a fan blade beneath this chest. He heard the rush of blood in his ears, felt his temples throb like something alive.

I'm sorry, Amanda, he thought before saying: "Let's just get it over with."

*   *   *

"My...God," J. Fullard Wallace had muttered when he saw Nicole sitting in his waiting room. He felt the area around his temples grow hot and clammy; a heavy throbbing started in his throat and worked its way down to his stomach where it settled and began expanding.

"My God," he said again.

Nicole hadn't noticed him yet; her head was still hung low, reading a magazine in her lap. He followed the curve of her face down to her supple neck, gazing at her hair, her pronounced but delicate jaw-line, her lips. He watched her as she slid her tongue out between them and dragged it slowly over both of them, first the bottom, then the top, before withdrawing it back into her mouth in an imperceptible gesture. He traced the shape of her breasts beneath her shirt, thought he could see a hint of nipple underneath. He felt himself go hard as his stomach burned and his mouth dried up.

"God in Heaven," J. Fullard Wallace said aloud, this time hearing himself, realizing that if she were to look up she would see him, sweaty face and shortness of breath and all.

He retreated quickly and quietly to his office, shutting the door silently behind him, and sat down to gather his thoughts and calm himself.

The urge to relieve himself was incredible; just close the door, lower the blinds, pull it out and tug on it a while, spraying the bottom of his desk in pearly-white ribbons before zipping back up again, leaving the stuff to dry and crust off in yellowish flakes over time. But he opted against it, deciding quite deliberately that Fate had dropped this into his lap for a reason, and the man who would attempt to deny a bitch like Fate was a common fool. Wallace had learned in life that Fate was a lady who occasionally got her kicks strapping one on and sticking it to you hard, but other times, J. believed, if you stroked her just right, you could get the old cunt to put out for you.

* * *

"Well open the motherfucker," Laney said to Miller, who was lightly tapping the upstairs window on the western side of the house, testing the resistance of the glass. All three of them were clutching the trunk of the oak, with English in the middle. His left foot had found a small groove at the base of a thick limb, but his right was floundering alongside the length of the trunk, kicking bark down onto Laney's face.

Miller, his feet less than six inches from English's head, continued to tap the window pane.

"Looks to me like we either break it or we don't," English said. "Don't see much sense in tapping it all day."

Miller sat in silence, looking past the glass and into the great room. On one of his solo journeys out to the Wallace place, Miller had ventured up to the front door, planning, had someone answered, to be asking permission for him and his friends to hunt deer on and around the Wallace land. But no one answered, and Miller quickly circled the house, inspecting the windows and doors, finally finding what he was looking for on the back kitchen door. A small sticker, yellow and black, with the image of an irate wasp painted in the middle of it. Above the pissed off wasp read the logo "Beehive Security." Beneath the wasp, "these premises protected."

The next morning, from a pay phone on campus, he had called Beehive Security and explained that he wished to have a security system installed in his home. When Miller asked for an estimate, the gentleman at the other end of the line informed him, as Miller had known he would, that it would depend on the square footage of the house, the number of rooms, the number of doors and windows, whether it was a one story, two story, or three, and etcetera. Miller rattled off the statistics to the Wallace home. Two-stories. Sixty-two hundred square feet. Eleven rooms. Twenty-four windows. Five doors. The Beehive man said that it would run somewhere in the neighborhood of four to seven thousand dollars. Thank you, Miller had said. And just before hanging up, he would add, almost as an afterthought, where would the main control unit be installed. By the door you and your family frequent most often, the man had said. "We're breaking it." Miller announced, tapping the edges of the pane once more.

The Beehive Deluxe Home Protection System, which was the one the Beehive man had said Miller would want in a house this size, ran off radio waves, and was virtually impossible to defeat. It would take months of practice and thousands of dollars worth of equipment to do it, neither of which Miller had the benefit. Miller saw the small fixture sitting firmly in the upper right hand corner of the pane, its single wire running within the glass. He was surprised the thing hadn't gone off already, considering how many times he'd thumped it with his knuckle. He placed his hand against the glass, palm spread as widely as possible, and was about to push the entire pane out of the frame when he heard the telephone ring inside the house. He moved his hand.

"What is it?" English asked.

"The phone."

"Break it, already," Laney said.

The telephone rang again.

Miller pressed his eyes against the glass and saw a birdshit-white phone sitting on an end table next to a couch. He listened as it rang a third and fourth time.

"Will somebody please tell me what we're waiting for?" Laney asked. "This is not comfortable, case you were wondering."

Five rings. Six rings.

Miller felt his pulse quicken, his mouth grow thick and clammy.

Seven rings.

"I tell you what, Miller," Laney continued, "why don't I come up there and break it? That way, you can get even closer to the phone and hear it real well. Answer it if you want, fuck around with whoever it is. Tell 'em the old lady's getting humped by the mailman or something, I don't give a shit."

Miller listened as the telephone rang for the tenth time, then fell silent. His head had started to pound slowly, rhythmically.

Miller replaced his hand on the glass. He was unable to take his eyes from the telephone, now sitting quietly beside the couch. He began to press forward into the glass.

And then it occurred to him, and he paused. But only for a second.

The idea of coming this far only to only to turn back was an anathema to him. There were rules.

Shards of glass fell to the ground at the base of the tree.

"Watch it," Laney yelled up the tree, ducking falling glass. "A little warning, how about it?"

Miller quickly stuck his hand through it and pulled the miniature appliance off the jagged window pane, ripping the wire from it and discarding it on the ground. The alarm made no sound.

"Now we're cooking with gasoline," Laney said, already beginning to climb the tree.

"Get your head out of my ass," English said. "I don't—"

"We're in and out in three minutes, guys. Three." Miller said, trying to estimate how long he had been sitting there tapping the window. Two minutes, he thought. Three at the most.

He pulled himself through the window and turned around to help English, who was followed immediately by Laney.

"Mother *fucker*!" Laney screamed, pulling his arm away bloody from the edges of the window pane. A thin cut, the length of a pencil, lined Laney's forearm. Blood was flowing freely down to his wrist and palm. Miller watched it hit the brown carpet beneath them.

"Stop the bleeding," Miller said. "Keep it off the carpet." Laney nodded and held the shirt tightly to the cut with his other hand. He then reached over and flicked English in the ear, allowing the shirt to fall to the floor, followed by several drops of blood.

"That's for kicking bark in my face, faggot."

"Blow me," English returned, before Miller jerked him around to face him.

"We've got five, maybe ten minutes before the police get here. Listen. I just shattered the window of a million dollar home. What do you hear? Nothing? That's because it was a silent alarm. It was probably lighting up the whole station from the first time I touched it."

English's eyes went wide with terror. Laney's mouth fell open.

"So move," Miller commanded. "Paulie, get downstairs and see if you can turn the thing off. It'll probably be by the door leading from the kitchen to the garage. Destroy it if you have to. Do not answer the phone if it rings. Rocky, you get to the foyer and watch the road, let me know the second you see anything, anything at all, coming up it."

"Oh my God," English said. "We're going to jail. We're going to fucking jail."

"Nobody's going to jail. Don't panic. We're smarter than they are. Remember that. Now move."

They did. Laney and English ran down the stairs, Laney to the front foyer, English towards the kitchen. Miller began going through the bedrooms, searching for Wallace's computer. He counted off the seconds as he searched, finding it in the bedroom farthest from the great room on count number twenty-two. It was a stand-up unit, situated snugly on the floor beneath a large, oak roll-top desk.

Miller glanced at it quickly and found that he'd been right about at least one thing: Wallace's computer had no receptacle for floppy's or CD-Roms, which meant that whatever information it held had been transferred via zip-drive. No disks or diskettes meant no downloading. No copying.

Which meant that, in the absence of hours and hours to decipher the invariable myriad of passcodes and electronic locks, there was only one way to get to it.

He removed a small, multi-head screwdriver from his back pocket. By the time he had reached fifty, he had unscrewed the computer's cover, and was carefully working the little plastic screws which held the hard-drive in place.

English burst into the room, wild-eyed, breathing fast, a picture of panic. "I ripped it out of the wall."

"Is Rocky watching the road?"

English nodded. "Please hurry, Mill—Adrian. This isn't a game anymore."

"No," Miller said, finally freeing the last plastic screw, gingerly lifting the hard-drive out of the C.P.U. and setting it on the floor beside him. "A game it is not."

He lifted the cover to the computer and began fitting it over the rest of the unit, sliding the little metal fingers through one another until they clicked home.

"Find a cordless phone somewhere," he said. "There's got to be one. Check by all the toilets and beds. Look on the couches and chairs in the living room. When you find it give it to Rocky and tell him to get into the woods as far away from here as possible, but make sure he sticks close enough to the road to see. There are three lines to this house, one for Wallace's personal phone, probably somewhere in the master bedroom—maybe on the bureau—and the other two to the rest of the house. Have him watch the road and call when he sees something." Miller wiped a sheen of sweat off his forehead with the back of his hand. He reached into his front pocket and removed a folded 3X5 card, tossing it to English. "Because he will see something. Those are the numbers to the three phones. Don't waste time."

Fifteen seconds later he heard the front door open and close, then English yelling, "he's gone."

Miller nodded to himself in the empty room, sliding the now functionless computer unit back into its original position, replacing the swivel chair, calculating. Always calculating. *Figure two, maybe two and a half minutes from the first window tap—which is most likely when the little lights and buzzers started doing their thing at the police station—till the pane being shattered. Four minutes since they entered the house. Another one, one and a half to get back out. Six to ten to find the truck and get back on the main road. Fourteen to eighteen minutes, and that was pushing it. How many miles was it to the nearest police sub-station? Fifteen? Twenty maybe? How many miles to the nearest patrol car, making rounds on this side of the mountain?*

Miller continued to click off the seconds in his head as he exited the room and made his way down the hall to the nearest bedroom.

So long as no one ever suspected he or Laney or English of anything—and there was no reason that they would—there was no need to attempt to conceal the break-in. Let Wallace sweat about who may or may not have done it. In another ten minutes it wouldn't be Miller's problem.

Miller set the disks on the floor, and ran down the hall into the master bedroom. There he grabbed a pillow from the bed, removed the pillowcase, and unzipped it. He removed several handfuls of cotton stuffing and tossed it to the floor. He carefully placed the hard-drive in the center of the pillow, and then wrapped the pillowcase back around it.

"Paulie!" He yelled. "Paulie! Get up here!"

He heard English's footsteps running up the stairs, taking them two or three at a time by the sound of it. He was excited and scared. Good. Miller wanted it that way. You made less mistakes when you were on edge.

"What?" English ran into the room, his face and neck drenched in fresh sweat.

"We're going."

"What about Rocky?"

"We'll meet up with him at the truck. We've got everything we need." He held up the pillowcase like it some sort of captured prey.

"It's all going to be under lock and key," English said. "Passwords and booby traps out the wazzoo."

"We'll worry about that later. Right now we're leaving."

The telephone rang.

English froze. Miller's head jerked around the room sporadically, as if searching for a means of escape. The phone rang again.

"Oh, fuck," English said. "Time to go."

"I'm thinking." He paused for a moment, then said, "answer it." He pulled off his shoe and handed English his sock. "Put it over the receiver."

English did. "Hello? Rocky, thank God. Just one? Go to the truck. We'll meet you there."

Miller began shaking his head, took the phone from English.

"Take the truck and get out of here," he said into the receiver. "Pick us up at the underpass two miles out. We'll be moving through woods so you're going to have to wait. Stay there for two hours. If we're not there, leave. Go home. Study. Take a nap. You don't know anything. You haven't heard anything. Lose the phone. Understood? Good." Miller hung up.

English said, "one car. Two cops. Coming up the road at about twenty miles an hour. We've got two minutes, tops."

"Time to run." Miller and English sprinted side by side down the hallway towards the shattered window in the great room. In Miller's right hand he carried the pillow-wrapped hard-drive, in his other he clutched his shoe and sock.

"Start climbing." He said, sitting to slide them back on his foot. "When you get down, head for the woods. Don't wait on me."

English nodded agreement and began feeding his lower body out the window, careful not to touch the sharp fingers of glass. He had just found his footing on the oak when he heard the wail of the siren behind him.

*   *   *

After a few quick squirts of breath freshener and a dab or two of cologne—Cool Water, $60.00 an ounce, and apparently the fragrance of choice for younger women these days—on his neck and shirt, J. Fullard Wallace left his office and entered the reception area. His manner was composed, his expression neutral. An attorney for over three decades, he was accustomed to concealing the truth.

Nicole caught his figure out of the corner of her eye and looked up at him. He was handsome enough, she supposed, to be as old as he probably was.

She smiled and stood, feeling as though she were on stage in an important performance. She decided that she and Miller were no longer even; he was going to owe her for this one after all.

Wallace extended his hand. "Fullard Wallace," he said. Nicole shook his hand and offered her own name. Danielle, the secretary, watched from her desk. Wallace felt as though she might be judging him. There was a slight lull as he searched for the right thing to say.

"Was there something I could do for you?" He said finally, his smile never wavering. He extended his arm towards her seat and invited her to sit down.

"I hope so," Nicole said, lowering herself into the seat and crossing her legs at the knees, Wallace expending considerable effort to keep from looking down her thighs. "But I'm not sure. I'm a law student at Chicago—a 2L—and I'm still vacillating as to which arena to channel my energies."

"I see," Wallace offered.

Nicole continued, making it up as she went along, as easily as though she were tying her shoes.

"I'm fairly certain I don't want to work in the solicitor's office—always a baker's dozen back on the caseloads, but the idea of living by the billable hour while drowning from all the frivolous litigation middle-class suburbia seems to be churning out these days doesn't exactly tickle me either."

She smiled, and J. Fullard Wallace found himself wondering exactly what it was that might tickle this young woman.

"In any case," she continued, "I was downtown shopping last weekend and saw your firm, and it reminded me of a fundraiser I attended not too long ago. We were briefly introduced…"

She let him fill in the blanks there, knowing that he would.

From his seat next to her, he could smell her breath, and found himself wanting badly to taste it.

"Well," Wallace chuckled, "the first thing you need to know is that no litigation is frivolous. It all pays the bills." They both laughed at that, and Wallace said, "but all kidding aside, that's no small undertaking. Have you spoken with many other lawyers thus far? Gotten their take on things? As you're no doubt well-aware by now, the law's a many-edged sword." He smiled at her. "By the way," he said, "is Lopatka still teaching Admiralty at Chicago?"

Nicole suppressed a grin. He was testing her, making sure she was telling the truth about being a law student.

"Yes," she said. "He and his wife, both. She does torts and labor law, though I never had her. I opted for Burkhardt; the class started later and about the only thing I enjoy more than being in bed is hitting that snooze button."

And after a little more congenial banter, he led her to his office.

*   *   *

"Oh fuck," English said. "Miller—"

"Freeze! Do not move!" The voice was booming from behind English, enveloping him, it seemed. English thought the whole world must be able to hear it. He felt the words hit his exposed legs and back like rolling thunder off the hills.

"Climb down slowly. Keep your hands where I can see them! Do not move your hands inside the window!"

English was numb with fear. He felt his bladder weaken and thought he was going to piss himself. His hands were as heavy as cement blocks. In front of him, Miller was crouched down on the floor, beneath the level of the window. His eyes were darting around the room like a rabid animal, thinking.

"What do I do," English whispered.

"Do not speak! Climb down the tree slowly." The cop's voice was deep and gruff, as though he were speaking through a mouth of gravel. English thought it was growing closer.

Without hesitation, without a word, Miller sprung forward from his haunches as smoothly and noiselessly as a falcon from his perch and placed both hands on English's shoulders, gripping his shirt in his fists, and jerked him through the window in one fluid motion. The two boys lay face down on the floor and covered their heads with their arms and waited for the sound of gunfire. None came.

"Go," Miller said. "The hallway. Now."

English didn't need to be told. He began worming across the floor out the great room and into the hallway, his knees whispering across the carpet. Miller returned to the window. He glanced out and saw the first cop, a large black man, sitting behind the dashboard of his patrol car, talking into the radio. The lights above the car were spinning blue and red like wild. Another five minutes and there'd be twenty cops all over this place.

The other cop, Miller saw, was a woman, tall and thick, built like a linebacker. She was standing at the trunk of the car, putting on some sort of vest.

"The silly bitch," Miller said beneath his breath, "is suiting up." And following that came its unavoidable partner, "they're expecting a full-fledged shoot-out."

He felt his heart kick it up another notch. His wrists pulsated, and his head started to throb louder at the temples. He lowered his head and glanced around the room, not sure what it was he was looking for, hoping he'd know if he found it.

"Miller," English called from the hallway floor.

"It's Adrian, dammit," Miller said. He stood and ran down the hall, stepping over English on the floor, and entered the master bedroom.

"Adrian, what the hell are you doing? We've got to get out of here. We can say it was just a prank or something. Maybe they'll go easy…"

Miller emerged from the bedroom with a handgun as big and black as anything English had ever seen on television.

"Good shit where did you get that?"

"No more fucking talking. None. Stay here." He began descending the steps two at a time, the gun in his right hand, the pillowcase in his left.

"What are you going to do?" English asked, sweat falling freely from his face and neck. "If they see that they're going to think we're real fucking burglars. We could be shot for God's sake!"

"They think that anyway. We've stolen his hard-drive. There's no turning back from that. What we need is leverage."

English's face looked like someone had kicked him square in the crotch.

"Listen, man. You've lost your mind. We've got two ways out of here: surrender or shoot our way out. That's it. There's no third. *And I am not about to get into a fucking shootout with the goddam cops because you wanted to steal some fucking lawyer's computer!*"

"Hold this," Miller said, throwing the pillowcase up the steps. "And keep your head down. You'd look pretty silly at the altar without it."

English was about to respond, but the altar thing had done its trick. Altars meant weddings and weddings made him think of Amanda, and suddenly English didn't care about right or wrong, good or bad, he just wanted to get as far away from here as possible, any which way he could.

English lowered his head to the floor and covered it with his hands. If he just got out of this without too much trouble, he'd never, ever do anything like this again. Never. This was it. Fuck Miller from here out; fuck Miller and fuck his stupid games. They weren't fun anymore. They weren't anything but bad.

Dear God, he thought, please let me make it out of this all right.

*   *   *

Wallace's office is, like his house, vast and spacious, decorated with expensive art work procured on expensive vacations in countries whose people are starving by the day. His newest acquisition—a Degas, original, illegible signature scratched across the lower right corner—hung proudly behind the sofa opposite his desk. It was purchased in Italy three years ago, where Wallace had written a forty thousand dollar check against the firm's account for it, less than five feet from a woman sitting on the corner, holding her three small children as she begged for money for food and diapers. Wallace had dropped fifty Lire into her plate—shifting the painting from one arm to the other as he reached for his wallet—the equivalent at the time of twenty-five cents.

J. Fullard Wallace believed indulgence and extravagance were, in moderate measure, good for one's soul.

Upon entering the office, Wallace sat Nicole in one of the large chairs facing his office, and proceeded to sit himself behind his massive desk, which, Nicole noticed, was freshly polished to a deep luster. She caught her reflection in it and checked her hair.

"Well now," Wallace said, pulling open a drawer, "now that we can breathe a bit easier, let's see what we can dig up for you, shall we?" He removed a manila file and set it on the desk before him. He picked up the phone, hit a button, and said, "Danielle, hold my calls." Smiling, he shut the drawer and opened the file.

"Mr. Wallace," Nicole said, recrossing her legs, listening to the big clock in the corner count off the seconds, "if you don't mind my saying so, I'm a little uncomfortable here. Like this." She almost laughed when she saw him flush. "Do you think maybe we could go somewhere else?"

"Somewhere...else?" Wallace repeated. "You mean out?"

Nicole nodded. "Or whatever. But not here. It's just so..." she looked around the office and wrinkled her nose, "confined. Don't you think?" Before Wallace could answer, Nicole opened into a smile, and thought she could almost see Wallace's muscles tense.

"I don't see why not," Wallace said, clearing his throat. "What did you have in mind."

"I was thinking about something more along the lines of an interview. Just a few questions and answers. I'd much rather do that than look through your files. Files aren't exactly exciting, are they? That's why they're kept in files, and not on coffee tables and mantles, isn't that so?"

"An interview?" Wallace smiled. "Of course. If you think that would help you the most."

"I think so."

"Where would you like to go then?" Wallace asked, standing, straightening his tie.

"Oh, I don't know. You pick. Somewhere not too noisy."

Wallace chuckled. How young the mind is at twenty-whatever. How very young and fresh and wonderfully tempting the mind is. Sweet God, to taste you just once.

"How would lunch be then, Miss Henderson?"

"Lunch would be wonderful. And I've never been one to shun familiarity. Do call me Nicole, won't you?"

"Nicole it is," Wallace smiled.

Wallace was flipping through a datebook, mumbling the names of several restaurants. "Your father," he said, pushing a button on his phone and buzzing Danielle outside, "wouldn't happen to be an attorney in the area, would he?"

Nicole nodded. "David Henderson."

Wallace's expression faltered; perhaps, Nicole surmised, to consider the implications of what he was considering implying.

Danielle's voice came through the intercom. "Yes, Mr. Wallace?"

"Danielle, ring *Starfish* and reserve my usual table. For two, please."

"Yes, Mr. Wallace. Shall I tell them what time to expect you?"

Wallace was looking at Nicole. "Forty-five minutes," he said, and his eyes never left her.

* * *

Miller was crawling through the Wallace dining room on hands and knees. The pistol had been shoved in his belt; the cold steel of the barrel poked his thigh as he moved across the floor like a frog in water. As he crawled, his hands were lost to their wrists in the plush blue carpet.

Miller made a mental note to have this kind of carpet in his own house one day. He stopped crawling and listened for a moment. Behind him, the rest of the house seemed unnaturally quiet. Like the calm before a hurricane, he thought. Miller rose to a single knee and peered out the window behind the drapery, removing the gun from his belt, holding it with his gloved hands.

They were shaking, his hands, and he concentrated on controlling that.

The front yard was empty. He had counted off forty seconds since descending the staircase with the gun. That gave him three, three and a half minutes tops before the backup arrived. Not much time.

The female cop's head peered in from the right side of the window. Miller saw her gun raised next to her cheek. She had not seen him yet, hadn't separated her reflection from his image, and then, for a fleeting second, their eyes met, and Miller thought he recognized a flicker of understanding there, even a hint of resolution. There was a momentary instant where the woman seemed confused, disoriented as she stared into the window and saw a face beyond her reflection, one that wasn't hers, and it had thrown her. Their noses were, for that second, less than four inches apart, divided only by a thin window pane.

Miller saw the woman's eyes widen, their whites growing wildly at the edges, and then she began to move her head backwards, leveling the gun at Miller's head as she did so. Miller quickly ducked, waited for the explosion of the gun and the piercing slices of glass on his back. It didn't happen. He crawled quickly through the dining room into the living room like a child running from a spanking.

"Three minutes," he said aloud. He held the gun before him and looked at it curiously. It was a Rossi .44 Magnum, five-shot, fully loaded, and heavier than it looked. Miller hadn't shot anything other than a hunting rifle in years, but he knew the .44 could punch holes the size of fists through people. It was big and noisy and blew sparks out the barrel when fired, and it would do the trick if it came down to it.

"Okay," he whispered to himself, still crawling, "Girl cop sees boy robber, gets scared, doesn't shoot. Why? A, because I'm devilishly handsome and she sees a future for us. B, because she's waiting for backup. C, she doesn't want to kill me, just wound me, and a shot to the face would probably do more than wound me. Or D, some reason I haven't thought of and never could in a million years 'cause I'm in *waaayy* too fucking deep."

He was crawling towards the back door. He crawled across the hallway and into the family room, *(way to deep)* off carpet and onto hardwood where his knees and the heels of his hands *thump thumped* and echoed off the walls, and he peered above the window sill into the back yard.

Empty.

"Where are you, sugar," Miller whispered. From this window he could see virtually the entire back yard. He could see the dense forest beyond the yard, rimmed with ripening blackberry bushes and fledgling pines. Higher up he could see the billowy white clouds rolling across a pure blue sky. Back down here, where he and his troubles were, he could see the blue and red of the squad car flashing far down to the left, reflecting off the side of the house like angry rainbows on the western side. He waited another ten count, listening for noises within the maddeningly quiet house, then placed his hand on the doorknob and unlocked it. Another ten seconds after that and he had opened the door.

"Two minutes," he whispered aloud. He crept along the length of the house, towards the flashing car. His feet struck gravel and crunched it down like new snow. His grip tightened on the handle of the gun; the muscles in his forearm burned as he wiped at the sweat on his forehead with the back of his sleeve.

He reached the corner, peered around it, saw the black cop standing by the oak, grimacing into the sun and looking up at the great room window. He might as well have been looking up at the sky, searching for stars. From here Miller could see he was a big man, two-forty, two-fifty easy. Droplets of sweat decorated his neck and forehead. His armpits were soaked through with wetness.

And his gun was drawn.

Miller pulled his head back and pressed it against the house. He glanced to his right, watched the door to the living room, watched the far end of the house for the woman.

The cop had his gun out, ready for business. The woods behind Wallace's house were maybe thirty, forty yards away, a distance he could probably make. From there he could cut south and make it to the river, follow it until he reached the interstate. There was a rest-stop another half-mile or so down the road where he could call someone to come get him.

But to what end? English was somewhere inside and scared shitless. No telling what he might do if she draws a bead on him with that cannon of hers. He's liable to run, screaming his innocence, get himself shot.

Think, Miller thought, sweat running over his eyebrows into his eyes…chest tightening like a fist—lungs forcing breath as hot as steam out his nostrils.

Think.

The gun's metal was heavy and warm through the latex glove. He looked down at it. It was shining black in the waning sunlight, like blood beneath the moon.

He could surrender. Drop the gun, put his hands on his head, come around this corner on his knees. Go to jail for years, be someone's guy-gal in prison. Learn auto-body or masonry between gang rapes and maybe find a job on the outside once his time was served.

He dismissed this notion as quickly as it came.

He peeked around the corner again, saw the cop standing there, speaking into his radio.

Goddam cops. A gun and a badge and they own the fucking world. And these two here for God's sake. A Nigra and a dickless tracy running around with graduate equivalencies, barking out orders.

Surrender, and take your chances with the courts. It was a prank, a mistake. You've got a clean record, you're an honor student. You're going to Yale Law one day. Lose the gun and surrender. They're liable to kill you if you don't. They do this sort of thing for a living.

No, Miller thought. Not a chance. Not me and not now. I will not have my life dictated by the odds. My world will not exist that way within the reach of my arm.

So be it, he thought, then turned the corner in a cloudy haze and felt himself leave this world of the tangible and step into a sea of blue on a great whoosh of wings and air and stillness where there was no noise and no movement and where the gun in his hand felt hollow and distant even as it fired over and over again.

Miller heard the gun's roar like an echo, the sound rising like words in a dream. He felt the recoil in his elbow from a million miles away. And he saw it all happen from some disembodied third-person perspective.

The first bullet went through the cop's large black nose like God's own particular grudge, erasing it in a small cloud of pink and black.

The second shot missed and struck the tree.

The third bullet hit the policeman—stumbling backwards now, gun dropped, clutching his bleeding face—in the stomach, and lodged itself somewhere in his intestines. He doubled over, wrapping his arms around his gut for protection, his mouth hanging open, drool falling from his lower lip like melting icicles, his head lowered. Miller, numb, seeing and hearing nothing but the cop's head, a black dot at the end of a soundless tunnel of light, took two long steps forward and shot twice into the top of that black dot. Bits of tight curly hair—wet, greasy, from blood or gel, Miller couldn't tell—and bone sprayed outward, striking the oak tree and Miller's chest. He felt their sting like bees. Tissue splattered his shirt and the surrounding grass, sprinkling the lawn like dew. A large piece of scalp split and sprayed the ground in a helter-skelter pattern that made Miller think of shattered tail-light glass.

"Urrgh," the cop managed, then fell to the ground. Miller, still surrounded by stillness, still in that blue, heard a scream from somewhere on the other side of the house, then placed the gun next to the man's pulpy ear and fired once more. The shot muffled by the fleshy skin there, followed by a sound like water dripping inside the dead cop's skull.

Miller dropped the gun to the ground, then took the cop's gun from his side. This one was heavier.

"Well," he said aloud, "that was fairly fucking irrevocable."

"*FRANK!!*" the female cop screamed. She was in front of the house, running this way from the sound of it. Miller quickly ran behind the car and rolled beneath it, the smell of black earth and engine oil filling his nostrils, pulling him back to the here and now.

The woman, black flak jacket firmly in place, rounded the corner at full steam, her gun in hand and leveled before her, and stopped dead when she saw what had been her partner.

"*FRANK!* Oh God oh shit Frank. Hold on. *HOLD ON!*" She ran to the car and dove inside. Miller felt it rock above him with her weight.

"This is Officer Carlisle in Hillside Estates. I'm at the Wallace place. There's an officer down. Repeat. Officer down and needs emergency medical assistance immediately. *Get a fucking ambulance up here now!*"

"*FRANK!* Hold on Frank. Hold on. I'm coming." Miller saw her ankles in front of his nose as she stepped out of the car, first the left, then the right. He placed the pistol against the back of the right one as it touched the ground, at the base of her calf muscle where it tightened into a knot to support her weight, and fired. The bullet exited the front of her ankle in a meaty red ball, splitting the two bones like an ax through a cherry twig. The woman fell with a scream, her foot hanging on stupidly by a single pink cord of tendon. Blood sprayed back into Miller's eyes and mouth. He could taste the iron in it.

He began crawling out from beneath the car, then saw that she was swinging on her back towards him, pivoting on her hips, using her one good foot to rotate her body in his direction like the hand of a clock. She extended her gun and fired. The side of his face was struck with an enormous gush of air and the tire four inches from his ear began to hiss. He backpedaled rapidly out from under the car and jumped inside of it.

He stuck the gun out the driver's door and fired twice. From somewhere deep in his consciousness the realization *I'm in a gun fight with a fucking cop* struggled to the surface and Miller pushed it away.

He waited. He didn't hear anything. No movement. He slowly stuck his head around the corner of the car and saw the woman aiming at him. She fired three times, shattering the front windshield over his shoulder. Glass rained down on him like hail.

Miller stuck the gun around the corner again, estimated her position, and fired twice more. His elbow rocked with the recoil. He heard her scream, poked his head out, saw her clutching her chest, blood spurting up between her thin fingers like a geyser. Her breathing came in harsh rasps, a hissing suck sound. The gun, Miller saw, was lying next to her in the grass.

She continued to breathe with sucking sounds, like a torn balloon deflating.

Her diaphragm, Miller thought. I hit her diaphragm. She's suffocating. Drowning in air.

Her or me, he heard somewhere in his mind.

It came down to her or me, so it had to be her.

Had to be.

But there she was, gulping at the air like a landed pike.

Dying.

Fuck her.

He climbed from the car and approached her, kneeling down beside her. She looked up at him through eyes that were already going glassy.

"I'm sorry," he said. Her fingers, as thin and delicate as a little girl's—strange on a woman so thick—were covered in blood. Her breathing became more rapid, almost violent. It was an effort in vain. The chest cavity is useless without a vacuum.

Miller leaned over and whispered into her ear, softly, "if it means anything to you, I didn't plan things this way."

She made no indication that she heard or understood him.

"This does complicate things, however," he whispered, watching the woman die. "I...I hadn't counted on this." Miller looked down at the woman and cocked his head a little to the left. "Can you hear me? Do you understand what I'm saying to you?" He redirected his attention to the house and waited for English. "You've raised the ante, you silly bitch."

The woman's eyes met his. The color in them seemed to fade as Miller watched. "C-c-cover..."

Miller stared at her. "What?"

Her lips struggled to form the word. She looked like a goldfish sucking at air. Her tongue thrashed madly behind her teeth. "C...cov—"

"Cover?"

"Cov..." a thin fountain of blood spewing out between her lips, "-c-c-c-cov—" she was doing something with her hands, pointing, touching the outside of the hole there.

Her chest. She wanted Miller to cover her chest, plug the hole, help her breathe.

Bad idea.

He told himself not to look at her, not to think about her dying there beside him, to imagine a trout or a flounder lying on the hard wooden dock beside him at the lake, flipping around in the air in a futile search for water, dying by the second. He had read somewhere that the Nazis were able to kill the Jews because they thought of them as bugs. First bugs, then dogs. Some had trouble killing dogs. No one minded when it was bugs. But he stared down at her regardless. He was unable to tear his gaze away.

You're not a murderer, Miller, his mind forced upon him.

No, he thought. I'm not.

Fuck.

He hesitated a moment, saw her eyes rolling like marbles in their sockets, and reached over and squeezed the woman's hand reassuringly before returning to the police car and ripping open the glove box. He pulled all the contents out and found what he was looking for. The instruction manual to the car was still in its plastic case. Miller tore it with his teeth and opened it into a large patch of plastic. He ran back to the dying woman and placed it over the gaping hole in her chest. There was a whispery popping sound as the cavity was plugged, the plastic sucked into the wound.

Although she was still badly injured, the woman was breathing now.

Miller cradled the gun in his hands and sat next to her, no longer looking at her but past her, into the woods. He was unaware of how much time had passed when he heard the distant wail of sirens riding the cool, thin air, and felt English tapping his shoulder.

*   *   *

Wallace was no fool.

You didn't get to be one of the top litigators in the entire state by being a fool. He took pride in being able to smell shit a mile away, and thought that right now, steering his mint green BMW in and out of traffic on the way to *Starfish* in the trendy Bucktown neighborhood, he was sitting in a mound of it.

J had fucked his way through that thing in the 60's they called the sexual revolution like a jackrabbit on speed. Now this little girl thought she could snow him with this looking for direction line of nonsense.

Nicole Henderson wasn't the first young lady to make herself available to him. It was a fact of life in his profession, or any profession, he imagined, where publicity and money play a part. That woman down in Atlanta didn't offer her daughter to Rob Lowe back at the Democratic shindig in '88 because he was a nice guy. And the fellow from Aerosmith that his granddaughter liked so much, the one with the lips that made Mick Jagger look like an oriental, he didn't check himself into a clinic for sex addicts because he was handsome. Power and prestige and cash spread more legs than all the love in the world combined. If you doubted it, it's because you lacked all three, and haven't had the pleasure of tasting that side of life.

He had to admit, however, that he hadn't thought someone like Nicole, whose own father possessed plenty of all three, to be taken away so totally by it, but perhaps seeing him at the fundraiser had had some arousing effect on her, or—and more probable, if he were to be entirely honest with himself—maybe she was planning a career in politics and wanted to start building her network early; J. had gotten his share of underage ass that way, too. Some eager little co-ed licking stamps for congressman blah-blah's reelection campaign wanted to separate herself from the pack, wanted to get noticed, was willing to lick a little dick behind closed doors to do it. Who knew? And, J. thought, imagining what it would feel like to have her spread herself across his face, to wiggle his tongue up through wet fur and push it into that sweet thatch of honey, who the fuck really cared?

But imagine. Her early twenties and already doing this sort of thing. What was happening to kids these days? They forgot they were kids by age fifteen, that was what. Where did they learn how to grow up so fast? Claudia had been a virgin until their wedding night, something not too uncommon back then. But it was a different scene these days. J. had had flings with married women who'd had upwards of ten, twelve affairs over the course of their marriage, sometimes two and three at a time. And Christmas. God in Heaven did they turn it loose at Christmas time. Something about the holidays, the office-parties, all the booze, it made married women want different dick. And lots of it. It was rampant, and it nearly made him sick to consider it.

It was the television, that's what it was. J. fully believed that. That Reno woman wasn't so far off the mark when she called for some sort of regulation of the shit that qualifies for prime time these days. The beshitted television, he had seen his own grandkids sit in front of it, watching endlessly. Mindlessly. Just sitting there, getting programmed like a bunch of senseless imbeciles. It taught them to do everything except read and add. How to fuck, how to steal, how to kill, you name it—it was a device from hell, and that was the truth of the matter.

But, J. thought, let's not be too hasty here. No reason to let a little something like principle get in the way of what was shaping up to be one hell of a memorable time. If David Henderson had been such a balls-up parent that his daughter felt like punishing herself and him and whoever else in the world she was lashing out at by twisting the covers with someone three times her age—a sad state for a woman so obviously well-bred—J. figured he could just chalk that up to professional courtesy. Thanks, Dave. Catch me at the club, I'll buy you a drink sometime.

What was that little saying they used to pass around the halls back in school? Whores like queens and queens like whores? You wanted to make a slut smile, you bought her a nice dinner, opened her door for her, took her to a show or something; whatever, so long as it made her feel different. But if you were looking to keep daddy's little princess coming back for more, you let her feel forbidden. You talked dirty to her in the middle of it, maybe come on her face if the mood hit you. Slap them across the ass so hard it left the imprint of your wedding band. Whatever it took to give them that nasty feeling their pristine little lives were missing.

But he had to be careful with this. Unlike the usual little number that J. spent an hour with here, a weekend with there, Nicole Henderson's father was a powerful man, and that could turn sticky. David had lots of friends in all sorts of places, and word traveled quickly about this sort of thing. Just ask the former Prez. what poking around in the briar patch did for his career, not to mention posterity.

Wallace considered that. Imagine, the rumors circulating around the healthclub locker rooms and the country club golf courses; hey, have you heard, J. Fullard Wallace got caught doing the Lewinsky with—you're not gonna believe it—Give up? David Henderson's daughter. Yeah, the David Henderson from Pierce and Stillright. Something else, isn't it? Imagine his wife'll leave him, take him to the cleaners over it. Man gave up his family for a quick piece of pie, and why? Because it was young. Young and tight. Hope he enjoyed it, that's all I can say. Must be awful to be old.

Yeah, J. thought. It probably would be if God hadn't bothered to make such a thing as little girls. Whenever he slid his cock into some twenty-something it was all he could do not to come right there on the spot. Their skin was so goddam smooth and flawless, their legs so lithe and pliant; and their faces…Lord but it never failed, their faces invariably twisted into some sort of wild mask when he found that sweet-spot of theirs for the first time. The young ones, they had never had dick the way a seasoned man like J. worked it.

Nicole Henderson was twenty-four, and that was pretty bad given that he was fifty-eight, but J. had been known to reach pretty deep into the cradle before. What was that little blonde's name from a few years back? Allison? Alicia? Amber, maybe. Whatever it was, she wasn't a day over seventeen. You want to talk about stupid? Get caught doing something like that, and the state gave you ten to twenty to think about it while large men with no real fondness for lawyers took turns renovating your colon.

But like every sin and vice, the young ones were their own compensation. J. looked over at Nicole, who returned his glance with a smile that said everything J. wanted to hear.

J. smiled back and wondered what his colleagues would say if they knew what he was doing. The smug bastards would talk about it over scotch and soda and then go home to their wives and moralize a bit. And who could really blame them. After all, *look* at what he was doing. Here he was, lollipopping around town with someone whose average day consisted of things like study sessions and Seinfield reruns, and they both knew where tonight was taking them. The goddam slut, he should spank her little ass and take her home to her father, that's what he should do. That's what he *would* do if he was interested in doing the right thing, per se. The prudent thing, in any case. But right now, prudence wasn't steering J.'s wheel. Prudence hadn't even come along for the ride.

But still, J. didn't think it too judicious to shoot for anything more permanent than a three hour session with lovely little Nicole. All things considered, once around on this ride was apt to be the best bet.

Of course, if he was only going to get one shot, he was damned sure going to make it a good one. Hump till his fucking eyes crossed.

* * *

"Miller... what have you done?" English stood beside Miller, who was still down on his knees, sitting next to the policewoman. The woman's eyes were vacant still, and there was a steady stream of blood flowing from both her ankle and her chest. But she was breathing.

"Mill—"

Miller reached out and grabbed English's leg, squeezing him hard. "No names, dammit," he said. "No…no names."

English, the pillowcase holding the hard-drive still clutched firmly in his right hand, nodded blankly, staring down at the sprawled figure of the woman.

"What have you done?" He whispered.

Miller rose slowly to his feet. "They'll be here soon." He glanced down once more at the policewoman's body, offered her a smile for lack of anything better to do.

Miller turned and looked at English, wondering if his own cheeks were as pallid as his. He paused for a moment, looked up a bit and over English's head, towards the house, then surveyed the surrounding tree line.

"This went about as bad as it could go," he finally said. English—thinking he heard something different in Miller's voice, something foreign, something like fear—turned away from Miller and dropped down next to the woman. He reached out to her, to touch her, to reassure her in some way, but Miller's voice stopped him.

"Don't touch her," he said. "Stand up and walk away from it. Pretend you didn't see it. We've got about a minute before this place is crawling with fucking johnny bluesuits."

"We can't just leave her here. She'll die."

"What do you suggest? Carry her through the woods? Say we found her like this?"

Miller walked back over to English and stared down at the woman. The woman—whose badge, Miller noticed, said her name was Officer Carlisle—would survive this ordeal because of Miller's plastic bag, and would later tell the doctors that at that moment, when Miller had stared down at her the way he had, his gray eyes opened wide and empty, she had thought that she had been staring up into the depths of hell itself.

"Lifeless," would be the word she would use to describe them. "Utterly lifeless and without remorse."

Miller kneeled down next to her, lowered his mouth to her ear. The wail of the sirens grew nearer.

"What are you doing?" English asked. "We've got to run. We've…we've got to run far."

Miller waved him silent. He redirected his attention to the cop. "Can you hear me?" He whispered into her ear. "Don't try to speak. Save your strength. Just nod if you can hear me."

Miller and English watched as Carlisle, her face drained of color and sprinkled with beads of sweat, managed a slight nod.

"Good. Listen closely. Your partner is dead, Office Carlisle. You know that. You've seen our faces. Now you and I, Officer Carlisle, we're both intelligent people. We both know what's going on here."

Carlisle's eyes widened in terror, her lips began quivering. "No, no. Be still," Miller continued. "I've only got a few seconds to say this. You're alive right now because I helped you. Nod if you agree."

Eyes white with fear, she nodded again. Don't, she thought incoherently, don't let him say his name. If they told you their name it was over. If they told you their name they didn't plan on you being around long enough for it to matter.

"Good," Miller continued. "Before I leave, I can pull the plastic off your chest, and it'd be like pulling your plug. Like a light, Officer Carlisle. One last flicker and then nothing ever again. Your parents or husband or whoever will i.d. you on a cold slab butt-ass naked with a toe-tag and you'll ride a steel tray down the river Styx. I can do it as easily as I tie my shoes and go home and have a nice meal. I know you don't want that, but I can't allow you to identify us. I'm sure you understand my position."

Miller held her fear-crazed eyes with his own. "If you give me your word you'll forget our faces, we go now and give the ambulance a chance to save you. If you don't, we go now and let the ambulance find two dead cops instead of one. The penalty for killing one cop is the same as for killing two. It's an i.v. and a nice long nap either way. You're the only one that stands to lose anything here." Miller paused. "Are you understanding this?"

Carlisle nodded. She stretched her mouth open, her chin shaking convulsively, and whispered, "my…word." She nodded once again.

Miller smiled down at her. "Good. I'm going to trust you, Officer Carlisle. Don't let me down."

Miller regarded her a moment longer before adding, "Hold your hands firmly to that plastic. The ambulance will be here any minute now, I imagine."

Miller took the pillowcase from English, motioned with his head towards the trees, and began running towards them with everything he had.

Before following, English retrieved both Wallace and the dead cop's gun from the ground and stuffed them down his jeans, wedging them tightly against the small of his back and pulling his shirttail out over them.

Miller didn't see him do it, which was how English wanted it.

Camaraderie was over. It was time to think about insurance.

* * *

As English broke for the woods, keeping his eyes focused on the brown and green treeline even as it began blurring from the tears, he heard the sounds of sirens—near, and growing nearer by the second—rolling over the hilltops and across the woods.

And so he ran. Despite how badly he wanted not to, English ran because he knew that he must; there was one dead policeman behind him and another pretty close, the sirens were getting louder and he didn't know how he could explain his way out of this one. They would be taken to jail. Charged with robbery and murder. Cop killing.

And so they ran, Miller in front by twenty paces, jumping fallen logs, ducking briars and limbs, twisting around trees and sprinting down hills and along creeks until they reached the highway. Neither boy spoke as they ran. English would not have been able. He felt as though he had just lost—*just thrown away*—everything in the world that was important to him. His family, his future, Amanda, his life. It would all be different now. Nothing he had imagined for himself—no career, no wife and kids, no house in quiet suburbia—would ever occur. And it was the fear of this more than anything that kept his legs moving one after another, when the muscles there felt as though they were going to tear and his stomach had tied itself into acidic knots. He was not running to save himself, to escape punishment for what he and Miller had done. He was running to preserve everything he knew and loved.

It had reached that point now, he realized, where he had one foot on either side of the line.

* * *

They had eaten lunch at *Starfish*—Wallace saying a silent prayer as they were seated that David Henderson's daughter didn't have a moral qualm about drinking, it being his experience that fourth in line behind power, money, and prestige when it came to helping women out of their clothes was alcohol.

As if she had known, Nicole had responded by ordering throughout the course of the meal—Yellowfin Tuna for her, lobster tails for him—three crown and cokes. J. had indulged in four Bombay martinis himself.

Neither of them would have said as much to the other, but both Nicole and Wallace reflected during the return drive to the firm that lunch had gone well. Nicole thought that she had done a rather nice job of getting the old man hot, especially once the drinks started coming with some measure of frequency.

That was when she was at her best.

As for Wallace, he congratulated himself for his fine performance. He had put on quite a show as the brilliant legal scholar, and could plainly see that he had impressed her. Her eyes had lit up when he had mentioned the fact that he owned horses, and kept them boarded in stables in the mountains just across the state line. When he had asked her if she rode, she shook her head, but had quickly added that she had always wanted to learn but had never found the time.

Wallace decided now was the time to test the water; float a test-balloon, as they said in politics.

"It's interesting that you should say that. I was just thinking that if you had time, and were interested, of course, we could perhaps continue this interview on the backs of some of my finest thoroughbreds. I have two mares that are sheer silk to ride upon."

"Perhaps," Nicole replied.

"Because it makes sense,"—ballsy now, laying it thick—"that an up-close perspective of the…off-duty, if you will, life of an attorney would help you to better make an educated decision. Give you perhaps a more…comprehensive perspective. After all, take away the lawyers and the law is rendered inept."

Nicole had waited a moment before saying, "Why not?"

*   *   *

The three of them drove home in virtual silence. English had nothing to say. He felt empty and sick. His insides were numb.

Laney hadn't known what to say when they told him what had gone down. I didn't do it, he repeated silently again and again. I didn't do anything. I wasn't there when they killed…

—*killed killed they killed a fucking cop*—his mind repeated mercilessly.

But I didn't do it, he reiterated. I wasn't even there when it happened.

And then another thought: I'm the get-away car. I'm the fucking wheel-man.

Laney had his foot buried to the floor, propelling the old truck down the barren side-road as fast as he could push it, the big engine whining from beneath the hood. He would occasionally glance over at Miller and

English sitting beside him, hoping one of them would look up and meet his stare and maybe offer some encouraging words to make things seem better, or at least have some suggestion as to what they were supposed to do next. But they didn't; English was simply staring out the side window, watching the world go by at eighty-five, and Miller's head was back against the back window, his eyes closed. Laney couldn't tell if he was sleeping or not.

Miller didn't speak because he could find no good reason to do so. These were problems that weren't going to be solved by three different and panicked opinions being shouted back and forth in a pick-up truck. He needed time to think. Space to sort this out. There was no connection whatsoever between any of them and Wallace. There just wasn't. And no reason one would ever be suspected. Why would the police even begin to look their way?

The answer was simple: they wouldn't. The state of Illinois was a big place; Wallace was a big man. The search and investigation—and it would no doubt be an exhaustive one—would overlook the unknowns.

But that brought him to an interesting point. He checked his watch. It was a little after six. They weren't completely unknown, were they? Directly perhaps, but stretch things just a touch and you'd reach Nicole, who, if things were going as planned, would probably be at dinner with Wallace right now, or maybe at the cabin at Grand Beach, where Wallace would more than likely come to know Nicole in the biblical sense. The police—presumably having arrived at the massacre back at the Wallace home—would have begun searching for him by now, would have called the office and asked about him.

But they won't know about the cabin, Miller thought. At least, not just yet. It was possible even his wife didn't know about it. Miller had to assume that they would, as the search intensified, discover it, but the odds of that happening tonight were probably fairly slim. And at any rate, Miller thought, there isn't a phone there. They'll probably take Mrs. Wallace, if they can find her, into protective custody for the night, and, if

Nicole does her part, reach Mr. Wallace sometime early tomorrow morning. And if that's how it turns out, it ought to be ok. He'll be no more the wiser, and will probably shed a hell of a lot more tears for his missing harddrive than the dead cop. The police will ask him where he was the night before, to which, unless he wants to admit spending the night with a strange girl, he'll have fashioned his own alibi.

But this thought snagged Miller. It had been the only snag since the beginning, the one he hadn't been able to get around from the word go.

There was a connection.

Nicole.

If for some reason something went wrong on her end, and they didn't end up going to the cabin, or the police were able to get in touch with him before they got there, the police could and would use Nicole as one of their starting points for their investigation. A long shot, but one they could ill-afford to ignore.

Miller tried to follow that road in his mind and didn't find it going anywhere he wanted to be. Check out her friends, who she hung around with. A man like Fullard Wallace no doubt had plenty of after-hour appointments with young women in his waterfront hideaway, but even a rookie detective would raise an eyebrow at the fact that Wallace's house was being looted at the same time he was so conveniently otherwise engaged.

Miller decided that he would have to risk calling Nicole on the cellular. He didn't want to do it, but he no longer had an option. If she said everything was fine, then he'd let things run their course until morning. Wallace would do everything in his power to hide Nicole's existence from the police, thereby unknowingly burying the only way they would ever connect Miller, English, or Laney to any of it. He'd be doing their work for them. Even if he did the math and suspected Nicole of having something to do with it, he would be knee-deep in his own lies and unable to say anything.

All English and Laney had to do was keep their mouths shut, and there were ways to encourage that. Everyone had their buttons. English's, for example, was five and half feet of blonde over blue.

And if Nicole hadn't been able to pull it off...No. He shut that part of his mind, the doubting part, off. There was no point in dealing prematurely with the ifs of the situation. He'd wait until he got home, and then he'd go to a pay phone and call. If things had run as planned, there'd be no problem. All they had to do was keep their mouths shut, and they'd be in the clear.

Almost an hour later, English climbed silently out of Laney's truck and into his Mustang once they reached The Beverage Station. He glanced out his side window towards Miller, who was looking back at him with a neutral expression on his face, then started the car and left.

As he got into his car and headed for Amanda's, he didn't care if he ever saw Miller again.

* * *

Mr. and Mrs. Peterson were, thankfully, gone when English arrived. He let himself in with his key and walked into the kitchen. "Amanda?"

No answer.

"Amanda? Are you home?" He walked through the living room, down a short flight of stairs, and opened the door leading to the garage. In the corner of the garage sat the nautilus equipment where she normally worked out, but no Amanda.

He went back up the stairs and heard water running above him. He climbed another set of stairs and knocked on the locked bathroom door at the end of the hall.

"Who is it?" Amanda's sweet, almost lyrical voice called. English felt his mood lift at the simple sound of it, and was overcome by the sudden urge to grab her small body and pull it in to his own.

"It's me."

"Hi, gorgeous. Let me rinse the conditioner out of my hair and I'll be right out."

English's stomach lurched. His mind swam sluggishly within his head. His hands felt weak. He leaned up against the door and closed his eyes. The world whirled.

When Amanda opened it several minutes later, a towel wrapped around her body and another around her hair, she saw him lying on the hallway floor, eyes staring vacantly at the ceiling, silvery tears running down his cheeks onto the carpet.

* * *

Miller angled himself inside the phone booth and pulled the heavy glass door closed. He deposited a quarter and a dime, and dialed the number to the cellular phone. He whistled quietly as he listened to it ring. Once, twice, a third time. After eleven rings Miller hung up.

He checked his watch. Seven forty-five. He deposited more money and called Nicole's townhouse. There was no answer there, either. He made a third call to his apartment and checked the messages. None from Nicole.

Which meant she was with Wallace, bless her soul, and everything was going to be fine.

* * *

On the evening of the seventh of October, several things would happen in quite different parts of the Chicago area, all of which would be, eventually, strung loosely together by one Michael A. Palto in an attempt to bury a local college student.

At the moment—11:19 P.M.—Michael Palto is nodding off a bit in front of the television in his living room. He is sitting upright on the couch, his eyelids resting comfortably together, his lips fluttering slightly prior to each snore. In his lap rests a partially reread law review article from one of his legal journals dating several years back.

Also at that moment, the author of said law review article, and Mr. Palto's personal hero, was having the second of what he very dearly hoped to be many angel-weeping orgasms compliments of Viagra and a severely drunken and amazingly uninhibited Nicole Henderson.

By midnight, Palto's wife, Jenny, would have trudged barefoot from the bedroom, through the kitchen and its icy linoleum and into the living room to retrieve her F. Lee Bailey and take him to bed.

By midnight, Nicole would be screaming horribly in a cabin at Grand Beach, trapped and terribly frightened, frantically punching at the numbers on the cellular phone with badly shaking fingers, misdialing twice. Finally she would get through, and the phone at the other end would begin to ring.

Or so Michael A. Palto would soon come to believe, and, subsequently, attempt to prove in a court of law.

*   *   *

J. Fullard Wallace and Nicole Henderson arrived at J's. Place at 3:54 P.M, Thursday, October 7th. This you know. What occurred inside the cabin was of little concern to Miller, who only cared that the two reach the cabin before the authorities reached them, which they did. He assumed their evening together, once having reached that point, would come off without a hitch, which it did not.

What transpired within that cabin forms the framework of the beginning of the end. Had things gone differently, as they by all odds should have, Miller's plan would have most likely succeeded.

Neither Miller nor English were ever able to get the entire story from Nicole, who was too badly shaken to ever work her way entirely through it. Both of them were able to glean bits and pieces during various conversations with her, but a full, flowing story was, ultimately, not to be.

Both English and Miller put what pieces they could together to formulate their own theories about what may or may not have happened in the ominous seclusion of the Grand Beach cabin that evening, behind the closed and locked door of J's. Place.

The facts of the case are these:

They walked up the four steps leading to the wrap-around porch, Nicole's arm laced through Wallace's, and stopped, as was Wallace's custom, to admire the view. Even Nicole, woozy from the effects of the alcohol, had to admit that it was breathtaking. The water seemed to go forever, stretched like pure silk as far as she could see, out to where it met the horizon and disappeared in dazzling hues of orange, yellow and red. Tall and short trees alike reached towards the crystal blue sky, their limbs wrapped densely with dark and light green leafage. Nicole inhaled the clean air and felt its coolness against her naked legs.

"No matter how often I'm out here, I never quite get used to the way it looks," Wallace said, standing closely behind Nicole, his large hands resting on her shoulders, swallowing them. "At night it's so quiet you swear you can hear the trees growing."

"Mmmmmmm," Nicole responded, leaning back into Wallace's large frame. Wallace smiled, stiffened, then, for the first time, realized with a sense of accomplishment that he was finally going to get to do something about that stiffness with the cause of it, and this thought caused him to smile even wider.

"Let's go inside, shall we?"

Before Nicole turned to follow Wallace, she saw a doe and her fawn walk across the road in front of the cabin. A nice touch, she thought. How quaint.

Inside.

The front door opened into a large, spacious living room. The floors were a natural hard-wood color that matched the walls. A sofa sat at the far end of the room, facing a fireplace dark with soot. Flanking either side of the sofa were two chairs pointed towards the fireplace at an angle.

Nicole noticed that a silvery spring was barely visible beneath the tan fabric of the easy chair on the right.

Behind her, where Wallace stood, a large bar stretched virtually the entire length of the room, with several stools situated in front of it. The front door was at the end of one bar, and at the other end another door stood closed. The bedroom, Nicole assumed.

She glanced around looking for a stairway. From the outside it had looked as though it might be a two story. She didn't find one, and upon looking up, saw why. The ceiling was high, vaulted, peaking in the center the way some churches do. An old chandelier hung directly above her head, two of its twenty bulbs burned out.

"Would you mind," Nicole said, remembering the phone, "giving me the keys. I left my bag in the car."

"I'll get it. Did you want a drink?"

"Please. And don't make it weak. And I'd just as soon get it myself, if you don't mind."

"Vodka?"

"Whatever," Nicole said.

Wallace poured them both screwdrivers and took a seat on the couch.

"It's unlocked."

She sipped her drink and winked at him as she stood. "You understand," she said. "Girl stuff." She walked slowly towards the door, turning down his offer to help her with the steps, balancing herself by holding to the wall, and returned a minute later.

"Is there a bathroom to be found in this charming little chalet, or do all the manly men just find the nearest tree?"

Wallace pointed to the closed door. "In the bedroom." He watched as Nicole walked past him into the bedroom, her bag slung over her shoulder, and wondered if it wouldn't be possible to just skip the small talk bit and cut right to the chase. If she didn't want him she wasn't stopping him, and J. had learned years ago that the two were one and the same.

But man was she young.

"*Real* young," Wallace murmured under his breath, setting the drink on the coffee table and kicking his feet up. But again, *so what?* No one had to know. He sure as hell wasn't going to say anything.

And what of Nicole?

What of her? She's so lit you'll be lucky if she doesn't pass out in the middle of it, much less remember it to tell in any case. And why would she tell, anyway? The way she was sucking down that crown at lunch, and now the vodka...kinda makes you wonder if ol' Dave's girl doesn't have a bit of the Irish in her, doesn't it? I mean let's face it, this is a girl whose capped off a few in her day.

Well, yes, it did, and yes, it was, but that was irrelevant. That was her problem. If she wanted to drink herself into a rehab center for rich neglected twenty-somethings before she saw thirty that was her choice. It didn't have anything to do with him.

No, it didn't, but it did bring to mind another problem. One that did matter to J. Fullard Wallace. Mattered a great deal.

Claudia. He couldn't very well spend the entire night out without any sort of explanation till morning. That would hardly do. He could call Mike Reardon and have him call Claudia at home, tell her J. had to fly to Washington on an emergency call or something. Reardon owed him a favor or two, (he had sold similar lies to Mike's wife, Regina, a few times in the past) and Claudia would buy it. She was trusting to a fault, and accepted his obligatory trips with a smile for the most part, especially in election years. Of course—and J. knew this—her amiability was at least in part due to the fact that she expected him to retire in another year and sit around and watch soap operas and game-shows with her all day, play doubles tennis with the Mitchellsons and shop all the best sales, a prospect that was less appealing to J. than having his scrotum pierced.

But that was another matter. Right now he needed to concentrate on getting in touch with Reardon.

As Wallace was leaving to use the phone in the car, Nicole reappeared from the bathroom. She had brushed her hair through, giving it a rougher, tasseled look that Wallace found wonderfully suggestive.

"Didn't you say something about horses," Nicole asked, and Wallace forgot about calling his wife.

Instead they spent the next four hours riding through the hills on horseback, trotting and cantering for miles. For part of the time they rode separate horses, for part they rode together on one of Wallace's larger studs, leading the other behind them. During this time Wallace let Nicole ride in front, holding the reins, and he sat snugly behind her, his arms wrapped around her marvelously small middle. By 7:30 P.M. it had grown dark, and they headed back towards the cabin. They stopped momentarily by a calm stream and allowed the horses to drink. Here Wallace and Nicole took several shots from a flask of Jose Cuervo he had thought to bring along (fresh lemon and a salt shaker in a side saddle-bag). They toyed briefly with the idea of building a fire and pitching a tent, which Wallace had also brought along, but decided to return to the cabin for the duration of the night. It was, as Nicole had pointed out, not wanting to be too far from the phone she had planted in the bathroom should something go wrong, supposed to rain throughout the night.

And so they had returned to the cabin, returned to whatever might happen there. Nicole knew what Wallace wanted, and wasn't sure yet as to what the best method might be for avoiding it. He didn't strike her as the type to grow too pushy on her, but still. One never knew.

Except about some things. And one of the things Nicole Henderson knew was that she was not going to sleep with J. Fullard Wallace, tonight or any other night. Favors to friends only went so far.

But she could play the game until. Tease him, pull him along. Let him feel her breath on his ear. Offer him the hollow of her neck to smell. It was fun in a way, and sadistic in yet another, and both were reason enough to let things go a little further.

So they lay together on the couch, drinking and talking idly about things of little importance. J suggested they roll a joint, and Nicole hadn't resisted. Another good sign, as far as he was concerned. They smoked and drank for another hour, the room gradually filling with the acrid smell of marijuana smoke. Nicole held it in her lungs until they burned, then let it out slowly through her nose.

"It's imported," Wallace said, inhaling, holding, letting it go.

"It's good," she said. "Smooth."

At a little before ten, J. decided he had had his fill of the meaningless prattlings of a drunken, stoned woman. It was, in his learned opinion, time to move on to other things.

Nicole had felt it coming, had, in fact, known how he would do it before he did it, and was therefore not surprised when his hand found its way beneath her shirt and his mouth its way onto hers. What did surprise her was that she didn't resist. Perhaps the alcohol and the dope…perhaps the minor thrill she suddenly noticed herself experiencing…

She tried to think about it further and lost it in the haze. Whatever. She was here. He was here. She knew what came next.

They went at it for a while on the couch in front of a crackling fire, before Nicole—eager to slow things down a bit—suggested they do a line or two. J. hesitated, flustered, and declined. Nicole shrugged, removed the vial from her purse, and proceeded to pour and shape two inch longs on the coffee table with a fingernail.

"Do you do that often?" J. asked, watching Nicole snort the lines, one through each nostril.

"Not as often as I do what comes after." She wiped at her nose with her wrist, dangling the vial from her fingers. "Sure you won't have any?"

"Nicole,"—stern, almost parental,—"I haven't in my fifty-eight years touched anything stronger than marijuana."

"Tonight can be your first for two things, then," she said, pouring another small pile onto the table, shaping two more lines.

"One of us," she said, sniffing as she nodded towards the coke, "is going to do those. If you don't, I will, and if I do four lines in one sitting

I'll be unconscious in half an hour. And J," her hand sliding over to his, her mind reeling, turning inward, her vision narrowing, every nerve-ending in her body firing and crackling from the drug, "this will be so much more fun for both of us if I'm not unconscious."

Wallace stared down at the cocaine and then back at Nicole. Without rebuttal he leaned over and snorted the lines, amateurishly, taking them both through his right nostril, wincing at the sting and exhaling sharply, blowing half the drug off the table into the carpet.

Nicole laughed and J., feeling perhaps emblazoned by his concession, led her to the bedroom. There was a period of ten seconds or so where he had to stop, as his heart rate increased wildly, but it wasn't anything with which to be concerned. It was much like the feeling he got on election night and the numbers were going their way. A little excitement, nothing more.

It wasn't until later, about five minutes after he had slid himself into Nicole's young, silky warmth that he realized something was wrong. His mouth went dry, then filled completely with saliva, running from between his lips. He was on top of her, hammering away wildly and screaming through clenched teeth, spilling himself spasmodically within her when he felt that pain again, deep within his chest. It was a sharp, tearing pain, like a thin pin had been shoved through his front and back at once, meeting at the middle in a silvery jolt of electricity. He jerked upwards, let out a high, frantic yelp which Nicole understandably took as pleasure, then slowed his pace. He had to stop. Something was wrong here. This had never happened before. He was suddenly…very dizzy.

J. slowed his rhythm, then stopped. He looked down at her—her head tilted back, mouth open, legs spread and lifted high, bent at the knees, heels imbedded in his back—and watched sweat fall from his forehead onto hers. He stared at her a few moments, still hard, still inside her. Their scent hung strong and heavy in the room. Her hands were on his chest, twisting and tearing at his nipples, grabbing fistfuls of chest hair. He saw her flat stomach shining with their sweat and began moving back and forth again.

But...wait—just wait a minute. His arms...oh God in Heaven his arms were beginning to feel...*numb.* That wasn't supposed to happen.

(Breath...Can't get breath)

"Is something wrong,"—Nicole, between breaths.

(Dear Heaven ...)

"—J?"

(Breathe I can't breathe why can't I breathe)

"J, are you all right? You're scaring me—?"

Wallace shook his head. "I...I need to rest a minute."

"Fine," Nicole said. "Roll over."

His ears began ringing. "What?"

"You can rest if you want," she said, dizzy, lost, confused, flying on instinct, naked in bed, the familiar feel and shape of a man above her, somewhere she had been before. Drunk beyond remembrance, beyond regret—somewhere else she'd been before.

"I'm not through yet," she said.

Wallace gazed down into those bottomless eyes of hers and smelled the alcohol on her peppery breath and felt her erect nipples rubbing his belly like kisses from sandpaper and felt his body respond the way it used to when he was thirty years younger, the way he hadn't thought it capable until the Timmons fundraiser, until dinner at *Riva,* until this afternoon when he had walked into the reception area of his office and had seen all the forgotten dreams of his youth sitting there reading a magazine.

She unwrapped her arms from around his back and pressed her hands against his chest. "Don't tell me you're finished."

"Wha... no, no not at all," Wallace gasping for breath. "It's just that—we've been going...I'm afraid..." another gasp, "I'm afraid I'm not as young as I used to be...and we've been proceeding at"—Gasp—"...at a rather furious pace."

"We aren't playing bridge."

She rolled them over to the right, towards the center of the bed, and positioned herself on top of him. At twenty-four, Nicole Henderson was young, virile, blessed with stamina and endurance that members of older generations have long since forgotten. This, of course, did not occur to Nicole. She was drunk and used to fraternity boys who went all night and wanted more in the morning. The lights were off and it was dark outside, and she was unable to see Wallace's face twist into an unnatural mask of fear and confusion as the outer walls of his heart began ripping. First a tiny hole no bigger than a pinpoint, then tearing like paper across the elastic fibers, seeping blue-red blood the color of ink into his chest like water from a tap. Nicole was unable to see the unmistakable look of pain as he suffered the heart attack his doctors had been warning him of for the past five years. She felt his hands tighten around her thighs in agony as she lifted herself up, down, up again through the heat and the breath and the moans. She heard his breathing come in even greater gasps, felt his legs tighten beneath her buttocks, heard his knees crack like icicles falling on cold pavement, and thought nothing of it. It was normal. They were, after all, fucking. When he screamed it startled her for a moment, but then she, too, ironically, felt her muscles tighten past their limits and her hips tingle and grow flush as she reached a climax, before falling, falling, falling down through that gray haze and finally landing atop Wallace's still body.

She lay there for over a minute before speaking, drunk and high, exhausted, her breath and heart returning to their normal rates, and it was then, when she spoke and received no answer, that she realized what had happened.

And it was then that Nicole Henderson began screaming.

CHAPTER 15
59 Days Before   (October 8)

The phone rang throughout the apartment only twice before Miller answered it. When he hung up, he noticed his hands were shaking. As he pulled on his jeans and sweatshirt, grabbing an extra pair of each, he walked down the hall to English's room. He wasn't here, which meant he was spending the night on the couch at Amanda's. That was fine. English wouldn't be anything but a hindrance with what Miller had to do now.

He had told Nicole to get dressed if she hadn't already. He'd told her to go into the living room and sit on the couch. He'd told her to stay away from the alcohol and the coke, to make sure the front door was locked, and to stay quiet.

Miller drove quickly but legally out of Illinois and into Grand Beach, Michigan, that night. He made one stop, at an all-night Wal-Mart three miles from the apartment. He carried his purchases—two bags of lime, two bottles of bleach, a case of tall kitchen trash bags, two batting gloves, and a hacksaw—out of the store in two trips and loaded them in the trunk before driving away.

Another mile down the road and he tore the receipt into tiny pieces and threw the pieces out the window over the course of the next five miles.

Including the stop at Wal-Mart, it took him a little over two and a half hours, with an additional twenty minutes of searching for the correct dirt roads once he had steered off the main road. He took several wrong turns, and had to consciously keep himself from losing control.

This one had him worried.

He finally found the road with the mailbox—*J's Place,* it declared stupidly as his headlights flashed across it—at the end of it and sped down it to the cabin. It was barely perceptible beneath the light of the stars, and even with that was little more than a gray outline against the surrounding trees.

He skidded to a halt, opened the trash bags, fitting one over each foot and tying it tightly around his ankle. He put both batting gloves on. He leapt from his car, taking the steps to the porch in a single jump. He banged on the door, his heart and mind racing.

"Nicole! Nicole open up. It's me," he called, sliding his hands into the batting gloves.

The door flew open almost immediately. "Miller!" Nicole screamed, throwing herself into him. He hugged her tightly and worked his way inside, closing and locking the door behind them. Miller could tell she'd gotten dressed in a hurry, probably frantic. Her shirt was wrinkled and untucked, her hair matted against her sweaty face. The smell of her skin was strong and familiar.

"It's okay," he said. "It's all right. It's going to be all right."

"It isn't all right," she sobbed, her arms wrapped tightly around his neck, her face buried in chest. "I think he's dead, Miller. Honest to God I think he died from it."

Miller untangled himself from her and held her face in his gloved hands. "Listen. Everything's going to be okay. I'm going to take care of this."

Nicole's eyes were a watery brown.

"Shhhh," Miller soothed. "Sit down here. I'm going to see what's going on, and you stay here and wait for me, all right? Can you do that, Nic? Just sit tight and wait?"

Nicole, sitting with her legs folded beneath her, nodded. Miller smiled and rested his hand above her head, brushing hair away from her eyes. "Trust me, Nicole. I'll take care of everything."

He bent over and kissed her head before entering the bedroom. Her scent was shampoo and sweat.

Once inside, he closed the door behind him and flicked on the light. He felt his throat tighten at what he saw. Wallace's body, beaded over with sweat like a waxed car in the rain, lying rigid in the middle of the bed. He was sallow and pallid, almost gray. His arms were down by his side, as though he were sunbathing; his legs slightly bent at the knees. His face looked normal, Miller thought, except for his eyes. They were somewhere between open and closed, their lids simply suspended half-way. Miller could see their whites even from the other side of the room. They glowed a sick yellow beneath the light.

As he approached the bed, his hands, he noticed, had begun trembling again. He could feel the sweat working its way through the gloves.

And then he saw it. It was slight at first, almost imperceptible, and he realized that he had been seeing it from the start without noticing it.

Wallace was breathing. There was a gentle raising and lowering of his rib carriage as it struggled to expand.

Miller cleared his throat and sat down on the side of the bed, next to Wallace's supine figure. It occurred to him that, if he played this perfectly, he might be able to turn things to his advantage.

"Mr. Wallace?" He spoke softly, his face inches from Wallace's. He wet the back of his right forearm with his tongue and lowered it above Wallace's nose. A gentle flow of air cooled his skin.

"Mr. Wallace? Can you hear me?"

There was a low groan, followed by the audible click of his eyelids pulling apart. The sound made Miller shiver.

"Can you hear my voice? Can you hear me talking?"

Wallace managed a weak nod. His eyes were dark slits.

Miller didn't move. He kept his eyes on Wallace's, taking care not to touch him.

"Wicked fuck, wasn't it?" Miller looked around the room, not sure for what. "She do that thing with her teeth? I remember the first time she did that with me. Came like a goddam badger."

No answer.

"Do you know where you are?"

There was no movement. Only the harsh sounds of breath being pulled through his nose and past his dry lips into his lungs. Miller thought he sounded like a motor winding down.

"Mr. Wallace," Miller repeated. "Do you know what has happened to you?"

"C...C...Clau" a hard-fought breath, "—dia," he whispered.

His wife.

"She's all right," Miller said. "She's fine."

Wallace responded with another feeble nod. Miller looked around the room and his eyes fell on the cellular phone Nicole had brought with her. He thought about calling an ambulance, maybe leaving an anonymous call before leaving. But he needed time to clean up. Traces of Nicole were all over the cabin. Miller was going to need hours to erase them, hours Wallace didn't have.

Miller looked down at Wallace again and was wondering why God hated him so much, when he was struck with an idea. He picked up the cellular and set it on the bed, beside Wallace.

"Wallace, I'm not a doc but my guess would be that you had a heart attack. You probably already knew that." He picked up the phone and showed it to Wallace. He punched in "911" and turned the phone in Wallace's direction, let him see the numbers on the digital display. "You overweight, over-aged suburban folks running around like postgrads, drinking and smoking and fucking the way you do, my guess is these heart attacks aren't much of a surprise when they finally come."

"You see that green button there, Mr. Wallace? The one that says 'send?'"

Wallace was staring at the phone in Miller's hand. Miller thought he saw him nod slightly.

"I want to push that button for you, save your life, but there's something you've got to do for me, first."

Wallace's head rotated slowly to the right and fell on Miller. He lifted his hand off the bed, slowly, an injured bird struggling for flight, and Miller moved the phone away.

"No, no, Mr. Wallace. It doesn't work that way. We're going to play a little quid pro quo here, you and I. You give me what I want, I call the ambulance, let you take your chances there." Miller looked at him lying there, stared as deeply as he could into those eyes. His index finger danced over the 'send' button slowly, hovering, waiting. "Are you understanding me, Mr. Wallace?"

Wallace nodded again.

"Good. Now like I said, I'm not a doctor, but I don't think it's much of a stretch to suggest that you don't have a hell of a lot of time. So please, for both our sake's, don't dick around."

Miller leaned over, lowered his face until it was less than six inches from Wallace's. "I need your password, the one you've got on your hard-drive. Say it so I can make the call and save your life."

Wallace's mouth fell open. Miller could see beads of sweat forming at his temples, literally growing out of his leathery skin before running down his face and into the sheet.

"Time's ticking," Miller said. "The password."

Miller waited a count of ten before shrugging, then standing from the bed and walking off, into the bathroom. "Fine. Lie there and think about it for a while. I've got time."

The boy's voice echoed into the room to Wallace from within the tiny bathroom. And something else…another noise. What was it? A sound; familiar, something common. Something he heard everyday but never really noticed. Wallace tried to turn his head further but could not. No matter.

But wait…

There.

It had become clear now. His heart, pounding in his ears...

...Dear God, he wanted it to be pounding. He wanted that sound to be his heart hammering away, pumping the blood through his chest and his limbs and his neck in great, healthy spurts, instead of...

...Instead of a muffled tone, almost like two rough surfaces, rubbing against one another.

And slowing down.

Water.

The boy was running water in the bathroom. Washing his hands. No, Wallace realized. His hands were in gloves. He was washing his gloves. Tightening them. Rinsing away the sweat. No traces here, no sir. Can't have that.

"Is there a great deal of pain? I've been told that heart attacks are akin to kidney stones."

Louder now. The boy's voice was getting louder. Closer. And...the patterns of his words, the almost total absence of any accent, seemed vaguely...familiar? That even, level way he had of talking to you, without too much emotion or inflection. Wallace had heard it somewhere.

"...a career in law," Miller was saying, "I'm thinking very seriously about attending Yale Law School when I graduate next May. Of course that's still months away, but you can never start planning too soon, can you? Right now I've got the LSAT, which is no blowjob in the bathroom, let me assure you."

Wallace struggled to remember but drew a blank. He looked up to see the boy hovering above him.

"You know about planning, don't you," Miller said, setting the telephone on the table next to the bed. Wallace turned his head to see it, saw the 911 resting on the display.

"You've planned everything for a long time, haven't you? The campaign, Patterson, and everything else. Even this cabin was a piece of the puzzle, wasn't it? It's not on the maps, it's not listed at the county registrar. Probably haven't paid too many property taxes on it either, have you?"

Wallace thought he actually heard the boy laugh at that.

"This is a nice little love nest. The shit that's probably gone down here. If the walls of this place could talk…" The boy moved in closer, his mouth less than an inch from Wallace's ear. Wallace could smell garlic and pepper on his breath.

"I don't feel bad for you," he whispered. "Not at all. But I don't want you to die." He reached over and got the phone. "That would make things immeasurably more complicated for me." Miller paused, held Wallace's eyes with his own. "But you're going to have to give me what I want."

Wallace didn't move. He remembered now.

Give me what I want.

That total detachment. Ice falling from the words. He was amazed he could have ever forgotten; the kid had given him the creeps from the start. A fundraiser. For Timmons, God bless the man. The boy had approached him, friendly, admiringly even. Something about Wallace's birthday party. It was the same fundraiser he had first seen Nicole—

And Wallace made the link.

Goddam, Wallace thought.

The boy had been pulling his leash from the start.

"The password, Wallace. To the information on your hard-drive. Give it to me."

Wallace stared at him, his face a neutral mask struggling to breathe.

"I need your password, Wallace. And believe me, you need to give it to me. Otherwise I walk, which means you don't."

Wallace nodded, opened his mouth, and forced a single syllable out of his lungs.

Miller lowered his face, turned his ear to Wallace's mouth. "What?"

"El…El…"

"El what," Miller said. "El-Shaddai? Elephant? Eleven? What?"

"Elm…Elm Street," Wallace finally managed. When he had said it, he was wracked by a series of violent coughs. Miller pulled his ear away wet with saliva.

"Elm Street? The password is Elm Street? As in Nightmare On?"

Wallace nodded, and it clicked for Miller. Elm Street was the street Kennedy had been riding down in Dallas when someone or ones had decided it was time to change chiefs.

Miller looked down at Wallace, lying beneath him, staring hard at the phone.

"A politician to the end," Miller said.

Goddam if he doesn't know, Wallace thought. The son of a bitch saw what everyone else who was too stupid and too idealistic and too blinded by their own ego missed.

Wallace gestured at the phone with his head, made an effort to say something and failed.

Miller held it up before Wallace the way he might have held a piece of meat up before a hungry dog, and pressed the "off" button. "I'm sorry, Mr. Wallace, but I'm afraid this doesn't end nicely for you." He slid the antenna down and folded the phone closed, then laid it down on the nightstand next to the bed. "I wish I could call someone, but I've got hours of work to do here before morning, and miles to go before I sleep...miles to go before I sleep."

Wallace looked up through half-opened eyes and saw the boy looking off somewhere else, across the room at something. J. remembered the kid introducing himself to him now. What had his name been? Something Jewish. Rosenberg, maybe. No. That wasn't it. But close. Something berg.

Wallace, his mind receding into the vast unknown, his field of vision slowly getting dark around the edges, came up with a picture of Claudia and reached as deeply within himself as possible and managed, "H....H....Help me...puh-puh...*please*." His mouth twisted into a violent ring as he gasped for air.

Miller picked up the pillow next to J's. head and held it over his face.

"This won't hurt, Mr. Wallace. Don't fight it. Just let go and see which of the religions has it right. Stephen King once said God was probably a big Mickey Mouse doll. Wouldn't that be disappointing?"

Miller lowered the pillow onto Wallace's face, pressed downward and leaned his weight onto it. He felt the impression of Wallace's nose beneath his hand, felt it give under his weight. There was very little resistance from Wallace. His wrists snapped once as he tried to lift his arms, and that was it. When Miller had counted to two hundred, he removed the pillow and re-licked the back of his forearm.

No air this time.

For the second time in twenty-four hours, he had killed a man.

Miller left the bedroom, pulling the door shut behind him, and walked over to Nicole. She had laid down on the couch, her knees pulled to her chest.

"Can we leave, Miller? Please. I really want to go home. I want to go home now."

Miller touched her face with his hand, rubbed it softly. Her skin was damp with tears. She leaned over into him, her head pressed into his stomach, and began crying again. Miller held the back of her neck with his hand, stroking it softly.

"Sssssshhhh. It's going to be all right, Nicole. It's going to be all right."

He placed both hands on her cheeks and looked into her watery eyes. Streams of tears fell freely down her face. Her eyes were red and puffy.

"I'm going to take care of things. I promise. I'm going to take care of it."

She nodded weakly, and Miller cupped his hands gently over her ears and kissed her on the forehead. "Don't cry, Nic. Nothing's going to hurt you. I promise."

"Take me home, Miller. Please take me home now."

He nodded. "Are you drunk?"

She shook her head. "No. Yes. A little, I don't know. Is he dead?"

He sat down beside her and smiled tenderly. "Let's go home."

Miller led her out to his car, where he sat her down in the passenger seat. As she sat, she noticed her left earring was missing and didn't care. She didn't think to tell Miller because it seemed irrelevant, though it's doubtful Miller would have thought so.

Later, when it was found, it proved to be anything but.

"I've got to come back tonight," he said as he sat down behind the wheel. "I have to take care of this."

"I heard you talking in there? Is he still alive?" Nicole asked.

"He's dead," Miller said. "I was talking to myself."

Nicole covered her face with her hands. She sounded exhausted, on the verge of passing out. "Can't we call the police? Let them handle it? I didn't do it on purpose, Miller. Nobody's going to think I had anything to do with it. He was old."

Miller shook his head. "We can't, Nicole."

"Why not?"

"We just can't."

"Miller—"

"Things went bad in Kenilworth today," he interrupted. "I'm not going to worry you with the details. You'll read it in the papers soon enough. Your father will probably be one of the first to know." He started the car and turned it around so it was facing the road. "But there are going to be a lot of people looking for Wallace in about four or five hours. Lots of questions are going to be asked. They've probably already started. He was a real heavy-hitter, Nicole. That's why we had to have him occupied in the first place. We had to have him gone in such a way that he would keep it quiet. That was the only way to cover our link to you."

"And now he's dead, Miller. Because of all this."

Miller put his hand on her leg to comfort her. He was still wearing the gloves. "It's not your fault, Nic. It...it just happened. It could have been anybody, even his wife. He had a bad heart. It's like a time-bomb, just ticking away inside. If it hadn't happened tonight, it would have happened tomorrow at one of his country clubs while he played squash. It just came at a bad time for us."

"I gave him some coke."

Miller shook his head. "You offered it. He took it. It's not your fault."

"They'll trace it to me, Miller. They have to. They're going to see someone was with him here tonight."

Miller nodded. He was aware of that. "They won't suspect you. They don't even know you. Guys like Wallace have entire harems on call."

"His secretary saw me, Miller. We spoke to each other. She commented on my hair."

Miller fell silent. Had he really hoped no one had seen Nicole with Wallace the entire day? Had he seriously entertained that notion? That she could wait for him at his firm, go to a public restaurant with him, ride around in the car with him, and not attract any sort of attention whatsoever?

No, he hadn't. He had counted on Nicole being seen with Wallace, making it that much more necessary that Wallace fabricate some sort of believable story as to where he had spent the night. His alibi needed to hold water. And Miller had known that it would. Wallace would be a veteran when it came to this running around business. What Miller hadn't counted on was Wallace's bum heart.

And now he was dead, hours after his house was robbed and a cop killed in the process.

This was turning into a case-study in foul play. The police were going to question everybody even remotely involved with Wallace. The people where he worked, where he ate, where he drank. The secretary could describe Nicole. Someone at the restaurant would confirm it. How long before they discover his cabin and give it a look? Ten, twelve hours at the most? And then what? A bedroom with sheets and smells that scream sex. Half-burned logs in the fireplace. Fresh dirt in the living room carpet. New tire-treads in the dirt out front. By the time Miller finished class tomorrow the police would be where he and Nicole were right now, looking for the next step. A young girl in her early twenties, attractive, auburn hair, Miller could imagine the secretary telling the police. They'd go through Wallace's calendar. Check all his social engagements from the past year. If this was just a one time thing, which they would logically assume, given her age and the fact that no one could place Wallace with her before that, he must have met her somewhere. Ask around. Pass the word. Make public the description. Sooner or later someone somewhere was going to come forward with Nicole Henderson's name. A mutual friend of Wallace's and David Henderson's, perhaps. Or someone else who had happened to notice her at the Timmons thing.

"Do you go to a lot of political functions with your father?"

"Some, why?"

Some. Great. Half the state party probably knew who she was. Nicole wasn't easily missed.

And did Miller really expect that female cop to keep her end of the deal? He had killed her partner and damn near her and she was going to keep her mouth shut about the thing?

No, Miller knew, wondering why in the hell he hadn't just let the woman die, she would not.

When you looked at it like that, the road from Wallace's corpse to Miller, English and Laney was a short one.

Oh man, he thought. Why oh why didn't I let that cop just quietly bleed to death?

Because, Miller thought, in no mood for the irony, I wasn't a cold-blooded killer at the time.

But you are now, a voice inside said calmly, void of emotion. You're not a student anymore. You're a thief and a killer. You're on the other side of the line now, where the rules are all different. And you can't learn them in a textbook.

And you can't arrive late.

"Don't worry about it, Nicole. Just don't say anything to anyone. This whole thing is going to blow wide open in the morning, and before tomorrow's over it'll be a statewide news item. Probably bigger. The only thing we can do is keep it from coming our way. No matter what you hear, you don't know anything. Just...just don't say anything to anybody."

Nicole was shaking her head, her face red and puffy, her eyes raw from the tears. "No more, Miller," she pleaded. "No more lies. I can't do it anymore."

"I'm afraid you don't have a choice, Nicole. None of us do." They drove on in silence for a full two minutes. Finally, Miller, the night's shadows washing across his face as he steered the car around the base of the mountain down the red-dirt road, "we're in this until the end."

"The end?" Nicole repeated quietly. "Where does it end, Miller?"

He didn't have an answer.

* * *

After dropping Nicole off at her place, Miller returned to the cabin. The darkness was black as tar and thick with the sounds of the forest. He aimed his headlights at the front door of the cabin, then got out of his car and opened the trunk. The silence was deafening, and the stillness of the heavy night air became painfully real.

From his trunk Miller removed first an industrial broom, which he let fall on the ground next to the car. Next came the items from the Wal-Mart: the lime, twenty-five pounds of the stuff, followed by the bottles of Clorox bleach. He removed the hacksaw and tossed it aside to the ground. He carried the lime and the bleach to the porch and set them on a step. He then removed a small fold-away shovel he kept in his trunk for when he and English went camping, and a dust-buster vacuum cleaner.

He checked his watch. It was twenty after four. He gave himself two hours to finish here, another two to get back to the apartment. That would put him back around eight in the morning if he hurried. His alarm would go off at a quarter till nine, and he would get up, shower, and head to class like every other day.

But he would have to work fast. He put the gloves back on and went inside the cabin, leaving the door open behind him. The car's headlights shined brightly through the door into the living room, casting an eerie yellow glow over the upper half of the room, leaving the lower half cloaked in shadow.

Miller went into the bedroom, saw Wallace's unmoving form, crossed the room and stood next to it. He looked at Wallace's closed eyes, licking the back of his forearm again and placing it before Wallace's nose. Nothing.

Miller reached down and wrapped his arms around Wallace's back—the skin still warm, damp sweat having already evaporated from it, leaving it sticky—then lifted him to the seated position. He pulled Wallace's torso off the bed, letting his legs drop to the floor with a solid thump.

Miller dragged him from the bedroom, through the living room, and out into the hot yellow glare of his headlights. Poignantly aware of the time, *lack* of time, he realized, he backed carefully down the steps and turned abruptly right at the bottom of them, pulling Wallace's limp corpse into the woods. It took ten minutes to drag the body fifty yards into the forest—Wallace's heel giving him some trouble on a branch twenty yards in, the foot becoming wedged somehow in a fallen oak limb, twisting with a hollow popping sound as Miller jerked the corpse free—and another twenty minutes to tow it down a sharp embankment he had backed into. He found a clearing and laid the body on its back, then returned to his car.

After turning off his head lights (the irony of having his battery die out here did not at all seem funny) he got the fold-away shovel and one of the bottles of bleach from the porch and carried them to the clearing, setting them beside the body. He made another trip to the car and returned with the bag of lime.

It was another hour before he was satisfied with the hole. It was positioned off to the edge of the clearing, back behind a freshly fallen pine. Four feet long and as many deep, it would be found rather quickly if the police decided to dig this far from the cabin. But it didn't matter; if they were digging they'd be doing it with bulldozers and dogs and they'd be going a hell of a lot deeper than he had time to dig with his shovel.

Miller split the bag of lime with the shovel and covered the floor of the hole with an inch-thick layer, then spread Wallace out in it, face down this time. He positioned Wallace's arms at his sides, lifted the bag to pour another layer atop the body, when he was struck with a sense of irony and found himself compelled to see it through. He set the bag of lime on the ground next to his foot, dropped into the hole, straddled Wallace, and, with some effort, turned the corpse over. The man's face was staring up at Miller, his eyes looking hollow and glassy, a scene that would have been disconcerting were it not for the measure of comic relief he had stumbled upon.

Miller brushed the lime off Wallace's face and pulled his eyelids further apart, bits of lime falling into Wallace's eyes, gathering on the whites like dust. He pried open Wallace's mouth, gripped the lower jaw in his right hand—his fist cupped around the bottom set of teeth there, his gloved fingertips pressing gums as dry and tough as old beef—and, with a swift jerk that ripped tendons and tore the corners of his lips, left Wallace's mouth gaping wide, dangling, a facial attachment that didn't quite fit.

Miller climbed back out of the hole and stared down at Wallace.

"Nothing personal,"—unzipping his fly, freeing his prick—"but it isn't often one gets the opportunity to piss on a lawyer." Miller released and aimed his stream into Wallace's open mouth, listening to it fill, the sonorous pitch growing higher as the cavity grew full, then overflowing, splashing Wallace's cheeks, his nostrils, then, with intention now, the eyes.

He was about to cover the body in lime when he remembered the hacksaw.

Fifteen minutes later he was kneeling in the hole next to Wallace's body, sawing through Wallace's right wrist, his own hand wrapped around Wallace's fingers to keep the man's arm straight. A single jet of blue-red blood as black as ink beneath the moonlight spewed like a faucet in all directions, dousing Miller's shirt, his face, his hair. It was warm against his skin, and salty in his eyes. When the saw hit bone it stuck, skipped up and down a bit, then began slicing through as though it were working on wood. Miller felt it as he pumped the saw through the splintered bone and out the other side, and Wallace's hand came off in Miller's with a sickeningly moist rip. Miller sat and stared at it for a moment, amazed at how fake, how rubbery, it looked. The ring finger still sported an over-sized gold ring which, Miller noticed upon inspection, read *Class of '55* across the side in script. Miller turned the hand over in his own. The skin looked as smooth and soft as velvet, save for the tips of the index and middle fingers, which were rough with whitish calluses. The tell-tale signs of a golfer.

He stared at it a little longer, hefting it like a paper-weight, realizing the magnitude of what he was doing. But there was no turning back, no starting over. He felt his stomach burn with nervousness, felt his hands begin to shake again. He had set-up one of the more powerful men in Illinois, and when things had gone wrong he had killed him. That was the situation. Anything else was just garnish.

"Well, so be it," he said aloud, then set the hand on the ground outside the hole, where it sat, semi-open, palm up, as if waiting for something to hold.

Forty minutes later and the other hand, along with both feet, lay next to it. Miller's shirt was stuck to his chest and stomach with blood, and his neck and arms were caked in it.

He decided then that if he was going to go to the trouble of making Wallace's body as anonymous as he could on such short notice, the fellow's teeth had to go. So he took the butt-end of the saw and smashed it into Wallace's face a few times, splitting the lips and turning his nose into pulp. He clenched his own mouth tightly shut and hammered away at Wallace until his shoulder throbbed and the place where Wallace's face had been was a shiny red smear. The smell of blood began to pervade the air and make Miller sick. Bugs swarmed around his head, lighting on Wallace's face and getting stuck there.

With his index finger he reached past the torn tissue and bone splinters into the moist, torn hole that had been Wallace's mouth. He felt jagged, broken teeth above and below his finger, projecting out like stalagmites in a cave.

He looked around for something harder to do the job with and found nothing. There wasn't anything he could do about it; he was running out of time.

He quickly climbed out of the hole and poured a layer of lime over Wallace's front, taking care, for the sake of theater, to lay it on particularly thick at his genitals. He covered Wallace's head completely with it—the black powder mixing with the blood and forming a brownish soupy mixture—then opened one of the bottles of bleach and poured it over the lime. The fumes from the bleach burned his nose and made his eyes water. When the bottle was empty, he added more lime on top of that, then filled the hole with dirt. He then took the shovel and scattered the excess dirt around the clearing.

He wiped a sheen of sweat from his forehead and stepped back to look at the grave. The night air was thin and clean, pregnant with the green smells of nature. Miller leaned his head back and stared up at the moon and surrounding stars. Those same stars had been shining down last night, when the worst of his worries was a nasty Poli Sci exam. They looked like candles burning holes in velvet.

He looked at the grave again, the earth there black and fresh, raw from the blade of the shovel, and Wallace lying underneath. A pauper's grave.

What did you have when you buried a lawyer up to his neck in dirt?

Miller ran the shovel over the grave to smooth it out a bit, laughing in the moonlight.

Not enough dirt.

"Case closed, counselor," he said, and laughed loud enough to send the forest teeming with life.

He pulled several rocks and log pieces over the grave, trying to situate them randomly, aware that none of it would matter in the end. They'd find the body, and they'd identify him. They could extract a strand of hair from his razor or shower drain at home to run a DNA test. The hands and teeth routine wasn't likely to do much more than buy him a little time.

So he gathered the hands and feet into the empty lime-bag, stuffing the empty bleach bottle on top of them, and ran through the woods back into the cabin, where he opened the second bottle. He found Wallace's shirt lying across an arm of the sofa, tossed haph-hazardly the way men toss their clothes when they're taking them off for a reason. He doused it in bleach and began wiping down all the surfaces of the cabin. The coffee table, the mantle, the wooden armrests of the chairs, the bar, the small tables at either end of the couch, the bathroom and kitchen countertops, the nightstand beside the bed, the doorknobs, the headboard, all the glasses, everything was washed with bleach. Miller did this for an hour, rubbing the rag over everything, every surface, then doing it again.

By the time he was finished, the morning's sunlight had begun to wash over everything, breaking through the clouds and the treetops in rays the color of bone.

It was ten minutes before eight.

Miller carefully wiped down the second empty bleach bottle with Wallace's shirt, then tossed it into the empty lime bag. He stuffed Wallace's clothing into the bag, then stripped down to his underwear and balled his clothes up, setting them on the passenger seat. He then tied the lime bag closed with a knot and set it on the passenger floorboard. His forearms and torso were stained red, but he simply covered them with the extra sweatshirt he brought, having run out of bleach inside the house. He pulled on the spare pair of jeans, got in the car, and drove it to the end of the driveway. There he left it running, and ran back to the cabin where he used the industrial broom to brush away Wallace's and Nicole's footprints. He erased as many of the tire treads as he could, but knew that it would be impossible to get them all. He had driven up and down miles of road back in these hills in the past five hours, and nothing short of a good rain would cover them all.

When he had brushed his way to his car, backpedaling, taking care to drag the broom over impression his bag-covered feet left, he unscrewed the head of the broom from the wooden pole connected to it, and threw the dirt-laced bristles into the forest. It would be found in the first ten minutes of the investigation up here, but that was unimportant. What mattered was that there was no dirt from these hills in his car. Between classes today he would take it by one of those quarter wash places and vacuum out the carpet and upholstery.

He returned to the pinto and tossed the pole into the backseat. It was now five after nine.

* * *

Miller pushed his pinto close to eighty for most of the drive back to the apartment, its engine whining in protest. The skyline burned brightly off to the right, and shortly after Chicago's towering presence began to loom in the newfound light of the East. It was ten-fifty.

As he pulled up in front of the apartment at twenty after eleven, he noticed English's Mustang wasn't there, and found himself grateful. One of the few things about the last day or so that had rolled his way.

English was going to have a lot of trouble with this.

English might turn out to be something he needed to worry about.

He carried the lime bag and his bloody clothes close to his body. As far as he could tell, no one saw him.

He entered the dark apartment without turning on a light, making his way through the kitchen by memory, finding a large trash bag and stuffing his bloody clothes into it. He set it along with the lime bag in the floor of his closet, behind a shoe tree. He then stripped off his clothes and climbed into the shower. He spent forty minute scrubbing every inch of himself, the dried blood going runny and washing down the drain in varying shades of pink. He showered until the water went cold, and then he showered some more.

When he got out of the shower at a quarter after twelve, he walked naked across his room and sat, dripping wet, on the edge of his bed. He stared at the gold rectangular outline the day's light formed around his closed blinds. A patch of it rested on his knee, warming him there, the water drops on his skin shimmering all the colors of the rainbow.

As he sat there, considering how all of this might play out, trying to prepare himself for tomorrow, and tomorrow's tomorrows, he wondered if the kindness and empathy he'd demonstrated with that lady cop would prove to be his fatal flaw.

* * *

After his two o'clock, Miller crossed the campus to the Business Administration building to see if English had made it in today. He stopped Mitch Doreel on the way and asked if English had been in class. Mitch said he hadn't.

Miller walked back to his car slowly, rehearsing the events of the past twenty-four hours. Since yesterday morning he had broken into and robbed the home of one of the most influential men this side of the governor, shot and killed one policeman and seriously wounded a second—but not before having a nice face to face with the woman—and buried the dead body of that influential man after soaking it in lime and Clorox.

Lord, Miller thought.

I couldn't have fucked myself better if my dick bent.

Miller felt the cool autumn breeze feather over his face like a freshly washed sheet, watched couples pass him by, holding hands on clouds of cologne and hair spray, students flying solo from one class to the next, textbooks and bookbags in tow, their hair pulled back in pony-tails and crammed up under baseball caps, the sum of their worries little more than term papers and frat. parties.

Miller watched them go by the way a man in prison watches children playing in a park.

Sometime later he reached a car wash and spent an hour and a half sterilizing the pinto. When he was finished—when he was certain every crumb of dirt, every flake of dried blood, had been removed—he stopped by *Honest Jim's Tire and Brakes* and had all four tires replaced, paying cash. On the off-shot the cops canvassed every tire place in the city in search of the matching tread, he kept the old tires. He drove sixty miles down the interstate until he found an off-ramp that looked fairly quiet. He exited the freeway, drove around until he found a playground, and dumped the tires there.

On the way back to the apartment he stopped by his parents place in the suburbs. Once there, he asked his mother if he could borrow her blender and muffin tin. When she asked him why, Miller said he wanted to do something special for Tracie, and that Tracie's simply adored blueberry muffins.

* * *

When he got home the answering machine had three messages for him. Two from Tracie—missed you at lunch today, call me when you get in, love ya—the third from Amanda's folks. They were worried, wanted to know if English had seen Amanda. Miller listened to them all and returned none of them, lying down on the bed, staring up at the ceiling, counting its cracks.

Where the hell was English?

Well, with Amanda, that much was obvious. There wasn't really any dire reason he had to see him now, but Miller was worried about him. He debated calling over to the Peterson place to see if they were there yet but decided against it. No need to get the Peterson's any more worried than they already were. Chances were, English would be pouring his heart out to the girl in some soda-shop booth like a catholic in confession and she would be crying and hugging and listening and telling him how he had to stop hanging around Miller cause Miller was bad news and always had been and probably always would be and English you don't want to go down with him when he goes cause he's sure to go sooner or later and when he does it'll be messy.

Yeah, Miller thought.

Messy this might be.

* * *

From the Chicago Tribune, Friday, October 8… (PAGE 1)
POLICEMAN KILLED, ONE WOUNDED, IN HILLSIDE ROBBERY
…an apparent burglary at the home of prominent Chicago area lawyer and Democratic Party activist James Fullard Wallace climaxed in the brutal slaying of a Sheriff's Deputy, and sent another to the emergency room, fighting for her life.

Deputies Franklin Delano Hudson and Officer Susan Carlisle reported to the Wallace address after the security system at that home was breached at precisely 4:16 P.M., and appeared to have interrupted the robbery in progress shortly before 4:30 P.M.,…

Deputy Hudson was shot at close range four times—three times in the head—and declared dead shortly after by arriving medical personnel. Deputy Carlisle was shot twice, also at close range, and survived only by pressing a plastic sheet over her chest. She is listed in critical condition at Cook County Hospital…

As of this writing police report having found no prints thus far from within the house, nor have they located the weapon believed responsible for the murder of Officer Hudson. Officer Susan Carlisle's weapon was also missing.

The unknown assailant(s) apparently fled on foot into the surrounding forest. An initial inspection of the surrounding area revealed several fresh drops of motor oil collected on the leaves of a fallen fir tree about a mile and three quarters south of the Wallace estate. The tread marks of a vehicle weighing between a ton and a ton and a half were found leading to and leaving from the oil sample…

Neither Mr. or Mrs. Wallace were available for comment...

Miller read over the article twice before falling asleep in his bed, the paper folded across his chest.

As he slept, the hard-drive sat in its pillow case, wrapped tightly and held shut with a rubberband, beneath his bed.

*   *   *

A little before six and Miller was ripped from sleep by a sound that, if it was ever there, was gone when he awoke. He rubbed the remnants of sleep from his eyes and called Tracie. He sat on the edge of his bed and let his legs hang over the side as the telephone rang. He thought of the hard-drive, and the newspaper article, about Wallace's body lying beneath four feet of dirt and Clorox and lime. He thought about Nicole, and how scared she had been last night, and how removed from the situation she fancied herself. And Nicole's father, David Henderson. He knew Wallace. He would be questioned. How long before the police noticed the drive was gone, and that thousand dollar paintings were still hanging on the walls of the Wallace place untouched. Silverware so fine you could comb your hair in the reflection was still lying in their drawers, the shrimp-forks here, the butter-knives here, engraved grapefruit-spoons here and so on. How long before the police figure it all out and start asking real questions?

Traci answered the phone after four rings, and the two talked about everything under the sun save what was on Miller's mind.

When he hung up, he gathered Wallace's parts from the lime bag in the closet and went into the kitchen to get started.

*   *   *

Two hours later Miller pulled the third batch of muffins from the oven and set them on the counter with the rest. As he was mixing the batter for the fourth and final batch, he wedged the cordless into the crook of his neck and dialed Amanda's number. A man answered several rings later.

"Is Amanda there please?"

"Who's calling?" A gruff, don't-piss-me-off voice.

"Miller Dispenberg. English's roommate," Miller said, rinsing the blender out in the sink, pouring the pinkish liquid down the drain, then picking bits of flesh off the blades. He flicked these down the drain as well, then filled the blender with hot water and vinegar, letting it soak.

"She's not in. There a number you want me to give her?"

"She has it. Do you happen to know when she might be back?"—wishing he could recall the question as soon as it had been asked, knowing it sounded like an implication that the man had no control over his daughter. Apparently John Peterson thought so as well.

"What is this in reference to, son?"

"I'm looking for English. He hasn't been home and I thought he may be there."

There was a long pause, followed by a heavy, sad sigh.

"They've gone off somewhere together. Amanda hasn't been home since yesterday. Her…her mother's worried to death something's happened to her."

A real tough guy, Miller thought. Her mother's worried to death. He just takes her messages. English was right. The man was a top notch asshole.

"I'm sure they're fine, Mr. Peterson. English wouldn't let anything happen to her." John Peterson seemed to be reaching for something. Miller could imagine him standing in their big, cold hallway in an expensive three-piece and five hundred dollar shoes, a Rolex dangling from his wrist like a weight and his Mont Blanc poking its ugly white head out of his breast pocket like a pimple, still asking himself where he went wrong as a father, not realizing because it wasn't in men like him to realize that sometimes things just happen and there isn't a whole hell of a lot you can do about it.

Things happen to you. Sometimes the best of us end face up, eyes wide with wonder, someone pissing in our mouths.

"I'll—I'll tell her you called, son," he finally said.

Miller nodded to the empty room. "Thank you, sir."

But Peterson had already hung up.

Thirty minutes later Miller was out the door, on his way to Tracie's for the evening. Along the way, he stopped and fed muffins—120 of them—to the ducks at the park.

CHAPTER 16

58 Days Before   (October 9)

Saturday morning. Miller and Tracie hadn't gotten back to the apartment until a little after one (English still gone), and she had stuck around for another two hours for some one on one in Miller's room. When they were finished she took a shower to wash him off and out of her, and Miller waited for her—Tracie placing a premium on the after-fucking cuddling routine, Miller partial to the pre-cuddling fucking, and so obliging—reading a few pages of *Sniper's Moon* by Carsten Stroud. A damned good book, that. It was the kind of book you wanted to read over and again; Miller had already read it twice before. He liked Frank but loved Sonny. To this day he wanted to bang Tricia in that same hotel where she and Sonny had made love to get back at Frank, three stories above the wavering blue-gray of the Atlantic, the ocean breeze whipping through the window and over their bed. Jennifer, his ex-fiance, had told him that said something about his character—relating to Sonny the robber and not Frank the cop—right before she broke up with him a year or so ago. Miller figured he knew what she was saying but didn't give it a lot of thought. It was just a book.

He had rushed out to buy Stroud's second novel when it hit the shelves, a dud named *Lizardskin* that read more like a history of Montana and Indians; getting through it was oddly akin to trying to jog through mud. Miller figured Stroud's success with *Sniper's Moon* set him up well enough financially to where he could afford to moralize a bit in his second one, and decided he'd wait till he read the third before forming any lasting literary opinion. Until then he simply reread *Sniper's Moon*, admired Frank in a lot of ways but wanted to be Sonny in a lot more, and told himself Jennifer and her wacko family could go fuck themselves in their fundamentalist asses.

When he realized he was reading the same sentence over and over without processing the words—Tracie having already slipped, naked, clean, fresh and smelling of soap, beneath the sheets, curling up against him, a leg lying atop his, her strawberry blonde hair whispering over his shoulder and chest—he tossed it and went to sleep.

The next thing he remembered after setting the book down on the nightstand was staring into the blood-red numerals of his alarm clock and trying to figure out what they said.

He gradually shook the webs of sleep and dreams from his head and was able to make sense out of the little red bars of light that stared out at him so accusingly. It was 5:40. Five-forty in the morning, for God's sake. He hadn't slept more than two hours.

He rolled back over towards the wall, shunning the clock, and closed his eyes. What he needed to do couldn't be done until later this morning anyway, and if he didn't get some sleep somewhere he was going to collapse before long.

He lay there for another fifteen minutes, eyes burning, muscles exhausted, unable to sleep. He finally gave up, settling instead for a hot shower. He debated waking Tracie, seeing if she wanted to join him, but decided, for reasons he wasn't quite sure, against it.

As he adjusted the water, stepping in beneath the heavy, massaging streams, his head resting against the cold green tiles of the wall, breathing the hot steam in through his nose...

* * *

...a telephone in a nearby motel room with blue shag carpet and purple velvet drapes began to ring at 6:00 A.M., splitting thick walls of darkness with its sound. A shape beneath a double layer of thin white sheets moved in jerky motions, an animal in hiding, as if in protest of the noise.

The phone continued to ring. The shape beneath the sheets moved again, this time more deliberately. A naked arm appeared. A bare foot fell out from under the sheets and hung limply off the side of the bed.

The hand at the end of the arm dropped down slowly like a crane, homing in on the relentless ringing of the phone, and lifted the receiver the way a bird of prey lifts a fish from the water. The hand guided the receiver towards the shape under the sheets.

"What is it?"

"Wake-up call, sir."

"Oh…right. Thanks."

The line went dead.

"Who was it?" Another shape, pressed firmly against the other, larger one, shifted its weight slightly. There was the gentle whisper of sheets, a kiss of skin on skin.

"Wake-up call. Go back to sleep. We've got the place till eleven."

There was no movement in the room for a very long time. The stillness settled over the couple in bed like a cloak, the smell of sweat and raw flesh hanging heavily in the air. Finally, a voice rose up in the darkness like bubbles in a pond.

"I love you, English. No matter what happens, that won't change. I promise."

*   *   *

Six-thirty and the telephone rang again. English clicked on the bedside lamp and answered it on the fourteenth ring, barking a "who is it" into the receiver. Amanda's warm body lay still next to his. He could feel her hair on his shoulder like fine lace.

"Sorry to be the bearer of bad news, bud, but folks are looking for the two of you." English didn't open his eyes. He thought briefly about just hanging up and dealing with it all after a few more hours of sleep, and probably would have if it would have done any good. But Miller would just call back.

"How'd you find me?"

"Remember the prom four or five years back? You raved about the size of the beds the next day? I took a wild guess and got lucky."

"I told the desk clerk not to forward any calls, the stupid son of a bitch."

"No offense taken, if you were wondering. It's not his fault. I leaned on him a bit, said I was Amanda's father, mentioned words like "kidnapping" and "minor" and "accessory" a few times. He was much more helpful after that. Some people just need their morning coffee."

English felt a yawn coming and fought it. It didn't matter one bit what Miller had to say; he was going to hang up and get busy sleeping a good chunk of the day away real soon. "Not to be rude, Mill, but I'm paid through eleven so if you don't mind—"

"Not problem, man. I just wanted to touch base with you about last night."

English slid his free hand across Amanda's naked back, over her buttocks and down the back of her thigh. Her skin was smooth as oil. He looked at her closed eyes, wondered how any girl could be so unguarded and so beautiful at once. "Last night was wonderful," English said.

"I'm glad you two enjoyed yourselves. Nicole and I weren't so lucky."

"That's a first."

"You thought about her folks, English."

"Nicole's?"

"Amanda's."

"Oh. Not much, why?"

"Well they've been thinking about you. You two have a story worked out?"

"No. Maybe. I don't know. I haven't given it much thought. To hell with them. She's twenty-one. She lives at home for convenience."

"Just checking. Did you say check-out wasn't until eleven?"

"Yeah. Why?"

"Go back to sleep. Enjoy the next four and a half hours. Bad's gotten worse, and you and I are dick-deep in the middle."

* * *

English pulled up alongside the curb in front of Amanda's house at a little after five that evening. They had left the motel two minutes before eleven that morning, returned the key, and had gone down to the pier from there. English drove through a McDonald's on the way for lunch, and the two sat on the dock and ate their food and watched the water rise and fall with the passing breeze.

English always found it peaceful there, listening to the clear of the water fold over itself like layers of silk, slurping and tickling against the rotten wooden legs of the dock beneath him. Farther out, as far as you cared to look, the sun would drip down on the hammered-copper surface of the water and turn everything brown and red and gold, layering across the water like a blanket of leaves on a forest floor. The air would blow past him gently through his hair, through Amanda's hair, feathering her long yellow strands out behind her in fiery arcs of gold, the current pulling the red to her cheeks, making her eyes tear at the corners. Gulls and ospreys would call to one another or nothing at all as they coasted above the water.

…"He didn't say what he meant?" Amanda had asked, scooting her tiny frame as close against her boyfriend's as possible, allowing her legs to hang from the edge of the dock, inches above the water.

"No. Only that it's gotten worse."

She didn't ask him why he had done it, why he had allowed himself to be pushed into something like this, or why he had allowed it to go as far as it had gone. Why it was still going, for that matter. She had already done all that. She felt as though she'd been doing it for years with English, asking him why he'd allowed himself to be pushed into something by Miller, wondering when it would end.

They had spent most of yesterday screaming and shouting and crying and holding one another until it was all out on the table, and Amanda had made the decision then to stop asking why and simply do whatever English needed her to do to help him through this. He was good and decent and innocent and in the end that had to count for something. She didn't know of anything she could do, except be there for him, listen to him, hold him and love him. He was going to need that as these next days came to pass.

Amanda shoved that thought far from her mind and laid her head on his shoulder. There was a soft breeze blowing in off the water, leaving a fine mist on her face as it passed over them.

They sat side by side and watched the sun settle into the far reaches of the lake, a great orange ball dropping slowly beneath the surface, setting the water on fire.

They didn't speak much, and about all English could do to keep himself from crying was to hold Amanda while she did.

At ten minutes after five they pulled up in front of Amanda's house, roughly twenty four hours (that's one thousand four hundred and forty minutes late, English thought) after her parents were expecting her.

English whistled between his teeth. "Man, we're definitely late."

"Just a little."

"What are they gonna say?"

"Probably nothing at first. My father will be disappointed. My mother will do a lot of yelling. At me for a change. It's not a revelation or anything. They found my pills years ago. Mother suspected us before there was anything to suspect."

"They still at each other's throats all the time?"

"Enough. Mom screams and he screams back and she goes through the house slamming doors along the way, and eventually things calm down until the next day." Amanda bit at her thumbnail nervously and eyed her front door. "I don't want to go in there."

"Then don't. We'll run off together right now. I've got at least twenty bucks in my pocket."

"How many Big Macs will that buy?"

"With or without fries?"

Amanda made herself laugh for his sake. She let herself out and circled around to his window.

"Call me," she said, and disappeared up the drive.

Chapter 17

57 Days Before   (October 10)

English rose from bed at twenty after eight as he did every Sunday morning, showering and dressing for church with Amanda and her mother (no doubt moderately disappointed with his decision to take her daughter to some strange motel for the night, and so blatantly at that).

Yeah, well, sorry about that, Mrs. Peterson, but a man's gotta do certain things sometimes. Fucking get over it.

He was on his way out the door—black slacks, white dress shirt with red pin-stripes, black tie paisley'd over in red, black suspenders—and almost bumped into Miller, who was returning with the morning's paper.

"Saved you the funny pages," Miller said.

Mixed emotions upon seeing his roommate. He had been disgusted with Miller the day it all went down—had come to fear him even, to fear what he was capable of—but it was a feeling that began to subside surprisingly quickly. He had wrestled with traces of it this morning—in the shower, getting dressed, talking to Amanda on the phone and telling her he'd be late—had tried, upon finding its remnants weakened, to re-instill it to a certain extent, knowing, believing in any case, that it was the right way to feel about everything that had happened in the mountains. But seeing him again now in the living room they had shared for the previous three years had killed that effort, had killed the motivation behind it. Miller was just Miller.

English said: "Thanks. I gotta run, man. I'm late as usual."

Miller, stretching out his arm, handing English the paper, "you seen this yet?"

English shook his head.

He folded it over. "Give page two, section A a quick read."

English took the paper from Miller and turned to the page. "I assume it's in there?"

"In much detail. I wasn't lying when I called you at the motel. Things have gone and gotten complex on us."

"Nicole?" English asked, scanning the article.

Miller nodded. "About as bad as it could have gone, it went. If there's a God up there, He had the day off this Thursday. Or hell, maybe he's just not on our side. Wallace had it coming eventually, if he was fingering even half the pies I think he was. Either way, it really couldn't get a whole lot worse than it is now."

"I don't have time for this right now. I'm always late and if there was ever a Sunday I needed to be on time, this is the one. If—" English found the headline and felt his face go numb—"Oh…my God. It says Wallace is missing…what the fuck…"

"You're closer than you think. Nicole fucked him to death."

"What do you mean she fucked him to death?"

"I mean I hope it was good for the old bastard, cause it was his last."

"He's *dead*? How…?"

"Heart attack. Can you believe it?"

"No," English said, his voice wavering like straw in the wind. He stumbled backwards until he reached the couch and fell to a sitting position. His head was beginning to throb.

"Well, it's true. He's off to that big court in the sky, where we all represent ourselves and there is no appeal." He paused, let English digest it all. "Nicole's taking it badly, too. She thinks Wallace may have o.d.'d on her coke. She may talk, English."

"She can't. Miller, you have to keep her quiet."

"I'm not sure I can."

English's voice was reduced to whisper. "She's...she's got nothing to lose from this, Miller." He dropped the paper and let it fall to the floor. "She could open her mouth and send us to jail forever. This was all just a game with her to begin with. Aside from a little coke, there's...there's no penalty for her. No reason not to talk."

"Not a pretty garden to be tending, is it?"

There was a lengthy pause.

"Miller, what are we gonna do? We...we can't...what about the—"

"—they already know about the cop. And they're getting pretty suspicious as far as Wallace is concerned."

"What'd you do with him?"

"I buried him in the woods." No emotion. No inflection of any kind.

"You what!? What the fuck were you thinking? They'll find him for sure now. This isn't fucking t.v. They're going to comb through those fucking woods and they're going to find—"

"—What the hell was I supposed to do with him? He was dead, English. As in living no longer. The son of a bitch upped and died on us; there wasn't a whole lot I could do about it."

"You could have dumped him in the lake."

"They would have found him there, too. They're going to find him. There's really no way around that."

"Holy shit. Now what? Now just what in the hell are we supposed to do?"

"Nothing we *can* do except wait. When the police discover Wallace's hard-drive was the only thing stolen, they'll investigate his firm, any business dealings he's had in the past ten or twenty years, the Timmons campaign, the Party probably, and anything else the man was involved with. They'll find out he was crooked. Half his business associates will probably run and hide, and the other half will be on the phones with their attorneys, as soon as they hear about this. It'll be obvious what we were in there for. The only thing that won't be obvious is who we are. They won't think to look our way, unless..."

English had already made the mental leap. "Unless Nicole says something."

"Right. If that happens..." Miller shook his head.

"I've got to talk to her."

"I was going to suggest that. She likes you, English. She may listen to you."

"She will. She has to. There's no other way."

Miller wasn't sure about that, but he didn't say anything.

* * *

English left for church and Miller went back to bed. English wasn't adjusting to this too well, yet. Things were getting worse in a hurry and he was on the verge of falling to pieces. But he wouldn't crack. Miller knew that about him. English had a strength to him he didn't know he had because he'd never been tested.

Well, thought Miller, this ought to do the trick.

The paper had been full of all sorts of cheery news this morning. On page two, there was another story on the break-in at the Wallace place. No new leads, but the investigators were now fairly certain that there were three and not two intruders, as was initially thought. Three sets of footprints had been discovered in the forest surrounding the Wallace's property, two running together, clearly fleeing at a high rate of speed, the other trailing off into a different direction altogether. Police speculated that the lone set, the set that ran towards the road, may belong to the driver of the get-away vehicle.

The length and depth of each set of prints seemed to indicate that all three were males, between 5'8 and 6'5, and weighing anywhere between 160 to 225 lbs.

Neither Mr. or Mrs. Wallace had as yet been reached for comment.

Miller had read through the article without too much difficulty. So far they didn't have anything damaging. Three men, each around six feet tall.

No surprise there. Nobody was going to suspect a malicious trio of lady dwarfs anyway. Of course, as he had told English, it wouldn't be too long before they discovered exactly what had been taken from the Wallace house, and then their investigation would get a lot more specific, which, provided Nicole didn't crack and blow everything, suited Miller fine.

But there was something else on page two, something which had Miller worrying a great deal these past three days. A smaller column—no picture, no bold headline gave anyone interested an update on the status of the deputy shot at the scene. Miller had read this column twice, and was now thinking about it intently as he lay in his bed, wondering what his next move should be.

After taking three bullets at the hand of an as yet unknown burglar in the Wallace home, Deputy Carlisle, it had read, gained consciousness for the first time late last night. Because of tubes running down her trachea into her lungs and another down her throat to feed her, she had been unable to speak, but lay with her eyes open as her husband, an automotive assembly-line worker, held her hand and read to her from a romance novel by Kathleen Woodiwiss.

Miller rolled over, then sat up frustrated. An as yet unknown burglar. As yet unknown.

Not yet, but soon. His mind replayed a t.v. news clip he had watched with his father two nights ago, a sound bite of Kenilworth's thin, no nonsense police chief as he was coming out of the station. *We don't have them yet, but we will, and you can bank your house on that.* Miller had felt the determination festering behind the man's words, the raw hatred cops feel for cop-killers burning like a clear flame. You didn't do that. Cop-killing wasn't something you walked away from. It was beyond the pale, outside all natural and moral laws. Raped an old lady? We'll talk about it. Fucked your daughter? Call a shrink. Whack a Haitian adolescent and eat her brain? Try this jacket on, get used to the color white. But kill a cop and you're going down. No ifs ands or buts about it.

And no bullshit rules.

Kill a cop and it becomes personal.

We don't have them yet, but we will. And you can bank your house on that.

As he sat there on the edge of his bed, a dark mass shrouded in shadow, he looked down at his hands, at his fingers, at his fingertips.

Thank God they didn't have his prints. That was one problem, at least, they didn't have to worry about.

What was going to be a problem, Miller was beginning to see, was that there were ghosts he had hoped forgotten that may very well be coming back, telling tales he could never afford to be told.

Miller repeated silently the final line of the article on the cop: Doctors say her prognosis is good, and a full recovery is expected.

Miller thought: We made a deal, Officer. We made a deal that saved your life.

Don't forget that.

Because I haven't.

And you can bank your house on that.

*   *   *

English drove to church that morning in a daze, the events of the past three days swarming through his head in a colorless blur, patched together by interludes of fear and pain, sorrow and regret. He didn't ask why anymore; he had done little else since it happened and it hadn't done any good. He didn't know the answers and had lost sight of the questions.

He would have to see Nicole, talk to her, beg her, anything. She liked him, she would listen to him—she had to. There just wasn't any other way.

He pulled off the main road and onto the smaller, single-lane street that would eventually lead to Amanda's church. His palms were clammy, his mouth dry.

(I buried him in the woods)

Just like that. Wallace had died, and Miller had done the natural thing. He had stuck him in the ground. Planted him in the dirt. He had hidden him, like a broken dish you didn't want your mother to find. Only if— no, time to stop deluding yourself. If nothing else, at least be truthful with yourself—*when* they found him…

Then what?

They'd put it all together. Wallace was distracted for the night, because someone wanted whatever is in his computer. Wallace was literally caught with his pants down, because someone wanted what was in his computer. Wallace died, and whoever it was that wanted whatever it is that's in that computer suddenly panicked, and they buried him in the woods. Nice and neat, that little theory. It was the natural one for the police to suspect first, the most obvious one.

And it was right as rain.

English felt his stomach flutter as he grew nauseated. His head began to throb in time with the wheels rolling down the road.

(I buried him in the woods)

He was sweating. His throat tightened, and he loosened his tie. From his glove box he produced a rag and wiped it across his forehead, his cheeks, his neck. It came away soaked. Wallace was dead, and there were no two ways about that. The cop was dead, and that was pretty final, too. The other cop might die, and as much as he didn't like the way it made him feel to admit this to himself, his life would be so much better if she did die.

But right now, about all he could do was make sure that whoever was looking for answers didn't come looking at him. Which meant…

Nicole. She had to keep quiet. She had to keep her mouth shut, or it could destroy them all.

—*Please, English. Please…you have to do what's best for you here…you can't trust him.*

Amanda's voice, like rain falling on a garden, soft and unrelenting.

Chances are Nicole was pretty badly shaken, understandably on the verge of letting something slip somewhere, if not cracking outright. And she was unstable anyway. You would have to be a card short of a flush to do some of the things she did. Who in their right mind would agree to fuck some grandfather just because they were asked? Who did that? How could someone so beautiful hate herself so much?

And the inevitable corollary to that question: who in their right mind would agree to rob some grandfather, just because they were told there might be something hidden in his computer?

And take it a step further while you're at it—Who in their right mind would knowingly be a party to murder, as well as a party to the cover-up of that murder?

Who, English?

Who lets themselves get pulled around like some…some fucking dog on a chain? Who barks at will and shits at will and spends all their fucking time worrying about where someone else's will is taking them?

Who does that, English?

Who hates themselves that much?

Who, English?

Who?

And English Mason pulled his Mustang to the shoulder of the road and puked until he thought his gut would tear.

Chapter 18

56 Days Before   (October 11)

The rain fell on the city of Chicago in thin gray sheets, twisting and bending what little light the sun was able to force through the thick clouds above into a series of distorted shadows that danced across the sides of buildings and over the tops of cars.

When the alarm sounded English smashed it quiet with his fist and buried his head beneath the blankets. As if she had known this, Amanda called less than five minutes later—getting Miller, who hammered on the wall that separated their bedrooms, waking English—reminding him to be at school today, that they were meeting for lunch at the pizza place across from the nursing building, calling just to make sure he hadn't decided to skip, telling him that she would be there and was wearing his favorite outfit.

English reluctantly agreed, saying it was only because she would be wearing that outfit that he would be there, then racked his brain trying to remember which outfit she was talking about.

I love you, she had said.

I love you more, he had said back.

Impossible, she had returned.

Amanda, English had said—feeling it all slip away, everything, all he knew and loved and wanted and wished for, all he could ever hope to have and ever want to do, all the bright lights and loud noises of the future, the career and the kids and the sharing of Christmases and Thanksgiving between in-laws, slipping, drifting, falling away from him, beyond his reach, back further and further until he could only sit and watch them, stare at them like jewels glistening under glass, his stomach reeling with nausea, his hands sweaty and cold—nothing is impossible.

And that, he realized, hanging up the phone and vomiting onto the carpet in his room, was what he was afraid of.

That nothing was impossible.

That there was a way out of this, that Miller would find it, that it would all start again someday.

Because nothing was impossible.

* * *

After class Miller returned to the apartment and locked himself in his bedroom. He closed the blinds, then slid a C.D. into his player—Nine Inch Nails' *The Downward Spiral*—before going to work on the hard-drive.

Two hours later—*The Downward Spiral* still spiraling, Miller humming along softly as he worked—and Wallace's hard-drive had replaced his own. Wallace's computer was now Miller's computer.

He flicked it on and waited while it clicked and hummed to life, the screen flashing, running Wallace's various virusscan programs, flashing some more, then settling on Wallace's screensaver, a picturesque mountain-stream scene that Wallace had apparently found on the net somewhere and liked enough to download.

Miller sat. And thought. A dead cop, maybe (hopefully) two. A dead and mutilated bigwig politico. And all for this. For Wallace's hard-drive, a little black box with its hairlined ridges and grooves in which traveled all the infinitesimal blips of data and energy and memory spinning at the speed of light, carrying their secret universes in spaces the size of atoms.

Miller moved his mouse around the screen a bit, clicking on various icons on Wallace's screensaver. He found one labeled 'File Navigator' and double-clicked, then sat back and waited.

He didn't have to wait long.

*   *   *

Earlier that morning, as Miller Dispenberg sat in his Colonial American History course, Detectives Michael Callahan and Jerry Mitchum—Mitchum taller, heavier around the middle, with dark brown hair and a matching mustache that needed trimming, his partner with lighter hair, wider shoulders, a clean-shaven bulldog's face, hard and box-like—were walking through the front door of the law offices of *Rogers, Stiles, and Wallace*. Illinois Bureau of Investigation had faxed over a list of Wallace's properties in the state—a couple of rentals in the burbs, a condo in the city—and Mitchum and Callahan had done some nosing around, lifted a few rocks, asked a few neighbors a few questions.

Now, inside the firm, Callahan hung in the background and flipped through a magazine while Mitchum approached the receptionist, a pretty blonde with blue eyes and a small nose who greeted him with a pleasant smile and a strong whiff of a perfume Mitchum couldn't place but found particularly pleasant.

Mitchum, returning her smile and offering his badge—"good morning. I'm Detective Jerry Mitchum. This is my partner Detective Mike Callahan. We'd like to ask you a few questions regarding one of the senior partners at this firm, Mr. J. Fullard Wallace. Do you have a moment?"

The receptionist held her smile with obvious effort. She seemed confused, almost flustered. "I...I can call someone to help you if you'd like. I'm not sure what I could tell you..."

"Please. There's no need to be alarmed. These are just routine questions we have to ask so we can go back to the office and fill out a lot of boring forms. It'll just take a minute."

She glanced at her watch, a gesture of habit, and nodded politely.

"I'll help if I can," she said then, reverting to familiar terrain, something she knew, "would you or your partner like some coffee?"

"No, thank you. I don't drink it and it makes him edgy."

"Oh," the receptionist replied, as if in apology.

Mitchum flipped open his small notepad and removed a pencil from his coat pocket. "When was the last time you saw Mr. Wallace?"

She thought about it for a moment before saying, "Last Thursday, before he went to lunch."

"And what time was that?"

"About noon I suppose. It varied from day to day."

"Were you at work Friday, October 8th?"

"Yes, sir."

"Please," Mitchum said, waving his hand, "it makes me feel old. Call me Jerry."

The receptionist nodded.

"Mr. Wallace didn't come in to work Friday, the 8th?"

"No. He didn't call either. He almost always calls if he isn't coming in. Even on Saturdays."

"Does Mr. Wallace work on many Saturdays?"

She nodded. "At least two a month."

"And did he come in this past Saturday?"

"I don't know. We have a temp that comes in Saturday mornings. I'm only here during the week."

"To the best of your knowledge, has anyone here seen him since Thursday?"

"No," she shook her head, "I don't think so. Mr. Rogers tried to call him at home, but there's no one there because of that break-in. Do you think he's in some kind of trouble?"

"Don't think so, Mrs…"

"Danielle Raleigh. And it's Miss." She said, holding up a naked ring finger.

"I'm sure that will change before you know it."

A gentle, attractive blush.

"To your knowledge, has anyone here or outside the firm heard from Mr. Wallace since he went to lunch Thursday?"

She shook her head. "Unless his guest could tell you something, I don't know."

"His guest?" Mitchum repeated.

Miss Raleigh nodded. "He went to lunch that afternoon with a young woman."

"A young woman?"

Miss Raleigh nodded. "She said she was doing research, I believe. For a paper of some sorts."

"Do you know the young lady's name?"

"I believe she said it was Nicole. She was a very pretty girl. I'm afraid I don't have a last name."

"Had you ever seen her before?"

"No, I don't believe so. Of course, it's unusual for his guests to meet him here at the office. He's usually very adamant about that sort of thing. He finds it unprofessional."

"Yet he had arranged for this woman to meet him here?"

Danielle shook her head. "I don't think he was expecting her. She simply walked in on her own and asked for him."

Mitchum was writing in his pad. "Could this have been a niece, a family friend of some sort. Maybe the daughter of a colleague? Or a client, perhaps?"

Danielle fiddled with a ring on her right hand, avoided eye-contact with the detective.

"I don't think so. From what I saw, this was their first introduction. But he did seem somewhat pleased to see her."

"Like maybe he had seen her before?"

"Yes," Danielle nodded, "yes, it was exactly like that."

"Do you think—"

"But something else," Danielle interrupted, then apologized, stopping in the middle of her sentence.

"No, no. Please. What were you saying?"

"Something she said to me. It sounded strange then, when she said it, but I wasn't exactly sure why."

"What was it, Miss Raleigh?"

"Well, I don't know if it was true or not, but she said she had met him at a fundraiser for Brian Timmons, the candidate Mr. Wallace is grooming for Senate."

Mitchum stopped writing and snapped the notebook shut. "Thank you very much for your cooperation, Miss Raleigh. You've been very helpful."

"Well I'm sorry I couldn't tell you more, it just that—"

"Not at all. You've given us a good deal. Do you think I could speak with one of the senior partners, please?"

"Certainly. I'll ring Mr. Stiles."

William Peter Stiles III. rounded the corner several moments later with the air of one extremely important who has just been interrupted by someone frustratingly unimportant. He was a short man, overweight, with thick greasy slabs of black hair combed back on his head. His nose was pinched, his eyes little more than dark slits complemented, if you could call it that, by a single furry eyebrow that stretched across his forehead like a black caterpillar. He had about him an off-putting air that set both detectives off from the beginning.

"Gentlemen," he said, extending his right hand. Each detective shook it.

"Mr. Stiles," Mitchum said, "I'm Detective Mitchum, this is Detective Callahan. May we speak with you in your office for a moment please? It won't take but a second."

"I'm very busy, gentlemen. If you don't mind, we can get this over with here and then we can both get back to our day."

"If that's what you want," Mitchum said, reaching for his notepad and pen. "But," he said, leaning closer to Stiles and whispering, "some of the questions may originate from, shall we say, situations you may find a little personal."

Stiles regarded them both for what seemed like a very long while, then abruptly turned and began walking down the plush hallway towards his office.

"Follow me," he said over his shoulder, without looking back.

* * *

The screen read:
ENTER RETRIEVAL CODE
Elm Street, Miller typed, and pressed the ENTER key.

* * *

Stiles's office is as large as Wallace's, almost big enough, Callahan thought, to play a pretty fair game of frisbee-toss in. He could fit about twenty of his own cubicles into it, and never mind the money that went into decorating the place. There were no puke green file cabinets with squeaky drawers to be found in here, no yellow post-it notes fastened with carry out pizza magnets, no electric pencil sharpeners that didn't work. Stiles tastes ran to the Oriental. And the expensive. From the thick draperies to the different oriental patterns that littered the carpet all helter-skelter like pillows in a cathouse, to the authentic Japanese vases with geisha girls painted on them in loud, flamboyant colors, the room, aside from the phone, computer, and fax machine on Stiles' desk, looked like it could have been in some emperor's castle centuries ago.

Callahan glanced over at Mitchum and could see that he too was impressed with the office. He seemed particularly engrossed with a painting that hung over a sofa on the wall opposite Stile's desk. Callahan stared at the painting, trying to figure out what it was. Lots of blues, with violent flashes of red and orange circling in towards the center. It looked to Callahan like someone had tried to paint a picture of the sun dropping into the ocean.

"It's a Van Gogh," Stiles said, as though he were explaining electricity to a child. "I presume you've heard of him."

The policemen ignored the sarcasm.

Stiles positioned himself in his chair, crossed his legs, and pressed his hands against his tie, taking several seconds to fiddle with the knot and straighten the clasp before looking up at either policeman. Finally, exhaling tiredly, he said, "pray tell, what was so important that we cloister ourselves away like little rabbits to discuss it?"

"He do that after he went nuts?" Mitchum asked.

"I'm sorry?"

"That," Mitchum said, pointing at the painting, "he paint that after he whacked his ear?"

"It was,"—Stiles drumming his fingers on his folded leg, brushing lint from his pants—"created in the early stages of Mr. Van Gogh's depression. But surely you aren't here for an art history lesson?"

Mitchum said: "If you don't mind, my partner here and I would like to ask you just a few questions about a partner at this firm, a Mr. James Fullard Wallace."

"By all means," Stiles said, "let us get on with it. I have" he gestured theatrically at his desk with his hands, indicating the mounds of papers and folders, "much to do today."

Mitchum nodded. "I'm sure you're a very busy man, Mr. Stiles. We'll only take a few minutes of your time. When was the last time you saw Mr. Wallace?"

"Thursday morning. Here, at the office."

"Did he seem to be in good spirits?"

"He seemed in ordinary spirits."

"Is he ordinarily in good spirits?"

"He's ordinarily in ordinary spirits."

"You didn't notice anything out of the regular, anything strange?"

Stiles shook his head and sighed. "He seemed fine."

"Did you happen to see his lunch date for the afternoon?"

"I wasn't aware that he had one."

"Your receptionist said he did. A young girl, maybe early twenties. Name of Nicole?"

Stiles's face was expressionless. "I have no knowledge of anything of that sort."

"He ever say anything about her, mention her, talk about her at all?"

Stiles sighed. "Detective…"

"Mitchum."

"Of course. Detective Mitchum, I have no knowledge whatsoever of the "her" you are referring to. I've said that. If I had ever heard J. say anything about her, mention her, or talk about her at all, I would have at the very least some knowledge of her, and, as I have now told you twice, I do not." He reached across his desk to an Oakwood pencil holder, rummaging through, as though searching for something in particular. "I hope that is of some help to you."

Mitchum nodded. "To your knowledge, Mr. Stiles, does Mr. Wallace have a habit of running around?"

"Running around?"

"Screwing women other than his wife."

Stiles cocked his head to one side. "J. is an exceptional lawyer, one of the best I've ever worked with, and I've worked with many. Of his personal life I neither know nor care. I do know that he is happily married. Has been for many years now. I also know that he very often lunches with women other than his wife. So do I. So do most lawyers at this firm, as well as many others, I should suspect. It's called business, detective. Nothing more."

"Business," Mitchum repeated.

Stiles nodded.

"Mr. Stiles, I'm sure you've read the paper these past few days. You've heard what we've all heard about Mr. Wallace's home being burglarized, about an officer of the law dying in the line of duty out there."

"I've read about it, yes. There was a second officer on the scene as well, wasn't there? Perhaps she saw something."

"When she's up to it we'll ask her. But what I want to ask you is this: what do you suppose whoever it was that broke into Mr. Wallace's home wanted? Do you have any ideas on that, Mr. Stiles?"

"None whatsoever."

"They didn't take a thing. Not even the guns they used to shoot the two officers. We found them in the woods. None of Mrs. Wallace's jewelry. None of the cash sitting out in plain sight on Mr. Wallace's bureau. Almost two hundred dollars. Nothing."

Mitchum waited a few seconds, then said, "except the hard-drive out of his computer."

They'd been looking for a reaction to that, and they'd gotten one, but it had been quick. Stiles' face had gone flat as stone for half a second, before reverting back to its previous bored, mildly irritated countenance.

"I have no idea what it was they were after, Officer Mitchum. I can tell you that I hope very deeply that you find whoever it was that did it and put them beneath the jail for a very long time."

"We're gonna try. Does Mr. Wallace have any enemies that you know of? Anyone that would want to harm him or his family?"

"I never heard anything of that sort. J. is a well-liked man, Detective. He is very easy to get along with. Very comfortable to work with. Everyone I know is extremely fond of him. He's a virtual hero in this part of the state."

"He's pretty active in politics, isn't he?"

Stiles nodded without speaking.

"The receptionist out there said something about a campaign he was helping run? You know anything about that?"

"Of course. J. has an active part in Timmons's bid for the senate. He's been an officer in the state Democratic party for as long as I've known him. Everyone knows that."

"Right. You involved with that at all?"

Stiles shook his head, fiddled with his tie. "I vote on occasion."

"Any of the other members of this firm involved with that campaign?"

Stiles shrugged. "Perhaps, gentlemen. Perhaps not. The attorneys at *Rogers, Stiles, and Wallace* are not bound by some silly law to report their personal lives to me. My sole interest rests entirely with their billing sheets. This is a law firm, not a prison."

"Of course." Mitchum turned and looked over his shoulder at Callahan.

"I think that's all, Mr. Stiles. I do appreciate your time."

Stiles stood and escorted them to the door. He shook Callahan's hand, and was shaking Mitchum's when Mitchum suddenly said: "Does the name Julie Anders ring a bell with you by any chance?" He was a cop, and one of the first things they taught cops was to ask questions on the way out. People were less guarded when the cops were leaving.

For the first time since meeting him, Detectives Jerry Mitchum and Mike Callahan got a satisfactory reaction from William Peter Stiles III. His eyes went wide and his lower jaw dropped like a rock off a rooftop, and—for the smallest fraction of a second—his expression went from that of bored and unamused to genuinely startled.

"Mr. Stiles? Julie Anders. The name. Mean anything to you?"

"No, it doesn't." The lawyer's face was back to granite, though for Mitchum and Callahan it was now cracked.

"Not that I can recall at this time, in any case," the lawyer repeated.

"Are you sure, Mr. Stiles?"

"Of course I'm sure. I've never heard of her."

"How about Deborah Ringer? Or Tabitha Star?"

Stiles eyes turned inward and his face closed up and went glassy.

"I'm afraid this conversation is over, gentlemen," Stiles said. "I really must get back to—"

"Funny," Mitchum interrupted, "we just spoke with Julie Anders yesterday, and she seems to remember you. Said she, Tabitha, and you had a real nice time at a little roadside half an hour outside the city. Said the three of you get together now and again to 'party,' as she put it. Talked about things like drugs, rope, videotape. Now," Mitchum said, leaning into Stiles a bit, cutting into his space, letting the little man feel his presence, "how confident are you that you're the only one with a copy of those tapes? Young girls scare easy, Mr. Stiles."

Stiles wiped at his forehead with his shirt sleeve and fidgeted with his tie with his other hand.

"You're an intelligent man, Mr. Stiles. Nothing the women say will stick for any length of time, certainly not legally, but imagine the personal fall-out from something like that. I would think the repercussions of something like a couple of twenty-somethings stating on the record that they've had combination sex with you around a bong in a condo somewhere would be disastrous."

"Disastrous," Callahan repeated.

"Course," Mitchum continued, "I could be wrong. Maybe you and your wife have some understanding about that sort of thing." He shrugged. "You find all kinds, these days."

Stiles regarded both men with nervous eyes then gestured silently with a nod of his head. Mitchum recognized the nod. He'd seen it on lawyers countless times before. Time to fall back. Talk settlement.

The detectives followed him back into his office, where Stiles closed the door behind them.

Stiles sat in his chair again, behind his huge mahogany desk. His right hand found a open and began doodling with it on a blank piece of typing paper.

"The ladies you mentioned and I have met on several occasions," he said, staring down at his hands. "Nothing serious. I'm a married man, you understand. Twenty-eight years this next month. We've got five kids. Eight grandchildren. It would…it would just kill her if this ever…" a wide gesture with his arms—"left the office." He sighed and poked at the paper with the pen. "Just a little fun every now and again. They…they are a bit more uninhibited at that age, yes? Fresher. You understand. It's not a regular thing with me. I'm not one of those who…keep something of that sort...on retainer, shall we say? The fact is that yes, I've had my clandestine fun here and again. It really is quite harmless, and I fail to see where that's pertinent to your investigation."

"Wallace involved with this?"

"Occasionally, yes. It's harmless, really. They enjoy the attention. And the money."

Mitchum pressed further. "Where do you go for these little get togethers?"

Stiles fidgeted with his hands, then forced them to remain still. There was a full minute of silence as he struggled to regain his composure before he said, "various places. But generally next door. Grand Beach. He—Wallace—owns a little cabin there a couple of hours from here. It's very secluded. No phones. No internet. No television."

"No need for them by the way it sounds," Callahan added.

Mitchum removed his pen and handed it to Stiles. "Write down the address."

Stiles looked dumbly at Mitchum's outstretched hand. "I don't know that it has one."

"Then draw me directions. You should know 'em."

Stiles took the pen from Mitchum and, removing a blank piece of notebook paper from a drawer, sketched out a map to Wallace's cabin. When he was finished he handed the drawing to Mitchum, who folded it like a business letter and slid it into the breast pocket of his coat.

"This will remain confidential, I trust, gentlemen?"

Mitchum was looking at the painting again. To him it looked like a child had gotten into the watercolors. Or like a madman's impression of a world closing in on all sides.

"We'll call you if we need any more. This ought to be enough, though. For now."

Stiles eagerly escorted them to the door, Callahan first, followed by Mitchum.

"Hell of a strange painting," Mitchum said on the way out.

* * *

Miller's monitor flashed the following message:

MAIN MENU
Timmons Campaign Fund

Miller sat before his computer and waited for his heart rate to slow. He felt the sweat dripping down his sides, felt his temples throbbing rhythmically. He pressed enter and watched as the screen blinked for several seconds before displaying Wallace's information.

"Dear God," Miller said after several minutes of reading. He scrolled down, read some more, then scrolled another several pages down.

"Oh dear God..."

*   *   *

The two detectives had been gone less than five minutes when Stiles reemerged from his office and marched down the elaborately carpeted hallway, past color prints of Watson, Palmer, Zoeller, and Nicklaus at the Masters, and to the receptionist's desk. Danielle was typing dictation when he reached her.

"Miss Raleigh," he said, startling her. "Those two gentlemen, the detectives? What exactly did you tell them?"

Danielle shrugged. "Only that the last time I had seen Mr. Wallace was Thursday, and that was when he had gone to lunch with that young lady."

"Which young lady was that?" Stiles snapped. Danielle recoiled from his tone. She noticed there was sweat on his forehead and neck, and he seemed to be short of breath.

"I don't know," she said. "I'd never seen her before."

"Did you tell them where they were going?"

"I couldn't. I didn't know. Mr. Wallace rarely tells me."

Stiles stared blankly at her for a moment before nodding. "Very good." He pressed his suit down with his hands, dabbed at his forehead with a monogrammed handkerchief. "If they should happen to return, under no circumstances are you to talk to them at all without my being present. Is that understood?"

"Yes. I'll notify you the second they come in the door."

Stiles smiled. "Thank you, Miss Raleigh. Carry on."

Chapter 19

52 Days Before (October 15)

Miller walked into his Voting and the American Electorate class without acknowledging Professor Johnson-White's presence, took his seat and laid his head down on his desk. He had spent the night in bed alone—Tracie having stayed at her place to study, Miller thankful for that—thinking about Wallace, about the hard-drive and what it contained, about English and the way he was liable to handle all this, about Nicole and her ability to keep quiet. He had gotten less than two hours sleep last night, and was paying the freight today.

He didn't feel badly for Wallace; he had been telling the truth when he whispered that to the old man. If the guy had taken it home to his wife he wouldn't have been in a position to have been with Nicole to begin with.

Johnson-White was saying something about having a cold, about there being a film in lieu of a lecture, and that they would be tested on the film's content. Miller kept his head on the table and his eyes closed, and waited for the lights to go down.

* * *

Mitchum and Callahan pulled into the driveway of *J's Place* a little before noon.

"There's his car," Callahan said, pulling it up next to the BMW. It sat where Wallace had left it, some twenty feet from the steps leading to the wrap-around porch.

Mitchum radioed it in.

"Hi, Madge. Yeah, this is Mitchum. Got a tag for you. A Beemer. It's a vanity plate, reads *HARVLAW*." He spelled it. "Yeah, I'll wait."

"Kind of overkill, don't you think?" Callahan said, opening the door and getting out of the car. "Pretty obvious whoever's car this is ain't a plumber."

Mitchum shrugged and held the receiver. "Last thing we need is to find some important piece of evidence here and have one of this scumbag's friends get it thrown out for improper search and seizure. We find out the car's registered to Wallace, we can probably get by with a just-cause argument to search it. The man's been M.I.A. for a week now without a trace. That makes him a suspect in any book."

The radio in Mitchum's hand buzzed to life in a cloud of static, then Madge's voice crackled through.

"1997 BMW IS, license number *HARVLAW* registered to J. Fullard Wallace of 117 Wallace Lane. No outstanding tickets, case you were wondering about that. Anything else, Jerry?"

"Nope. That'll do it. Thanks, Madge. Love your body."

"Prove it, cowboy."

"One day," Mitchum replied, then joined Mike, who was standing next to the passenger window of the car.

"Time to see if anybody's home." Mitchum said, crossing the driveway and climbing the wooden steps. He turned around and saw Callahan had walked towards the end of the cabin, and was staring out over the water. The sun broke over the tips of the trees of the foothills and filtered through the branches in golden oranges and yellow browns. The air was thin and blue, and a breeze blew in off the lake, bringing with it the smell of pine cones.

"Hell of a view," he said. "Can't really blame them, you know?"

"I blame them."

"Yeah, but you can see his point. Wanting to get it on with a coupla centerfolds out here. I bet they boffed right there on the porch while the sun came up over there." Callahan sighed and shook his head. "Things could be worse."

Mitchum smiled and knocked on the door. "You ought to be a porno producer, Mike. You've got the eye." He rapped on the door again. "Wallace? This is the police. We need to talk to you. Open up." He continued knocking for several minutes, then removed his gun and took several steps back.

"Care to join me?" He called to his partner, who was still staring transfixed over the surface of the lake, admiring the view. "I know it's pretty, but we've got work to do."

"Foot or shoulder," Callahan said, ascending the steps in a single leap.

* * *

He was leaving Voting and the American Electorate when he heard his name being called from behind. He stopped and turned around, distantly aware that he recognized the voice. Recognized, but couldn't place it at first.

Then he saw her, and he understood why he'd had trouble with the voice. Amanda Peterson wasn't one to purposefully initiate contact with Miller. They both knew she didn't care much for him, a sentiment he couldn't imagine having improved these past few days.

"Hey, Amanda," he offered, his voice neutral and non-confrontational.

"I was wondering if we could talk," she said. "Not here. Someplace else."

Miller nodded. "Yeah. Sure. You want to get a cup of coffee or something?"

"Actually, no," she said. "I was thinking about a drive."

Miller shrugged. "Sure. I'm done for the day, anyway. You?"

"No," she said, walking in the direction of the stairwell, Miller following her, "but I'm taking the day off. This is more important."

"This is a first," Miller said. "You ever skipped a class before?"
"No. We'll take my car. I'm parked around front."

*   *   *

English was sitting in the lazy-boy in the living room of Nicole's townhouse. Nicole was sitting on the couch, wearing faded jeans and a white Chicago Law t-shirt. English was wearing his standard; blue jeans and a flannel untucked, blue and green, and faded loafers he had worn since high school. He had his feet pressed closely together before him on the beige carpet, his torso hunched over his knees. His hands were folded together, as though in prayer. In front of him, beyond Nicole and the couch, English could see the hallway that led to Nicole's bedroom.

Nicole, her legs folded up beneath her the way girls do, wrung her own hands together without knowing it, her neck bent over, her voice thin and raspy. English decided closer would be better for this; he stood and sat down next to Nicole, on her left, and even here, like this, he thought she smelled like summer rain.

"I wake up at night a lot," Nicole was saying, her knuckles popping with the syllables. "I just wake up and lie there in the darkness. And I can see him. I can see him looking up at me, English."

English listened, not knowing what to say or even if he could say it.

"Sometimes I think I can still feel his hands against me, and they're cold. I took three showers that night when I got home. Three more the next day." A shiver climbed her spine and she shook it away. "I can't get rid of it. I... I just can't get it to go away."

"It will, Nicole. Eventually..."

She shook her head. "No, English. I...I can't. I can't keep doing...whatever we've been doing. I...I just can't. Things have got to stop. It has to go away." Her hands were pressed against her ears. "I can't sleep, I can't study, I can't eat without feeling like I'm going to puke."

English nodded silently. For the first time since they had sat down, he looked over at her and noticed her nails were unpainted, and didn't think he had ever seen that on Nicole before. He saw her auburn hair hanging down between their faces. He lifted his hand and touched it, soft wisps of silk laced together into one. He pulled his fingers through it and away from her face. She didn't move.

"I'm sorry we got you into this, Nicole. I never wanted you to get hurt. It—everything—got out of hand."

She nodded slowly. "This wasn't you're fault, English. I know that now. I guess I've known it, but just didn't want to admit it. It's difficult to look at yourself in the mirror when you know what you'll see, when you know you won't like it. He's so easy to trust."

"I did it mostly because he asked me to. Isn't that the most ridiculous thing you've ever heard? Doing something like that just because someone asked you if you would? But I've never been good at telling him no." She looked at him and laughed, and for a second English thought she might be mocking him. "I don't imagine anyone is."

"You know I used to think I was in love with him?" She said, laughing ironically between closed teeth. "I had a crush on him all through high school—two years younger than me and I was in love with him. Then I went to college but I still saw a lot of him. He just always seemed to be there. My second and third years of college…God I was so crazy about him. It makes me sick to think about it now. I used to think Miller Dispenberg was the best it could get for a girl. And,"—sniffling a little and rubbing her nose with her thumb—"he may be. But not for me. Not anymore. What I'll do for him—what I've done for him—it scares me. It scares something horrible, English."

"He's got a way…" English said.

"No," she said, shaking her head, "it was more than that with me. I really loved him. Part of me still does, I think. Some part deep inside that I'll have to learn to ignore, or to hide away from myself. But it's a bad love. It's that part of love that's unhealthy, that makes people do things they know they shouldn't do. It's that part that makes you not care anymore. It's a disease, really. An addiction."

She buried her face in her hands and pushed her bangs up over her forehead. "I'm sorry you're involved with this, English. But you have to understand there's no other way."

English didn't say anything. He was wondering where she was going with this, getting the feeling that he wasn't going to like wherever it was.

"My father can get a deal to keep me out of it. I haven't talked to him yet, but he knows everyone and he can keep this quiet. He's done it before."

English felt for a second that she might have slapped him. "You're not considering—"

"I've no other choice, English."

"Holy shit, Nicole. You're ratting. You're talking about fucking ratting on us. My God—Nicole…? You can't do that. It'll land me and Miller in jail for the rest of our fucking lives. Laney too." English fell back against the seat. Something like rage pulsated behind his eyes. He had begun to perspire. "You can't be serious."

She tried to smile for him but could not, and settled instead for wiping away the tears that had begun to fall resolutely down her face. When she spoke again, after what seemed to English to be many hours, it was thin and weak, her voice strained. "It doesn't ever get better, English. Once you do it? It never goes all the way away."

English wasn't hearing her; he felt the pressure inside the room grow and weigh down on him, felt his stomach reeling and his throat constrict.

"The memory,"—Nicole, not looking at him, staring off at someplace on the opposite wall—"The wondering what it might have been like. How it would have felt inside you, growing, kicking." Her voice trailed off to an unknown place, and she seemed to consider something deeply. English stared at her bewildered.

"What the fuck are you talking about, Nicole? Miller? Is that what this is all about? Cause if it is, please for God's sake think about it. Please! They're not fucking around with this thing, Nic. Miller shot a policeman and he did it on purpose. He could get the death penalty for that. Are you aware of that?"

Nicole shook her head slowly back and forth, said: "Miller won't get caught. He's smarter than anyone—even you—gives him credit for being. You're the one I'm worried about."

"Nicole,"—his voice rising several notes, "listen to me for a second here. Just listen to me. If you tell your father you were involved—"

"He can get me out of this—"

"Any deal your father cuts—"

"He can make sure that—"

"Any deal your father cuts is going to include you fingering me, Laney, and Miller. And once you do that it's the end of the fucking road for us. You can't do it, Nicole. Find another way. Go to therapy or something. Fucking-A, Nic, do some coke or something. I'll do it with you if that'll help. But this, you can't do it. You just can't." He was facing her, his face only inches from her own, and he found himself wanting to grab her head between his hands and shake it hard.

"Oh, English," Nicole said in a tone of pity, "you've always been such a good friend for him. Does he tell you that? Does he thank you for always being there?"

"Nicole—"

"Do many people tell you that's one of your flaws? Amanda, perhaps?"

"This doesn't have anything to do with Amanda." Not good; losing his patience. Need to stay calm.

The sound of Amanda's name even remotely connected to this whole affair overwhelmed him with disgust and guilt all at once. "And no, I don't think loyalty is a character flaw."

"Loyalty isn't a character flaw? Silly English. You sound like George Bush." She laughed. "The old one. Not the new one."

"Listen, Nicole, talk to me here. Talk to me. I don't know what's going on inside you right now, and I mean it when I say I'm sorry, on behalf of everyone involved. But telling your dad won't—"

"So loyal..." she paused, and seemed to consider her words. "That night, after the fundraiser, I think that's one of the things that made me do it. You've always been so kind to me, making me promise not to drink too much, trying to convince me to stay away from the pot and coke, the pills. Why, English? Why are you so sweet and decent to me, when I haven't done anything to deserve it? How many times did I try to get you high with me? How many other guys have tried to get me high for the same reasons? But not you. You never let me get that low. You always admonished me." She paused, then issued a quick, cynical little laugh. "Do you remember the time you drove me home from Cliff's place a few years ago? I nearly passed out in your passenger seat, one too many. Anyone else would've driven me out to the lake and had their way with me—hell, I was practically fighting with you to get you out of your pants. But not you. Not English." She looked at him closely, and for a very long second English thought that she was going to kiss him. "Do you remember that?"

He remembered. "There's nothing wrong with you, Nicole. And besides," he said with a shrug, "you're my friend."

"I know, English. But you're wrong, there's a lot wrong with me. I let him use me again, and that policeman is dead. So is Wallace, and it doesn't matter what Miller says, I had a part in it. And if I don't stop now, I'll let him do it again. And again. And again. Until eventually it'll be me that's in all the trouble." She sighed, stretched her legs out in front of her. "Like you, English."

Nicole laughed, then looked at him with a kind of pity in her eyes. "Do you really think," she said, "that he hasn't thought this through? That he doesn't have some...some plan in case they come knocking on his door? Think about it, English. When's the last time he got caught for anything? She pressed her hands together and laced her fingers through. "He's invisible, English, and it's no accident."

English didn't have anything to say to that, and was afraid of what he might find if he looked.

"It isn't in him to feel regret. He doesn't have a conscience, English. He's like stone on the inside. Cold, unfeeling stone. On the outside he pretends to care, pretends to feel, pretends to have emotions and to love, but you get past that and he's ice. Two years ago, when it happened I told him I wanted to try to make things work out between us. That I didn't want things to change. Or I guess I did want them to change, but not in the way things like that usually do. I didn't want to stop seeing him. My father has plenty of money and we could have gotten, I don't know, we could have stayed together. I wanted him to think of me as…as more than someone who was always *there*. Like Amanda and you. Your relationship is so perfect."

English shook his head. "My relationship with Amanda is a hell of a long way from perfect, Nicole."

"No, it's perfect. It always has been. There's probably some shrink out there that would tell you that's why I tricked you into bed. I was trying to have what she had, only on the surface, where the sex and games are, where it seems I always look for things. And I guess I was looking for something like that with Miller, too, only Miller's not like you." She brought her knees back up to her chest and wrapped her arms around them tightly. "Miller's not like anybody."

* * *

She'd pulled the car into the parking lot of the Tremont Inn, a small, nicely-landscaped motel twenty minutes outside of the city. She and English had come here once, years ago, back before he had moved out and gotten his own apartment.

"Ok," Miller said. "I give up. What's going on?"

Amanda turned the car off, leaving the keys in the ignition. She turned and looked at Miller.

"Why did you pull English into this?"

"Oh for…Amanda, I'm not going through this with you. Are you serious? English is your boyfriend, not your child. He's a grown man. I couldn't pull him anywhere he didn't want to go."

"You killed that cop, Miller. Don't you feel the least bit badly about that?"

Miller raised his hands. "This conversation isn't going to happen," he said. "If this is what you were looking for, you could've saved yourself the gas. He shouldn't have told you anything. He's always had a problem with that, ever since the two of you got together. He'd rather play house than be a man sometimes. But if that floats his boat then that's just gravy, but I'm not going to compound the error by discussing it with you."

"You'll get caught, you know."

"No way. Not possible."

"What about Nicole?"

"What about her?"

"She'll crack."

He shook his head. "I don't think so."

"Why not?"

"Because she's categorically in love with your boyfriend, and she'd never send him to jail. She harbors fantasies of the two of you breaking up and the two of them collecting social security together one day."

"She might do it to get at you."

Miller shook his head. "I don't think so. Not Nicole. That's not how she works."

"People do strange things in crises, Miller."

"Yes, that's true. But this isn't a crisis yet. Wallace is dead because his heart couldn't keep up with his prick. And yes, his hard-drive is missing from his computer, but so what?"

"If she talks," Amanda said, "she'll put both of you under the jail for the rest of your lives."

Miller didn't say anything for a moment. He glanced out the window, tapping his fingers on the dash. He felt Amanda's stare as heavy as stone on him.

"What do you want me to do, Amanda? Kill her?"

She didn't say anything, which said a great deal for Miller.

"I can't do that," he said.

"That's not what I want," she said. "Although we both know you could do it."

"For the record, princess, I didn't want any of this to happen. I saved English's life up in those fucking hills. That cop—the one you're so torn up over—he wasn't up there to slap our wrists. Yes, it may have been my idea to go there in the first place, but I sure as hell wasn't looking for the brand of trouble we found, and no one twisted your boyfriend's arm, in any case. He was intrigued as much as I. But he fell apart when the heat came down, and that cop would have blown him out of his shoes had I not retired him early. You might thank me."

"Thank you," she said, which took Miller completely by surprise. "Thank you for saving English's life when it counted." She pressed her hands together, interlaced her fingers.

"You care about him, I know that. But you're bad for him, and if you're honest you'll admit that you know it's true. You're dangerous, Miller, and there's no point in your denying it because you'd only look silly and dumb."

He looked at her.

"What do you want, Amanda? You want me to say it went bad. All right. It went mind-fuckingly bad. You want me to apologize. Fine. I'm sorry. You'll never know how sorry I am. You sit there in judgment but you've no idea what I go through each day. You think I'm free of guilt here? Do you think it doesn't haunt me?"

"No. I never said that."

"Then what?"

"I want you to help me," she said.

"Help you do what?"

"Help me get him out of this. English. I want you to help me make it so English can walk away from this. If you truly care for him, you should want that, too."

"Sure," Miller laughed. "You got a magic bottle you need me to rub, I'll be glad to. Some chant I can say to make this all go away for him, let me know. It's not like I'm sitting on the answers here without sharing them, Amanda. I'm in this shit too, case you missed the flash."

"You have the hard-drive, right?"

He paused. "If I do?"

"No," she said. "No ifs. Let's dispense with all the rhetorical nonsense. You either have it or you don't. If you don't, say so and this conversation is over. If you do, tell me."

Miller shook his head. "Sorry, Amanda. No soap. We'll do this theoretically, and only theoretically. You push for more than that and I'm out of the car."

Amanda met his stare with her own. She steeled herself and said, "o.k. Fine. For discussion's sake, can we assume you have the hard-drive?"

He looked at her, then looked away. Out the window, at a pair of birds diving and looping after one another.

"For discussion's sake—speaking only academically, you understand—let's say that yes, I know where it is."

"Is there money on it?"

"Let's say for discussion's sake that there's an ever-loving shitpile of it."

"So you were right about Wallace. About him stealing from the party?"

"Let's assume so for the moment."

"What have you done with the money?"

"Let's assume, for mere discussions sake, that I haven't gone shopping yet, and that the money's safe."

"Good." She grabbed her purse from between their seats and opened it, moving quickly before she changed her mind. She produced from the purse a single pass-key and set it on the dash. Miller saw that it had the insignia "Tremont Inn" scripted across it.

"I think I have a way that both you and English can get out of this," she said. "But I need your help. Interested?"

Miller spread his hands, shrugged his shoulders.

"By all means," he said. "Color me rapt."

"Well you should be. If this Mr. Wallace truly does have money floating around out there in some nebulous account somewhere, then there might just be a way."

"I'm all ears," Miller said, his expression one of bemusement. "And it isn't a nebulous account—it's real money rotting offshore."

Amanda said: "I don't trust you, Miller. I don't trust you and I don't particularly like you. I'm not going to insult you by pretending that I do. And I'm not going to risk English's one shot by saying too much. You're going to have to meet me halfway on this."

"Halfway where?"

"The answers," she said, "are in room 700." She pointed through the windshield towards the inn. "It's all the way in the back, second floor, on the right. Fourth room from the end."

She picked up the passkey from the dash and handed it to him. He took it cautiously.

"What's your game here, Amanda? This isn't like you."

"We don't have a lot of time," she said. "You're either in or you're out. Room 700. Go there. Wait. When you hear the knock, open it. Or say that you want no part of it and I'll drive us back to the university. If you ever share any part of this conversation with anyone else, I'll flatly deny it. I've never lied to anyone in my life, Miller. My credibility is flawless."

"Yes," he said. "That's true." He stared at the passkey, turned it in his hand, the way you might turn a letter from your doctor the week after your biopsy, filled with hope and trepidation and everything in between.

"What's in room 700? The cops? Are you wired?"

"Really, Miller."

He sat there and considered it for a while, then, without a word, he got out of the car.

Amanda watched him walk towards the inn, saw him disappear around the corner of it. She gave him another five minutes to get into the room—five minutes which seemed like hours to her; five minutes in which she pushed all thoughts of everything save the task at hand away—and then she got out of the car, locked it, and walked to room 700.

* * *

"I didn't know the two of you were—he never said anything about it."

She shook her head. "Are you surprised? Listen to yourself, English. If you don't do anything else, listen to yourself. He's got another side to him, and it's always, always dark there." Nicole folded her hands together and blew a few stray strands of hair out of her eyes.

"I have mirrors, English. I'm aware of how I look. I'm beautiful and smart and rich and I can go all night and then do it in the shower the morning after. If you read the magazines in the check-out lines that's supposed to be all there is. I could have any man I want. But not Miller, and that seemed so...so *Millerish* to me that I thought I could change it. That I was the one with the right stuff, whatever that might mean, to navigate the waters of his mind and somehow raise my flag once I reached solid ground. I thought that if I could do that, no one in the world would ever be able to uproot my place there. No one would be able to take him from me. But of course I was wrong. Just one more who felt too much and fell too fast. A statistic, another number. It bothered me but I didn't make too much out of it. I thought if I made him happy enough he'd come around and decide we had something good."

She looked at English and suddenly burst into laughter. "You know, I've never even told him this. He thinks it was what I wanted, too. If he was here listening, he'd be shocked and amazed. Imagine, Nicole Henderson talking about having feelings for someone other than herself. Hard to believe, isn't it?"

"I've always known there was more to you than that."

She regarded him with a wan smile. "Until I got you into my bed. I suppose I shattered your resilient impression of me somewhere around the time I removed your cummerbund." She laughed. "Your silly pink cummerbund."

English looked away; it had taken work to bury his evening with Nicole beneath as many old memories and new experiences with Amanda as possible, and, though he was occasionally visited by some fleeting glimpse of recollection of that night, (and, in truth, infrequent moments of arousal had accompanied these memories, along with generous servings of shame) a night of decadence in which neither his flesh—defiled by Nicole—nor his consciousness—warped and twisted by enormous amounts of alcohol—emerged unscathed, hearing it referred to out loud, in the open, touched places that were still raw.

English put his hand on Nicole's knee. She leaned her head over on his shoulder. "If I had it all to do over again, I would have seen him for what he truly is. I wouldn't have let it go as far as it went."

"Nicole," English said, "what did you mean when you said the memory doesn't go away. That it grows and kicks—"

"Didn't you know?" Nicole asked.

English shook his head. "Know—? No. What?"

Nicole didn't say anything.

"Didn't I know what, Nicole?"

Nicole nodded as she stood and crossed the room to the window, where she sighed and wrapped her arms around her middle. English could see a new group of tears welling up in her eyes, saw her fight them back with the skill of one who has done it many times before. She looked somehow smaller there, standing before the window like that.

"I had an abortion," she said, parting the hanging silk drapes and staring out into the parking lot. English could see a wedge of gray sky above Nicole's head. "Miller made a mistake and took me to the city to erase it."

English felt his jaw drop. "When was this?"

"The beginning of last year. He paid cash and waited for me and took me to my apartment and tucked me in the bed. He sat up there and studied while I slept. I remember thinking how sweet that was. How nice it was to be cared about like that. I wonder what he would have done if I had gotten sick from the procedure? Or if I had decided to keep it. What if the only way to erase his mistake was to erase me?"

She looked back at English, then away. "You think I'm bitter? That I'm being too hard? I'm not, English. If anyone knows what he's really like, it's you." She turned away from the window and pleaded with her eyes. "Don't let him use you, English. Don't let him position you like some piece in a game. You're smarter than that. If anyone can keep that from happening, it's you, English. He's smart. It's scary how smart he is. He's always thinking about the next move and covering his last one. But you're smart, too. You're not so deep that you can't save yourself."

"Nicole, you've got to keep quiet about this. Just this one thing. I won't let him near you afterwards. I swear to God. I'll help you anyway you want. Whatever you ask. But you've got to—"

"Be careful, English. You have to think like him. That's going to be difficult for you. It's where he has the advantage."

"Nicole, please!" He was desperate now.

Nicole covered her face and shook her head. English—torn between an urge to hurt her and an obligation to comfort—crossed the room and wrapped his arm around her shoulder and held her close, her body shuddering against his, her tears falling down her face onto his shirt as softly as rain on the tops of trees.

* * *

The lights from the various squad cars flashed across the side of the cabin like a giant Christmas tree, bathing everything in deep blue and blood red. Both detectives thought it was overkill—there not being anybody out here to arrest—and it wasn't like they were on the highway or in a residential development where they had to make their presence known. About the only thing they'd be scaring here would be the squirrels.

Two guys from forensics, John Kepler and Travis Sandstone, were busy going in and coming out of the cabin, running over every inch of the place with their brushes and chemicals. Several others were busy taping off the periphery and photographing the cabin from various angles. Callahan was leaning back against the hood of one of the cars, drinking a Pepsi out of the can, thinking the same thing Mitchum was thinking.

What Mitchum was thinking was this: where was Wallace? Everything pointed to his having been here. His Beemer was pulled up in front. Forensics had been through it and had lifted five different sets of prints. There were two sets, however, that were the clearest—the most recent. One was Wallace's. A copy of the pattern had been faxed not ten minutes ago to the Feds and had been positively matched against Wallace's, digit for digit. Every lawyer is printed before he takes the bar.

But the other set wasn't so clear. The tips were smaller, thinner than most men, the pads of the fingers held close together, like a woman's. Add to that the fact that the last time anybody they were aware of had seen Wallace he was leaving for lunch with a young attractive woman and that Wallace, or whoever had been out here, had most certainly gotten it on with a woman in the bedroom, and things started to fall together. Semen samples that would more than likely match Wallace's blood type. Vaginal secretions that Mitchum was willing to bet a month's pay hadn't come from Mrs. Wallace. And with this thought came it's inevitable partner; who had Wallace left his office with that afternoon?

A woman. A young lady, early twenties.

The receptionist at Wallace's firm had said she thought the name she gave was Nicole.

Nicole who? Mitchum thought. And where was she? Where would Wallace have met her? The secretary said something about a fundraiser. Where were they now? Left in another vehicle, perhaps? Mitchum thought it unlikely. Neither he nor Callahan liked the way this was turning out. Too many things didn't sit right.

Like the bleach.

The smell had hit Mitchum and Callahan like a shot with their first step past the front door. Both men had known what had happened; it was common. Someone had decided they didn't want their presence known, had washed the place down with some sort of cleanser. Mitchum and Callahan had seen it before. It made for a bit more of a hassle finding a viable print sometimes, but generally, in a place as big as this with as many surfaces and crevices and angles as this one had, something was missed somewhere.

In this case, the something came in the form of an earring. A shiny golden earring as big and flat as a quarter, lying innocently beneath the couch in the living room. Kepler had lifted a partial print that didn't match any of the five from the BMW and faxed it off only seconds ago. Mitchum and Callahan—Callahan finishing his Pepsi and crushing the can, tossing it onto the floorboard of their LTD—were still waiting on the results from the lab.

Callahan watched Mitchum across the dirt driveway. He was squatting down on his haunches, talking to Sandstone, who was busy scraping something that looked like mud off the surface of the drive. Callahan joined them.

"What is it?" He asked.

"Hard to be sure," Sandstone said. To Callahan it looked like crumbs of mud, or topsoil. Sandstone gathered several more samples of it and dumped it in a bag and sealed it. "Need to break it down and run a few tests first. But I'm pretty sure it's lime."

"Lime?" Mitchum repeated.

"Yeah, you know. The kind you use in a garden. Keeps the weeds under control. My wife's always spreading it around her flowerbeds."

Callahan and Mitchum looked at each other and came to the same conclusion without a word. Before either of them could speak, another uniform, Dan Murphy, was hollering something from his car, where Kepler sat as he awaited the news on the earring.

Mitchum and Callahan looked over at Murphy.

"Is there a match?" Mitchum called.

Murphy shook his head but his smile didn't fade. "They got seven positive points, but it isn't anywhere on file. We've got a virgin."

Callahan was staring off at some place out across the treetops.

"Looks like we're going hunting for buried treasure," he said.

CHAPTER 20

51 Days Before   (October 16)

By five that morning, the dogs had found Wallace's grave. Fifteen minutes later four cops with shovels had unearthed what was left of him, and had him tagged and bagged and on his way to the Cook County morgue. Along with the hands and feet, most of his face had been gone, as were both of his eyes.

By noon, tissue-samples confirmed what Callahan and Mitchum already knew, and the networks had the story.

*   *   *

For English Mason things got better slowly. He had been able to extract from Nicole before he left a promise not to say anything to her father until he could think of something better than *Dad, Miller, English, and Laney are the ones who killed the cop and robbed Wallace's house, and by the way he died putting it to me so hard his heart called it quits.*

For the first time in a long time he found himself thinking about things other than the Wallace incident—life had begun proceeding at its ordinary pace again, the rhythm of things began to return; his thoughts and emotions were gradually rising above the fog that the Wallace thing had left them in.

He decided he owed much of that to Amanda. For him, it all came back to her. Her steady resoluteness and unfailing loyalty had a way of bringing out the optimist in English, and he couldn't help but think that maybe, just maybe, things would turn out all right from all this. Wallace's body would be found, yes, but heads weren't likely to turn his and Miller's way. Except for a bit of Laney's blood—

—and how easily, English thought, could they really trace that, after all? This wasn't the movies. Laney wouldn't be registered with the F.B.I or anything, his blood-type and fingerprints and distinguishing marks filed and logged in some gargantuan database somewhere—

—they hadn't left anything behind at Wallace's house. Other than a dead policeman, and another close behind. Other than a massacre.

Yes, but still. There wasn't anything indicating them specifically. No physical evidence, no motive…

…But there was a witness, wasn't there? And if she lived, she'd be a compelling one indeed. Her face hadn't been more than a foot from Miller's near the end there.

But Miller had shot her up something terrible. He'd left a gaping hole in her chest and blood squirting out of her legs like water from a hose. No way she was going to make it.

No way she could make it.

And then there was Wallace's cabin, the little chalet in the woods. Miller wouldn't have left anything behind there, either, except the body of course, and the obvious signs of the cover-up. But that was all right, so long as nothing pointed them this direction.

Laney had too much to lose to say anything, and Miller would take it to the grave. He and Amanda had resolved without words to speak exclusively of other things, which only left Nicole. And Nicole had promised not to talk. Not yet, in any case. But time was passing, passing, always ticking itself away, and English felt confident that Nicole's memory of the night—or at the very least, the sheer vividness of those memories—would ebb a bit as the days turned into weeks into months. The urgency for absolution, for *cleanness,* as Nicole had described it, was bound to subside.

It all pretty much came down to that, and as such English had done a fairly decent job of compartmentalizing the fact, convincing himself that no one would look their way, that the search would pass around and above them, and in the end they'd make it through.

But these hopes were not without their price. Amanda didn't simply pump her boyfriend full of promises and possibilities. There were rules. She was brutally frank with him as she laid it out. One of them was leaving the apartment, and if English couldn't bring himself to tell Miller than she by God would. If Miller wouldn't leave, English would, even if it meant moving back home. When she had said it she did it with the kind of fierce determination a mother has when defending her child, and English had taken her small frame in his long, wiry arms and pulled it into his own and laughed aloud, not because of what she had said but because she had had the stuff to say it at all. The emotion he felt for her sometimes shook him to the bone. Her beauty, her devotion, her ability to lift him from bottomless depths and take him for rides in those sky-blue eyes of hers, everything about her made English realize how much he needed her, how far he would go to keep her safe.

It was at that perfect, crystalline moment that English Mason resolved to do whatever it took—barring nothing, absolutely nothing at all—to give them a happy ending out of all this.

He marveled, later, at how profoundly changed a man could be after making a decision like that. Once you decide that there are no limits, that the rules are someone else's problem, all you've got left is freedom.

* * *

Nicole rolled out of bed at a quarter after five—eyes burning, a mild headache forming at the base of her neck—wearing a white tanktop and panties, sitting up slowly without turning on the light so as not to wake Buck. She reached across the cool of the sheets until her hand found him—hair, warm skin, his arm—and listened to his light snores.

Her first class was Wills and Estates and it didn't begin until nine, but her father would be on his way to work in another hour and she needed to get this over with as soon as possible.

She thought briefly of English, and thought it was strange that she should. She then rubbed her eyes, stood slowly, and, finding a pair of sweats on the floor next to her bed, slipped them on. She went into her bathroom—barefoot, the linoleum cold against her feet—and splashed several handfuls of cold water onto her face, avoiding the mirror, not wanting to see herself this early. She left the bedroom and walked down the hall to the kitchen to call her father.

When he answered, she began by saying: "I'm in trouble,"—no emotion, a client to her lawyer—"and I need you to help get me out."

* * *

David Henderson was not a man to waste time. He listened to his daughter's story, asking questions as he needed, and then hung up. He was on the telephone to Roger Soraski, a partner with *Fielding and Fielding*, a thriving small firm on the other side of town that specialized in defending the very rich and very guilty. He and Roger had come up through undergrad at Berkeley in the same fraternity, and had finished law school the same year, Roger from Berkeley, David from Stanford. When David had heard back in the early eighties that Soraski was accepting an offer with *Fielding and Fielding*, he had had his family out to the house for several days while their stuff was shipped from the coast. Now, over a decade later, they played racquetball together a couple times each month, once at his country club, once at David's.

The phone rang four times before Soraski's wife answered it in a sleepy voice.

"Hi, Hannah. David Henderson. Is Roger in?"

"Oh, David. How are you? No. He left about ten minutes ago. Have you tried the car?"

"No. I'll do that. Sorry to wake you."

"Oh, no problem. I was getting up in a few hours anyway. How's Julie?"

"She's fine. I'll have her call you sometime. Maybe we can have dinner later."

"That'd be lovely. I spoke with her some time ago at the Dreyers thing and…"

"Excellent. I'll pass it along. Good-bye." David Henderson hung up the phone without another word. He went back to the kitchen table and removed his appointment book, found the number to Roger's Mercedes, and dialed it.

Roger answered on the second ring.

"It's me." He said.

"Roger. David. I have a problem I need to discuss with you. Are you free at all today?"

"Oooh, Dave. Bad day for me today. I'm in conference with the Himmel people all week. Can it wait until next week?"

"It can't wait until lunch."

"That serious?"

"Cubed."

Soraski coughed into the phone, then sniffed loudly. David could hear the sound of horns blaring in the background.

"You'll have to excuse me. I've got an awful cold. Damned weather still plays hell with my sinuses every winter." There was a pause, which David used to thumb through several more numbers in his book, earmarking those he'd be needing. "Call me at my office in half an hour."

"Thanks, Roger."

When he hung up, David Henderson called his secretary, Melinda, and told her to cancel all of his morning meetings and appointments.

* * *

"And that," David Henderson said as he finished repeating the story his daughter had told him only hours before, still sitting at his kitchen table, drinking vodka with lime, the phone wedged between his left shoulder and ear, "is it. She had no idea what it was she was doing."

"Well," said Roger, "it won't be pretty, but you're probably going to be o.k."

David knew that, but he breathed a sigh of relief anyway. It was still good to hear.

"So long as your daughter cooperates all the way. We're talking about kids she's known all of her life here."

"She'll cooperate."

"Has she said as much?"

"No, but she knows it'll come to that. She isn't stupid, Roger. She knew what she was doing when she approached me. She positively despises me and everything I stand for. Always has. That she's reaching out to me is illustration enough as to how serious this is. She's well aware."

"How did she react?"

"She didn't. Nicole's reaction is no reaction. She understands what she's involved with here. She's a victim here, Roger. Nothing more. I don't want this approached from any other angle. She's my daughter."

"Hey, David, in my business they're all victims. Guilt is about as important as the color socks they wear. Didn't they teach you that up in Stanford? Innocence and guilt are irrelevant abstractions. Less than formalities. A paper-term."

"As long as we're on the same page with that."

"What I understand is this: Your twenty-four year old daughter was involved in a romantic relationship with J. Fullard Wallace—"

"—Encounter," Henderson interrupted.

"—a romantic encounter with J. Fullard Wallace before which they had smoked marijuana and ingested cocaine. Somewhere during all this she realized the guy had died in the middle of it, so she called for help on a cellular phone, then sat in the living room crying while this Dispenberg kid made plans to bury the man and wash away their fingerprints. She was then driven back to her house by this same kid, who immediately went back to this cabin and disposed of the body. He did this because the day before he and a couple of his buddies had broken into and robbed Wallace's house, killed at least one cop and maybe another. That pretty much sum it up?"

"That's what Nicole told me this morning. And I believe her, Roger. She's absolutely terrified."

"I'm not interested in whether you believe her or not, David. You're her father. There's a disincentive for your not believing her. And she should be terrified. This is serious business. You've seen the news. They're combing the state looking for whoever robbed Wallace's place. Her name tied to it can do nothing but harm her."

"Her story will stick in court, though," David said. "She thought she was on a date. She went to bed with the man, and while it doesn't fill me with fatherly pride, it isn't a crime. They did do drugs, but—"

"The coke thing could get a little sticky from a legal standpoint, but we probably won't have to deal with that. They'll slice and dice the old man when they dig him up and find the dust in his system, but any deal we cut will simply have as a predicate that Nicole neither admit to drug abuse nor submit to a drug test. Don't lose sleep over the dope. She's got information they want, and they'll be willing to deal to get it."

David heard Soraski cough into the phone. "But you're going to have to resign yourself to a couple of things. I'm speaking as a lawyer here, David, and not a friend. If you want to keep the D.A. away from your daughter, she's going to have to swear under oath before God, country, and the Almighty Press to what you just told me. She had prior knowledge of the crime, and in the eyes of the law she's an accessory. In order to get out of that, the D.A.'s going to want a great deal in return. According to what you've told me, she's got it to give, but all three of those boys will have the right to stare her in the eye when she testifies. Their lawyers are liable to try to discredit her, make her say some pretty unflattering things about herself. It's a lot to ask of a young lady."

"It is. It's also her problem to deal with. I'm interested in keeping her out of jail."

"And you feel Nicole will tell all for the D.A. in exchange for immunity?"

"Without a doubt."

"Fine. I'll get on it and call you in a few. Until then, inform your daughter that she's to say nothing—absolutely nothing—of this to anyone. Not a word."

* * *

At twenty minutes after twelve, Roger Soraski sat behind his huge desk in his huge office and dialed the number to Ben Kingford, a former assistant to the D.A. who was now working as chief legal counsel to Proctor and Gamble. Roger knew Ben from the early days when they'd go up against one another in court, where Ben had earned Roger's respect by winning a case against him here and there. The two didn't see each other much in a professional capacity anymore, but Roger made a habit of keeping in touch with everyone he knew once or twice a month. Even if it was just a phone call or an e-mail. You never knew when you might need somebody.

Kingford's secretary forwarded Roger's call to Ben's office, and Roger heard his voice on the line after the second ring.

"Ben. Roger Soraski here. How've you been?"

"Overworked and undersexed, Roger. What's up?"

"Funny you should ask. Remember that fellow you had clerking for you some years back, Michael Palto?"

"Sure. Shit, that's been a while. Ten, fifteen years or so. Chicago D.A. Brightest son of a bitch you care to come across. Knew it even then. He knows it, too. What about him?"

"Well, I have a piece of news he might be interested in. It's about this Wallace thing."

"Fullard Wallace? Hot item. What do you know about that?"

"Nothing I'm at liberty to tell you, I'm afraid. But you knew that. I was thinking you might pass it along to him that a dime's been dropped in my direction, and I might be interested in passing it along to him if he wants to talk about it."

"Why can't you call him yourself? He's in the book."

Soraski rested his feet on his desk and chuckled into the phone. He glanced out of his window overlooking the city; a gray cloud of smog hovered on the horizon like a storm.

"My ethics impede me."

"Unethical? You're involved with the case, then?"

"Have him call me if he's interested. If he's not, tell him too bad."

"Oh, I imagine he'll be interested."

"Thanks. Oh, and Ben?"

"Yeah?"

"Call me at the house sometime. You and the wife should come by for drinks. We've added a deck behind the pool and the sunsets are simply marvelous."

* * *

Michael Palto was on the phone with his wife when Sara entered carrying the message. He flipped it casually onto his desk, thanked her, and finished his conversation with Jenny. Before hanging up, they made plans to build a fire in the living room and eat dinner naked on the floor in front of it when he got home.

When he hung up the phone, he read the message, and misdialed twice before he could get his shaking fingers under control.

* * *

Michael Palto called the law offices of *Fielding and Fielding* as soon as he had gotten off the phone with Ben, who had called as soon as he had hung up with Roger.

When his secretary buzzed him with the message, Roger was leaning back in his giant leather chair, his feet perched up on his desk, his arms folded behind his head, smiling, a man in love with his profession, in love with the game.

"Soraski."

"Mr. Soraski. Michael Palto here. I'm told you have something to tell me."

"Mike. Please. Call me Roger. How are things in the D.A's office?"

"Busy. Did you want to talk about this?"

"Well, I may, and I may not. A lot of that depends on you, Mike."

Palto was sitting at his desk with a pen in his hand, poised to write. "I don't suppose it'd be too much to ask for any and all information you may have pertaining to the Wallace case. He was found dead this morning, you know."

"I heard that too. A shame, really. Such a selfless old man. Good as gold, Michael. Good as gold."

"I'm sure he would have been pleased to hear that from you. Do you want to talk?"

"I always want to talk, Mike. One of my favorite things to do."

"What can you give me?"

"Well, Mike, I'm not really in the giving game. They've got churches and charities for that. I'm more interested in trading. Something for something. Do you have something I might want, Mike?"

A pause. "I'm listening."

Roger, examining his nails, said, "How's the D.A.'s office-supply of immunity these days? If you have some you'd like to spare, I'd be willing to have a sit down with you. See what I might have that you might want."

"You've got a source connected to Wallace," Palto said. "Ok. Fine. I'm interested. Is your source involved with the crime?"

"Have you ever heard of granting immunity to someone who wasn't involved?"

"I can't guarantee anything, Roger. If you're withholding information about Wallace's murder—"

"Whoa. Hold up there, cowboy. Who said anything about a murder? You prosecutor's—everything's a murder or a rape. No one ever has an accident. I haven't heard anything about any murder. In fact, I've heard different."

"What have you heard?"

"I'll give you a taste. The old bastard died of natural causes, if you can believe that, Mike. Ironic, isn't it? They get Capone on tax evasion, he dies of syphilis. Sometimes there's just no justice."

"Natural causes? He was found buried out by one of his properties. There was lime and Clorox all over his body. Someone dumped him in a hole like an animal."

"Everything you're talking about may well be true, but it all happened after the man died. Call the coroner's office and see for yourself. I think you'll see he had a heart attack."

"Do you mind holding while I confirm that?"

"Not at all."

Three minutes later and Palto was back on the line. "A massive coronary brought on by extreme hyper-activity. What does your source know about it?"

"He died fucking, Mike. There're worse ways to go. Wanna make odds the broad wasn't the Mrs?"

"I can promise your source leniency in exchange for full and immediate cooperation."

"Leniency? From the district attorney's office. I'm overwhelmed. Come on, Mike. You and I both know that amounts to a hill of shit on a hot sidewalk. I want a guarantee for immunity, and I want it in writing, signed by you, the judge, and as many witnesses as it takes to move a piece of paper through that bureaucracy you're running over there. I want an authorized copy of it delivered by courier to my office, and then you and I can sit down and hash this out."

"Who've you got talking to you, Roger?"

"The tooth fairy. You want to deal, or do I go back to making four hundred an hour and watching you guys chase your tails on the news?

Either way I'm eating prime rib, porking the wife, and sleeping like a baby tonight."

Palto sighed. "Somehow I don't have any trouble believing that."

"Ah, wisdom from the common man. Just a working Joe in a suit, is that it? A burnt out humanitarian, hungry for the big one. The olive in my martini bigger than yours? Your briefcase heavier than mine? Save it for the courtroom shitter, Mike. I don't have time for it. Those of us not on salary have to earn our money."

"You carry a briefcase, Roger? I thought it was all done on powerbooks and palm-pilots these days in corporate town."

"You want to deal, or just trade pleasantries all day?"

"I could nail you for obstruction."

"Horseshit, Mike. This isn't a murder case, and even if it was, before you could sharpen a pencil to fill out the forms I'd be acting counsel for who or whomever is involved, and then all this is privileged. I'm trying to help you here, Mike, but these threats, they cheapen the process."

"What are you getting out of this? You planning on defending whoever's responsible?"

"Mike, I'm hurt. I want to see justice done, just like you. I thirst for equity and fairness. I crave victory for the side of righteousness and covet proper punishment for those in the wrong. I lust to see the scales of justice balanced, and the blindfold firmly in place, and justice for all, and thine is the kingdom for ever and ever, and anything else you idealists carry a flag for. Whatever. What I want is my source protected. If you can't do that, just say so and we can quit wasting each other's time. I will tell you this, however. You can only win by doing this. If I gave you the name of my source this very minute and let you guys do your thing, he'd walk anyway. We're talking about a bystander here, Michael. Someone who knows what happened and is very, very scared. I'm willing to drop this case in your lap in exchange for this individual's complete and unquestioned immunity, but not for anything less. Not for a handshake, not for money, not for a blowjob from the mayor's goddam daughter, so don't embarrass yourself with any elementary bullshit law-school counteroffer. This is as good as it gets and it doesn't get this good again. So the clock's ticking, Mike. Pay your money and place your bets."

Palto thought about it for less than ten seconds before answering: "all right. I'll have the papers to you by mid-afternoon. One source protected by law. Unabridged exemption from any and all charges filed relating to this case or any other that may be extend from it. But I get to meet with him tomorrow morning. Here, in my office."

"How's 8:00?"

"Fine."

* * *

Because he was in class, English didn't know Wallace's body had been found until that evening; he'd been over at Amanda's for dinner.

When he had heard it on the 6 O'clock newscast, English had excused himself and he and Amanda had abruptly left.

Miller, however, had been sitting in the darkened living room of the apartment, bathed in the thin blue light of the television, a shimmering silhouette in the center of a room that rippled and pulsed like it was under water. He was nursing a glass of orange juice when channel twelve news had broken into *Wheel of Fortune* to report the story.

Miller listened to the newscaster speak, a wave of calmness and serenity overtaking him when it was over. For days he had known it would be coming, this point of no return, and had simply not allowed himself to think about it. There were other things to worry about. Like figuring out what to do with the information on Wallace's hard-drive.

That—his trump card—had the potential to change everything. But now that the moment had arrived—when he had heard on live television along with the rest of Chicago that Wallace's body had been found buried near his cabin in Grand Beach, that whoever had buried it was most probably involved with the murder of Deputy Frank Hudson—

there was little, if any, noticeable change. He didn't start sweating. His heart rate stayed the same. If anything changed, things got clearer. That was the only way Miller knew to describe the feeling he got sitting in the old stolen frat house chair in his living room, listening to a mildly attractive blond woman talk about how the police were working harder than ever, around the clock to solve this case.

Clear.

No, that wasn't quite right.

Alive.

Even when the woman reported stonily that the district attorney, one Michael Palto, believed that someone who had allegedly been intimately involved with the entire Wallace affair, who knew who was responsible and why, was willing to cooperate in exchange for immunity, Miller had felt nothing but relaxed and focused.

He listened to the rest of the broadcast, learned nothing new, then flicked off the television with the remote, burying the room in blackness.

Three things, he thought, listening to the sound of perfect stillness all around him. First, cover your tracks. Make sure that if they come to you, they don't get anything easy. He'd done that. He'd walked in trashbags and worn gloves and washed with bleach and fed the ducks over a hundred high-protein muffins. He'd done everything he could do in that department, save one. Something needed to be done about the lady cop. That was shaping up to be an issue he'd have to revisit.

Second, find out who talked. No mystery there, really. It could only be English, Laney, Amanda or Nicole. You could scratch English and Amanda right off the top. That twosome would never utter a whisper. Even if English did get weak and felt like he couldn't take it anymore, Amanda would never let him talk. Girls like her were wives and mothers from the start. Her instincts to protect what she loved were as much a part of her as her x-chromosomes. She may be timid and shy, but she knew what she wanted out of life, which was a ticket to tomorrow with English, and she would never allow anything to jeopardize that. If anything brought her out of her shell and gave her the will to fight, it was the thought of something happening to her boyfriend.

That left Laney and Nicole. Laney had as much to lose as any of the rest of them. And while he was prone to floundering around in a sea of denial at times, he wasn't so stupid he didn't know the deal. He was the wheel-man.

Which meant it had to be Nicole. Fucking Nicole and her rich bitch lay-me-down attitude towards everything. For all her drug-induced wild nights and reckless bedroom abandon, Nicole didn't have much of a stomach for disturbance. If it was fun she wanted lots of it, whatever it might be, but once it lost its allure it was time to move on.

So. There was something else he'd have to deal with presently.

Third, find the exits. Make arrangements. He hadn't wanted to go that route, but if it came to the point of forced relocation, better he rather than the state plan the accommodations.

So the stakes had been raised. Things would move very quickly now.

But first things first.

Miller stared blankly out at the empty space before him, seeing nothing, hearing nothing, thinking only of Nicole.

Fucking Nicole.

Chapter 21

50 Days Before   (October 17)

The card, a small, flimsy piece of cardboard wrapped by a string around the damp stem of the rose, read, "I'm sorry," in thin, wispy letters.

He had been dragged from bed a little before ten by the heavy drumbeat of someone—impatient, English decided, trudging down the hallway in his sweats, shirtless, his right eye still glued shut from the night's sleep—banging on the door.

He opened it to reveal a gentleman he'd never seen before, and as his still-sleeping mind struggled to find something coherent to say, the man stuck out a glass vase with a single rose—in the midst of bloom, damp with water droplets, thorns adorning its stem all the way down, looking larger in the water—to which English responded by taking the flower and saying, stupidly, "thanks," as the delivery boy left.

"Goddam you Nicole," he said aloud now, reading the note—*I'm sorry; please forgive me*—snapping the bright red flower off its stem and slinging it across the room. It struck the face of the far wall with a thud, falling to the floor silently, a whisper of the past, a long wilting descent much the way English imagined birds who die in mid-flight must fall.

"Goddam you into hell."

*   *   *

That same morning, hours earlier at 7:45 A.M., Roger Soraski and David Henderson walked briskly up the steps to the Chicago courthouse, through the large mahogany doors, and down the long, serpentine hallway towards the elevators. They walked importantly, with a purpose—men who were used to attracting respect, to getting what they wanted—stopping once they reached the office of Michael Palto, District Attorney for the city of Chicago.

* * *

They were shooting hoops at the courts behind their apartment complex, English and Miller, their shirts off, both of them sweating despite the cool Chicago air.

English dribbled the ball and shot from the top of the key. The ball hit the rim and ricocheted into the yard. Miller ran after it.

"You think about it much?" English asked.

Miller returned with the ball and shrugged. "Some. That cop dying and all…it's not what I had planned." He spun and shot at the basket, listened to it whoosh through the net like a child's whisper.

"Nice shot." English said.

Miller gathered the rebound and dribbled slowly. "I've relived that second over and over again, English. Turning the corner…seeing the cop…firing. Neither of us had any time to think. I don't know why I did it. I really don't. It was like something inside of me knew how serious a thing it was we were doing up in Wallace's house, and was willing to do anything to avoid that. But it didn't work out."

English stood in silence and listened.

"He would have shot me, English. I'm convinced of that. He had his gun drawn and ready for work."

English allowed himself a moment to consider how much better off he and everyone else would be had that actually happened.

"Do you believe in God, Miller?"

Miller looked at him crossly. "Where's that come from?"

English shrugged. "I've been thinking a lot about that stuff lately."

Miller said, "no. I don't guess so. Not really. Not a God like most people do. Guess I'm not a good Jew. But there's something running things out there. Has to be. You ever pick a flower, or look closely at a housefly, or think about the way your body takes in a hamburger and packs everything it can't use into neat little bundles of shit before kicking it out—I don't know how anyone could ever be aware of anything like that and not think that there's something out there."

"Amanda thinks He's active in our lives everyday. She says He's got a plan for everyone, each individual, all of us."

"Well," Miller said, shooting the ball, "Amanda's a good girl, and you should do what you have to do to hold on to her."

English shook his head slowly. Robins sang in the trees above him and he ignored them. "I don't see how He could have let something like this happen."

"Because that's the way it goes. It's not a perfect world. Read your Bible. Look at the flood, or all the plagues—people died who probably shouldn't have, children, the elderly, the crippled. Herod plows through a town slaughtering all the little baby boys. Next to that, knocking off a cop isn't so terrible."

They took turns shooting in silence, neither knowing where to start, or even if they wanted to.

"How do you see this turning out, Miller?"

Miller shook his head. "I don't know, man. It won't be pretty, if it comes this way. But," he said, shooting, missing, rebounding and shooting again, "there's something you need to remember, whatever happens. There's a back door to every house, English. There's no such thing as a dead-end. You may not be able to see it some of the time, but it's there. Even if you have to knock out some of the boards and bricks to get to it, it's there if you know where to look." He spit into the grass. "That's what separates those that get caught from those that don't. Everybody thinks its some mutated criminal gene that allows people like Jack the Ripper or the Zodiac killer to run around on the loose forever, doing what they do at their leisure, always keeping one step ahead of the authorities. But they're wrong. Ted Bundy had the I.Q. of a genius, and you see where it got him. Free Fries if Bundy Dies, The Bundy Barbecue and all that. Our own Hillside Strangler was purported to be of superior intelligence, but it didn't do him any good, either. Not in the end. He died just like a common idiot, holding his breath in the gas chamber, as though the oxygen were on its way."

"Those that survive have qualities the others don't. They have the raw intelligence, the mental agility, to find the ever-elusive back door. So much of the world is filled with blatant idiots, English. We're a society of lotion-skinned softies trying to make it in a very hard world. We've outgrown evolution and replaced it with technology and geometry. Our lives are governed and managed by bureaucratic clock-watchers and overpaid office-managers. Two hundred years ago our ancestors were fighting Indians and carving countries out of the wilderness, and now most Americans can't make it to work without their morning coffee. But even here, in this cyberkinetic age of supercolliders and virtual reality, it's the same thing. It's not a world of men anymore."

He sighed, shot the ball up from the top of the key, and missed completely.

"Will," Miller continued. "Will is something else entirely. Will adds a whole new dimension of problems, an entire set of variables. The willingness to do whatever it is that needs to be done. Whatever it takes. Will is what makes us what we are. Stones don't have it. Computers don't have it. Will, English. It's our will that separates us from the rest of the universe, and it's with will that we answer the question of who we are. Look at that Rudolph character down in the Appalachians. The Feds had every available agent out there, combing the woods with infrared and heat-seekers and deep-space satellites, and still they can't find one man in the woods. And it's because of will. Eric Rudolph had will. All the Feds had is an objective. It's the game of the most determined, and the most determined wins."

Miller stopped, stared hard at English. "I have will, English. All they have is an agenda."

English considered that a while, wondering how in the hell he had managed to get himself involved in the game of the most determined with Miller Dispenberg, unquestionably the most determined person he'd ever met.

"I'm worried about Nicole," English finally said.

Miller nodded. "So am I. Do you think your talk did any good?"

English thought a moment about mentioning the rose, but he held his tongue. Somehow, it seemed like the smart thing to do. It seemed like the sort of thing Miller would hold back if he had it.

"I don't know," he finally said, understanding that he was now a full-fledged player in this game of the most determined, and that the teams weren't completely decided yet.

"I just don't know," he repeated.

* * *

They left the courts and walked up the hill that led to the drab brown apartment buildings. They pushed each other around a bit, the shorter one popping the tall kid's head quite hard from the looks of it, and him countering with a blow to the other one's stomach. Then the shorter, thicker one, the one Mitchum and Callahan had learned from University files was Miller Dispenberg, popped the taller one in the head and broke into a run. The other, who was by virtue of exclusion English Mason, followed, until they were over the hill and out of sight.

And this is how things looked—from two blocks away, through binoculars, sitting behind the badly cracked dashboard of their LTD—to Detectives Mitchum and Callahan.

* * *

Like most Saturday mornings, John Peterson had left his wife and daughter and home sometime between eight and nine and was now entangled with Patricia in her bed, the sheets twisted and knotted around and between their feet like rope. The air around them hung heavy and stiff with the smells of sweat and skin. The pink and white bed rocked and creaked in rhythm with the blaring stereo from the corner of her bedroom. Patricia's legs were pointing up, arrow-straight at the knees, her toes spread like claws and reaching for the ceiling. John Peterson was a picture of focused intensity. He heard the classic rock blasting—*gimme the beat now and soothe my soul, I wanna get lost in your rock 'n roll and drift awaaaayyyy*—against his back as it rose up, down, and up again, felt the bed rise and fall beneath his relentless hammering, heard Patricia's muffled yelps of pain and pleasure as she bit his neck and clawed his butt and whispered fuck me, fuck me, oh for the love of God in Heaven fuck me, and felt as though he were in college all over again.

When they were finished, they would usually take long showers together, where they would, on occasion, succumb to another fit of lust and hit the tiles for another round, the water washing over their bodies like rain. Other times, he would shampoo her hair and she would wash his back, and then she would sit at the end of the pink and white bed in a silk robe he had bought for his wife but had on a whim given to her, toweling her hair dry as he dressed back into his suit to leave for the office. Occasionally she would stand as he was finishing, letting the silk robe part slightly down the middle to reveal a thin stripe of soft pale flesh, hot yellow sunlight washing over smooth pink skin, and delicately tie his tie for him, brushing her hips lightly across his crotch as she did so.

It was this that had first tipped John's wife as to what may be going on during those Saturdays at the office. When you lived with the same man for nearly three decades you learned his habits. You picked up on the little stuff. You came to know how he did certain things, even if you weren't aware of your knowing them. You learned how many ice cubes he put in his morning orange juice, how his shoes were arranged in the closet. You learned where he tapped the razor on the sink as he shaved, and you learned how he tied his tie. If he suddenly began asking for cream in his coffee instead of just sugar, you might wonder. If he came home with his tie tied differently than he had tied it that morning, a foreign scent surrounding him like mist in the Napa, you might wish you could wonder, but you would probably know. And Julie Peterson had long since stopped wondering.

But it hadn't been until now that she was in a position to do anything about it.

Chapter 22

49 Days Before   (October 18)

Trust in the hour, Stroud wrote. The hour of the wolf.

The hour of the wolf—when the revealing light of the sun is at its furthest point and time seems to rest—is when the hearts of men turn inward and black, and hatred and vengeance roam its bloody corridors like wild dogs. It is in the hour of the wolf when housewives, lying in bed and staring at their husbands sleeping like lumps of warm meat, begin to think of long kitchen knives glowing silver in the darkness. It is in the hour of the wolf that the lonely sip their solitude and think of bridges stretched high above dark rivers, imagining what it is like to fly. It is in the hour of the wolf when the jealous think of loved ones being held by another and decide that dead is better than gone.

And it was, as he had known that it would be, in the hour of the wolf that Miller, sitting upright and naked in his bed, cloaked in darkness, the blacks of his eyes glowing from the sodium-white street-light beyond his window, decided what it was that needed to be done.

*   *   *

Church with Amanda let out at noon, from which English and Amanda drove back to her house for Sunday dinner. The dinners of late had been a little forced, with Mr. Peterson saying even less than usual to English, because, no doubt, of the stunt he had lured his daughter into, and Mrs. Peterson trying to make up for her husband's aloofness by making even more uncomfortable small-talk at every opportunity. English and Amanda would eat their meals and indulge her mother and ignore her father and exit stage left for the living room as soon as possible.

Today the two of them ended up lying side by side on the floor in front of the television—English suggesting they go to his apartment, Amanda, on the chance Miller may be there, refusing—where English would flick the remote through the channels, bouncing from ESPN to MTV and back to ESPN again. Amanda lay there and entertained herself by playing with her boyfriend's hair and reading one of her lab manuals.

English made it a general rule of his not to be in the same room as Amanda's father for any longer than was required to get Amanda and go, but that didn't pose too much of a problem these past few days. He had skipped dinner with his wife and daughter the past two weeks, locked inside his study. When he did come out it was only for long enough to gather his coat and umbrella and leave, without a word, out the front door. Such was the case today, as English and Amanda, lying on the floor, their legs intertwined, him watching a football game while she poured over a chapter on intramuscular medications.

"I think I'm going shopping for a bit today. I have to pick up a couple of things I have on layaway at Field's."

"Can we wait until halftime?"

"I was thinking I'd go alone. I have a few other errands to run."

English hit the mute button on the remote. "Like what?"

"Just stuff."

"Well, we can do *stuff* together. We do *stuff* together all the time. I'm a pro at *stuff*."

"Yeah, well, *stuff* a sock in it and watch your game. I have some things I need to pick up."

"Just wait till this quarter's over and we'll go."

"I have something I have to pick up alone," she whispered with a smile.

"Alone?"

"Honestly, English," she rolled her eyes. "For us to use alone."

"Oh," he smiled. "Right. By all means. I could use a nap anyway. Why don't you come over on your way back."

She nodded. "I'll meet you at your parents, then?"

"Come by the apartment."

"I don't think so."

"Amanda," English said, tired of the same old scene, "don't start this again."

"When he moves out, I'll come by. Until then, we can do things here or at your parents' house or nowhere at all. I'm not coming by the apartment."

"I'm not in the mood to argue," English said, rising, flicking the television off and tossing the remote to the couch, "call me when you figure out what you're doing."

"Where are you going?"

"To my apartment."

"I thought we had a deal."

"Yes, we did. The goddam deal went this way. One of us moves out. It's been all of two days since we decided this. Do you honestly think either of us has had time to find somewhere else to live, Amanda?"

"What's wrong with your parents' place?"

"Nothing. I'm sure they like it fine. But I'm not moving back home with my folks after having lived somewhere else for four years. We'd all go fucking nuts. Call me when you feel like being reasonable."

And he was out the door without another word.

*   *   *

When she reached Watertower Place she went inside Field's and paid the balance on a sweater and pair of jeans she had on layaway. She then left Field's and walked down to *Sugar and Spice,* a lingerie shop English professed to love but refused to enter. They would walk by the window at a crawl, and he would stare at the mannequins, whistling under his breath and mumbling R-rated comments, but she could never convince him to come inside with her, even if she offered to buy (and wear) whatever he picked out.

Amanda had seen a small, white teddy on a mannequin in the window several weeks ago, and had made up her mind a few days ago to buy it for English. She knew he loved her in teddies, and she knew he especially loved her in white teddys. The boy had a thing for white female undergarments.

It was as she was walking in the lingerie shop that she saw Nicole. There wasn't any reason she should have seen her, really, just that she was a familiar sight amongst all the strange faces and bodies floating through the mall. She was alone, off to Amanda's right, facing away from her, walking towards the escalator which led to the second and third floors. She was carrying a shopping bag from the Gap in one hand, her purse in another. Amanda debated calling out to her, to say hi or something, but didn't really feel an obligation to talk to her, particularly while she herself was in the process of buying something from *Sugar and Spice*. Nicole's incessant talk of sex embarrassed her, and she would probably just make some lewd comment about lingerie and its possibilities, and generally cheapen the whole thing.

She had made up her mind to pretend she hadn't seen her and simply keep going when she saw Miller, sitting at a table at the food court, fifty or so feet from the escalator Nicole was now ascending. He was sipping a coke and looked as though he were waiting on someone. She most definitely did not want to speak to Miller, and knew that if he saw her he'd come over. She began turning away but stopped when she saw something that, for reasons she could not define, chilled her to the core.

Miller had seen Nicole, and was following her from his table with his eyes. His face had taken on the qualities of stone; whatever he was thinking about he was entirely focused on it. Amanda stood motionless and watched. She had seen that look on him before, and it scared her every time. She thought he looked like a man without a soul when he looked like that.

Now, as Nicole was halfway up to the second floor, Miller's head rotated slowly to keep with her. Amanda's eyes bounced from Nicole to Miller and back to Nicole, stepping off the escalator on the second floor, and then it occurred to her. Nicole hadn't seen Miller.

Miller then set his coke down on the table, rose to his feet, and began making his way to the foot of the escalator. He moved like a man very much intent on getting what he came for. He was a presence; a great, dark, enigmatic presence whose very existence turned Amanda cold.

Amanda walked several steps outside of the lingerie shop, clutching her Field's bag firmly in one hand, and thought about just forgetting it, finishing her shopping and getting back home. English had been obviously upset with her, and she didn't want to let that sort of thing sit unattended too long.

Bit she kept staring at Miller's back as he rode slowly up the escalator, watching his unmoving head, unable to see but knowing he was looking at Nicole. She thought about that blank, empty look she had seen in his eyes as he had been sitting there, watching, just watching. She thought about going to a payphone and calling English, then wondered what in the world she would say to him. I saw Miller and Nicole at the mall, please hurry? He'd think she was nuts. He already thought she was paranoid when it came to Miller.

Without knowing exactly why, acting upon a hunch, Amanda too stepped onto the escalator, and began her ascent to the second floor.

* * *

Miller stepped off the escalator and walked slowly after Nicole, about fifty feet behind. When she would stop and look in a window or go inside a store, he would lean over the railing and stare down at the masses of people beneath him, shopping, talking, laughing. Couples would walk below him holding hands, swinging their arms in unison, almost skipping it seemed, without a care in the world. Old men made their way with the help of canes, their seasoned bones finding strength from the pleasure that comes from waking up alive yet another day. Babies rode in strollers and sucked their thumbs, ignorant of such temporal qualities as time and life. People argued, kissed, bought and sold. Nicole made many stops in various clothing stores as she worked her way down the length of shops, and each time Miller, masked by the crowd, would pause and wait, wait and pause, and pass the time watching others pass theirs.

It was a long way down, he thought, from here to there. He stared hard at the people below him on the ground level, tried to estimate how many feet above them he was. He imagined Nicole down there in the crowd and wondered how many Nicoles, stacked on top of one another, it would take to reach from the floor of the first level to the railing of the second. Five, maybe six. A pretty nasty drop, in any case.

Someone falling that distance would more likely than not have a lot of trouble afterwards.

Someone falling that distance might not make it.

As he thought about these things, Miller failed to notice that down below, amongst the tide of shoppers rushing this way and that were others doing as he was. Watching, waiting, and watching some more. He either did not notice or did not consider as particularly important the man on the bench, his shoulders hunched, smoking a cigarette and reading the paper. The man who would occasionally glance above his paper, in the general direction of Miller, and would just as casually return to it. This man who, when Miller began drifting behind Nicole again, would walk that way as well.

* * *

Amanda followed Miller for only a minute before deciding that she was being silly and that whatever it was Miller was doing was probably stupid and childish and she wanted no part of it. So she turned around and began walking back to the escalator to buy the teddy—having decided not to say anything about their fight when she let herself into English's apartment with her key, stripping down to the teddy and waiting for him in his bed—when a man in old jeans and a Notre Dame sweatshirt was suddenly beside her.

"Amanda? Amanda Peterson?"

Amanda stopped and looked at the man, someone she was sure she'd never seen before in her life.

"Yes?"

The man was looking at her through gray, neutral eyes. His face was covered with the shadow of a beard. Amanda noticed his hair was thinning in the front, and his lips were cracking from the cold weather and Chicago wind.

"My name is Michael Callahan. I'm with the Chicago Police Department."

He showed her his identification. "You're friends with a young man named English Mason, isn't that right?"

"I'm his girlfriend. Is there something wrong?" She was suddenly very scared, aware of all the people around her, of the precious little space between her and this man standing in front of her, talking about her boyfriend. Talking about English.

"That's what we're trying to find out, Amanda." He removed from his pocket a crumpled piece of office paper and handed it to Amanda, who accepted it warily.

"Why don't you have him give me a call sometime? That first number is my number at the station. The bottom one there is my home number. I don't give that one out much, so that makes this kind of special. You tell him he can call me anytime, night or day." He offered her a smile.

"What's this about?" Amanda asked, hoping it sounded sincere as she looked at the numbers. "What does he need to call you for?"

"Just have him give me a call." He lingered a minute more, as if to say something else, then said: "Goodbye, Amanda."

Amanda stood holding her shopping bag and watched the man walk off.

"He didn't do it," she said before she was aware she was saying it.

Callahan stopped and turned around.

"What's that?"

"Whatever you're trying to blame him for. He didn't do anything." Her lip had started to quiver, and her eyes went watery.

"I'm not blaming anything on him, Amanda. I just want him to call me and talk a little."

"About what?"

He answered with a shrug that seemed more ominous than careless.

"Whatever he might want to talk about."

Callahan turned and walked away, and Amanda, her eyes beginning to blur, ran for her car.

* * *

Mitchum, for his part, confronted Miller outside *Britches*, while he was waiting on Nicole to finish up inside *The Limited* three stores down. They had followed Miller from his apartment, had planned to corner him together, to shake him up a bit and scare him, see how he handled it. Palto's information might have been way off. It wouldn't be the first bad tip they'd gotten.

But after talking to Amanda and seeing the way she was fighting back the tears at the mere suggestion that her boyfriend was in some sort of trouble led Callahan to believe that the suits might have gotten it right this time. Someone wasn't telling the truth.

It was Mitchum's job to arrest Miller. He'd gone about approaching him much the way Callahan had with Amanda, surprising him from behind, badge out, cutting through the shoppers and browsers the way cops cut through crowds. But Miller wasn't Amanda.

Mitchum had been about twenty feet behind Miller when Miller had, as if he'd sensed Mitchum back there, turned and glanced over his shoulder, locking eyes with Mitchum. The two men had stopped there for a moment, something like understanding passing between them. Mitchum was considering his options when Miller had, in a manner too casual for the situation, sidestepped into the clothing store to his left, his eyes never leaving Mitchum's.

It took Mitchum less than fifteen seconds to reach the store. He swept through the racks, glancing under the rows of long dresses and body suits, checking behind the purchase counter, in the supply rooms, the dressing rooms, the break room.

But there was nothing. No Miller. He was simply gone.

* * *

Miller drove home considering his options. They were fewer now than this morning. Nicole had done her damage. She had laid herself out on the table for them and they had picked her apart and come up with his name.

Way to go, Nicole.

Anytime I can help you out, just give me a ring. I'm there for you, babe.

And so now he faced the *ifs* of the situation. It came to him that he could run, and when he wondered where, the practical, logical part of him replied "anywhere".

So he had very little choices, really. Stay or go.

Which, of course, was no choice at all.

Stay, and the best he could hope for was a good lawyer who could poke holes in Nicole's story. But then, there was Laney to worry about as well. And that cop, breathing and eating through tubes in the hospital, just waiting. And who was to say how deep English's loyalties might run. Fear could do strange things to a man.

So run it was. Throw a dart at the globe and go. He'd already bounced most of the stolen money out of Wallace's accounts in Brazil and Switzerland and into his own in Antigua and Barbuda. It had taken all of three hours on the computer; he'd done it over a week ago, the afternoon he danced down Elm Street and into Wallace's secret world. It'd been easy; Wallace had included the appropriate passwords and account numbers and points of contact in his files. Miller had called the bank the next morning from a payphone on campus—nine dollars and seventy-five cents per minute—to confirm the balance, and had actually lost his breath when they quoted him the right amount.

But if he went that route he'd be all but confessing his guilt. Might as well leave a note behind telling the hows and whys of the whole deal. Organize it nice and tidily like Wallace had for him. If he ran, he'd have to keep running. There'd be no looking back. He'd be giving up everything…his family, all the years in school, law school, politics; all of it. Tracie, too. He'd be living in some foreign country with a new name and no history and whatever future he created for himself.

This was true. But if it came to that, Wallace's cash would go a long way towards making a nice future.

Besides, if he was here when it all went down and it broke any way but his, he'd lose everything anyway. The money wouldn't do him any good in prison.

So when you thought about it in those terms, there weren't all that many directions to go. Only one, to be honest.

He checked his watch and knew they'd be waiting for him at the apartment. If he went home that'd be it. They'd arrest him and handcuff him and the process would begin, on their terms and at their pace. His father would get him a lawyer, but Miller would watch it all fold out from the defendant's point of view, the accused from square one.

He came to an intersection and considered it one last time. To go to the airport he'd need to turn around, hit the Kennedy. To go home he'd keep going straight.

He thought of Wallace's badly mutilated body in a pit of lime in the woods, now in some morgue somewhere, exhibit A in the state's case; he thought of English and Amanda and Laney and Nicole and Officer Carlisle and Frank Hudson, whose brains flying through the clear day's air had made him think of comets and shooting stars; he thought of Tracie, and wondered if she'd come with him without any notice, but knew he couldn't afford the risk of taking her; he thought of his parents, of his mother in particular, who'd find a way in all this to blame herself for her son's misguided ways. He thought of his ex-fiance, and before he got too far with that he slowed the car, pulled a U-turn in the intersection, and headed for the airport.

And then the utility truck broadsided him, sending him through the windshield in a dazzling array of colors and noise, and Miller stopped thinking about everything altogether.

* * *

"Slow down and tell me everything," English was saying.

They were in his room, he and Amanda, she sitting on his bed Indian-style, him pacing back and forth. The pacing made it that much harder for Amanda.

"Don't go getting yourself all worked up—just try to remember what he said." He rubbed his hands back and forth together and hung his head, as though he found something intriguing about his feet.

"He told me to give you that piece of paper, and to tell you you needed to talk to him. To give him a call, he said."

English held the phone numbers in his hand, rubbed them between his thumb and forefinger. "He didn't say what about?"

"No. He acted like he knew you'd know. There wasn't any doubt in his tone at all, English. Not any. He was quite sure of himself—he looked almost pleased. Like he had solved a riddle or something."

"A riddle. That's not far from the truth, is it? A riddle. Oh holy fucking shit what am I going to do?" He continued to pace, then stopped in his tracks, glanced up at Amanda.

"It was Nicole," he said in a whisper. "She cracked. The stupid fucking *bitch.*"

"You've got to call him, English. There's no other way."

"That goddam cock-sucking dirty ass-eating whore. I don't believe it. I don't motherfucking believe it! That stupid fucking *cunt*. She fucking promised she'd give me time to figure something out."

"You talked to her about this?"

"Well of course I talked to her about it. She's part of it. She fucked Wallace to death. If the dumb whore had been frigid we wouldn't be in this mess right now."

"When did you see Nicole?"

"At her condo a couple days ago. It doesn't matter when, Amanda. It apparently didn't do me an ounce of goddam good."

"You're going to have to call him," Amanda said.

"And say what? And don't say the truth, Amanda. Don't hand me any of that girl scout wedding-night virgin horseshit you're so fond of. This is real life. *My* real life, and the last thing I want to do is fuck it up because of some…some fucking fairy tale called the truth." He ran his hands through his hair in exasperation and continued pacing.

"What else can you do? They *know*." Her voice was quivering, shimmering, like a delicate layer of ice. "They found out somehow…they—if Nicole talked to them then she probably told them everything. They'll know you weren't really the one in charge, that—"

"This wasn't some military assault here, Amanda. It was just something we did that got out of hand. Nobody was in charge."

"Miller was."

"Dammit, no he wasn't. And even if he was, even if he was Amanda, what do you want me to say? Officer, I didn't know what I was doing. Miller made me do it? Just following orders? Come on. I'm twenty-three, Amanda. They're not going to buy that victim shit."

"Why not. Is that so far from the truth?"

English threw up his hands in disgust and began walking out of the room.

"Where are you going?"

"To get the cordless."

"You're going to call him?"

"No, I'm going to call my broker. Of course I'm going to call him. What choice do I have?"

"What about Miller? Are you going to tell him?"

English considered it a moment before nodding. "I have to, Amanda."

"He'll talk you out of it. You know he'll try to manipulate you into doing whatever will benefit him the most. He won't care what it'll do to you."

English looked at his girlfriend and saw her eyes filling, and watched helplessly as the tears began to glide softly down her pink cheeks. She wiped at them with her hand and forced a smile, a gesture meant for him, for comfort, for support, and he knew it. He wanted to say something meaningful then, how sorry he was, or just how much he loved her, but instead he simply turned away.

* * *

He wasn't aware of any pain, just noise. Things got very bright for a moment, like he was standing in the center of the sun, and Miller imagined that this must be what it's like in hell.

As he neared the ground—the gray-black asphalt slamming into him, the smell of blood and copper deep within his chest—he thought vaguely, distantly, that if he could just get his hands up he'd be all right.

* * *

"Callahan."

"This is English Mason."

"Mr. Mason. Glad you decided to call. Can I call you English?"

"That's fine."

"Great. Are you free later this afternoon, English?"

"I'm not sure."

"Well, think about it real hard." There was a pause. "You go to Chicago, that right?"

"Why does that—"

"Helluva school. Champion debater, a 3.8 G.P.A. Damn near top of your class. Probably thinking about a job a lot lately, am I right English? Thinking about getting into the real world and making some real money, wear a tie, track your 401. Bet your folks're awfully proud of you, son. Especially your old man. Probably bores the pants off the neighbors and relatives around the holidays, doesn't he? Imagine how all of this breaking loose is going to make him feel. Imagine what it'll do to your mom to see you go to prison instead of work."

"I didn't do anything wrong."

"That's not entirely true, English. People who should be alive right now aren't, and all the signs are pointing in your direction."

"I didn't kill anybody."

"Maybe you did, and maybe you didn't. Maybe it was your friend, Miller. If that's the case, you don't have to worry too much. That's what I thought we'd get together and talk about."

Another pause, this one excruciatingly long.

"When?"

"Now's good with me, son. I get paid for this kind of thing."

"What do you want me to do?"

"There's a bowling alley on the corner of Windsong and Hampden, across from the mall. Inside is this little sandwich shop, off to the right a bit. I'll be there in ten minutes. You want to talk, meet me there. I'll wait half an hour. After that I'm gone and we'll do this by the book. That means arrests, lawyers, bail hearings, newspapers, all the fun stuff."

"I'll be there."

"Look forward to it."

* * *

English walked into the bowling alley forty-minutes later—Amanda telling him once more as she left that he was doing the right thing, that she'd wait for him at her house, for him to come straight over when he was done—past the mid-day bowlers standing around smoking and bullshitting and needing a shave, coming to the sandwich shop at the end of lane 14.

He saw a man several booths down along the far wall, nibbling from a basket of fries drenched in mustard, and knew it was Callahan. He wondered if this was part of being on the wrong side of things, walking into semi-crowded establishments and spotting the plain-clothes cops as easily as if they were in uniform.

Callahan caught English's eye and wiped his hands on his napkin as English reached his table. He extended his hand, and English shook it.

"Glad you decided to come by, English. I wasn't sure."

"I told you I'd be here."

He wasn't sure how much he should say, or when he should say it, or anything at all, really. He knew police were trained to extract information out of people by coming across as their friends, or by putting up an informal, unattached front. He didn't want to open his mouth and say something that could sink him, but something Amanda had said rang true. If they wanted to, they could have just arrested him and saved the questions until later.

"You've got a smart girlfriend. Pretty, too." He regarded English for a moment, then smiled. "We're both men, right English? We're on the same wavelength here, aren't we? I won't keep you any longer than necessary. I know you'd rather be off with her somewhere than sitting here with me, and you can be sure I don't live to work on Sunday afternoons, but we've got this mess to clean up, and I thought you might be able to help me."

English shrugged. "I'll try." He felt like a fool, scared of saying the wrong thing, scared of not saying enough.

"That's best for all concerned." Callahan took a swallow of his drink and motioned for a waitress. "You want anything?"

English shook his head.

"Another coke, light ice." The waitress smiled and left in a flurry of cheap perfume and sour hairspray.

"Why don't you tell me about Miller Dispenberg?"

English shifted uncomfortably in his seat. "There's not much to tell, really. We're friends. Roommates."

"Close?"—raised eyebrows with this question, its asker leaning forward on the table, hands folded together, elbows apart. English remembered his dad telling him once that when you wanted to appear in control, always fold your hands and give the impression of listening. Callahan looked that way to English right now.

"Pretty close, yeah. We've known each other for about eight years," folding his hands above the table.

"What's he like?"

"What do you mean?"

"Well we've done a little nosing around. He's smart, we know that. He's got a fairly regular girl, young lady named Tracie also going to Chicago. Why don't you start with his interests, his hobbies—what does he like to do, other than rob houses?"

"We didn't rob Wallace's house."

"Then you were there."

"You know I was there. You wouldn't have confronted my girlfriend if you didn't, and I wouldn't have bothered coming down here if I wasn't."

Callahan nodded, as if he approved. The two faced each other in silence for half a minute before Callahan opened his hands, as if to say *well?*

"He's very smart. He'll probably graduate number one in the Poly Sci. department, go to law school at Harvard or Yale or some place like that, graduate from there and make an ass-load of money."

"How did he know Wallace?"

"He didn't."

"That's not true, English. You don't want to lie to me, so don't. We've got proof that he knew Wallace intimately, or had at least been inside his home before. You and he and this Laney character cut a path from the entry-window to Wallace's study. Once there you stole his hard-drive. What was on it? Who were you boys working for?"

English looked at him. "We weren't working for anyone."

"Then why the hard-drive? What's on it?"

A full minute passed. English watched them tick away on his watch. Amanda had given him that watch three or four Christmases ago.

Callahan moved his drink aside and leaned forward, lowering his voice.

"Level with me, son. Level with me or so help me I'll arrest you right here and cart your ass downtown faster than you can say ten to twenty."

English summoned most of what he had and met Callahan's stare across the table.

"I'm telling you what I know, Detective."

"You're not telling me anything I don't already know. Talk to me about computer hardware. Why the hard-drive?"

The game of the most determined, English thought.

"That's all I'm saying without a deal."

"A deal?" Callahan repeated, surprised or disgusted, English couldn't tell. "What kind of deal?"

"The kind where I've got immunity," English said, his stomach reeling. "The kind where what I say isn't ever used against me in court. The kind you came down here to give me rather than simply arresting me. You know I was at Wallace's. My guess is I haven't been arrested yet because you want to work a deal with me in exchange for my testimony."

Callahan was shaking his head. "Not a chance. We don't need to deal with you. We've got Laney and Nicole."

"Nicole wasn't there," English said. "She was the one fucking the old man into the grave, remember? And if Laney was enough you wouldn't be here shaking me down."

Callahan took another swallow of his drink and glared at English.

English played his hand a little heavier.

"You may have Laney, but he can only give you so much. I live with the guy. I know him. I was there when the plan began." He hesitated, then said, "And I know why. I know who approached Miller about the hard-drive to begin with." It was complete bullshit, but it was all he had right now.

"Something you need to understand here," Callahan said after a moment. "There's an us and a them in this, and you're either with us or you're with them. The good guys or the bad guys, English. There's nothing in between. You live with the fellow? So what? That means shit to us. We're not here to cut deals, kiddo, and you'd do well to remember that. This isn't t.v. If you're looking to save your ass, you start singing, earn my gratitude. That's how this works, and that's the only fucking way it works. Someone gunned down a cop in cold-blood up in those hills that afternoon, English. Someone shot him at point blank range. Blew his brains all over the grass. That man had a family, son. Little kids that don't understand why daddy didn't come home from work that evening. Why daddy's never coming home again. He's got a wife that cries herself to sleep every night over his pillow. Did you know that?"

English shook his head in silence and tried not to picture Hudson's children.

"How does that make you feel?" Callahan asked, pressing.

"Awful. The whole thing makes me feel awful. I'd…"

"You'd what?"

"I'd give anything to undo that. I swear to God I would."

"Then why didn't you come to us and tell us what happened? Did you think you were going to get away with it? Did you think you could kill a cop and nobody would notice?"

"I didn't kill anybody," English said, lowering his voice to a harsh whisper, "and you know it. If you thought I killed him, we wouldn't be sitting in a bowling alley sandwich shop right now."

"Maybe you didn't. But your friend did. And you knew it, but you didn't do a damn thing. You didn't do anything to stop him and you didn't—"

"I was inside when it happ—"

"You still live with him, son. You still pal around with a cop-killer. You shoot hoops with him, break bread with him, breathe the same air as him."

English lowered his head and bit his lip.

"You didn't say a word. To the law you're an accessory after the fact, and for that you can go to jail."

"Which is why I need a deal, Detective Callahan," English said, standing, "and until I get one, this conversation is over. You want to arrest me, let's get it done. But I've said all I'm going to say without a lawyer."

English walked several steps away, then turned back.

"Have you spoken to Miller, yet?"

Callahan shook his head. "Can't. Not till he gets out of the hospital."

"Hospital? What are you talking about?"

"You haven't heard?"

"Heard what? What's happened?"

"Your friend lost a jousting match with a truck not far from the mall this afternoon. E.M.S. had to peel him off the pavement."

So that was it. Their case was on hold until they knew whether Miller was going to make it or not. Which bought English some time.

The game of the most determined.

"Which hospital?" English asked.

"St. Teresa's," Callahan said.

And English turned and walked away, a full-fledged player in the game of the most determined.

* * *

English stopped by Amanda's house long enough to pick her up, and the two left directly for St. Teresa's hospital. On the drive over, English relayed to Amanda what Callahan had said, and what he had said to Callahan, and was surprised to find that he was able to do so as easily as he did. As he spoke and Amanda listened, he was aware of a certain lightness, an imperceptible lifting of the weight which had settled on him over the past several days. It was relief, he supposed. Comfort in the fact that now, for better or for worse, it could finally end. Amanda had been right all along. Callahan had been right this afternoon. It, everything, all of it, was Miller's doing.

As they turned into the visitors lot at St. Teresa's, Amanda slid her hand across to his, then pulled it to her mouth and kissed it.

"This is going to work out."

English looked at her and tried to smile, then something Nicole had said to him three days ago—English sitting next to her on the couch, touching her leg softly, asking first then begging in an attempt to purchase her silence with anything he had, all of this remembered through a cloudy haze—occurred to him.

"*He's always thinking about his next move, and covering his last one.*"

It's scary how smart he is, Nicole had said, crying, shivering. *Scary.*

No, English thought. He was dimly aware of the soft sound of Amanda's voice next to him, but it reached him through water, fuzzy and jumbled, incoherent mumblings.

(*It's the game of the most determined, English…and the most determined wins.*)

(… *It's scary how smart he is*)

Yes, English thought. Sometimes it can be.

(*Will is what makes us who we are…*)

"I know what I have to do now,"—English, shifting the Mustang into drive and steering out of the parking lot.

"We're not going to see Miller?"

English shook his head. "I finally know, Amanda," he said, pulling out of the hospital parking lot and merging with the flow of traffic. "I finally know what I have to do now, and it doesn't hurt. That's the amazing thing. It doesn't hurt a bit."

* * *

Looming four stories above the Mustang as it sped out of the parking lot and merged with the unforgiving flow of traffic, Miller Thadius Dispenberg lies on his back, alone in the small white room, his eyes closed. His body is an arc of dull humming pain. His right arm is broken. His right shoulder, on which he'd landed, was shattered in the impact and will need surgery. His skull is fractured in seven places; four from the accident, another three by the doctors to allow room for his brain to swell. His head is bandaged loosely, wrapped in cotton strips which cover his right eye. The skin along the right side of his face is gone. His jaw is broken in two places, and he swallowed two molars when he struck the concrete.

He was given four units of blood upon entering the emergency room, and has been receiving fluids via an i.v. in his right forearm since they admitted him. He is to be watched temporarily, long enough to regain what fluids he lost, long enough to regain consciousness, and then discharged and arrested.

The shade is pulled in room 412, the sun kept outside. It is dark inside, the air sterile and clean. It seems thin when Miller pulls it through his nose, oddly cool.

When the door opens off to his left, sending elongated shadows dancing across the far wall, Miller's eyes remain closed. He recognizes his mother's scent, her soapy, mildly floral fragrance that is strongest in her hands and face. He feels the room's dimensions shift and change as she approaches him, feels the heat from the hallway light on his face, then loses it as the door closes itself with a click behind his mother.

The chair squeals against the floor as she pulls it closer to the bed, creaks in its metal joints as it adjusts to her weight. Though he is awake, aware, and in pain, he keeps his eyes closed. He feels first her lips and then her fingers on his face, listens to the gentle sounds of her crying. Her breath is steady, but her hands tremble against his cheek. Still he does not open his eyes.

"Mama's here, Miller," she whispers to him. "You're going to be all right, sweetheart. The doctors say you're going to be fine." She runs her fingers through his hair and touches his face again. "I love you, darling," she tells him, and though he hears it, he remains still.

The door has been opening and someone entering the room every few minutes for the past two hours. Miller assumes it is nurses or doctors or both, checking on him. Before she left a few minutes ago, his mother had spoken briefly with one, and had been told that her son would eventually be fine, but that the damage to his right hand would most likely necessitate his having to learn to write using his left. Miller had heard this and wanted to smile. He had taught himself to do that in the tenth grade.

He has caught fragments of their conversations coming and going; once, when his mother had left briefly to try to reach his still unaware father, who was somewhere on the back nine at Cabbagepatch, Miller had intercepted a few casual words spoken to the police outside his door by what he assumed to be a doctor.

He had been heavily sedated in the emergency room, and had risen out of the depths of unconsciousness like a swimmer in a pond, rising to the surface steadily, a bubble climbing towards the sunlight, feeling the warmth and hearing the muffled sounds coming from above the water. He had woken entirely some ten minutes ago, but was keeping this detail to himself for now. When the doctors were satisfied the drugs had worn off—when he was awake—they would explain to him his situation, and then inform him that the police intended to arrest him for the murder of Deputy Frank Hudson, the assault with intent to kill Deputy Officer Carlisle, breaking and entering Wallace's house, the usage of a firearm during the commission of a crime, and a whole slew of charges in relation to the disposal of Wallace's body.

Once this happened, things would move along in fast-forward, a furious blur; if he didn't have his thoughts clearly organized and his account of what exactly had occurred and in what order down pat—if he was anything but flawless—he ran the risk of being caught off-guard. And more than anything, he could not afford to stumble now.

If he was going to win this, there could be no mistake. He was in trouble, now. Real trouble. Permanent, adult trouble. The kind civil-servants sucking breath-mints typed in black ink on forms that followed you around till you died. Things had gone bad from the word go—but it wasn't over yet. There were still cards left to play. Paths as yet unventured.

But he needed time to think first.

And so Miller Dispenberg lay motionless on his bed, let his mother smooth his hair and stroke his face, and thought.

Chapter 23

48 Days Before   (October 19)

By what was perhaps an unrelated coincidence, Miller Dispenberg had his bail hearing the same day Julie Peterson, unbeknownst to either her husband or daughter, sat down in the office of Attorney-at-Law Steven Blann and began the preliminary procedures necessary to file for divorce.

Miller's father, who had finally been reached on the links two hours before his son was arrested in his hospital room, had hired an attorney, a mousy man with an excellent record named Walter Williams. Williams had argued on Miller's behalf, who was *in absentia,* requesting that bail be lenient, given the fact that his client had an unblemished record, that Miller Dispenberg was an honor student at one of the most prestigious universities in the nation, that he was still unconscious in a downtown hospital. Michael Palto had taken exception, citing the particularly heinous crimes of which Dispenberg stood accused as ample grounds for the court's denial of leniency. Judge Furr listened to both men, scheduled the arraignment for November 3, and set bail at twenty-five thousand dollars. Mr. Dispenberg wrote Bulldog Bondsmen ("We'll get you out of the Doghouse, no bones about it!") a check for twenty-five hundred, and signed a promissory note for the balance, plus eleven and a half percent interest.

When the judge was finished, Palto walked briskly from the courtroom, a man propelled by ambition, and, in a deeper sense, a personal obligation to bring to justice the man who brought down, at least indirectly, J. Fullard Wallace.

* * *

"I don't want to get into it right now, son," Miller's father, Wesley Dispenberg, was saying as he sat hunched over his knees in a squeaky hospital chair next to Miller's bed.

"I know you're innocent of these…these outrageous charges. We're going to do whatever's necessary to get you off. Your mother said Williams is one of the best. He'll be over here shortly."

Miller lay still, his free eye open now, its white a bright pure red.

He nodded softly and said, "Thanks, pop," before losing consciousness again.

* * *

The bottom of the front page of the *Chicago Tribune* carried the following headline: **SUSPECT INVOLVED IN WALLACE DISAPPEARANCE RELEASED ON BAIL.**

Throughout the article, Miller was named twice, and the dead policeman, Deputy Frank Hudson, three times. The final line of the article read: *Miller Dispenberg, recovering from a car accident in St. Teresa's Memorial, was unavailable for comment.*

* * *

English parked his Mustang at the Quik-Stop and waited. The sky was hanging low and heavy this late in the afternoon; there was a bite in the air so cold it stung. English left the engine idling and kept the heat on.

He flipped through the radio stations and tried not to look at the clock in the dash. It was 4:30.

At 4:33, the gray L.T.D. pulled up beside the Mustang, and English climbed out of one and into the other.

* * *

Amanda sat and cried and counted the days on her calendar for the hundredth time. It was late. Her time, it was due on the fifteenth this month, and it hadn't come.

She had started taking the pill almost five years ago when it had become clear that she and English were going to be graduating from kissing to everything else, and she was never, ever a day late. You could set your watch by it. Every twenty-eight days, almost to the hour. Amazing how a pill a fifth of the size of a vitamin can change your body like that.

But this month the due date was the fifteenth and here it was the eighteenth which meant it was three days late and that couldn't mean anything good no matter how you looked at it.

She hadn't worried at first, not really. The thought was there as she went to bed that night, but she slipped a pad in her panties and expected it would be there by morning. Saturday the sixteenth had her a little worried, and she racked her brain trying to remember if she had missed a day somewhere. She checked her case, saw that all of them, today's included, were gone. She spent a short while obsessed with trying to remember all of the times she and English had been to bed, but didn't get far before deciding it was futile.

By Sunday she had resigned herself to the fact that things happen to you, like it or not, and eventually there comes a point in time where looking back and wondering why loses its meaning, not to mention its appeal, and all you can do is look forward and deal with whatever is coming. So she stopped wondering, stopped crying, and began figuring out the best way to handle it. She decided almost immediately that she would have it. The idea of getting rid of it left as quickly as it came; part of English was inside her, growing, on its way to becoming perhaps a little boy with eyes and lips like his, with his crooked smile and his boyish little laugh, or maybe a little girl with blond pigtails that would bounce up and down and catch the sun. Either way, she was keeping it. Deciding that had been the easy part. Convincing English that it was the best thing to do was apt to be something else entirely.

But that was yesterday, and today, October 19, she knew how to go about doing it. It had only been three days since Amanda Peterson had missed her period, but she knew.

She knew.

* * *

English stood in the hallway of the apartment and opened the door to Miller's room. He stood there for a while, not walking in but only staring into the room.

Miller's computer sat on his desk in the corner, beneath the window. A heavy absence lingered in the air, the dimensions of the room oddly different, as though when Miller had left it last he'd torn a piece off and taken it with him.

It smelled like Miller, too—a scent he couldn't express in words but one which was unmistakable. Soapy and brusque, thick beneath all that; it was an oddly pleasant, comfortable smell, a familiar companion to him these past eight years.

He reaffirmed to himself that he was doing the only thing he could do. He told himself he had no choice. Something Amanda had said yesterday had given English the idea, and that fact alone—that her mind was even equipped to think in those terms—had left English feeling uneasy. He didn't like learning knew things about her this late into things. They'd been together nearly seven years; he felt he had a right to know her completely.

She hadn't come right out and suggested anything concretely, but she had mentioned Wallace's hard-drive, and the possibility that Miller had been right, that there had been money on it.

She'd asked English if he'd talked to Miller about that. English had said no, he hadn't, and was surprised that it hadn't even occurred to him. He'd been so consumed by what had happened in Kenilworth that he'd forgotten the reason they'd been there in the first place. Money. That's what it was all about. The alleged money on the hard-drive. Miller had the hard-drive, and hadn't said anything about it to English either way.

But Miller knew the rules, didn't he? To the game of the most determined, Miller Dispenberg knew the rules better than anyone.

"He wrote them," English said aloud in the still apartment.

Yes, he thought. It's his game. They're his rules.

I'm playing by Miller's rules. Every step of the way, just like Nicole said. I'm just reacting, waiting, hoping.

And then Amanda's voice, as soft as a bolt of satin: *did you ever find out if Wallace was stealing from the campaign? Did Miller ever say?*

No, Miller had never said, because that wasn't one of the rules. You don't compromise your position. You don't make decisions based on emotions. You move fast. You stay hidden. If you have to hit, you hit hard. Not like you, English.

That's right, he thought. Not like me.

I've been led from go; lead by Miller, led by Nicole, led by Officer Callahan.

Still he remained in the doorway.

Led by my own fear.

The bed on the right wall, a basket of freshly washed and folded clothes in the center of it. The American Flag hanging on the wall above the headboard, his high school wrestling singlet hanging from the right hand post, the black and gold laces from his old wrestling shoes on the left. A portrait of Pele sat above the American Flag. When he was eleven he had taken a pen and scribbled *Pele* across the bottom of it in an autographic flair.

On the opposite wall hung two posters, one of a disheveled, black and white Einstein, with the famous quote beneath it, "imagination is more important than knowledge." His best quote, Miller had said the day he bought that poster. That had been their freshmen year of college, English remembered. Back when a night drinking beer and watching George Carlin on tape was a big deal.

"Back before I had to testify against you in a murder trial," English whispered to the empty room.

The other poster was of a mansion built on the shores of a lake, with a series of rare, expensive automobiles parked before it. "Justification for Higher Education," read the caption beneath it. The good life, was its implied message. That's what Miller used to call it. Said he was going to have it all, and English had never doubted it. That—The Good Life—it seemed to English, was reserved for people like Miller; people with the brains and the ambition to make their wishes reality.

The Good Life. The irony of it all was enough to make you cry.

Lying flush up against this wall, in the corner beneath the window, was Miller's desk, upon which rested the computer. Beside the desk, to its left, was a bureau, upon which rested several pictures. One of the Dispenberg family at the beach, taken several years ago. Mrs. Dispenberg a few pounds lighter, his sister Cori minus the breasts that bounce this way and that when she walks now. One of Miller and English, taken out at the lake several summers back. One of Miller's sloppy dog, Morgen. Miller was the only person English knew who framed pictures of his dog.

English walked into the room and felt a heavy sort of emptiness settle over him in there without Miller; he made himself look at the picture of the two of them, made himself remember the day it was taken. He had been wearing a black bathing suit, Miller a blue one. They were standing near the water. They were both squinting from the sun, and English, standing next to Miller who was brown year round, was badly in need of a tan. English stared into the picture, looked into his own eyes, and tried to imagine what might have been going through his mind the second the camera had clicked and whirred and captured that moment in time forever. Nothing came. He looked at the picture beside it, a framed one of Al Pacino he had cut out from a magazine interview. English remembered him doing that. It had been just after Miller had seen *Glengarry Glen Ross* and had gotten on his Mamet kick.

Next to the bureau was a two-drawer metal file cabinet that held all Miller's V.H.S. tapes. English slid the top drawer open and looked over them. Aside from the tape that Miller had put the Reverend Berry thing on, the rest were originals. *Glengarry Glen Ross, Scarface, The Getaway, Reservoir Dogs, The Edge, True Romance, Pulp Fiction, Swingers, The Untouchables, Hoffa, Escape from Alcatraz.* English had read somewhere that you could tell a lot about the American man by taking a peek inside his medicine cabinet. English thought you could probably learn a lot from someone just by looking at the kind of movies they watched, too. Even if he didn't know Miller, he'd be able to look at this and know Miller had a thing for David Mamet, Al Pacino (*say hello to my lil' frin, joo whores*) and Quentin Tarantino. If you'd seen the movies you could go a little further. The owner of these tapes had a certain respect for violence, for men that said their piece and went their way. He believed in blood. Paying a price didn't bother this person if the reasons were right. The owner of these movies believed that the game of the most determined was something worth winning.

English glanced back and made sure he was alone. He wondered how many times he had been in this room, around this stuff. A hundred? A thousand? More, probably. Even back in high school, Miller used to let English and Amanda borrow the bed when his parents were out, back before Amanda got the guts to let them use her own room. Funny how you remember those kind of things.

How many pictures had been taken of him and Miller together, how many movies had they seen, how many parties had they gone to, how many beers had they capped off together? How many cigars had they smoked, how many times had they gone to the lake and fished, how many trips to beneath the bridge to talk about whatever was on their minds. They'd spent the past three and a half years in school sitting on that bed and talking over beers about how, when they were older, they were going to buy a beach house together somewhere on the East Coast one day and vacation with their wives and kids together. All part of The Good Life. All part of The Plan.

How many plans, English wondered. How many dreams?

Funny how everything ends when it finally does. So fast. And so damn final.

English tried to dismiss these thoughts and sat himself before the computer. He flipped the on-switch and waited several seconds before realizing nothing had happened.

He pressed the 'on' button again, then once more, and still nothing happened. English slid the chair back and looked beneath the desk. There, at the baseboards, was the thick, black cord, running out of the socket and up the wall, an inch-long piece of electrical tape pressed across it every few inches.

English got down on his hands and knees and crawled beneath the desk, running his hand up the cord and into the hole in the desk-backing that allowed the cord to feed into the computer's plug-port. When he reached the hole he wormed his fingers through it, feeling for the back of the computer. Instead, he felt an array of wires and microchips, and he understood what had happened.

English crawled out from under the desk and stood. He lifted Miller's monitor off of the computer unit, and set it on the floor at his feet. He hadn't needed to, but he turned the computer around to confirm his suspicions just the same. The hard-drive was gone. They'd come in here in the last day or so when he was gone and taken it.

He turned the computer back around and replaced the monitor atop it. He backed away from the desk a few feet, and stood motionless in the silent room.

Something else occurred to him and he lifted the monitor again. It was light; too light.

He wasn't surprised. In truth, the surprise would have been had he been able to simply waltz in here and wander around Miller's hard-drive. The moment things started going awry Miller would have restructured. He would have begun measuring options, calculating odds, preparing alibis, establishing fall-back positions. The data would be moved. Miller's rules. Move fast.

But to where?

English thought about that.

He knew enough to know that information loaded onto a computer's hard-drive, even once deleted, left a trace. There was always some electronic footprint left behind, however well-hidden. When you deleted old databytes, you weren't truly destroying them, but were simply tagging and covering them with new databytes. If you had the technology and the know-how, you could uncover "deleted" material as simply as you might remove a glove from your hand.

Miller knew that too.

So, English concluded, the only entirely safe course of action for Miller would have been to never load Wallace's information onto his own hard-drive at all.

Floppies, then. He could have pulled the information up from Wallace's hard-drive onto his screen, perused it, then copied it onto floppies. That would explain the lightness of the monitor. Miller wouldn't have chanced the police confiscating the monitor and somehow detecting what had been shown on the screen. English didn't think that was possible, but it was a possibility Miller could ill-afford to consider. After viewing the contents of Wallace's hard-drive, he would have most likely copied it onto floppies, then reloaded the information elsewhere. Wallace's hard-drive, along with the guts of Miller's monitor, were probably destroyed a day or two after the robbery.

But where would Miller have reloaded the data?

Someone else's computer. It would have to be another computer somewhere. Who did Miller trust enough? The answer was clear: no one.

Not someone else, then. Some*place* else.

If they came after his hard-drive—which they obviously had—and they didn't find what they were looking for on it, they'd be going through the same process English was going through now. Who did Miller trust? Who did he know? To which computers did he have access? They'd check his friends, his girlfriends, probably the university and his father's work.

But they wouldn't know Miller like English knew him. They'd eventually map out his history and his social circles. They'd have him profiled and pigeon-holed in an attempt to get a handle on his abilities and his aptitudes, but they wouldn't understand his mind. At least, not yet. Not this soon. They'd learn of his near-obsession with politics, but they probably wouldn't know that, on virtually every Friday afternoon since the '92 Presidential Election campaign, Miller Dispenberg visited the little local library down the road from his parents' place and surfed the net for several hours, reading everything from Newsweek to The Drudge Report. It was about a half-hour away, but he opted for the town library over the university because it was quieter and less crowded. And, unlike at home where all he had was a slow, noisy ink-jet, at the library they had laser printers, and provided you brought your own paper, you could print all you wanted for free.

* * *

English parked his Mustang in front of the library and walked inside. He'd never come with Miller during those Friday afternoons; the idea of sitting around a library at the end of an already book-filled week waiting for Miller to have his fill of the nation's political news wasn't high on his things-to-do list. He'd never even been inside the library.

It was a small building, single-story, brightly-lighted and overwhelmingly quiet, a strange contrast to the usually bustling campus library. When he walked in a woman who looked to be in her mid-50s greeted him with a warm smile. English smiled back, and asked her in a near-whisper where the computers were.

She pointed to English's left. "On the other side of those stacks there. There are only four, I'm sorry to tell you. What with all that's going on with the internet, sometimes you have to wait half an hour or more for one."

"Thank you," English said, and walked quietly towards the computers.

They were situated into the far corner, as if in afterthought, in two opposing rows of two. Three of the four were available, the fourth being occupied by a high-school-aged girl with pierced eyebrows who seemed extremely interested in whatever was on the screen before her.

English ignored her and, figuring one was as good a place to start as any other, sat at the empty one opposite the girl. The screen's wallpaper was the standard Windows '95 blue and white cloud scene. He moved the mouse around the clouds, settled on the "explorer" icon, and double-clicked. A list of folders appeared on the left-side of the screen.

Wallace's information was likely text, with perhaps some interspersed charts and graphs, so English was looking for anything with a ".txt" extension. He navigated down to the "msoffice" folder and clicked once. A "cache" folder appeared in the right window, and English double-clicked on it. A brief listing of all the files stored in the "msoffice" folder appeared, and English clicked on the "date modified" bar to list them chronologically. The most recent was over three months ago. He navigated back to the file-folder listing in the left window. He began counting the folders, and stopped at forty. It would take him days to go through each one, file by file then document by document, and then repeat the process on each of the other three computers. He needed a quicker way.

He closed the "explorer" window and returned to the desktop. He positioned the mouse in the lower-left hand corner of the screen and, when the "start-menu" popped up, English clicked on it. A vertical list of options appeared above his arrow; he clicked on "Find," then "Files or

Folder," then "Date Modified." Here he typed in '10-07 to 10-18.' The day of the robbery up through yesterday. English glanced at the numbers on the screen. Ten days. It had only been eleven days since it all happened. Eleven days that had changed his life irrevocably.

He clicked "find" and waited. A total of four documents appeared, and English opened and checked each of them. None were what he was looking for.

He returned back to the desktop, then slid over to the computer beside him and began repeating the process. Five minutes later, having found nothing on computer number two, he was sitting in the third one, next to the eyebrow girl, repeating the process again.

Eight documents were found stored between the seventh and the eighteenth this time. The second one, entitled—plainly enough—"Kworth," was 175K in size and had been saved on the 11th, one week ago yesterday. Four days after the robbery.

English felt his hands begin shaking. His mouth grew clammy and his stomach felt as if matches were being lit one at a time in there. He glanced over at the girl sitting next to him. She was still surfing the net, still staring glassy-eyed at the screen which, English saw, was a write-up of some metal-band, replete with vivid pictures and slogans. She didn't look as though she'd be finished anytime soon, so English simply turned the monitor away from her, angling it into the corner. He shifted in his chair a bit, made sure there was no one behind him, and double-clicked on "Kworth," saying a silent prayer that whatever else it was, it was all that Miller had believed it would be. For whatever else the information they had stolen and killed to obtain might be, it had become the linchpin of English's plan, conceived out of necessity, and nurtured by desperation.

The screen flickered for what seemed eternity, then produced the document. English began reading. It looked like a diary of sorts, with dates running across the top of each page. The first entry, the one on page one, was October 27, 1977, some twenty-plus years ago.

English hit the "page down" key a few times, scanned every fourth or fifth page. He had been doing this for about half an hour when he came upon a name that caught his eye.

No!—reading more closely now, the name popping up in several places, scrolling the document up-screen and finding it some more—*NO NO NO NO NO...*

English spent the next four hours reading all of it, every page. At the end of the final entry—October 2, five days before he died—was a list of foreign banks, access codes and dollar amounts. Large dollar amounts.

But beneath that something else. Following the last entry was a series of some twenty to thirty blank pages, which English scrolled down through just to be thorough. Then, at the bottom, was another entry, this one dated October 11, four days after Wallace died, and the same day the document had been saved here at the library.

It was another bank—The Island International Bank of Bermuda—with another account number and access code, another point of contact.

The balance read 2.1 million dollars. English felt himself smile and fought to contain it.

Over two million dollars. Tax-free.

He quickly upscrolled back to the previous lists of banks—Wallace's list of banks. There were three of them—these in Switzerland and Brazil—their balances registered next to their account numbers. The Royal Bank of Brazil: $600,000. The Crown Banking Corp. in Switzerland: $850,000. And The Swiss Anchor Bank: $650,000. Together they tallied 2.1 million dollars.

So that was it, then. Miller had been right. Wallace had been stealing and stashing. Miller had caught him, slipped inside his computer, and pulled the money across the Atlantic and above the equator, depositing it neatly into his own vacation fun-in-the-sun fund in Bermuda.

English minimized the document, went to the front desk and purchased twenty sheets of paper for a dime a piece, and returned. He printed the necessary pages—the ones with the account numbers and names of banks—then deleted the program entirely. He then went to the "recycling bin," found the discarded "Kenilworth" file, and deleted it again. If someone knew how and where to look, they could still retrieve it, but it didn't much matter now, anyway.

He had what he needed.

When he got back to the apartment, he turned all the lights off and crawled beneath the covers of his bed, and the fear and excitement was as real as anything he'd ever felt.

* * *

That night—John Peterson having called to tell his wife that he wouldn't be home in time for dinner, that he was at the office putting the final touches on a contract that was scheduled to be reviewed first thing in the morning—Julie Peterson decided she'd had enough.

So she called Amanda downstairs and explained things to her as best as she could manage through the tears.

* * *

The sound of the ringing telephone echoing throughout the still apartment like a siren's song pulled him from a dreamless sleep.

It was Amanda.

"Hiya, sweetheart. I was gonna call you in a bit."

Amanda was crying.

"English—" her voice fell off, a child falling from a cliff.

English sat up and rubbed his eyes.

"Amanda, what's wrong? Are you hurt?"

She managed a "no" between sobs.

"Okay. Listen to me. Calm down. Take it easy. We'll take care of this. I'm here with you, all right? Slow down and catch your breath. Just calm down and tell me what's wrong."

"My parents are getting divorced and I'm pregnant."

There was black silence on the line. "Well at least it's not bad news."

She laughed through the tears. "You're not mad at me?"

"Because your parents are getting divorced? No. Your father's an asshole. I hope your mother takes him to the cleaners."

"That I'm pregnant."

"If it comes out black I'll be mad. Other than that, I guess I was there just as much as you were."

"I guess…I don't know…I never forgot to take the pill, I promise, English. I didn't do this on purpose. I know some girls do and I know I used to joke with you about it and everything, but I took it every day without fail. Every day. I swear it, English."

"Whoa, Amanda, calm down, honey. I know you didn't. Nobody did. Things happen. I should've pulled out. We'll…we'll be all right, o.k.?"

"What are we going to do, English?"

"We'll take care of it. Can you come over?"

"I don't want to take care of it. I want to keep it."

"Then we'll keep it. Are you coming over?"

"Now?"

"Yeah."

"I can. You really aren't mad?"

"Don't be silly, Amanda."

* * *

Amanda arrived fifteen minutes after hanging up the phone. She let herself in with the key English had given her shortly after he and Miller had moved in over three years ago.

She walked down the hallway into his open room and into his arms. English held her for a minute, listening to her heart hammering against his chest.

"Your boobs are bigger already," he finally said.

She punched him in the stomach. "This isn't funny, English. This is your fault."

"My fault? You were there, too."

"If you weren't so adorable I could have told you no."

"Yeah, well, so what. We'll get through it."

Amanda looked at him and laughed. "We? You're sweet."

"What? You know I'll be with you every step of the way through this, honey."

"Really, English. Unless you were planning to pass a bowling ball, you'll simply be holding my hand."

"Hey," he said, taking her small face and cupping it in his hands, "I know this isn't easy, but we'll get through it." He kissed her. "It was going to happen sooner or later anyway, right? You were always talking about this sort of thing. Babies and motherhood and all that."

"Yes, but we were going to do other little things first, like finish school, find jobs and get married. We're out of sequence."

"We'll be all right." He eased her onto his bed and sat down beside her, figuring the direct route would be the best right now. He had a great deal to say. And they had an even greater deal to decide.

"Let me tell you about my afternoon..."

Chapter 24

43 Days Before   (October 24)

Six days after the accident, Miller took his first step. With the help of his nurse he made it into the bathroom, where he washed his face and shaved the heavy layer of stubble. He had to use his left hand because of the damage to his right arm and shoulder, but he took his time and got through it with only minor cuts. It hadn't taken long; only half his face had skin to shave.

He closed the door and, with effort and not a little pain, stripped and examined himself. Aside from the shoulder, his primary problem as far as function was concerned was his vision. He was still completely blind in his right eye; the doctors had placed the odds of his vision ever returning to any appreciable degree at fifty-fifty. They had him wearing a patch to prevent it from straining as it tried to work in concert with the other.

He'd had surgery on his right shoulder five days ago; they'd reset the broken Humcrus at the same time, which meant everything from his shoulder down to his wrist was immobile for the next eight weeks.

He'd been fortunate. The cranial trauma he'd experienced had been, as far as cranial injury goes, minor. He'd suffered a nondisplaced linear fracture, which essentially meant his head had been cracked open but the skull-plates hadn't shifted any, so it was simply a process of waiting for the bones to fuse themselves back together. The cerebral edema—the brainswell—was minimal, and aside from the too-frequent headaches that jackhammered through his skull, everything up there seemed to be functioning as normal.

But not so much so with his face. An oral-surgeon had reset his jaw, leaving behind a perpetual, almost metallic pain which seethed throughout the bones on the right side of his face and blossomed over his chin. They hadn't done anything about the teeth he'd lost yet, but it was a moot issue at this point. The doctors had said it'd be six weeks minimum before he'd be able to chew solid foods again.

The swatch of skin on his right cheek and around his right eye was gone, replaced with a clear synthetic strip of adhesive to keep the bacteria out while the scar-tissue formed. Miller stared at it with his left eye, not feeling much emotion of any kind. The meat beneath the adhesive looked raw and pink, a lot like beef in the grocery store cold-case. As long as he didn't make any gestures—no smiling or frowning or wincing of any kind—it didn't hurt, but it radiated a continual heat, and felt oddly wet beneath the synthetic strip.

So the face was the problem. The immobile shoulder and the broken forearm weren't any big deal—painful and inconvenient, but not apt to attract any real notice. Plenty of people walked around with an arm in a cast.

But he'd need to do something about his face before he tried to slip into the night.

He thought about this, and while he thought he began squatting up and down, up and down in the small, silver bathroom, flexing his calves, his thighs and hamstrings, tightening his left hand into a clenched fist, then opening it again. He did this continuously, until every muscle burned. He rested, then began again.

He was running out of time, and he'd need his strength.

* * *

English and Amanda were stretched out on the couch at his apartment when the telephone rang. It was Laney.

"English, what's up?"

"Not much. Just hanging out with Amanda. You?"

"Studying. Listen man, the reason I was calling…have you talked with this Palto guy yet?"

"Yeah, why?"

"I did too. Yesterday. He wants me to cut a deal with the state. Wanted me to, I guess would be more appropriate, because I already did. He said you did too."

"It's not something I'm proud of, Laney."

"So it's true then? You are going to testify against Miller?"

"I wasn't given much of a choice." A pause, and then, "he killed that cop, Laney. Killed him in cold blood."

"I know," Laney said. "I just wanted to touch base with you, see how…see how you were." Laney hesitated a moment, like he was searching for something else to say, or perhaps the right way to say it.

"Things have gotten really weird around here, English. I mean, they're reporters calling my place here. They were waiting for me outside Histology class yesterday. They've started calling my parents. You can imagine what this is doing to my father. His health is bad enough as it is…"

"It's all gone straight to hell," English agreed, ready to get off the phone. "You did the only thing you could do."

"I know," Laney said. "But…I don't know. I don't know what I'm trying to say. It's just that we grew up with Miller, and somewhere deep inside on some visceral level I feel like maybe we shouldn't have been so quick to jump sides. I have to prevent myself from asking if Miller would have done the same to us. He's…he's always been pretty loyal, you know?"

English thought about that for a long time.

"Yes," he finally said. "Miller's always been pretty loyal."

"Well," Laney said, "I just wanted to check with you, tell you I was thinking about you and all. I know you two were real close."

"Yes," English replied, "we were."

CHAPTER 25
37 Days Before   (October 30)

On the evening of the 30th Miller Dispenberg went through his stretching routine before the silvery mirror in the small, sterile-feeling hospital bathroom for the final time.

He was in the bed by ten that evening; the following morning, his parents were coming to take him home. He had very little time left, he understood, and as he closed his eyes for the last time between those stiff, antiseptic-smelling linens, he catalogued in his mind all the things he needed to do before the endgame.

Chapter 26

36 Days Before   (October 31)

His parents had picked him up from the hospital at a little before nine, and had taken him home to a hot breakfast of soup and warm tea. There'd been lots of warmth and reassurance and the almost tangible absence of questions. Wesley Dispenberg had been firm on the car ride over; Miller wasn't to be bothered with the arrest or the trial or any of what the papers were calling "The Wallace Incident" until he had sufficient time to rest.

He'd left his parents house—patch firmly in place over his right eye, his vision there still nill—around four that afternoon, after watching a few hours of television in the den with his father. The two hadn't spoken much; Miller's face and jaw hurt too much. There was the occasional snippet of small-talk about school or the game, and at one point Wesley Dispenberg made a point of telling his son not to worry for the moment about all that which was rapidly assuming shape and dimension around him. Miller had nodded, complicit in the understanding that it was all coming soon enough. Right now they'd find a way to be content, and to relax before the fire, sipping hot cocoa—Miller through a straw—in the comforting, familiar glow of the wide-screen t.v.

When he'd left, his father had been asleep on the couch, issuing gentle snores. His mother had been in the diningroom, pouring tiny pieces of candy into baskets for the night's trick-or-treaters, separating them. Hard candy here, chocolates here, licorice and gelatine-based candies here. She hadn't pushed him when he'd said he'd be back in a while, hadn't even asked him where he might be headed. He implied for a walk around the block, maybe down to the Magic Mart just outside their neighborhood for a slush-puppy.

* * *

Miller walked inside the Magic Mart and bought a pack of wintergreen tic-tacs, a twenty-ounce bottle of Mountain Dew, and a package of salt-substitute. As he slowly set the items on the counter, ignoring the counterman's awkward stare at his patch, he hummed a little tune beneath his breath... *one of these things just doesn't belong here, one of these things just isn't the same...*

* * *

English dropped Amanda off a little after eight that evening.

"Wanna come in for a few minutes?" Amanda asked when they pulled up in front of her house. Her blond hair was down tonight, cascading over her shoulders like a sun-washed waterfall. English looked at her and thought about the trial and felt his insides wrench.

Calm, he thought. Stay calm. This is going to work out somehow. It has to.

"I need to get home and shower up before the movie. Couldn't hurt to shave, either," he said, looking in the rearview and dragging his hands over the stubble. "I'm starting to look like an English major."

"That's my line."

"What is?"

"Looking like an English major. Remember? My father asked me what I was going to major in right before my freshman year, and I said English."

"I'm sure he loved that."

"He threatened to have me sent away to a convent. Ironic, in light of present circumstances, don't you think?" She winked at him. "Why don't we stay in tonight? We can watch something on tape."

"I still need a shower."

"You can take one here. I promise to leave you alone."

"Promise not to and I'll think about it."

"Come inside and we'll negotiate."

"Your folks home?"

Amanda shrugged. "It's a big house." She was smiling in that special way she had that made English's better judgment take five.

English peered around Amanda into the driveway and looked for her father's Mercedes. It was gone, as was the station wagon her mother drove.

"Where do you think they are?"

"Who cares?"

"My, my, Amanda. Feeling brave today, are we?"

"Come inside and find out."

There was a note inside on the kitchen table from Amanda's mother, saying she had gone to see her parents across town and would be back sometime around ten. That was good enough for English, who started for the steps, calling over his shoulder, "order a pizza while I clean up. There's some money in my wallet."

The guest bedroom where English stayed when he spent the night was at the end of the hall. He was heading that way, stopping at the linen closet to get himself a towel, when he noticed the door to Mr. Peterson's office was slightly ajar. You could see a thin slice of darkness between the door and the jamb, dead space separating the two.

Strange, English thought. He never leaves it open. He and Amanda had once, many moons ago, turned the house upside down looking for the stereo she was sure she was getting that Christmas. The checked every room of the house until they came to his office, which was locked. That was six, seven years ago, and since then every time English passed the room he'd give the knob a little jiggle, just to see if it was still locked. And always, without fail, it was.

But not today.

Today it wasn't even closed.

He thought about calling Amanda up to check it out with him. As far as he knew she had never been in there, either.

But he didn't. Instead he listened for a moment, heard her downstairs flipping through the channels in the living room, then he pressed the door to Mr. Peterson's office open.

He reached his hand inside and flicked on the light, half expecting to see dead bodies or mounds of gold in the corners—something to warrant all the secrecy and security. But all he saw was what he imagined he would see if he were looking into anyone's home office. A large wooden desk against the opposite wall, a computer sitting atop it. A swivel chair on a plastic runner. Bookshelves lining two of the four walls. A couple of ducks Mr. Peterson had bagged sometime or another, wings outstretched in eternal flight on his wall thanks to the taxidermist, gazing out at him through marbles where their eyes had been. Pictures of his wife and daughter on his desk. A calendar hanging by a thumbtack on the wall next to the computer. Papers all over the place, stacked on the desk next to the computer, on the floor around the swivel chair, on the bookshelves.

Nothing special, English thought. No reason to treat it like Fort Knox, in any case.

He was reaching up to kill the light when something caught his eye. A picture on one of the bookshelves, a bunch of men standing around some animal in the woods.

English walked forward a few steps, into the office, dimly aware that he was most certainly not supposed to be in there, and looked at the picture more closely. The thing in the middle was a deer, sprawled out and relaxed in the peace of the dead, its rack of antlers reaching towards the sky like oak branches in winter. There were four men dressed alike in green, rifles at the ready like Massachusetts Minutemen, two squatting on their haunches, the other two resting on one knee, beaming into the camera like they had just raised the Titanic, opened cans of beer resting on their knees and strewn around the deer like shotgun shells.

Tough guys, English thought. Buncha soft lawyers running around holding shotguns in manicured hands that stunk of skin lotion, drinking imported beer and shooting at everything that didn't wear orange.

There was Amanda's dad, second from the right, his shit-eating grin probably the biggest of them all. English looked at the deer, wondered what its last thoughts were. *Asshole lawyers*, maybe.

"Too true," English said aloud, then realized who the third man was, the one standing next to Amanda's father. The picture was probably a few years old, but the look was the same. That hair, even outside in what was obviously cold weather, it was still the same, as thick as carpet and blown-dry to perfection. And the way he smiled at the camera, like the Almighty Himself had just stepped out of the Heavens and told him Newton had it wrong, that the world really did revolve around him—it was the same look he and everyone else in the state had been seeing lately, staring up at them over their morning coffee from the paper and out of their televisions during dinner.

It was Wallace.

* * *

The taxicab pulled to a noisy stop downtown as night began its fall over the city. The lone figure in the heavy winter's coat climbed out slowly, paid the fare, and began walking. It was a short walk to the hospital, no more than a couple of blocks.

He walked carefully, as though he were considering each step before taking it, and as he did, it began to rain. By the time he reached the hospital and entered through the emergency room doors, it was both dark and pouring outside.

* * *

English's thoughts were a virtual blur on the drive home from Amanda's that evening. He found himself thinking—as if there was every anything else to think about these days—about the trial, and about the information on Wallace's hard-drive, the two hundred or so pages of narrative written by Wallace and meant only for him. It had run on like a journal in places, Wallace recounting war stories from all fronts, his sexual prowess and legal skills and courtroom victories and closed-chambers bribes and payoffs and blackmails—and, of course, the figures and access codes and bank information at the end of it all.

Wallace had never planned to leave Chicago permanently. He'd hidden the money offshore for use by him and his wife in their golden years. At the time of his death they were half a year into the building of a massive beach house in St. Lucia, complete with private airstrip, where Wallace and wife planned to spend the winter months.

And he was filthy. Beneath the tailored suits and six-figure education was a man intrigued, if not obsessed, with matters beyond the pale. English had had to reread several portions of the text to make sure he hadn't misread. Over the years Wallace and associates had engaged in numerous sexual orgies out at the cabin in Grand Beach, always with expensive women flown in from out of town. He had a penchant for pornography involving young girls, and had on several occasions paid handsomely for it. Once, back in '82, he and a colleague—a fellow attorney Wallace referred to only as Stiles—had flown to Maylasia for the express purpose of having S&M sex with a twelve year old girl. Stiles had found the experience so invigorating he'd wanted to purchase the girl to bring back to America, but Wallace had been able to convince him otherwise.

The contents of Wallace's journal had left him feeling numb, but what he'd seen in Amanda's father's study was possessed of far greater implications.

English's mind—for reasons he decided he would probably never know—returned over and again to the picture he had seen on Mr. Peterson's wall. He wondered what to do about it all, and supposed the easiest thing—the best thing for all concerned, and certainly for him—

would be to leave it alone, ignore it. He and Amanda would be leaving soon anyway.

He decided, opening the apartment and walking into its familiar, comfortable smells, that that's what he would do. Nothing. It wasn't his problem, and at a time when plenty of things were, he didn't need to create more for himself.

But an hour later, as he lay in bed, he found himself fumbling across his nightstand and turning the light on, rising from beneath his covers—clad only in underwear, the elastic strap of the jockeys ripped and hopelessly worn, the entire article hanging stupidly, looking absurdly large on him—and booting up his computer, tapping the keys slowly at first, then building inertia and writing quicker as he progressed. It was another two hours before he was finished.

When he was through, he printed and folded the letter—six pages, unsigned—three ways, slipped it into a business envelope, addressed the envelope to Detective Michael Callahan, c/o the Chicago Police Department, and stamped it. He took the letter, no return address, slipped it into the inner pocket of his ski-coat inside his closet, and went back to bed.

*   *   *

He rode the hospital elevators without a word, without movement. Two orderlies, a tall black one and a short white one, both looking like they were on the tail end of a thirty hour shift, leaned against opposite walls and struggled to stay awake. A nurse stood to his right, dressed from tits to toe in white, holding a clipboard with both hands in front of her, a stethoscope hanging from her neck like costume jewelry. To his left was an elderly man, dressed in chinos and a sweater, smacking his gums and holding flowers. None of them seemed to even notice the eye-patch or the cast. If there was anywhere in the world where the injured and broken fit in, it's in a hospital.

The elevator stopped on the fourth floor and one of the orderlies, the white one, got off. The other one got off on the fifth floor.

At the seventh floor he got off, hoping the nurse wouldn't follow him, knowing he would have to abort the whole thing if she did. She didn't, and when the elevator doors closed behind him with a whispery whoosh, he was alone.

The hallway was long and quiet, the walls two-toned brown and tan, the floor slick linoleum. Lights and shadows played along the floor at awkward angles; the silence was loud in his ears.

He walked down the center of the hallway quickly, gliding across the floor like a spirit, stopping when he reached what he was looking for.

The door to the supply room was locked as he had expected, but he was prepared for that. He checked up and down the hallway, listened for anything that might be coming his way. He thought if he listened closely enough, he could hear labored breath coming from the cubicle-like rooms off either side of the hall; the measured sound of air being pumped into tired and brittle lungs by machines, then pulled back out again in a whir of beeps and blips and charts and graphs.

In the door to the supply room, above the steel knob, was a pane of glass, half a foot wide, two or three in length. Reinforcing wire ran crisscross through the glass, anchoring it in the door. That would have been a problem, but tonight he had time on his side.

Twenty feet down the hall was a gurney, pushed up against the wall. The pillow was missing, but the sheets were there, blue and white paper ones that were tucked in tightly beneath the mattress. He walked down the hall towards it slowly, thoughtfully, as if pondering the health of a sick friend, or mourning the death of a family member. If someone were to see him he was just upset, wandering the halls, lost in thought.

When he reached the gurney he rolled it back down the hall, towards the supply room, and pressed it against the wall. He stopped and listened. Still no one. The dark rooms around him breathed rhythmically, like animals in the night.

He pulled the sheets out from under the mattress and let them hang down over the sides. They reached the floor with an inch to spare, pooling around the bottom of the gurney. He crawled up under it, folded his legs before him, carefully situated his cast across his thighs, and waited.

It wouldn't be long before somebody needed something from the supply room—a tired orderly, or maybe an unsuspecting nurse, and came down here and opened it for him.

* * *

It was hours later—almost midnight—when a shadowed mass surrounded by shrubbery, crouched low and cloaked in darkness, slid open the unlocked window to Nicole Henderson's bedroom.

* * *

She could do it, she told herself. He never listened to her anymore anyway, so all she had to do was act natural about it all. She only had to tell him this once; nothing said she was required to discuss it with him.

Julie Peterson walked down the hall to the door of her husband's study and knocked twice. When she heard her husband grunt "it's unlocked" she pushed it open, and shut the door behind her.

She took several steps into the center of the room and steeled herself. He was hunched over his computer, tapping keys and making notes from the screen onto a yellow legal pad in his lap. He didn't bother to turn around.

"I've filed for divorce, John."

The keys stopped tapping, but he didn't turn around. "I'm listening."

Be strong, she told herself. "I consulted an attorney and filed for divorce."

Silence.

"Who'd you get?"

"Steven Blann. One of the few you don't play racquetball with at the club."

"He's an eel, Julie. And probably Republican. Not a bad choice. When did you do this?"

"I did my part a few days ago. You've been doing yours for the past fifteen years."

John Peterson gave his wife the back of his head and said, "you won't be able to prove a thing, Julie. Not a single thing. I'm not stupid."

"No," she said. "I know you're not stupid. And I won't be trying to prove anything, except that Amanda and I will be better off without you."

She paused, debated whether to say what she felt forming in thought.

"One day, John, when your health begins to go or the money runs out, your little whores won't be around anymore, and all you'll be is an older version of the man I married, and you might think back to before you ruined everything with the only woman who ever really did love you, and loved you before you were either rich or a lawyer."

He shrugged. "If you came in here looking for a fight I'm going to have to disappoint you. I've got work to do." He cleared his throat. "You understand."

"Yes," Julie said, walking out. "I didn't come to fight with you. But just the same, I'm used to being disappointed."

As she left the study, closing the door behind her, she heard the keys tap-tapping once again. She locked herself in their bedroom and spent the night crying alone.

* * *

Miller lowered himself onto the blue-white carpet as if it were glass. Above and behind him, the night was a blanket of blackness with tiny holes of yellow-white light speckled helter-skelter across the sky.

He closed the window behind him, leaving it unlocked, and squatted on his haunches, listening to the silence, his eyes adjusting to the darkness as Nicole's furniture began to take shape throughout the room. The bureau against the opposite wall, her bed in the center of the room. And in the bed, beneath a mass of twisted blankets, Nicole's still figure, rising, falling, rising gently again. Buck wasn't there, which was good for Buck.

Miller remained motionless. A slow throb of excitement pulsed in his temples. Sweat formed on his forehead and neck.

He stood and crossed the room like a specter. When he reached the foot of the bed he stopped, and stared at Nicole's silhouette through the cool black air.

He stood there for a moment, just staring at her, at her subtle outline beneath the sheets, a feeling unfamiliar welling up inside of him. She was lying on her back, her legs partially opened, her face turned sideways, away from the window. He watched her, watched her breathe and sleep on that same bed where she had brought him countless years ago to teach him the secrets of fire and night, and the weight of their history slammed into him with all the force of an unwanted memory.

* * *

Nicole felt the dimensions of the room change, felt the darkness shift. She woke up in time to hear the fleeting whisper of sheets across one another, followed by the slight smell of mint and feel of hot breath on her cheek, and then she realized: Miller was upon her.

All at once he surrounded her, his hand over her mouth, his knees straddling her waist like a vice. Nicole didn't move. She watched wide-eyed as he lowered his face to hers—an outline of shadows falling upon her, an apparition moving through water—and turned her head as he pressed his mouth against her ear.

"Hello, Nicole." She could feel the pressure of his lips, felt them dance across her ear as he spoke.

She didn't answer.

There was silence for a long time as she felt him looking at her. His eyes burned through the darkness and held her to the mattress. Finally, slowly, he removed his hand from her mouth.

"Sorry about the wreck," she said without emotion, nodding at the cast. "How inconvenient. Must've hurt."

"Bad moves, Nicole." He whispered. "You've littered your path with bad moves."

Her voice cut the darkness like a blade. "I learned them from you."

He traced his left hand down her cheek, over the hub of her chin and down the center of her neck. He imagined he was opening her up, leaving a thin trail of red in his finger's wake.

"There are times," he said, his finger resting on the hollow of her throat, on the soft flesh there, "when I wonder why you made the choices you've made. You are…" he faltered, "so beautiful…so blessed. It didn't have to go this way."

Nicole stared up at him and spoke softly, "Flattery," she said, her voice a raspy whisper in the blackness, "has gotten you as far as it's going to. It didn't have to go this way for you either, Miller. But it did. For the same reason you did what you did up in those hills, I did what I did in that office. For the same reason you're bringing your best friend down with you," she paused, waited for a reaction to her words—"or instead of you, I'm doing what I can do to send you straight to hell."

Miller wrapped his hand around her throat. His face remained neutral.

"I'll scream," Nicole threatened.

Miller shook his head. "I doubt it."

They were both silent for a while, and Miller thought Nicole might actually be gearing herself up to scream.

Then she shifted beneath him, rotated her hips to the left a little with a grunt. "You're not so smart. I can scream at any time."

"It's not your way."

Quid pro quo. Miller's favorite game. Nicole didn't miss a beat. "This surprises me, Miller. I didn't think you were stupid enough to do this. You must be getting scared." She smiled up at him. "Panic doesn't become you. You wear it like a bad coat."

Miller cut his eyes from hers and glanced across the room. His eyes had already adjusted to the darkness, and he could make out various familiar objects. The vanity mirror in the center of the far wall. Her lipsticks and hair sprays and brushes and ribbons sitting pell-mell atop it. The bureau in the corner, a framed picture of the Los Angeles skyline at night above it. Miller smiled. Nicole Henderson, big city girl.

"Money doesn't always do the trick, does it, Nicole?"

"It does most of them."

"A car at sixteen, your own charge cards at seventeen, trust funds at twenty-one. Was it fun?"

"A daddy with lawyer-friends that can cut me a deal. Go on and say it. You aren't going to hurt my feelings. Being a little rich bitch has its high points." She smiled a raw, sardonic smile. Her teeth caught the moonlight and glistened. "Membership has its privileges." She pressed her palms against his knees and pushed him back a bit.

"What do you want, Miller? Why are you here? To keep me from testifying? Is that what you came here for? To scare me? Do you really think anything you could say or do would ever keep me from getting rid of you?" She let out a yelp that served as laughter and Miller slammed his hand over her mouth. She licked his palm with her tongue. When he moved it away, she blew him a kiss.

"What's your angle tonight, Miller? I know you have one. It's as much a part of people like you as your heart and your bones. Strategy, *monsieur artifice*? Come to practice your craft? Tell me, did you know Wallace would be dining at *The Golden Swan* that night, the night Michael Lifter took me there? I know you suggested the restaurant to him. Were you orchestrating even then, Miller?"

Miller didn't say anything. He listened to the empty space of her bedroom behind him.

"I've been subpoenaed," she said. "I assume you knew that."

She saw him nod. His fingers were on her face now. He traced her lips with his thumb, delicately, like a sculptor carving glass—he felt the exquisite, almost ethereal arch of her upper lip, felt it climb to its peak where it met flesh in a sea of softness and sweat, then down again till moistened creases joined it to the other...across the center, over the slightly parted opening that through the years had given him pleasure and pain alike, over the pouted flesh in the center, full and ripe, warm and pulsating with her heart.

"I'm going to tell them, Miller." She said it with defiance, like a convict on parole vowing to kill again. "Are you listening? I want you to hear it from me here, now, like this. I want you to look down at me pinned beneath you all alone in the dark like a helpless little bird and hear me tell you that I'm going to send you to jail for the rest of your fucking life."

"Your mouth is as filthy as ever," he said, but it had its effect on him. Nicole felt it on her hip.

"I'm doing the world a favor."

"A martyr, Nicole. How patriotic. I hadn't had you pegged."

"Fuck you."

"You still don't get it, do you?" He said. His knees were pulled in tight against her ribcage, beneath the gentle slope of her breasts. His free hand rested between them. When he spoke, he did so quietly, but with a kind of force that made her shiver.

"You lay there in all your refined beauty, a million emotions flying around in your pretty little head, wanting to scream for help but wanting to reach for me about as much, torn between security and wild abandon, and you talk your talk and promise to walk the walk when you get the chance. These songs you sing are old and dying, Nicole. I've heard this stuff before. You and Palto and everyone else in the world are so full of sanctimonious rhetoric it would make me want to puke if it mattered. As it is, it makes me laugh." He leaned over and kissed her mouth. She turned her head to the right to avoid him.

"Testify, Nicole. Tell your pretty tales to the jury. Cry when Palto throws you the signal.

Have your mommy positioned in sight of the twelve apostles so the two of you can dab your eyes in unison. But leave the monogrammed handkerchiefs at home. The middle-class loathes little rich girls like yourself, with your designer skin and your designer hair and your cunts lined with honey." He pulled his free hand up her side, beneath her night shirt on naked skin. She felt the rasp of his palm as it made its way across smooth skin stretched taut over ribs. Up to her neck.

"None of you understand this," he said. "It doesn't matter what any of you do. It doesn't matter what any of you say."

"That's where you're wrong, Miller. They've got you this time. They've nailed your Yiddish ass to the cross and you're too blinded by your ego to even see it. You are being tried by the district attorney for crimes he knows you committed. Crimes your best friend is going to say he saw you commit. If you think that doesn't carry weight you're as much a fool as you are a sociopath."

"Nobody saw me do anything more than break a window."

"That cop, the woman? She saw quite a bit more. And she's alive, Miller…" Nicole saw his demeanor change, saw the beginnings of a smile before it ended just as quickly. It was a smile she understood.

"So," Nicole said, surprised at her lack of emotion, "you've tied that loose end as well." She let out a half-laugh. "And no one in the world with a motive but you. You might as well turn yourself in. You're doing their job for them."

Miller's left hand was over her right breast now, her nipple, as hard and stiff as a pebble in the sea, was wedged between his fingers, and she wasn't fighting him. He stared down at her in silence for a while; her milky brown eyes looked black in the darkness as they caught glints of sodium street light from the window over his shoulder, reflecting it up in tiny crescent moons, ebony marbles speckled with gold. He felt her chest expand and contract beneath his weight, felt the muscles in her shoulders tense beneath his knees. He concentrated on his own heartbeat, talked it down.

Thump thump
thump thump
thump...
thump...
thump...

He could feel the emotion radiating off of her like heat. He could feel the raw energy in her tensed muscles, the hatred in her clipped words. And something underneath all that.

He pulled her shirt up and over her head in a whisper, tossing it to the floor. Her hair, fanned out behind her head like a veil, shone in the darkness, catching what light there was and turning it blue.

He lowered his mouth over hers and held it for a full minute. He felt her heart beating beneath his chest, could feel it accelerate as he kissed her and she kissed him back. Her taste was sweet and familiar.

When he stopped she pushed him back far enough to focus on him.

"You're still holding on, aren't you? To that silly idea that you're going to get out of this."

"Nicole," Miller said, his fingers on her neck, hers busying themselves with his belt, "I was never in it."

Sometime later, her breathing heavier, Miller beneath her, the watery blue light coming in from the window bathing their bodies and casting shimmering black shadows across the far wall, Nicole said, "this doesn't change anything. I still pray for you to die every night."

Miller smiled at that.

"You and I both know," he said, "that God doesn't listen."

Chapter 27

33 Days Before   (November 3)

Miller pleaded not guilty to the charges the judge read off, and the carnival began.

Promptly at 8:05 A.M., Miller Thadius Dispenberg was indicted by a grand jury on one charge of first-degree murder, one charge of aggravated-assault with intent to kill, one count of felony breaking and entering, and one count of obstruction of justice by means of evidence tampering, Wallace's corpse being the evidence, burying and disfiguring it being the tampering.

The judge discarded the charge of theft, having not been sufficiently convinced that Palto's assertion of a stolen hard-drive was correct, but the other charges stood.

The trial date was set for December 6. Jury selection was to begin immediately.

The next morning it would be in the *Tribune*, next to pictures of both Miller and Palto. Beneath that, a separate article would have Gambon leading Timmons by a margin of seven points with five days until the election. A quote from the Clerk of Deeds would read, "the people of this state are justifiably tired of business as usual and good old boy politics. The dramatic rise in public support for this campaign demonstrates this. We *will* win next week, and the good people of Illinois will once again have a voice in Washington."

Gambon was not quoted.

*   *   *

English had reacted to the news of Miller's indictment with a passive sort of acceptance. It hurt to see his friend fall, and fall hard, but Miller had a plan. English knew it with all certitude now, and so the few weeks between today and December 6th was all the time English had left to get everything in order. Enough worrying about Miller's intentions or his next course of action. He was tired of second and third-guessing Miller's motivations, of trying to empathize and predict, prepare and react. It was time to look out for Amanda. For the two of them. She was right; she'd always been right. If English allowed Miller's dirt to sully him, no one would feel it more than Amanda. That alone justified in English's mind any means of self-preservation.

He was finished being passive. There'd been a line drawn in the sand, and the other side was cooking with gasoline now.

So, English thought as he sat on the edge of his bed, the bedroom door closed and locked, the telephone receiver in his hand and the yellow pages opened in his lap, *it's unfolded like this: Palto and his office are well-aware that Miller, Laney, and I were there when Hudson breathed his last. They clearly knew of Nicole's connection, which had been, of course, the missing piece which tied it so tidily together for them. Nicole cut a deal, so Nicole gets to walk. Both Laney and I are testifying, and Miller knows it. He has to know it by now. And he's found Wallace's money, transferred it, and in so doing has confirmed—as if it ever really needed confirming—that he has a plan.*

"Will," English whispered to the empty room. It was everything in the world at a time like this.

And Miller had it. He had Will. And all they had was an agenda, a case, which included, among other things, the eye-witness testimony of English, Laney, and Officer Carlisle, who, according to the latest article English had read about her a couple of days ago, was doing fine, and was expected to be able to testify in the impending trial.

Will or no, English thought, flipping through the yellow pages, stopping once he found what he was looking for, it'd be difficult to beat all that, which, of course, meant one of two things. Either Miller was delusional, which English had never known him to be in all their years, or more likely, Miller had no intention of playing a losing game. If the odds were so hopelessly stacked against you, the only percentage was in not showing up at all. It was tough to lose when you didn't play.

English sat on his bed and thought about that for a long, long while before dialing the first toll-free number. He listened to it ring. When they answered, English asked his questions and placed his order, using his credit card. He then hung up, and repeated the scene five more times. By the time he was finished, his $5,000.00 credit limit was met and surpassed. After making the sixth call, he held the receiver down with his finger, wiped a sheen of sweat from his forehead and neck, and called Amanda.

Chapter 28

29 Days Before   (November 7)

And now, on November 7, sitting on the same dock they had fished from since middle school, English stumbled—fell into, he would later tell Amanda, much the way one falls into a covered hole in the ground—upon the defining moment of their crime, saw for the first time with clarity the path down which he would have to venture before all this was over, and he knew he had never really had a choice to begin with; you are what you are, and when all is said and done all you really have is a list of things you won't do. The rest is made up as you go.

Shortly after making his six phone calls four days ago, English had discovered, via the evening news, that the recovering Officer Carlisle had been murdered in her sleep, several days prior. A massive injection of saltwater into her i.v. while she slept unsuspectingly in her hospital room, a policeman standing guard outside her door. They were coming after Miller with everything they had for that one; had arrested him the morning after, in fact. But both his mother and father had corroborated their son's story, that he was asleep in the elder Dispenberg's chair in the family's living room all night. That and the absence of any physical evidence or eyewitnesses—how could someone wearing an eyepatch and a cast slip by an armed policeman, after all—had prevented the state from bringing charges against Miller. Thus far.

How English had missed that little detail he had no idea; it was simply another reminder of what he was up against, and of how engrossed he'd become in all that which was forming so convincingly around them. And through it all he kept focused on the one true thing—Amanda, what he owed her, what she meant to him—cognizant of the fact that she was—and always had been—the only harbor out there.

He was sitting next to Miller, holding his fishing rod, thinking this when Miller, his cast propped awkwardly in his lap, the plaster there having gone from a bright white to a dingy-looking off-tan, said, "you talking today, or do we just do this silent treatment thing?" And so it went.

The two boys sat and fished for another hour, bantering with one another, both skirting around the issue at hand, neither of them mentioning Carlisle, neither of them having to, each of them knowing the other's understanding of the situation. In the game of the most determined, you did what you had to do. English had come to realize this, and he hoped that, in time, he might be able to think about it without wanting to rinse his mouth out.

Miller had been testing the waters all afternoon, measuring his friend's attitude, the way he handled certain questions Miller would throw at him.

Miller had made a conscientious effort all afternoon to steer clear of talk of the trial for a couple of reasons. He wanted to see if English would bring it up, and, if so, how. Last week, at Nicole's place, she had said something to the effect that Miller was setting English up. The words had come out of her like a foul smell, like something she had found and been holding in for too long. Someone—Palto, her attorney, maybe her father—was putting ideas in her head, and Miller needed to know if he had done the same with English.

So he went along with English's brand of superficial conversation until it came time to stop going along and start finding answers. Once they were in the car, English asked him if he had thought about what he was going to do, to which Miller replied that he had thought of everything.

Miller was leading him. Baiting him. I've thought of everything, English. Does that worry you?

Finally, ten miles down I-80 on the lizardskin cut of road that twisted through 10,000 acres of evergreen pines and firs, with the brown hills rolling along either side of them like giant sanddunes, Miller turned to his friend and said to him, with a sense of something breaking, "I saw your name on the prosecution's list of witnesses."

"Yeah," English said. "I didn't have any choice, Mill."

"No, I don't suppose you did." He reached over and squeezed his friend's leg. "Hey, cheer up, man. I wouldn't be a friend if I said I didn't understand. I do. It's cold out there. You've got to look out for yourself." Miller cut his gaze away from English and watched the trees whir past the window at seventy.

"Everybody's got to do what's best for them, English. We all have to look out for the whore in the mirror," he said, still staring out the window. "Everyone in the world understands that. No one could ever blame a man for doing what he had to do, if he truly had to do it to survive."

The hills beyond the tree-line were a brown and copper blur, streaked and tipped with gold leaked from the falling sun. Miller rolled the glass down and stuck his head out into the air. The breeze whipped past his face and ears and feathered his hair back over his head.

"I love the air this time of year," he said, the wind tearing the words from his mouth. "It smells so clean. So new."

"Like football," English said.

"Yeah, like football," Miller said, almost wistfully. "You remember those games we used to have back in high school in your folks' backyard? You and me and Laney and Scott and Pat and all those guys?"

English did.

"Hard to believe anything can move as fast as time," Miller sighed.

English slowed for a turn in the road and then kicked it back up to seventy five, the big engine roaring like a hungry animal. They were alone on the long, winding road.

"You wanna get a case of beer before we go back?" English asked.

Miller shook his head. "I'll go in halves for a bottle of O.F.C. with you. We can take it up under the bridge. Throw rocks at the rats."

O.F.C. Outta Fuckin Control. If it had another name neither of them knew it. English shook his head and whistled under his breath. O.F.C. would make a night of it.

"How much you got on you?" He asked.

"Eleven bucks. A bottle's fourteen. You got a few and we're golden. I'll even spring for the smokes."

That made English kind of sad. He and Miller had smoked cigars on every occasion they had decided should go down as a special occasion; it didn't matter what. The good, the bad, the balls-down ugly. It made it special, sanctified things.

"Macanudo's?" English asked.

"Absolutely."

There was a long strand of silence there for a while, and Miller took advantage of it as he hung his head out the window and let it flap in the breeze like a seasoned hunting dog on opening day.

"This is changing wind, English," Miller yelled into the rushing wind. "Air that's moving south as it's pushed out by stronger currents from the North Pole across the mountains of Canada. It whips in over Lake Michigan and gets that water-cold to it, cleans things out."

English thought that made a nice image. Great gusts of wind swooping down out of the North to wash away all the bullshit that had accumulated so solidly in the past three months. Were that it was so simple.

They didn't speak much the rest of the way home, and neither of them said anything about the trial.

They stopped at the Quik Stop outside the city on the way back, the one where Speedy, a fifty something mildly retarded man still stuck in Vietnam, worked, and the two bought a sixteen ounce bottle of Olde America Genuine O.F.C. English gave Speedy three bucks for forgetting to charge them full price, and Miller sprung for a couple of Macanudo's. English also bought a family bag of salt n vinegar chips and a two-liter of orange Gatorade to wash everything down with, and they took the stuff out to under the Route 5 bridge and listened to the cars hum above them. They heard the familiar sounds of rubber skipping on the cement seams as they drank the liquor and smoked the cigars and ate the chips and threw rocks at any rat that happened by, and they treated the trial like a fat whore one had fucked while the other watched, and neither of them mentioned it again.

*   *   *

Hours later, the two of them were well into the O.F.C. before they lit the cigars. Miller had them resting in his breast pocket, next to the matches. He removed one of them and handed it to English with an unsteady hand.

"My lawyer says I could get into a lot of trouble hanging around with the likes of you these days," Miller said. "You're bad for my image." He inhaled his cigar and held the black smoke in his lungs for a count of ten. "Not like that's news, though."

"Imagine the time the papers would have with this little scene here," English said. "Defendant in a murder trial and chief witness for the prosecution sharing a smoke and some corn-liquor."

Both boys laughed at that, and the laughter was good and it was real, and it was something English wanted to remember. Them, like this, and all the times before and all the times after, with just a three-month blip of murder and deceit and betrayal in between. Just one little game of the most determined played between them.

"Too bad we don't have our zips," Miller said, changing the subject.

Their zips were their lighters, matching Zippos they had found at a hunting supply store in the mall many years back. They had been shopping for something for their moms, Mother's Day being the following week, and Miller had gotten the idea that if they were going to keep having their cigar sessions, they ought to have something special to light them with. So they bought Zippos instead of Mother's Day gifts. English couldn't remember what he had done about Mother's Day.

"Matches'll work fine," English said, taking the cigar from Miller and working the wrapper off with his teeth.

"That's not the point," Miller said.

They were on their rears on the long, cement bank beneath the Route 5 Bridge, like twin soldiers with their knees pulled up in front of them and their forearms resting across their knees. Miller had the O.F.C. precariously balanced on his cast. The Gatorade bottle was wedged in between their bodies. At the base of the slope, about thirty feet down at a meaner than average angle was a small creek that had as much shit and debris in it as any drain pipe under the city of Chicago. Miller and English had walked the length of it once back in tenth or eleventh grade, knee deep in brackish water that was as thick as mud in places, starting here beneath the bridge, following it through the surrounding forest for about three miles until it entered a long, rectangular-shaped tunnel beneath 294, the kind copperheads and wild dogs find attractive.

English was to Miller's right. His brown hair was blowing lazily in the gentle breeze, his eyelids hanging just a little lower for the alcohol. When the sunlight, waning in the setting sky and finding its way beneath the highway in rays the color of old bone, hit him just right, Miller could see the hint of anxiety in the lines of English's face.

"The point is to light the damn cigar, isn't it?" English was saying, "doesn't matter how it's lit."

"Lighting isn't the whole point. It's not the true point."

Directly across from them was another cement lean-to, a mirror image of the one they were situated beneath. The cement was the color of dirty chalk. Trails of water ran down it, dripping from the road above and the earth all around. It left the cement black. That was one of the reasons they had chosen this one back when they started coming here. For some reason or another, this side of things tended to stay a little dryer. Forty feet of air separated the tops of the two. Seven enormous cement poles kept

Route 5 above them firmly rooted in the ground. Graffiti adorned all of them like jewelry. *Fuck this…down with that…save a donut, killa cop…the poor will rise…so and so was here.*

"They'll rise," Miller once said, "when they quit painting underpasses and start getting jobs."

English lifted the bottle from between his feet and took another swig of the fire inside.

"God*dam* that stuff is potent."

Miller looked over at him and shook his head. "Wish you hadn't done that." He belched. "Now I gotta have another."

English handed him the bottle, almost eager to get rid of it. His mouth felt like he'd been gargling acid.

"Thought I had forgotten about it, huh? Tried to distract me with the cigar, didn't you?" English said.

"Hey, whatever works." He held the bottle by the neck for a while, staring into the clear liquid, sloshing it around a bit. His own eyes were beginning to droop some, and tiny beads of sweat had started forming around his temples. His naturally dark skin had lines cut in it around his eyes like seams in a stone. Too deep and too many for someone his age, English thought.

Miller found a rock wedged beneath his hip and threw it left-handed across the creek at the other side. English watched its sharp arc until it struck the concrete opposite them with a delayed echo. He'd been working his left arm, English saw. Practicing.

"Not too many rats around today," Miller said.

"Nope." English was still fighting with the wrapper on his Macanudo, trying not to break the cigar in the process. His head had started spinning ten minutes earlier, and now seemed to be taking on the properties of lead.

"Fucking thing," he said, spitting a piece of clear plastic out of his mouth. "Next time, we get the good ones. The one's that come in a tube."

When he finally got it lit he took a long puff on the cigar, holding the tar-soaked smoke in his mouth as long as he could manage, then turning to Miller and blowing it in his face.

"If you aren't going to drink," English said, "stop bogarting the bottle and slide it this way."

Sometime later Miller said, "it'll be dark in an hour or so."

The rain came then, a slow drizzle at first, then a steady downpour. It came in sideways under the bridge and the boys moved to their left to avoid it. The empty Gatorade bottle got dislodged in the process and rolled down the cement hill, tinkering and clanking like a cracked bell all the way down, bumping this way and that on chips of gravel and various other debris until it hit the rocks along the edge of the creek with a satisfying smash. Both boys had stopped to watch.

"You remember The Shark?" Miller asked once they were re-situated. The rain surrounded them, wrapping them inside their blanket of cement and steel, thick sheets of gray on both sides, warping and twisting the light as it faded behind the clouds.

"Vaguely," English said.

"Vaguely," Miller repeated. "I'm sure vaguely. Hope your memory's that bad at the trial." He'd meant it to be funny, but it had come out something different. Both of them wished it hadn't been said.

"Anyway," Miller quickly said, "I ran into her the other day."

The Shark was a girl named Kyrie Donovan, a hot little brunette all of nineteen that had taught Miller most of what he knew about the pleasures of women. They had met at a party the summer after high school graduation and, while he would never admit it to English or anyone else in the world, English thought Miller might have just fallen in love with sweet little Kyrie. The ironic thing was that her dad was a preacher of the fire and brimstone variety, a Holy Roller whose only daughter wasn't too holy but was known to roll around once and again. Her dad hadn't taken well to Miller being a Jew, even though Miller wasn't a real Jew, at least, not your garden-variety kosher-keeping Jew.

He knew about as much about the Hindu religion as he did the religion of his grandparents. The name and the nose was the essential totality of Miller's occasional claim to Judaism.

In any case, the time came as it always did that Miller decided little Kyrie wasn't worth the hassle anymore. She lived a good twenty miles away, and although at the end of that drive was a bona fide gymnastics lesson "with some of the nicest, fullest pair of lips ever seen on a white girl," as he said more than once, Miller, for reasons known only to him, got tired of it all. He called her up and cut it off.

But Kyrie had different plans. She came to his house at all hours of the night, called him up ten, fifteen times a day, followed him around on the weekends, even skipped work two or three times a week to wait out by Miller's car after school. When that didn't work, she took to calling Miller's folks and crying on the line with them, and when that fell short she started visiting English, just to talk about Miller. It all drove Miller nuts, and somewhere in there she picked up the nickname "Shark." It just stuck.

English held his cigar in one corner of his mouth and spit out the other, something he had practiced and mastered sitting in this very spot. "Imagine that was pretty awkward," English said. "Like that time Amanda and I ran into Mr. Ellerbeen in the skin-shop."

Miller was laughing and trying to swallow O.F.C. simultaneously, and failing both fairly well.

"I forgot about that," he managed. He'd brought O.F.C. up through his nose and had tears flowing freely from his eyes.

"Yeah," English said, shaking his head, remembering, "well I didn't. It took me months to get her to go in there with me, and when she finally acquiesces we have to go and bump into her fucking Chemistry teacher." He laughed at the memory. "I don't mean see him across the way or anything. I mean literally bump into the bastard, right there in the synthetic-cock section. Damn near knocked him and his life-size whatever the hell it was to the ground."

They sat in silence for a while, grateful for the time together, for the memories they'd made, for the presence of the alcohol to mask and distort the impetus behind the occasion. English said sometime later, how long he couldn't have said, "I heard she moved to Colorado."

"Heard who moved to Colorado?"

"The Shark."

Miller shrugged.

"You ever miss her?" English asked.

"I miss her pussy," Miller said. "That count?"

They both laughed. "Nice, huh?"

"As though you never knew," Miller said.

"Not I," English quickly returned, his face flush and his head feeling light. "I was with Amanda back then."

"That's true, sure enough. You were with Amanda back then. With Amanda you were. You've been with Amanda forever."

English pulled from his cigar and released the thick gray ribbon of smoke through his nose. "If I had, though," English said, "and I'm using the term 'if' here in it's strictest sense, but if I had nailed her, I do believe I would have enjoyed it."

"Think so?" Miller said.

"Oh yes sir," English said, smiling. "I do indeed."

"Well," Miller said, "in keeping with your current, Clintonian line of linguistic limbo, had you tumbled around with sweet little Kyrie, why might you have hidden it from me? I had, after all, moved on, as the saying goes."

English swallowed from the bottle, felt his throat burn before going numb. "I guess it might not have ever come up."

Miller seemed satisfied with this. Some things never come up.

Miller looked at his friend. English felt the stare and glanced away, pretended to be studying something intently across the creek. His head was full of cotton now, and his ears were ringing. He had grown suddenly uncomfortable out here with Miller like this. Like he'd revealed too much of what it was he held inside.

"She was a hot little number though, wasn't she?" Miller prodded.

English whistled under his breath. "Boy oh boy was she hot."

"And those lips," Miller continued.

"Great lips," English agreed.

"Nicest lips I've ever come across," Miller said.

English looked at him and tried not to laugh. "That was pretty bad, Mill. No more drink for you."

"You wish you had said it."

English was shaking his head. "You're too drunk to be Freudian," he said, spitting. They both watched it sail.

"Nice hang-time," Miller said.

After an immeasurable amount of time in which English thought he might have closed his eyes and dozed a bit, Miller touched his elbow. English couldn't be sure if it was the liquor or not, but he got a sense from Miller that he was opening something up, almost purging himself. Like he needed this time with him to set things straight, to get right with the world, the way a dying Catholic needs a last minute with his priest.

"I want to tell you something," Miller said.

English looked at him with blurred vision.

"Listen, Mill, if you're going to confess to me that you're a fag or some-such, don't feel like you have to. That's kind of the sort of thing you tell someone before you sign an apartment lease with them. Not after."

"Will you shut the fuck up for a minute? I'm being serious, here. You need to know this. Maybe it'll clear things up for you a bit, help you understand some of what's been going on these past weeks." He paused. "Maybe it won't though…I don't know."

He looked at English, as if to say, *do you really want to hear this?*

English nodded.

"Me and Nicole," Miller said, his voice flat and measured, "we have what you might call a history. As much a history somebody our age can have, in any case. Now, maybe you knew that and maybe you didn't, but you probably never knew the extent of it. And you might not want to, either. Hell…there are times I wish I didn't know some of what went on over those years. But it's true. Been going on since back in high school, off and on." Miller's eyes had turned in, gone somewhere else, somewhere far away. "Which of course led to that which led to this and before I knew it I was walking her out of a hoover clinic in the city, tucking her into her bed at home, telling her it was all right, things would turn out okay, that it was normal, lots of girls had abortions. Shit deteriorated after that, but I still think about it. I don't think about it a lot, but every now and again it comes back to me. Floats around for me to look at for a while." Miller cleared his throat and spit. English didn't say anything. "Not Nicole per se, but about what it all did to her. And I don't mean just the abortion. That probably wasn't even too traumatic a thing for her, or if it was, she never let me know. But that's the thing with Nicole. You can never tell with her. She's as unpredictable as she is compelling."

Miller stared out across the creek and exhaled a long, heavy breath. He ran his fingers backwards through his hair and glanced down at his cast.

"We slipped into some pretty crazy shit over the years," Miller said. "She's ventured down some different roads in her life, and to hear her tell it I was there leading her down every one. I don't think that's entirely accurate, but even so, I'm probably at least partly responsible." He paused. "To some extent I'm definitely responsible."

"You mean the coke?" English asked. "All the drugs? You forget, I was there for a lot of it."

Miller nodded. "The drugs, yes, and other stuff. She's bisexual, you know. Or was for a while. Not anymore, I wouldn't think. I didn't push her into that—I doubt you could ever really push someone into something like that who wasn't at least remotely curious to begin with—but that's just it. That's my point. We were close, always had been, so she confided in me. She told me things. We'd meet when the sun went down and walk each other hand in hand through the shame and the dirt of all of our fantasies and curiosities, and somehow the mutual denial in the morning made all the shame and dirt disappear."

"You guys had three-ways?" English asked, more intrigued than surprised.

Miller nodded. "Sometimes more. The others were always girls we'd meet out at a club somewhere downtown. Never anyone we knew or had a chance of running into during our normal lives. There's an entire underbelly out there, English. A whole culture of vice and sin and unadulterated moral decadence, and if you know how to find it and where to look once you get there you can pretty much take a whirl on any merry-go-round you like. We'd be out dancing and drinking and the rest of the business, and if she saw someone who piqued her interest, she'd approach them. Occasionally they'd agree. It was fun at first. Then we started mixing things in. Like the drugs, and the bondage. Just to push things a bit. One of the women we brought home was into S&M pretty heavily—cigarette burns, knotted rope, piercing—and we tried that a time or two. We videotaped a lot of it. As far as I know the tapes were never watched. We just had the camera running for kicks. It added something to it. None of it stuck for long, but she'd browsed through most everything by the time she walked the stage at Chicago. I was there with her, willfully going along, too zapped by the dust or the liquor to even consider what long-term effects it might have on her. For all her external strength and bravado, she really is a very soft girl who has lost part of herself to the shadows of night, and when she looks back at it all and feels the pain and the disgust and the regret, apparently the most salient thing she can recall is that I was there for all of it."

Miller didn't say anything for a while. English let him have the moment.

"She has a profound hatred for me, now. I represent something bad to her. Something she'd more than likely call evil. You'll probably hear her say that during the trial. That I'm not even human, but rather a thing so evil it needs to be locked up someplace dark until it dies. It's that hatred that's driving her through this whole stupid thing. She's out for my blood. You can see it in her eyes if you look right. She's excited. Turned on, almost. Like a lawyer at a ten-car pileup. I don't mind, though."

"What do you mean, you don't mind," English asked. "It scares the hell out of me."

"Well," Miller said, "as tight a spot as this seems to be, at least I know I'll be my sharpest whatever comes next. After all, if the world was with me in this, I might get lazy."

Chapter 29

26 Days Before   (November 10)

At 3:20 P.M., November 10, District Attorney Michael A. Palto called a press conference to announce that his office would not be seeking the death penalty against Miller Thadius Dispenberg for the murder of Deputy Franklin Hudson. When asked why, he cited the fact that, pragmatically speaking, it would be too difficult to convince a jury to sentence a defendant as young and charming as Miller Dispenberg to death.

Instead, a guilty verdict would carry a mandatory life in prison, without possibility of parole for forty-five years. Either way, Palto assured the press corps, society would be safe from Miller Dispenberg for a very long time.

*   *   *

Amanda parked her car along the curb outside the Robert Michel Government Complex and stepped out into the drizzle, her olive raincoat draping down to her heels. She opened an umbrella and crossed the sidewalk to the short flight of steps leading to the large revolving doors.

She stopped momentarily and reached into one of the deep front pockets of the coat and ran her finger over the paperwork for the thousandth time. The woman over the phone had told her she would need birth certificates, driver's licenses, social security cards and her checkbook. Amanda fingered each one in her pocket and felt a chill run down her spine. She told herself it was the weather, and started up the steps.

Chapter 30

25-2 Days Before   (November 11–December 4)

In the days before the beginning of it all, Chicago's weather took a turn for the worse. The heavy rains had begun in late August and continued off and on through the better part of September. In October the rains turn to snow, and the steel and cement that make up Chicago become covered in billowy layers of white that, for a short time, catch the sun from the glassy blue sky and turn the air cold and crisp.

Nicole's life during this time was as close to normal as could be expected, given the circumstances. Everyone knew she was the one who turned on Miller, and everyone knew she had hidden behind daddy while she did it. People either felt strongly one way or another about it or they didn't much seem to care at all. Laney held a grudge, and a few of the other guys that had considered themselves Miller's friends didn't look too favorably on one of their own feeding a friend to the law, but Miller was on a one-way road to somewhere they didn't want to be and Nicole was still here and still beautiful. Such things tend to wear down loyalties fast.

Nicole's father, David, considered his daughter's involvement a done deal. He and Soraski and Palto had hammered out an agreement that would have Nicole testify at trial to what she knew and would leave her out of it insofar as personal responsibility was concerned. If Nicole did it right, and David would see to it that she did, she would come out looking almost like a victim, a trusting sort whose friendship was taken advantage of on a cataclysmic scale by the manipulative Miller

Dispenberg, University of Chicago student and alleged cop-killer. It would not matter much at any rate, however. Part of the agreement had been that Nicole's name would never be mentioned by the prosecution to the press, and Illinois State Law barred cameras from inside courtrooms. Nicole would do her testifying, leave, and for all intents and purposes, remain anonymous to those not intimately involved with the legal proceedings. The hysteria surrounding the Dispenberg boy was feverish and growing by the hour. Nicole, one witness in a line of many, would slip through the cracks and be forgotten.

As for Nicole herself, as near as David could tell she seemed to be holding up fine. She didn't talk to him much, hadn't for as long as David could remember, and never mentioned the trial that was scheduled to begin in two days. On one of the few occasions she returned his call, he had tried to walk her through her part of it, but she wasn't having any of it. She had offered a terse "thank you" for his help and had hung up without saying anything more.

She was dating someone new now, a doctor named Chris Watkins that she had bumped into some time ago. It hadn't been long after Miller's surprise appearance in her bedroom and she had wanted something, anything, to help her take her mind away from him. So when he asked her to lunch she accepted. He was her senior by some ten years, and Nicole found that particular aspect refreshing. There was a certain, seasoned maturity to him that was lacking in most of the men she knew her age. He didn't press her for details about the coming trial; he didn't press her for anything at all. He appeared to be interested in her company for the sake of her company, and his mere presence did a fairly good job of keeping her mind off of everything that was going on around her.

Nicole didn't speak to Miller any more. She, like English and Laney, was under a court order not to. What happened in her room happened between them and neither would say anything about it. That understanding was as real and concrete as anything they had done in there.

But she spoke to English a good bit, much more than anyone else was aware. English approached her; never the other way around. He had a week ago followed her into a grocery store and asked her where she'd be that night. She said at home, but if he liked, something could be arranged.

English liked, and something was arranged. She met him that evening at the Hard Rock Cafe in the city, and the two spent an hour talking over coffee and crepes. Just talking, cutting through the preliminaries. Nothing major, nothing English needed to say. That would come later. Soon, but later.

They both knew that.

As they were leaving he asked her if she could meet him again the next week. Monday, to be precise. Amanda had a dental appointment that afternoon and would be busy there for several hours, so English had some time. She said yes. He told her he'd be at the ice cream shop in the city, the one in the bottom of the Sears Trade Tower, at half past three.

Nicole told him she'd be waiting, which she was.

That had been a week ago. Monday afternoon, with Amanda presumably at her appointment, English and Nicole in the Frozen Dipper Olde Fashioned Ice Cream Shoppe, sitting across from one another. Nicole sipped a chocolate shake; English nibbled on a sundae with nuts. It was ten before four.

"I wouldn't have asked you to help if I didn't need it in a bad way, Nicole."

Nicole was wearing black slacks and a red blazer hanging open in the front, revealing a stripe of white from a turtleneck beneath. Her chestnut hair reached down just past her ears and brushed delicately against her face. She looked clean and alive, as fresh as a winter breeze. She stirred her shake around with her straw and stared over English's head, at a clock on the wall in the shape of an ice cream cone. She was sitting erect, as proper as royalty.

"You're taking quite a risk here, aren't you? Being here with me, like this? Particularly now."

English nodded. "I am."

"Any particular reason why?"

"Like I said, I need this in a bad way. I'm running low on options."

Nicole shrugged her shoulders and sighed. "I never meant to make things difficult for you, English. Never you. Never anybody. But especially never you. I...I just wanted everything about him to go away. Forever."

"It looks like you may get your wish."

She laughed at that. English hadn't meant for it to be funny.

He studied her closely as they spoke, watching her movements, her gestures, her eyes, searching for some sign that he was getting somewhere with her. This cold, unfeeling figure of ice, carved of gold and dressed in style. It was difficult for him to believe that this girl sitting before him that he had known for almost a decade was the reason—at least, one of the reasons, the final reason perhaps—that this, all of this, had reached the proportions it had. English looked across the table at her face, perfect in its shape and wrapped in flawless skin. Her velvety brown eyes looked watery, a shiny liquid swimming beneath her heavy eyebrows, guarded by long, dark lashes as thick as rope. He looked at her full, pouty lips and remembered briefly what it was like to feel them on his own, across his back, on his legs.

He felt himself harden beneath the table and held his breath till it died. He couldn't afford to be distracted. Not here. Not with her. He was running out of time to make this work. Nicole tucked her hair behind her ears and stared at English straight on in that disarming way she had perfected years ago.

"What do you need from me, English? If there's some way I can help you, I'll try. I'll do what I can do." She flashed him a fleeting hint of a wicked smile. "And there's a lot I can do."

English felt his heart skip and leaned forward, forcing himself to remain calm. "What I'm going to need isn't much."

She lifted her eyebrows. "Well?"

"A ride."

"A ride." She repeated.

English nodded. "That's it. Just a ride."

"In a car or a bed?"

"Car. A fast one, preferably."

Nicole slipped the straw back into her mouth and pulled the shake up its length. English watched her do it and thought about fundraisers and cummerbunds.

"That doesn't sound too terribly difficult. The way you were acting, I thought I was going to have to poison somebody's wine or something."

"This will be easy for you. I just need a ride from A to B. I'm not sure when yet, but it'll be soon. And Nicole," he leaned forward and took her hands in his own. She let him, and leaned in a little herself, "I'll be counting on you. If you say you're going to do it, you can't back out. I have to be able to depend on you."

She smiled at him, a slight parting of wet red lips.

"You can." She leaned back in her seat and glanced down at her shake. She was considering something. English didn't say anything. He had known her long enough to know what was coming next.

A moment later—ice princess emerging, proving, as though it needed proof, that she was not all ribbons and curls—she said, "Of course, one favor deserves another, don't you agree?"

English played all his cards at once. "Anything you want."

"Anything is a big word."

English nodded. He knew that.

"Fine. We'll discuss it later." She glanced up at the clock again and said, "I imagine Amanda will be done getting her teeth cleaned or whatever she's doing fairly soon. You'd better run home in case the tele should ring."

English checked his watch and nodded. "Thank you, Nicole. And please, don't be offended that I haven't told you more. It really is for your own good. The less you have to worry about, the less—"

She held up a hand and interrupted him, her raspy voice and her deep brown eyes bearing down on him. "English, please, I've always had such a fondness for you. Don't disappoint me now. You may have taken me to bed, but that doesn't mean I'm a simpleton." She winked at him as she stood and slid into her coat. "I understand these things."

And understand she apparently did.

For English the days leading to the trial were difficult and long ones. Amanda reassured him that he was doing the right thing by testifying; his parents agreed. The cops agreed, Palto agreed, everyone in the world seemed to agree. English told himself again and again that whether it was the right thing or no, what he had chosen to do was the only thing he could do, the only way out he had.

But even still he was juggling. Even now, having decided to testify, having looked his closest friend in all the world in the eye under the bridge with their mouths wrapped around cigars and their livers swimming in O.F.C. and told him through his silence that he, English Mason, would be taking the stand and swearing the oath and spilling his soul for the world to smell, even now there was a game to play. He needed Nicole to make it work but it was something Amanda could never know. Not ever. If Nicole had been the kind of person to open her arms and willingly help without the thought of something in return, he wouldn't be in this situation now. He wouldn't have to be sneaking around behind Amanda's back, trying to string several very risky ideas together into one concrete solution to problems that were growing exponentially by the second.

But Nicole wasn't that kind of person; she saw herself as the victim in this, and she was owed.

English had known that when he started. If he wanted her help, he'd have to pay the freight for it. Those were the rules. That's how The Game of the Most Determined was played. The fact that he enjoyed it only made it harder for him. He told himself he was doing it for all the right reasons, that he was doing it for himself and for Amanda and in a very sick and twisted way for Miller, but in the end all that really counted was that he was doing it at all and he never, ever should have.

Nicole's note had been left in the mailbox of his apartment the next day, a corner of yellow legal paper ripped out of one of her notebooks and folded into an unmarked envelope. He opened it in his bedroom and recognized the script. Like her voice it was thin and feathery, a whisper across the page, a furtive alliance of letters and words.

Figured out my favor. King's Inn. Rm 308. Fri. Nt. 8.

The King's Inn. A quaint English pub in the city with singles and suites above it that provided a magnificent view of the city. He knew a couple of guys who took their prom dates there for dinner back in high school. He didn't know too many that stuck around for the rooms afterwards. You could rent a room at Motel Six every Saturday night for three months for the cost of one night at the King's Inn. Motel Six may not have the view or the air of regality that The King's Inn had, but it had a bed and a pisser, and you brought your own view.

But if it was class you were looking for, you probably couldn't do much better than The King's Inn. It was built for people who needed that type of thing.

People like Nicole. If she was anything at all, and she was many things, she was, externally speaking, class personified. She wore it like a perfume and the scent fit her well.

So there it was. They were to go to The King's Inn. For dinner or for rooms, English wondered, then decided probably both. It was going to cost him a mint, but of course, not going would cost him more.

English shredded the note and flushed the pieces down his toilet. He left to pick up Amanda, who would be getting out of her last class in another forty minutes.

When he got to the nursing building she was waiting for him patiently with her hair pulled back in a ponytail and her books pressed up against her chest. When she saw him round the corner she smiled at him and rushed to greet him with a quick, almost violent kiss that tasted like spearmint. They walked to his car hand in hand and drove to the apartment, where they plopped down in front of the television and argued over Geraldo reruns and MTV.

They were on the couch less than a half hour before English fell asleep, Amanda lying behind him, her legs enmeshed in his, his head pressed up against her chest while she played with his hair.

She reached over his side and took the remote from his hand. He grunted a bit and shifted around, snuggling up against her, melting into the couch. She felt his weight pressing her into the back of the couch as he started a light snore and she turned the television off. She lifted herself up with an elbow and looked down at his face, at this boy she loved with every part of her body and mind, at this boy whose baby was growing inside of her. She leaned over and kissed his face, softly on the cheeks and eyes, then lay her own head next to his and let herself succumb to sleep.

As sleep came, she thought about what her mother had said about the divorce, about how in a matter of months her daddy would be living somewhere else, maybe with someone else. She thought about how she was going to have to bring herself to tell her parents that she was pregnant, that although she had been on the pill for the better part of seven years something somewhere—mere frequency, she supposed—happened and here it was. She thought about what English would be going through once the trial began, how it was going to challenge everything within him to say the kinds of things they were going to make him say about Miller. But he would do it. He would do it and they would get through it together, and in time the sensationalism of it all would die and things would be fine again. He was as emotional and sentimental and idealistic as a girl, but he was practical enough to see it was the only way out. And if for some reason he lost sight of that, she'd be there to remind him. After all, taking care of him was her job, and, she thought, reaching her arm around his midsection and burying her hand beneath him, Lord knew someone needed to do it.

Chapter 31

The Day of ... (December 6th)

The Dispenberg family pulled up in front of the courthouse, Wes driving with his wife next to him, Miller and Cori in the back. Williams met them at the curb. They looked like they were arriving at the temple, all of them decked out in their Friday-best, looking expensive and clean and in need of sleep.

Miller was wearing his nicest suit, a gray pin-striped with his father's favorite tie. It was burgundy with tiny black and gray slashes going diagonally left to right. His mother had bought him a new white shirt and cuff links the day before, and had this morning in his old bedroom helped him get the sleeve over his cast and the links just right through eyes blurred with tears.

Williams was wearing an olive green trench, carrying his briefcase in his left hand and an umbrella in the right, looking about as much like a lawyer as a man could look.

The sky above them promised rain; it hung heavy and low, thick with gray and black clouds.

It was less than a minute before the flood of press poured down the courthouse steps in Miller's direction, cameras and lights and microphones sticking out of their mass like antenna on a roach.

Williams walked next to his client and reviewed the instructions. "Keep your head up and don't say anything. Don't smile, don't frown. If you feel you must speak, say no comment. They'll try to provoke you, just to get you talking. Ignore them. Save it for inside."

Miller nodded and looked over his shoulder. His father walked over to him and touched his neck. "Good luck, son."

Miller nodded. "Thanks, pop."

He looked over at his mother and sister, standing in the center of the big white walk and looking at the rushing tide of reporters like they were afraid of them.

"You better look after mom, huh?"

He hitched, as if he was trying to say something, and Miller saw him struggling with something deep. He finally touched Miller's back once more and said, "we'll be waiting inside," before leaving to join his wife and daughter.

The press hit Miller and Williams full steam and barraged them with questions.

—Miller, do you have anything to say to the family of the policeman?—

—Is it true you tried to convince the Henderson girl to sleep with Mr. Wallace—

—What's your opinion of the restraining order Mr. Henderson has served against you—

—Is it true you got the Henderson girl pregnant and paid for the abortion—

—Is it true you and Nicole Henderson had a child two years ago—

—was the robbery motivated by politics?—

Williams spoke up. The reporters gathered like crows around roadkill.

"My client has nothing to say at this time. We will have comments on the proceedings here today once today's session is adjourned. That's all. Let us pass, please. Thank you. Let us pass. That's all for now."

—Have you cut a deal with the state, Mr. Williams?—

—Are you planning an insanity defense?—

The questions came like bees, but Miller and his lawyer made it through.

"Mr. Williams," Miller asked as they walked inside the courtroom, leaving the press in the drizzling rain outside, "can I speak to English before we get in there?"

Williams shook his head. "Absolutely not. Until all this is through, he's one of the bad guys."

They walked down the hallway side by side, Williams all business and strategy and Miller's face expressionless. Men and women in suits and trench coats passed them and Miller felt their stares. That's the one, he heard someone whisper as he passed.

Yeah, Miller thought. I'm the one. The road to nowhere leads to me.

They stopped at a water fountain and Williams swallowed three aspirins.

"Headache?" Miller asked.

Williams shook his head. "Preventative medicine. Don't want to have to deal with one in here." He cleared his throat and spat into the fountain, not bothering to wash it down.

"Let's review what we discussed last night," Williams said.

"There's no need," Miller said. "I'm not going to forget."

"You're sure?"

Miller nodded. Williams had drilled him until after three this morning at the dining room table, doing what he called "Q+A" for over six hours, on the off-shot that he put Miller on the stand. Miller thought he could do it asleep.

The long hallway ended and they were at the doors of the courtroom. Miller pressed his tie against his chest and looked at his attorney. "Is he already inside, you think?"

"Who?"

"English."

"We'll find out in a minute. Listen, Miller, I wouldn't suggest trying to communicate with him in here. That means no hand gestures, no nod of the head, no fleeting smile, no cute little winks. He's not here to cheer you on. The closer you two look the stronger it makes the state's case. Stay away from him and let me take care of things, all right? I've done some digging and I'm fairly confident I can punch a few holes in his credibility."

"I understand," Miller said.

Williams opened the doors and he and his client walked down the center aisle and took their seats at the defense table. Palto and two other lawyers dressed in suits cut with a scalpel and fitting like mist were already seated to the defense's right. Miller saw the back of their heads and was hoping Palto would turn around for a little eye to eye, but all he got was the back view of his designer hair cut.

There were a few people in the courtroom; Miller recognized Mrs. Wallace from the news, and saw two of his professors, Dr. Aster and Dr. Allen, sitting together. Dr. Aster made sense; his professor for four different government and political science courses, she had always had a soft spot for Miller, but Dr. Allen was a bit of a surprise. Miller had only had him for one course, back during his freshman year. And it was a survey course at that, with little to no interaction between the students and the Prof. Miller figured maybe he was boning Dr. Aster.

Miller glanced again at Mrs. Wallace and their eyes met. She looked at him like he was a package air-mailed from Iraq with something ticking inside.

Yeah, well fuck you too, lady. If hubbie had kept his dick in check none of us would be here.

And so here he was. Miller Dispenberg at the bottom of a very long fall from grace, sitting in court waiting to be tried for murder charges by a jury of his peers. He glanced over at the jury box and wondered who would be sitting in the twelve seats when it all started.

He checked his watch. A quarter after eight. Palto was scheduled to call his first witness at nine sharp. Who would that be? English, maybe. No, he'd want to save him for last. The coup de grace. Wonderful.

His stomach hitched and he tried to calm himself by studying the courtroom. The ceilings were high and dark, and met the walls in gentle angles of brown wood that looked like either oak or cedar and smelled like leather and furniture polish. The judge's bench was at the front of the courtroom, raised on a platform, a huge, sweeping black bench with a swivel chair waiting patiently behind it.

And the witness stand. A single chair facing out, open to all who cared to look, the focal point of the entire room.

There it is, Miller thought. The infamous witness stand. What was it they called it on television? The hot seat? It wouldn't be long before people he'd known for most of his life would be sitting up there, sharing for the jury every negative thing about Miller that Palto had been able to dig up.

Miller wondered if in the final analysis Nicole would be able to go through with it, and decided that yes, she probably could. She'd probably be so happy about the whole thing she'd have to change her panties afterwards. And Laney. Laney, the guy that sold dope and fucked everything with two holes and a heartbeat. Laney the ivy-educated med. student with a future to protect. Miller knew Laney wouldn't enjoy it, but he also knew that there wasn't much of a question how Laney's testimony was going to go. Like everyone else Palto had gotten to, Laney had cut himself a deal.

But English. English was something else. Miller wasn't so sure English could say the kind of things he was going to have to say with Miller in the room.

Can you do it, English?

Can you sit there and damn me into hell after all these years?

Will you?

* * *

Ten minutes later and Miller listened half-numb while the judge, a middle-aged man losing his hair with nervous hands and a little stub of a nose, read off several pages of procedure for the benefit of the onlookers. The lawyers knew the drill. No smoking, no talking, no whispering, no note passing, no noise, no leaving for water or trips to the bathroom. If you got up and left you stayed out until the court recessed. No exceptions. Miller had glanced behind where he and Williams were seated five minutes before the hour and had seen rows and rows of faces. Some he recognized from school. Other's he'd never seen before. He saw an elderly black couple sitting near the back on the other side, their faces flat and brown with sorrow and pain, the man's bony arm draped over the woman's shoulders like a shawl. He figured it was probably the cop's folks. A shame about that. He hadn't meant for that to happen.

He saw Laney's parents a couple of rows back and wondered if Laney was there as well. Another star witness for the prosecution. He looked for English but didn't see him.

Professor Aster caught his eye and gave him a warm, reassuring smile.

There there, dear, she seemed to want to say. Chin up.

Palto made his opening remarks next and made a point of mentioning Miller by name as many times as he could. He said words like murder and evil, deceit and vicious, time and time again. He walked over in Miller's direction several times and pointed at him as he spoke, punching the air and bringing his hand down on the table hard. Miller sat through it and stared ahead at the space in front of him and tried to keep his head clear.

Williams went next, and talked about how it was bad that Officer Hudson had been killed, and bad that Wallace had died, but that there wasn't one single substantial shred of proof of evidence that his client was the one responsible. Williams accused Palto of engaging in rumor-spreading and hearsay, using innuendo and trying to manipulate the jury's emotions. Williams maintained that the prosecution would be unable to produce one witness who saw his client murder anyone, and everything else would be circumstantial. Someone has committed a heinous crime, Williams conceded in a low, mournful tone for the jury, and someone must pay. But an even worse, more heinous crime it would surely be to convict an innocent boy of such a crime, to rob him of his future, to condemn him to the common punishment of a common criminal. Would they, the members of the jury, be able to live with themselves if they, in effect, murdered an innocent person by snuffing out his future? A person, Williams continued, not unlike his client? If the prosecution, Williams told the jury, can give you proof that Miller Dispenberg killed anyone, then convict. But barring that, it's your constitutional duty to acquit him. The burden of proof rests with the prosecution, and it is a burden they will prove to be unable to bear.

The next thing he knew Williams was touching his wrist to reassure him, and Palto was standing from his chair off to the right, rising in the courtroom like Neptune from the sea, his shoulders squared and his back erect and his voice booming off the walls and ceiling like thunder.

"The prosecution calls Mitchell Huffington."

Who?

All heads turned as a man of about fifty stood from somewhere in the back and began walking towards the witness stand. Miller looked at him without too much interest and decided he had never seen the man before in his life.

He leaned over to Williams and whispered, "who is Mitchell Huffington?"

Williams, his eyes never wavering from the gentleman taking the stand, scribbled across a yellow legal pad, *hunter*.

Hunter, Miller thought. What hunter?

"Mr. Huffington, do you swear that the testimony you will give here today will be the truth, the whole truth and nothing but the truth so help you God?"

Huffington snapped out an "I do" as if he were marrying a centerfold. Miller watched him take the hot seat and adjust his tie. The black in it shone like ink. His shirt, Miller noticed, was freshly starched, and his hair was combed as nicely as a girl's.

Wonder if that's his only collared shirt, Miller thought. He watched the way Huffington's eyes ratcheted around in their sockets like a cat in a strange room, this way and that, trying to soak in everything all at once.

Terrific, Miller thought. The guy thinks he's on stage.

Miller sunk down in his chair a bit and settled in for a long morning. Sing, Huffington. Tell us what you know. Heaven knows *I'm* curious.

Palto had his hands resting on a stack of papers before him on the table, and was tapping them lightly as Huffington situated himself in the chair. After half a minute of silence, Palto began.

Miller sat stone-still and watched the proceedings before him as if he were a bystander and not the reason for it all. He checked his watch and felt a dull wave of apprehension wash over him as the Q+A with the happy hunter there wore on—apparently Huffington had been hunting around the Wallace property that afternoon and had seen three individuals fitting Miller, English, and Laney's description, skulking around the place.

The judge had said they'd be recessing at 12:30 for lunch—half past twelve was how the prick had put it, sitting up there in that big chair behind that big table wrapped in that big robe, no doubt dreaming of the days of yesteryear when men were men and women weren't and judges sat with powdered wigs and oversaw it all—which meant they had another three hours and fifteen minutes to go of this just to get to lunch. That's three and a quarter hours in judge lingo, Miller thought. A long time filled with nothing fun.

So Miller settled back in his seat and kept his innocent face on for the jury and watched Palto then Williams finish with Huffington, watched the state's procession of witnesses file past him and climb into the stand like they were settling back in the dentist's chair, not too thrilled to be there but excited about all the special attention they were getting.

They came and went one after the other—former professors, ex-girlfriends, Wallace's wife, Mitchum and Callahan—popping up from the benches behind Miller like prairie dogs when their names were called, little eager beavers just dying to do their civic duty and be good Americans, and Palto would take his turn with them after which Williams would take his, and it all happened in front of Miller in a blur of questions and objections and whispers and murmurs.

Palto then called David Henderson.

*   *   *

She parked her car behind, rather than in front of, the government complex this time and entered through the employee entrance in the back. She was aware that she was probably being overly-cautious, but as the trial progressed the amount of attention English was getting increased dramatically, and the risk of some picture-happy photog catching her going in or coming out of here wasn't one either of them could afford.

Amanda entered the building without looking at anyone directly, walking casually but with a purpose, as though she were a secretary returning from break. English had come alone last week to do the part she couldn't do for him, and if things went well here today this would be the last of it.

She checked her watch and saw it was a quarter after twelve, which was good. It was lunchtime in Governmentland. Odds were there'd be one person behind the counter to deal with every administrative red-tape problem of the modernized world, and she'd slip in and slip out without much notice.

As she walked through the lobby towards the elevator, she passed a mailbox and dropped the letter English had given her—the one addressed to Detective Callahan—inside. She wasn't sure what English was writing to the police about; he had been vague when she asked him about it, but she didn't suppose it mattered all that much.

When she finished at the government complex, she drove, per English's instructions, four miles to the First Federal Bank of Chicago. She made several other stops that afternoon; one at the Illinois Railroad Savings and Loan, another at Illinois Federal, another at First Chicago, still another at NationsBank, and finally—the last stop before returning home—one at Wachovia.

She followed English's instructions to the letter, and left the two athletic bags in the trunk of her car, hidden beneath an old blanket.

* * *

English had called Nicole the night he found her little note in his mailbox and explained that Friday night just wasn't a good one. It was hard enough to get away from Amanda during the week, but Friday night it was all but impossible.

He was prepared to back down and just wing it with Amanda if Nicole pressed it, but she didn't and they rescheduled for Monday, the night of the first day of Miller's trial.

Nicole had said she thought that was poetic. English thought, but didn't say, that Nicole was just plain mean.

But that was the way he felt about Nicole's whole idea of a favor; she knew he had had trouble with what they had done the night of the fundraiser, but she didn't care. Or if she did care, she cared in her own special way and didn't let it inconvenience her much. She didn't let a little thing like a friend's feelings get in the way of her fun. What she wanted was what she wanted, and everything else could take a number.

So English shoved all the shit down to his lizard-brain, where things like hunger and desire and fear registered, not allowing himself to think about Amanda or Miller or the trial or right and wrong or anything like that, keeping his eye on the brass ring the entire time, telling himself over and again that what he was doing he was doing for them, for him and Amanda, and that in the end—no matter what happened—the end would make the means forgivable.

He arrived at the King's Inn at a quarter till seven. It was seven degrees above zero, and he was dressed in jeans and a white polo sweater with little red pin stripes running horizontally across the chest. Underneath he had on three undershirts. When he had talked to Nicole Friday to see about getting this pushed back a few days, she had told him not to dress too formal.

No cummerbunds, was how she had put it.

English parked his Mustang in a city lot across the street and down two blocks, then double-backed to the hotel. He walked into the lobby, with its royal blue carpet and deep cherry-wood furniture, asked the man behind the desk if there were any messages for a Mr. Mason, and waited while the tall, lanky gentleman checked the boxes behind him.

"Yes," he said, his tight little mustache bobbing up and down with the words, "there is as a matter of fact." He handed English a folded slip of notepad paper and went about his business. Nice, the way money bought privacy like that.

English unfolded the note. Across the top was the King's Inn logo, the words *King's Inn* wrapped around an eight point crown. English thought that was kind of cheesy for such a nice place.

The message was simple enough. *Room 308. Regrets not accepted.*

Pretty cute there, Nicole. No regrets. That's your motto, isn't it. Do it all and never look back. Hedonism to the nth. No regrets.

English crumpled the note and stuffed it in his jeans pocket. He found the elevator and rode it to the third floor. When he knocked on the door of Room 308, Nicole answered it in blue jeans and a big, floppy red sweater. The sweater brought out the red of her lips. Her skin reminded English of newly fallen snow.

"Right on time," she said, touching his wrist with her hand, leading him in. The room smelled like her; mint and water, soapy with the scent of perfume—Moroc this time—hovering under it.

English walked into the center of the bedroom and looked around. It was a suite, with an adjoining living room off to the left. There was a large window directly opposite the entrance, with white draperies framing the view of the city beyond. In the far right hand corner of the bedroom was a brass fireplace. A little metal key stuck out of the floor for instant fire.

An entertainment system sat to the right, C.D. player, television, VCR, the works. Waiting atop the stereo was a bottle of champagne chilling in ice, crystal champagne glasses as thin as paper on either side. A large chandelier hung from the ceiling, all lights and little crystal goblets that cast rainbows on the ceiling.

The bed, a queen with pink and white sheets, a thick cream colored comforter and matching pillowcases, was to the left, beyond the doorway leading to the living room. It was arranged so you could lie there and warm your toes and see both the television and the starscape outside.

English whistled low under his breath. "This place must have cost a fortune."

"It did. But never you mind. I took care of all that."

He walked into the adjacent living room and stopped in his tracks. The entire far wall was glass from floor to ceiling, the shades pulled back and the lights from the city's skyscrapers shining in. English watched them twinkle like stars in a naked night and had trouble telling where the buildings ended and the sky began.

He walked across the beige carpet, past a couch and loveseat, past another entertainment system, this one bigger than the bedroom version, past a twelve-foot oaktop bar with four matching stools. He stopped at the glass and stared out over the city. He could see the distant movement of cars and buses, of shapes in windows and on balconies. From the third floor of The King's Inn, the city was a silent wave of lights and shadows crisscrossing the surface of some foreign terrain.

"Beautiful, isn't it?" Nicole asked, standing behind the bar. English heard a cork surrender with a loud pop, followed by the sound of liquid pouring into a glass.

"Where did you get the money for this?" He asked, turning towards her.

She shrugged and smiled. "Oh, a little here, a little there. You know how that sort of thing goes."

She brought him a glass of white wine. He sipped it, holding it in his mouth before letting it flow down his throat.

Surrender, he thought. Just surrender once more, for one more night, and see this through. For Amanda.

He looked again out at the looming city. If it wasn't for the circumstances, he could almost get into an evening like this.

"How long have you been planning this?"

Nicole didn't answer that; instead she took him by the sleeve and, flicking the lock on the sliding glass door, led him to the balcony. The wind cut through his jeans and pulled gooseflesh from his skin.

"See?" Nicole said, pointing at the ground with her toe. "Cozy, wouldn't you agree?"

English would. There, on a balcony that ran roughly fifteen feet long and protruded from the building about ten, sat a heart-shaped Jacuzzi, just big enough for two if the two were on good terms. Steam rose from the dark water as it bubbled and churned like something boiling. English listened to the bubbles and felt the hot steam cooling against his skin. About half the water's surface was covered in moonlight, making the water a milky gold.

Man, English thought. That is not a bath for strangers.

"A hot-tub?"

"There's a veritable slew of oils and perfumes underneath the bar. Isn't it romantic?" Romantic it was. English looked around him and saw they were isolated from all. The balcony had a four foot red-brick wall that ran its perimeter. Someone sitting in the water there would be lost to the world.

"It's freezing out here," was the best defense he could find, realizing that it was no defense at all. He gave up on defense when he left his apartment tonight. That he was here said more than any words he could use.

"That's why they call it a hot-tub. It's supposed to be cold out. Did you bring a suit?"

"You didn't say anything about it."

"Fancy that," she smiled. "I forgot mine, too. Good thing it's dark. Now, come back inside before we catch our death."

They went back in and Nicole ordered room service. Shrimp cocktails, lobster for both of them, caramel custard for desert. Another bottle of wine. English sat on the couch and channel-surfed with the remote and tried not to enjoy being there.

"Hey, Nic," he called over his shoulder, "you never answered my question. How long have you been planning this?"

"Since I was about seventeen," she said, joining him on the couch. "Were you at the trial today?"

"No. Were you?"

Nicole shook her head. "My father testified."

"I heard. Something about the invitation."

"Yes," Nicole said. "Palto's building his case rather nicely, from what I'm hearing. From all accounts he really is an exceptional lawyer. He's using Miller's past and present to paint for the jury a none-too-flattering character sketch of sorts, while at the same time he's tying Miller to Wallace and the fundraiser. He's apparently found a Wal-Mart clerk who's going to testify that Miller bought lime and bleach the night Wallace died and was buried."

English shook his head. "My God," he said. "They're going to put him away forever, Nicole."

"It'll be some time before he sees the light of day again, to be certain," she said. "And a great deal of me is only too happy to do my part. I'm just glad I wasn't there this afternoon. Apparently Miller's lawyer did a fairly decent job of making sure everyone in attendance knew I wasn't a virgin. Poor daddy. It makes me feel sorry for him in a way, having to sit there and hear that in front of all his colleagues." Nicole laughed. "Of course, it's kind of funny, too. When do you testify?"

"Wednesday? You?"

"The same. Kind of eerie, isn't it?"

"The whole thing sucks," English said. "I wish...I don't know what I wish. I wish to hell we'd never gone to that fucking fundraiser."

Nicole touched his leg and took the remote from him, clicking the television off. The room fell silent. English looked down at her hand, at her perfectly manicured nails, shiny in the light.

"That's a waste of time, English. Wishing. I've been doing it my whole life. It won't get you anywhere but sad."

"You, Nicole? What could you, with all you have, wish for?"

She touched his face then, and offered him a wan smile. "All I don't."

There was a knock on the door from the bedroom and Nicole got up to get the food.

English watched her go and told himself for the millionth time that no one knew he was here, that no one was ever going to find out. This was something he was going to do once—once more—and never again. He had walked in off the street and would walk out just the same, signing nothing and leaving nothing behind. When he got in his Mustang tomorrow morning he would drive away from The King's Inn and from everything that happened in it and two days later Nicole, like the trial, would be a memory he'd spend the rest of his life trying not to remember.

"Would you like our itinerary?" Nicole said, reappearing on the couch.

Why not, English thought, and said, "sure."

"Well, I thought we'd have dinner as soon as it cools. There's a table set for us in the bedroom. Then, perhaps a glass of wine or two in front of a cozy fire, and, if we're feeling daring, a midnight Jacuzzi under the open sky."

"I have class tomorrow."

"Yes, well, if I'm not mistaken your first one isn't until nine. I promise you'll be home in time to brush your teeth and gather your books."

English had anticipated a late one, and had his books already in the car.

"And then..." her voice trailed off.

"And then," English interrupted, nodding towards the couch, "then we migrate over in that direction, and you and I make the last one count."

Nicole looked at him without smiling and nodded. "And it is the last, isn't it, English?"

"Yes, Nicole. It is."

He thought for a moment that she might cry, and wondered if there was a chance that she understood what he was doing. Here, this, everything. Had she known all along? Was that what the big production—lobster and bedroom fireplaces and midnight Jacuzzis—was about?

"You will be there, won't you Nicole? At the courthouse?"

"Is that the only reason you came tonight?"

English would wonder about that for years to come.

"Does it really matter," he asked.

Her face moved closer to his, her lips slightly parted, her scent very strong throughout the room and around him, the scent of something free and unchained, something loose and running wild. He felt her breath on his face, then her mouth on his and was surprised to find how comfortable it felt there, how familiar all this was, as though the two of them belonged here together, like this, pocketed away inside some extravagant, waterside hotel with elegant trimmings, clumsily negotiating their way through an illicit encounter of breath and skin.

When her hand touched his chest and her weight was against him he could feel his blood rushing in his ears and her hair against his neck and there was nothing left in him that was willing to resist.

"No," she said, "I don't suppose it does."

Chapter 32

Judgment Day   (Dec. 8th)

The court was in recess and Miller and his attorney were in an anteroom with a table and three small chairs. Miller was sitting in one, and William's briefcase was in the other. Williams himself was leaning over the table with a pad and pencil, his coat folded over the back of the third chair. They had twenty more minutes before court resumed.

Miller was hunched over, leaning on his knees. He was rocking slowly, thinking.

"That forensics guy's testimony hurt us, didn't it?" Miller asked.

"It didn't help," Williams said. He didn't stop what he was doing. The man had a knack for dividing his attention three or four ways without cheating any one.

"I'm still stunned," Miller said.

Williams glanced up. "That your sweat was found on Wallace's corpse?"

"That it survived the lime and the bleach and the dirt," Miller said, throwing up his hands. "I'm just fucking speechless at that."

"It's liable to get worse," Williams said. He turned to his briefcase and removed a stack of papers, flipping through them with his thumb.

"The fact that Officer Carlisle isn't alive to testify—that she was murdered in her hospital bed—isn't going to help us, Miller. He won't be able to come right out and accuse you, but Palto's going to subtly and repeatedly tie you implicitly to her death. What you just saw in there isn't anything compared to how it's going to be. He's just getting started. I'll put your mother and father on the stand so they can corroborate your alibi, but in the end it isn't likely to count for much. They are, after all, your parents, and therefor have reason to lie." He glanced up at Miller. "Who stood to lose the most from her living, and subsequently testifying? Who stood to gain the most from her death, and consequent silence? These are questions he'll force every member of that jury to answer for themselves, without ever actually asking the questions. I'll object every time, but the jury isn't a machine. They're people, and they're going to hear half a dozen times that Carlisle can't be here to testify as to what she saw in those hills because she's dead, because someone injected a vial full of common saltwater into her veins. There are two hospital employees on his witness list, both of whom were working the night she was killed. If they testify they saw you there—well, you get the picture. It isn't a pretty one."

"No," Miller agreed, "it isn't pretty at all. But," he said, pausing, staring eye-to-eye with Williams in a manner so detached it chilled the attorney's blood, "it is prettier than the one I'd be looking at if she *were* in fact alive to testify, isn't it?"

"That," Williams said, returning to the stack of papers before him, "is a question the answer to which would necessitate my forming some judgment in regards to your innocence or guilt, which I have no interest in doing. The what if's of the situation aren't of any value here."

Miller didn't say anything. He knew that. He also knew the big guns were yet to come. Laney, who'd give the jury a firsthand, eyewitness account. And, of course, English, who'd be going up there to bury him.

Miller thought about the money. He thought about all the places that much money could help someone disappear; all the trails that kind of money could help cover. He thought about that a lot, lately.

"I may be able to get Palto to offer a reduced deal," Williams said without looking up. "Any chance you'd be interested in something along those lines?"

"I didn't think he was interested in deal-making."

"He may not be. When Laney and English take the stand and give the same testimony," Williams pulled one of the chairs around backwards and straddled it, facing Miller, "...it doesn't look real good. I can keep redirecting his witnesses, catch them in little embellishments of their version of the stories, try to raise a few doubts about their character or their reliability, mention the deals he's cutting them, and when it's our turn we can call as many people as we want to talk about how many tests you've aced and how many little old ladies you've helped across Main street, but in the end nothing we can do will change the fact that all we're left with is a dead cop, three boys who were there when it happened, and two of those boys pointing to you as the killer."

Miller was thinking about a little condo on a beach somewhere in Mexico—*we'll drink tequila, and look for seashells, now doesn't that sound sweet*...he had heard that in a song somewhere, and the words warmed him now—or perhaps a cozy little log cabin nestled down between two Swiss peaks. He was picturing the globe he had in his room back at the apartment, next to his desk, the one he would spin sometimes when he was sitting there studying, amazed at how big the world really was when you looked at it like that, and how if you found Chicago on the globe, you saw it was really just one city in one state of one of many, many countries. Just a little speck of dust, really.

"Miller?"

Miller looked at him.

"Do you want me to approach Palto?"

He was silent for a moment. "Would you recommend it?"

"With what we've got, where we are, yes, I would recommend it as strongly as any recommendation I've made in my career."

"I'd have to change my plea, wouldn't I?"

Williams nodded. "I think I can get him to accept a guilty by reason of temporary insanity. We can say you had blocked it out because of the severe shock, psychological trauma and whatnot, try to get a postponement long enough so that I can get you evaluated by a psychologist. I've got a couple that work well with me. I can't guarantee Palto though. He wants to win this, and Mike has never been big on plea-bargaining. After what went on in there this morning…" he shook his head, "I just can't make any promises. Of course, we don't need his permission to change our plea. But we're going to want his cooperation when it comes to sentencing."

Sentencing. It had a ring of finality to it, like *cancer*.

"There's going to be time in prison regardless, isn't there?"

Williams nodded again. "Our goal here is to minimize it."

Miller mouthed the words to himself. *Minimize*. To what? From forever to fifty years? Fifty years was forever.

Williams said, "we're due back in about ten minutes. I need to know so I can request a stay."

"And afterwards…tonight I mean. Would I get to go home with my family the way I've been doing? I wouldn't, would I? I'd be cooped up in some cell wearing gray and orange, sporting a number, watching the cement walls close in on me while some giant ape butt-fucks me into oblivion. No thanks."

Williams said, "If you reverse your plea, you'd most likely be held without bond until the trial is over. We'd request bail, but I'd be lying if I told you there was any chance we'd get it."

Miller wasn't listening. How many Chicagos would it take to fill up the world? A hundred thousand? A million, maybe? "Miller?"

It's a big world, Miller thought, before saying, "let's see what happens this afternoon before we do anything."

Williams sighed, and Miller could see he was beginning to grow exasperated.

"English Mason and Laney Taylor are scheduled to testify this afternoon," Williams reiterated, "and Palto's going to make them dance. I've seen him do it before, Miller, and it will only weaken our case. There is a point of no return when it comes to plea-bargaining."

"We're close to it, I assume."

"Perilously close, Miller," Williams said.

Miller rubbed at a spot on his wingtips. Beneath his coat, the arm inside his cast itched so bad it burned.

"Then what?"

"Well," Williams said, "if we continue—if we don't plea—once the Mason kid testifies the prosecution will rest, and then it'll be our turn."

"So we start tomorrow," Miller asked.

Williams nodded. "Unless the judge gives us a day's recess and schedules us for Friday, yes we begin our defense tomorrow morning."

"Let's wait a little longer. Give me one more night at home with my family. Let me have one more dinner with them. Say goodbye on my terms. Then we'll do it."

"I don't think you understand," Williams said. "Our position gets demonstrably weaker with each witness they call. Once Laney and English testify—"

"—Tomorrow," Miller interrupted. "We'll do it tomorrow. If it goes bad this afternoon, that's just something I'll have to deal with tomorrow. But I need tonight to be with my family."

Williams hesitated a moment, then nodded. "If you're certain."

"I am," Miller said, thinking that he was about as certain of this as anything in his entire life.

And the two of them walked back into the courtroom, Miller virtually oblivious to that which surrounded him, focusing instead on tonight.

Tonight he made his move.

* * *

Palto called Nicole Henderson and it was much of what Miller expected. She stayed cold and distant and aloof of anything personal, nailing down the facts and nailing them hard. Yes, she had been approached by Miller to distract Mr. Wallace. Yes, she knew Miller was planning to rob Wallace's house. No, she didn't know why, but she knew it was something he had been planning for weeks. That's right, weeks. It was Miller, Nicole said without emotion, who staked out both Wallace's house in Kenilworth and his cabin in Grand Beach before it all went down; Miller who slashed the tires of Mrs. Wallace's car to keep her from coming home too soon; Miller who picked her up from Wallace's cabin that night and took her home.

Miller Dispenberg, the defendant? Palto asked, pointing at Miller sitting in his seat, his legs folded beneath the table.

Yes, Nicole said, her cheekbones fine and solid, her hair and eyes shining in the light. That's him. Miller Thadius Dispenberg.

Again Williams put his all into damage control, but the futility of it was almost transparent. He was getting frustrated with the process and nowhere with the jury. Nicole held her ground like Miller had known she would; he was almost proud of her. She was in the center of the fire, forced by Williams to say some pretty unflattering things about herself, her morals and her reputation, but she said them matter-of-factly, as though she were in a room filled with girls in curlers at a slumber party and not in a courtroom that held her parents and her friends.

When the dust had settled and the words were no longer flying like daggers back and forth, Miller thought and was pretty sure Williams would agree that Nicole's version of the truth sounded all the more credible; there was no reason a twenty-four year old woman would sit there and denigrate herself so completely to perpetuate a lie. The jury felt it too. Nicole Henderson had told the truth, the whole truth, and nothing but the truth, goddam her soul.

Then there was Laney, and Miller went numb. He tried to meet Laney's eyes but Laney would have none of it; he sat tall and erect, looking every bit the part of an honors medical student, clean-cut, smooth-shaven—an ivy alumnus, after all—even a well-worn trace of indignation, Miller noticed.

Palto made a point of standing between Miller and Laney, keeping either from making eye-contact with the other, making it easier on the witness.

Palto asked, "did the three of you break into Wallace's house?"

"Yes," Laney said.

"Tell the court about that afternoon, Mr. Taylor," Palto said.

And so it went.

*   *   *

"The prosecution calls English Mason to the stand."

English took the stand and Miller watched him do it. The moment of truth, he thought. Can you, English? There's a backdoor to every house. Have you found yours? Have you learned the rules to The Game of the Most Determined?

English sat in one of his two suits, the gray one, wearing a blue tie with his golden *E+A* tie-tack while Palto circled from behind the table slowly, savoring the moment. This was it. His star witness, his trump card. Moments like this, Miller imagined, were what made all the bullshit a prosecutor puts up with worthwhile.

Miller sat erect in his seat with his hands folded over one another before his face. His foot tapped lightly beneath the table. Williams sat to his right, hands folded in his lap.

Miller was counting off in his head the number of countries in the world that spoke English as their primary language, then figured it really didn't matter. He could learn other languages.

When he and Williams had come back into the courtroom, Miller had seen in the benches behind his seat a number of familiar faces. The Dean of the Government Department from the University. The rabbi at the temple he'd stopped going to some six or seven years ago. The people who lived across the street from his parents. His father's sister. An entire row of people he knew from his classes. Tracie and her mother were there. Laney was seated near the back with his parents. English was with his, three rows in front of the Taylors. Amanda wasn't with him.

Miller found that exceedingly odd.

"English, can you recount for the court exactly what happened in Kenilworth the afternoon of the seventh of October?"

English sat stock-still in the chair, his hands linked at the thumbs across his lap. His eyes looked swollen and red. He was avoiding eye-contact with Miller like it was a disease.

Come on, English, Miller thought. Have a look. If you have to do it, do it like a man. Don't let them take that from you.

"Yes, I can." English said, his voice barely more than a whisper.

Palto circled the courtroom like a shark, finally lighting near the jury box, his hand resting comfortably on the mahogany beam in front of it.

"Please do."

English fiddled with his tie and shifted in his seat. His eyes were down, looking at something near his feet. He seemed to be searching for the words.

"English?" Palto prodded. "I know it's difficult for you. I know you two were close. But the court needs to hear what happened up there."

English offered Palto a nod and cleared his throat. Miller was directly in front of him, arms folded over his chest now. He stared at English hard, searching for the right emotions for this. Anger? Betrayal? Fear? Pity? He dug deep and came up with them all.

"We—me, Laney, and Miller—we broke into Wallace's house. We climbed a tree and entered through an upstairs window."

Palto moved, almost floated, slowly across the courtroom. "What happened while you were breaking into the Wallace residence?"

"We must have tripped a silent alarm, because the police were there by the time we were leaving."

"How long, then, would you say you were in the house?"

"Maybe five minutes. Long enough for Laney to find a cordless phone and make it to the treeline so he could see the road. We had time to go through a few drawers."

"Time to go through a few drawers? Were you looking for anything in particular?"

"Yes."

"And could you tell the court exactly what it was the three of you were looking for in Wallace's house that afternoon?"

"We were there to steal the hard-drive out of his computer."

A low murmur swept over the court like a swarm, then broke and settled into isolated whispers.

Palto waited. He was a patient man.

"And could you tell the court, English, why you were there to steal Mr. Wallace's hard-drive?"

"We'd been..."—English glanced out at Miller, focused on his eyepatch, that black barrier between his eye and the world, between the world and Miller's mind, and said, "we'd been hired to do it."

Miller and Williams both perked up. This was news to them. Both of them looked at Palto and came to the same conclusion. Palto had heard this before, which meant English had contrived it some time ago. Back when he cut his deal.

Which meant it had been prior to the O.F.C. under the bridge, Miller thought.

"By whom were you hired," Palto asked.

"We were never really sure," English said. "We never got a name. Miller was approached by telephone the weekend after the fundraiser."

"The Timmons fundraiser," Palto said.

English nodded. "The guy called the apartment, said he wanted to meet with us."

"Us?" Palto inquired.

English nodded. "Miller and me. So we met him the next day, at a coffeeshop not far from the campus. He offered us $50,000 to retrieve the hard-drive for him. He said he could provide us with the blueprints to the house as well as the codes for the alarm."

"Why you two, English? After all, you and Miller weren't exactly professional thieves up until this point, were you?"

English shook his head. "Miller asked him why us, and the man simply said that part of the $50,000 was that we didn't get to ask questions."

"Did he say why he wanted the hard-drive?"

"No," English said. "I thought it was probably related to the Timmons thing, but he never said anything to that effect. And we never asked."

Palto nodded, paused long enough for the jury to digest it all.

"And then what happened," he continued.

"We left. We were noncommittal. Miller and I talked about it for a while, as a joke more than anything at first. Then it got more serious. We began discussing things we'd do with the money if we had it, and somewhere in there we just decided to do it. It seemed harmless enough. Steal some lawyer's hard-drive for $50,000.00 It started looking like a real no-brainer."

"And then what?"

"Then Miller contacted Laney and Nicole, both of whom agreed. Neither of them knew about the money."

"Wait just a second," Palto said. "Are you saying that neither Laney nor Nicole had any idea of the $50,000 offer?" Palto asked.

"That's right. Laney did it for kicks...we knew he would, which is why we called him. We grew up with him. He's been that way since he was a kid, just doing things for kicks. We needed a third guy, someone to tail Mrs. Wallace through the city, learn her schedule, habits, things like that. So we called Laney."

"And Nicole?"

"All she knew was that we were going to be robbing the house. Her end didn't have anything to do with that part. She was supposed to distract Wallace, and that was it."

"By spending the night with him in his Grand Beach cabin," Palto said.

English nodded. "Yes."

"What happened then," Palto asked.

"Once we agreed to do it we got the stuff—the blueprints to the house, a map of the surrounding area, the alarm codes—in the mail a couple days later. They came in a plain brown wrapper with no return address. Postmarked from somewhere downtown. But we didn't care much. There was a typed letter saying we'd get a phone call at eight the following evening, which we did."

"Was it the same man as before?"

"It was. He's the only one we ever had any contact with."

"And what was the essence of that phone call?"

English hesitated, as if remembering. "The essence was," he said, trying to hide his distaste for Palto, "he told us that once we had the hard-drive one of us was to go to the same coffeeshop where we'd met, and order a cup of coffee and some eggs. We were to sit in a booth, sip our coffee and eat our eggs. When we were finished, we were to walk to our car, rest a foot on the back bumper, and tie our shoe. We were then to drive off."

"And did either of you follow these instructions?"

English nodded. "I did."

"What happened after that?"

"We got the phone call at home again. At the apartment. Same guy. Calling to arrange a trade."

"The hard-drive for the money," Palto said.

"Yes," English said, releasing a long-held sigh. "The hard-drive for the money."

"Now, English, if I told you I didn't believe you about the money, that I thought you were lying about being hired to rob the house in an effort to perhaps explain your actions in the hills that afternoon, or even to shift the blame to some extent, what would you say to me?"

"I'd say that you were wrong," English said.

"Yes, but could you prove it?"

English paused. "I think so, yes."

"How?"

"When the guy called he gave us instructions for the drop. We were to wrap the hard-drive in newspaper and cotton, then put it in a plain brown grocery bag. We were to leave our apartment at precisely midnight, drive down the interstate until we reached the Indiana state-line, and stop at the rest-area there. We were to leave the bag in the restroom, atop the back of the toilet tank in the first stall. A duffel-bag holding the fifty thousand was to be waiting for us in the garbage can inside the restroom."

"And did you follow those instructions, English?"

"We did. Miller and I, we both went."

"But not Laney?"

"No," English said, shaking his head. "Laney didn't want anything to do with it at this point."

"What about his share of the money?"

"I already told you, Laney never knew about the money. But he knew we were on the edge of serious trouble, and he didn't want anything to do with any of it afterwards. He wanted shut of it completely. He said he had too much to lose."

"And he was right," Palto said. "Pity you and Miller Dispenberg didn't see things the same way."

"Objection, your honor," Williams said.

The judge was nodding. "I was waiting for that. Mr. Palto, you know better than to moralize like that in my courtroom. Objection sustained."

"Yes, your honor." Then, to English, "You left Wallace's stolen hard-drive on the back of the toilet tank in the first stall of the restroom?"

"Yes."

"And was there a duffel bag holding fifty thousand dollars waiting for you in the trashcan?"

"There was, yes."

"Cash, English?"

English nodded. "Cash. Fifties and twenties."

"And what did you do with the money?"

"Nothing, at first. We were too scared. Everything was going crazy all around us."

"Where's the money now?"

"In the bank," English said. "We didn't spend any of it."

"You deposited all fifty-thousand dollars into a bank," Palto said.

"We put it in a safety deposit box to avoid a trail. Chicago National, downtown. About a week or so after the robbery. We were hoping things would cool down some. Obviously they didn't."

Palto had returned to his table, where one of his assistants handed him a small piece of paper.

"Your honor," he said, addressing the judge, "I'd like to submit this as exhibit E in the case of Illinois v. Dispenberg. Let the record show that it is a purchase slip for six months' lease on a safety deposit box subpoenaed from Chicago National and dated October 19 of this year, exactly twelve days after the robbery at the Wallace home in Kenilworth. Let the record also show that the amount found by the police department upon search is fifty-thousand dollars exactly, cash."

Palto handed the piece of paper to the judge, who, after examining it, handed it to the bailiff to be carried to the jury.

There was another low murmur throughout the courtroom, and the judge silenced them with the gavel. At the defense table, no one was moving.

"Now, English, I'd like to move back a bit. To the afternoon of the seventh. The day you, Miller, and Laney broke into the home of J. Fullard Wallace. You said you were given a list of the alarm codes, but yet you set off an alarm when you broke the window. How do you explain that?"

"I can't," English shrugged. "We broke the window, punched in the codes as they were given to us, and assumed the alarm, if there'd been one, had stopped. But the phone began ringing and shortly after Laney called from the road half a mile down saying the cops were coming. One car. Two officers."

"Officers Frank Hudson and Officer Carlisle," Palto said. "Both deceased now."

English nodded. "Yes."

Palto waited a few seconds to let that last bit sink in for the jury, then continued.

"Then what happened, English?"

English glanced at Miller again, at that patch, and searched his face for anything at all that resembled approbation. But there was nothing. His face was a stone.

"We got the hard-drive," English said. "I remember Miller was holding it when Laney called with the news about the cops. Things got tense, then. I wanted to leave…but Miller…I don't know. Miller was…it's like he was procrastinating. Like he didn't want to leave just yet."

"So what did you do, then?"

"I ran down the steps, and was going out the front door when I realized Miller was still upstairs. I called for him, and he came…" English stopped, chewed his bottom lip for a second as if deep in thought…"and he came around the corner with a gun."

"A gun? What kind of gun?" Palto asked, crossing the courtroom to his associate, who handed him a handgun in a plastic sandwich bag. A low murmur swept over the court.

"I don't know. It was a pistol of some sort. You know. A handgun."

"Did it look like this one?" Palto asked, holding up the gun.

"Yeah, I think so. It was about that size."

"Your honor, I'd like to admit this gun as State's exhibit F. In accordance with Officer Sandstone's testimony, it is the type of gun used to kill Detective Hudson on the afternoon of October 7."

Palto paused. "What happened then, English?"

"I asked him where he got the gun, what he was doing with it. He said not to worry about it, that we needed to get to the forest. I would have gone for the front door but it opened to the road and was too dangerous. So I ran back up the steps and followed Miller to the great room where we had come in, and I was climbing out of the window when the cops—when the police arrived."

"Miller was holding the gun at this time?"

"Yes."

"What happened when Officers Hudson and Carlisle arrived?"

"Miller jerked me back in the window and ran downstairs. I got...I panicked and ran into the Wallace's bedroom. I...I don't know what I was thinking or why..." his voice trailed off. Miller was watching intently, thoroughly intrigued, and thought English might cry. He felt a wave of pity for his friend. Breaking was bad enough. Breaking for the world to see left scars.

"English," Palto pressed, "what happened next?"

"I did some digging around...looked through some drawers, in the closet, underneath the bed, and I found—there was a gun under there and...and I grabbed it and ran down the stairs."

"What's that?" Palto said, unable to hide his surprise. English had thrown him, interrupted his rhythm.

"I said there was a gun there and I grabbed it," English repeated.

"You found a gun beneath the Wallace's bed?" Palto was standing motionless before English, his composure and his stance rigid.

Miller leaned forward and listened.

Miller glanced over at Williams, who was staring straight ahead. He looked at Palto and tried to keep from smiling for the sake of the jury.

English had tears in his eyes now. He blinked them back and continued. He tried not to look at his parents out there, told himself they weren't there, they weren't hearing this.

"I...I grabbed the gun and ran down the stairs with it," English said, plowing on, betting it all on this one hand even as he prayed to God that it would be enough. It had to be. It had to be enough. Anything else was too horrible to consider.

"I heard Miller behind me, in one of the rooms off to the right I think...and I circled around the stairs and went out the backdoor, through the living room."

Palto looked over at his associate who looked back through blank eyes.

"Your honor, I'd like a moment to confer with the witness in private if I may."

That was all Williams needed.

"The defense objects, your honor. This is Mr. Palto's witness, sworn to tell the whole truth, and it's painfully apparent that Mr. Palto would presume to muzzle him because he doesn't like what he's hearing. The defense has maintained all along the innocence of Miller Dispenberg, assuring the court that due process would find him innocent of the charges against him. It's our position that—"

"Mr. Williams," the judge interrupted, "the court is well aware of your position. Your client is the veritable community-pillar who's the victim of a vast some-wing conspiracy. Do spare the court your high tone, Mr. Williams."

"But your honor—"

"Please be seated, Mr. Williams. Thank you. And Mr. Palto, I don't have to tell you that Mr. Williams has a valid point. This is your witness, called to the stand by you, and under oath to this court to tell the truth as he knows it in its entirety. I'm afraid the testimony must stand."

"Yes, your honor. The prosecution has no further questions of this witness at this time, and we respectfully request a recess until tomorrow."

"The defense objects, your honor."

"Imagine that, Mr. Williams. The request for a recess is denied. Your witness, Mr. Williams."

Palto sat down quickly and began rifling through papers. He and the associate were whispering feverishly.

It was Williams' turn.

"English," he said, standing, "please continue for the court where you left off."

English nodded. "I went outside and I could…" his eyes closed, remembering for the jury, "I could hear someone on the other side of the house, over where the police car had been. I remember thinking they were going to shoot us, that they thought we really were burglars or something and they had come to take us down.. All I could think about was—" the tears were flowing now, silently, zig-zagging over cheekbones and around his nose, stopping at the chin before falling into his lap, "was my family, my girlfriend, and I thought about school and getting married and, and about my dad and all the hard work he and mom had done to send me through school and all this other shit that I was just...just throwing away and now the cops were going to shoot me down like—like a criminal because I was there at some stupid lawyer's house I didn't even know...I wanted to run to the woods but I was afraid to because the police were right there, right there around the corner so I turned the corner and tried to talk but the words wouldn't...they wouldn't...the words, they just wouldn't come and he saw me and he saw the gun and he started reaching for his and I...I—"

English's face fell to his hands. Williams moved closer to the witness stand, a look of paternal love plastered across his face.

The courtroom behind Miller was perfectly silent. Miller felt the people's presence behind him like a force. His stomach was turning. His palms were soaked.

Williams moved in, with love, for the kill.

"Did you shoot him, English? Did you shoot and kill Officer Hudson?"

He lifted his face and refolded his hands. His eyes were red and watery, his face swollen and shining from the tears.

"It was a clear case of him or me," English said, his voice faltering. "You have to understand that. It was a clear...a clear case of him or me..."

Williams said, "English, I have to ask you again. Please son, an innocent life is at stake here...did you shoot and kill Officer Hudson?"

"When it's something like that," English said, "when it's a clear case of them or you, you do what you have to do. You do what you have to do," he repeated, raising his voice for effect. "Anyone would. I know we shouldn't have been there in the first place, I know what we were doing was wrong, that we were stealing and the money only made it worse, but," he paused, lowered his head again for a silent count of ten, then raised it again, "but when it's a case of you or them, you have to do the right thing. For that one instant...for that one instant it was that case—him or me—

and I did what I thought was the right thing. I swear to God I thought it was the right thing at the time."

He stopped then, and simply gazed out into the court, the decided vacuous stare of one who is remembering something terrible.

"Did you shoot Officer Hudson, English?"

"I buried the gun," English said. "I buried it about a mile and a half down a dirt road that runs near the lake, behind a new development. Down that dirt road, on the left side, it's buried beneath a telephone pole. Maybe three feet down."

"English," Williams repeated, "did you shoot Officer Hudson? Did you pull the trigger on that gun?"

"Don't you see," English said, his voice laced with desperation now, "don't you see I had no choice. I...it was him or me. I keep telling you that but you don't understand. It was him or me. I had no choice. None. He took my choices away when he went for his gun. He was going to shoot me. He was going to...to *kill* me for God's sakes. What else could I have done?"

"English—"

English looked Williams in the eye. Williams knew. Williams knew English was writing fiction up there, and he was going along for the ride with a smile and a hard-on all the way. Fucking lawyers.

English opened his mouth but nothing came.

He wiped at his eyes with the back of his hand. Williams produced a handkerchief from his inner coat pocket and gave it to him. English took it and pressed it over his face, dropping his head. He felt the judge watching him from his left, felt the eyes of the jury plastered on him. He thought he could hear, from somewhere in the crowd, rising above the general buzz of whispers that hummed through the courtroom like a current, the sound of his mother crying.

"Mr. Mason, do you need a moment?" The judge asked calmly.

English lifted his face in the judge's direction and whispered, "may I"—sniff, wipe... "can I use the bathroom for a second, your honor?"

The judge nodded and signaled for the bailiff. "Escort Mr. Mason to the restroom and back when he is finished. Do not leave his side, not even for a moment."

The bailiff nodded and walked with English down the aisle. English glanced over at his mother and father on the way out. His mother's face was buried in his father's chest. She was sobbing. His hand was holding the back of her head, and English saw something he had never seen before in his life, an image he would carry until he died. He saw his father crying.

He followed English with his eyes and wiped tears from his cheeks; it took everything English had not to run to him and hug him, to tell him it wasn't true, that it was just a dirty lie he had to tell in order to ever get shut of this for good.

But instead he turned his head away the way Pilate must have turned from Christ, and he walked with the bailiff down the corridor to the restroom, carrying with him the same fears and prayers Pilate must have carried that day two thousand years ago: Dear God, please don't let this have been the biggest mistake of my life.

*   *   *

When he walked in the restroom he went straight for the last stall on the left. The bailiff sauntered in behind him, an older man somewhere in his sixties, tall and thin and looking very much like a pale-blue skeleton in his uniform.

"Hurry it along, son," he said, walking over to the sinks on the opposite wall from the stalls, washing his hands as he examined his gums in the mirror.

English ignored him, pulling and latching the stall door behind him. He was no longer crying. His hands were shaking and his stomach burned with fear. He glanced up above the toilet, near the ceiling at a small, rectangular window, black wires running through the glass for strength and protection. It was about seven feet off the floor.

He reached around the toilet tank and squeezed his hand between it and the wall. There was a brief second of mind-numbing panic as his hand came up with nothing but cement dust and cobwebs, but then he found it.

His fingertips touched cold steel and he wrapped his hand around the bar and withdrew it from behind the tank. A little over a foot long and an inch in diameter, English held in his hands one of his five pound dumbbells from the apartment. He had come to the courthouse a couple hours before it closed for the weekend last Friday with two of them, wedging one behind the last tank in each of the two first-floor bathrooms. But this was the restroom closest to the courtroom, which was good for him, because the little window faced the quieter of the two possible streets.

He'd spent four miserable days worrying about it being found. Monday the trial began and there was no way he'd get past the media circus without being noticed, and yesterday the building had been closed for Pearl Harbor Day.

Now, English thought, stuffing the pipe down the back of his pants, under his coat, now all I have to do is do it.

He flushed the toilet and waited a count of twenty before coming out. He measured his breathing and told himself, again, that there was no other way.

The bailiff was standing near the door, wiping at his hands with a paper towel. His nightstick hung from his left hip; his gun rested on the other one.

"Mind if I wash my hands," English asked.

"Quickly," the bailiff said. "They're waiting on you."

English nodded and approached the sinks. He turned on the faucet and ran his hands beneath the water, watching the bailiff in the mirror. He rubbed his hands together, waiting, looking for his chance, knowing he wasn't going to get a second one.

He began talking, his eyes never leaving the bailiff's.

"When we were fifteen we made a pact—nothing serious, one of those stupid things you do during the summer when you're too young to drive anywhere. Anyway, our pact was pretty simple. We'd always have the other's back. Always be the wing-man. It's almost a cliche these days, but in our little fifteen year old heads, we meant it."

The bailiff was watching English. He didn't say anything.

"Like on *Tougher Than Leather*. Man, for a while there that was our all time favorite. We'd watch it three, four times a day. Just pop it in and let it play over and over."

"Let's go, son."

English kept rubbing his hands under the water. He squirted a few shots of pink soap into the palm of his left and ran them back and forth, rubbing each finger up and down like a surgeon.

The bailiff was watching English rub at his hands. English had quit watching him and was concentrating on working the soap around his fingers.

"You ever see *Tougher Than Leather?* I'd be willing to bet you haven't. Not many people have. It's a firecracker, though."

"Hurry and finish it up there," the bailiff said. "They're clean enough."

English's opening came when the man stuck his right hand in his front pocket and pulled out a piece of chewing gum. English turned off the faucet as the bailiff unwrapped the gum. He shook water off his hands, and was getting himself a paper towel as the bailiff slid the stick of gum in his mouth, walking this way, towards English, to throw the wrapper in the trash.

English faced him, wiping his hands with the paper towel, and said, "you got anymore of that gum?"

The bailiff looked at him curiously.

English tossed the paper towel into the trash. "I'm trying to quit smoking, but my nerves are shot to hell today," he said, tucking in the front of his shirt, then the sides. "I feel like I'm going to puke," he added.

The bailiff nodded as if to say he understood, that his nerves had given him trouble all the times he had confessed to murder in open court too, and reached in for another piece of gum.

English reached around at the same time, tucking in his shirt tail, his eyes never leaving the bailiff's face, and pulled the dumbbell from his belt, bringing it around in a low, hard arc that caught the bailiff on the side of his left knee. The bailiff wilted like a flower, crumpling to the ground with a howl of pain, falling to his back and reaching for his gun. English lunged forward and slammed his foot on the bailiff's wrist, grinding it into the ground. The bailiff reached with his other hand for his nightstick, and English, his foot still on the man's wrist, reared back with the dumbbell.

"You've got a chance to make it out of this with a cracked knee, mister. You go for that stick and I'll smash your skull. Nothing personal, but if it comes down to you or me, it's gonna be you."

The bailiff's eyes were locked on English's. Something like understanding flickered in them. He nodded.

"Do what you're gonna do then, boy."

English crouched down, his right arm still cocked back with the dumbbell.

"I gotta have your gun. I'm sure you understand."

The bailiff nodded and lay his hands on the floor by his head. "You're not going to get away, son. They'll be in here looking for us inside of sixty seconds."

English took the gun and the nightstick and threw them in the trash.

"You don't concern yourself with that," English said. "Just concentrate on keeping still and quiet. You're on the clock."

He stepped over the bailiff and made for the window, then stopped, turning back to the bailiff on the floor.

"You can tell them what I said. It's why they never stood a real chance. He's my friend, you people aren't, and the lot of you underestimated that. That's about as tidy as I can sum it up."

He climbed atop the toilet tank and slammed the dumbbell into the glass with all he had. It shattered and rained down on his hair and back. It took another four whacks with the dumbbell to knock the wire framing out.

English checked the bailiff one last time. He was in the same position, lying on the floor, his hands resting patiently by his head, his eyes staring up at the ceiling, union wages and a uniform apparently not enough to warrant a cracked cranium.

Smart man, English thought, and pulled himself up through the window and out the other side. He had mapped this out the day he decided to do it, and had chosen this route because of its speed as well as location. This side of the building was the least active. There was traffic and a few people walking the sidewalks beneath the window, but of his choices this had been the best. Anything near the front of the courthouse was covered by the press, and the northern face of the building opened to one of Chicago's busier streets.

English reached over and grabbed a drain pipe running up the building. Another reason to take this route. The pipe was fairly thick and looked sturdy enough to withstand his weight, and it passed within inches of his window. Had he been in the other bathroom, he would have had to simply jump.

English shimmied down the fifteen feet to the ground in about ten seconds, tearing holes in the knees of his suit and scraping blood from his knuckles on the brick along the way. He hit the street running south on the sidewalk, down four city blocks, cutting in and out of people walking up the sidewalk, his tie flying up before him, until he reached Ashland Avenue. There he turned right and crossed over, dodging cars frenetically and sending off a cacophony of blaring horns and screeching brakes, then running for another two blocks. He didn't look back and he didn't slow down. He didn't allow himself to think that she wouldn't be there. She had to be. Anything else was too horrible to consider.

He came to the corner of Ashland and Pope John Paul and stopped, gasping for air, covered in sweat.

Nicole was waiting for him in her little red Miata. English saw her sitting behind the wheel, her lips parted in a smile and a large white bow in her hair, and he thought he'd never seen anything quite so beautiful in all his life.

* * *

English was only half in the car when Nicole slammed the accelerator to the floormat. He was thrown backwards, hitting his head on the dome-light.

"You said fast," Nicole said, running a yellow light as she crossed 35th Street, then turning right onto the Adlai Stevenson Expressway.

English was taking off his coat and tie and unbuttoning his shirt. "Just don't get a ticket whatever you do. Watch that car ahead."

"You just worry about changing. I'll take care of the driving, thank you."

English unzipped the Notre Dame athletic bag that was sitting on the backseat of the Miata. In it he had packed a pair of jeans, a plain black sweat-shirt with a hood, athletic socks, and a pair of old sneakers. The plane tickets were in there as well, six pairs of two each, along with $1,100.00 cash, three hundred of which had been his. The other $800.00 was Amanda's. English had cleaned out his account—$509.31—to help pay for the tickets. He raised the rest by selling his car two days earlier to a dealer for $6000.00 cash, a steal for a two year old Mustang with less than thirty thousand miles on it. But English had needed ready money and he hadn't had time to negotiate.

He stuffed his dress-shirt, tie, and pants into the bag. He balled his dress socks into the Dexters and laid them on top. He slipped the cash and tickets into the front pocket of the jeans. He threw the suit jacket into the back-seat.

"Your father have any need for a suit without knees?"

Nicole was cruising along at a flat eighty-five, barreling down the fast-lane, flicking her brights and laying on the horn at any and everyone who stood in her way.

"I will never understand why people feel the need to go sixty-five in the fast lane. There's a perfectly good lane right next door for the old and dead." She glanced over at English. "I hope wherever you're going has more sensible driving laws than Chicago."

"We'll both be going to the hospital if you don't watch out."

"I'll be happy to play by the rules if you'd like, darling, and we can do the stop 'n go for the next hour. My, don't we look cute in our tighty-whities?"

"Keep your eyes on the road, Nicole."

English pulled on the jeans and slid into the sweat-shirt. He pulled the tickets from his pocket and looked at them again. Each of the six pairs was wrapped together with a rubberband. He shuffled them around and put them in order. All were from O'Hare International Airport to various destinations, scheduled to take off anywhere from nineteen minutes to an hour and forty-seven minutes from now. Two to Winnipeg. Two to Mexico City. Two to A.B.E. in Pennsylvania. Two to Miami. Two to San Diego. Two to Madrid. All twelve tickets were one way. The flight to San Diego connected to San Juan. A.B.E. connected to Oslo. Miami to Venezuela.

"So where's home going to be?" Nicole asked.

"This is your exit. Right there, Nic. The Kennedy. See it?"

"I know where it is. I do live here, English." She jerked the Miata across from the far left lane to the far right, cutting off a series of cars and setting off a chorus of horns.

"Never drive angry," she said, slowing down to a seventy mile an hour crawl for the off-ramp. English held his oh shit handle and prayed.

"Care for some music," she asked, fumbling behind her seat. "I've got a few c.d.'s somewhere back here. Pearl Jam. Stone Temple Pilots. And that other band you like so much."

English was looking at the clock in the dash. He wondered if the police had reached his apartment yet. Would they have the interstate blocked? No, not yet. There hadn't been enough time yet.

Nicole was still looking for the c.d.'s, steering with one hand, the car swerving half-way out of the lane and back because of it.

"Nicole..."

"What was that band you were always going on about? Sang this, sang that. You went to their show once."

"I don't know," English said. "Try to stay on the road. We don't need Johnny Law pulling us for reckless whatever and finding me riding shotgun on the way to the airport."

"Fine," Nicole said, abandoning her c.d. search. "It was that group from New Orleans. You know the one."

"*Better Than Ezra*. How far till the airport?"

"Half an hour, depending on the traffic. How long before they send out the Cavalry?"

English looked out the back. "I imagine the Cavalry's been sent," he said. "Five or six minutes ago, probably. They'll go to the apartment first. Then my parents' house. Then Amanda's. Won't be long before they start checking airports and bus stations. They've probably put out a call to every cop around to be on the lookout for me."

Nicole pressed the car up to ninety then slammed the brakes behind a semi plodding along at a miserable forty mph. "Oh for—" she jerked them into the stall-lane and kicked it up to seventy, then eighty.

"Dear God, Nicole," English said. "You're gonna get us killed."

"Think how simple life would be then," she said, merging with the flow of traffic again, cutting off a van behind her and eliciting a round of horns because of it.

"Open the glove box and get the fuzz-buster. I'd hate to get pulled, aiding and abetting and all."

English slid the radar over his visor and plugged it into the lighter.

"Your old man know you're here?"

"He will. He took this car to work today. I had to go to his office to get it. The Jag's in the shop getting re-upholstered. Left him mother's Mercedes in its place. Can you imagine the look on his face? He'll spend the entire drive home wondering if his roll-on has too much aluminum in it. Serves the bastard right. You should hear the tone he takes whenever he speaks to me now. Ever since my testimony, he's decided he's somehow responsible for my fall."

"I heard it was pretty juicy stuff," English said.

Nicole laughed and weaved around a row of cars at ninety-five. In several places traffic on the Kennedy was stopped completely, and Nicole simply went around it in the emergency lane.

"I suppose." She shrugged.

"It really moves, doesn't it?"

"Oh, this is nothing. Let me know if we're in a hurry and I'll turn it loose."

He checked the clock. He had fourteen minutes before the first flight took off. He looked out the back again for police and didn't see any. His hands were shaking. His stomach was turning flips inside and he felt like he was going to vomit.

"I guess this makes me an accomplice, doesn't it?" Nicole asked.

"You're the law student."

"Lovely."

"After you drop me off go back to your dad's office and try to switch the cars back. If anyone asks you about this, you don't know a thing. Trust me, Nic, you don't want to have to deal with any of this after I'm gone."

Nicole swerved into the slow lane and passed a Corvette like it was going backwards. The driver, a model-type with mirror shades and rows of kinky blond hair that blew in the breeze like a mane, looked over at Nicole and gave her the finger while laying on the horn.

Nicole laughed. "The catty little bitch," she said.

Blondie looked at Nicole and blew her a kiss, then hit the gas and left the Miata a memory.

"I've always hated blondes," Nicole said. She glanced over at English and smiled. "Except Amanda, of course."

English caught a sign, a green and white blur to the right. "Seven miles to O'Hare." The clock said he had ten minutes before he missed the first flight.

"You never answered my question. Where are you going?"

"You're right," he said. "I never did answer that."

"Yeah, I thought you'd say something like that. You tell your parents?"

"No. They don't know anything about this. The last I saw of them they thought I was on my way to jail for killing a cop. I left them a tape, though. A video I made a couple of nights ago at the apartment, explaining everything, telling them why I had to do it." He paused, staring out at Chicago, at his home since birth. It was all he'd ever known. "Telling them goodbye, mostly."

"What if they turn the tape over to the prosecution, and they introduce it as evidence? Your parents might do that to try to clear your name."

"Can they do that?"

Nicole nodded. "It'll be tougher for the jury to convict Miller in light of your testimony, and Palto would simply spin it by saying you left the tape to exonerate yourself in your parents' eyes, or as a de facto alibi for yourself, but there's no question in any case that you've damaged the prosecution immeasurably."

English considered that a moment. "I hope so," he said, "but it's not my problem anymore. I did what I could."

"And then some. You took the fall for everyone. The sins of the world. No one deserves a friend as good as you, English. Particularly Miller."

"I don't know if it'll work or not. I did everything I could. I sacrificed everything I had. And in the end, I don't have a clue if it did any good or not."

"That's not true." The airport traffic began merging right and Nicole slowed down to join it. "You'll know that you can't be bought. You'll know the police don't control you. Palto doesn't control you. No one in the entire twisted system controls you. Whatever anybody says about you after you're gone from here, you'll know that you're the kind of person that will take a stand on what he thinks is right and not give a shit about the consequences. Most people can't say that, English."

English slid the tickets back into his pocket. He grabbed the duffel bag from the floorboard and tossed it into the backseat. All he had was the cash, the tickets, and the clothes on his back.

"Lucky them," he said.

*   *   *

"There it is," Mitchum said, pointing to the large white two-story set back on a well-manicured lawn. "2719 Centralia. Think he's home?"

Callahan pulled into the driveway and left the car idling. "Tell you in a minute."

He left Mitchum in the car and walked a pebbled path through a smooth rye-grass lawn as flat and uniform as green glass. When he reached the front porch he climbed the three steps and rapped loudly on the front door. *Bam ba-bam-bam!* The knock of cops.

He stood a ways back from the door with his hands at his sides. There was a hammock to his left, and a couple of deck chairs on the right. Dual ceiling fans sat still overhead. He listened to the sounds of the neighborhood behind him—kids calling to one another, the voices of women gossiping in driveways carrying on the wind, front doors opening and shutting—and glanced across the smooth sea of green over to the house directly opposite this one. It was just as big and just as nice and probably had a hammock and deck chairs on its front porch, too. Nice life these people led.

Callahan hammered the door again, intent on making the life of at least one of these suburbanites a little worse this afternoon.

He heard footsteps from behind the door, the click-clack of heels. A woman. She opened it and looked at him curiously, probably trying to remember if she'd called for a handyman. She was holding a cordless in her right hand.

Callahan showed his identification and asked the woman her name.

"Just a minute," she said into the phone, then, to the man on her front step, "is something wrong?"

Callahan answered. "We're not sure just yet," he said. "Are you Mrs. Peterson?"

Amanda's mother nodded her head slowly, feeling a cold panic forming in her throat. She tried to remember where Amanda was. At the campus? Over at English's?... No. Today was English's day to testify in that awful trial. She'd said she was going downtown to the courthouse to wait for him.

Before she could give voice to any of her fears, Callahan said: "Do you by any chance know where your husband might be, ma'am?"

"He's not at work?"

"Afraid not, no. We were hoping you'd have an idea where we'd be able to reach him this afternoon. It's kind of important."

Julie Peterson realized then that she was still holding the phone, her divorce attorney on the other end. She glanced down at it in her hand and wondered if she should consult him before saying anything to the police about John, and then the potential of the situation occurred to her.

"Is he in some sort of trouble?" She asked, letting Blann ride it out on the phone a little longer.

"You could say that, yes."

Callahan thought the woman was surprisingly cooperative after that. "Then yes," she said. "Yes I believe I might."

*   *   *

Nicole skidded to a halt in front of the baggage check-in and was getting out of the car when English reached across and touched her arm, saying, "I better do the rest alone, Nic."

She stopped and looked at him, and English saw something change in her eyes. She looked at him hard for a full minute, looking as if she were trying to find the right thing to say.

English felt the emotion of the moment in his stomach and his eyes and wanted to nip it quick.

"Thank you, Nicole. I owe you everything. I won't easily forget you."

"Do you think, English, that in another time, another life…you and I could have…" she turned away, then looked at him.

"I'm being ridiculous," she said, touching his face.

Her smell—so subtle and wonderful he found himself wanting to taste it—surrounded her.

He smiled at her. "In another life, I would probably be very much in love with you."

English leaned across the seat and kissed her cheek. She wrapped her arms around his neck and hugged him tight, kissing his neck once.

"You'd better go. It'd be a silly thing if you made it this far only to get caught."

"Take care of yourself, Nicole."

"Will you think of me often, English?"

"Yes. I expect I will."

"Then go. Go now and go fast. Don't stop until you get where you're going, and when you do, remember why you're there. You're one of the good ones, English, and you deserve all the happiness you get."

English slid out of the car and closed the door behind him without looking back. He walked with a crowd of travelers through the electric double-doors and into the baggage check-in. He quickly passed the various airline and rental car counters, into an enormous waiting area with assorted shops situated side by side along the perimeter. Bookstores, gift shops, video-game arcades, restaurants and bars, shoe-shine booths. English passed all of these until he came to the mouth of a large tunnel that led to Concourse A. People were milling in and out of the tunnel like cattle, suitcases and children in tow, jockeying for position on the electric floor.

English stopped at the entrance of this tunnel and checked his watch. Three minutes before the first flight took off. Twelve until the second one.

He was scanning the crowd, bouncing from man to woman to child and back to man again when he found her, over there, across the way, coming out of a ladies restroom about two hundred feet away, a suitcase in one hand and the two duffel bags hanging from her shoulders. She had made it.

English looked at her over the crowds of people pushing and milling all directions, and he felt his face flush and his heart pick up. Her blonde hair was brushed to one side and pulled in front of her shoulder. He saw her as she checked her watch and looked into the crowds of people for him, and English Mason allowed himself for the first time to believe that everything was going to be all right.

She didn't see him, not yet, but she knew where to go, and was halfway there when she saw him waving at her.

When she hit him it was full speed and she almost knocked him down.

"Passports?" English managed between kisses.

"In my purse."

They kissed again.

"Perfect," one of them said.

* * *

As she left the airport, swerving the Miata in and out of traffic on her way back to her father's office, Nicole thought about what English had said—about their being in love in another life—and supposed that the world was probably *filled* with other lives, filled with Englishes for that matter, and all she had to do to find one suitable was look in the right places.

She wondered why it had taken her twenty-four years to figure that out.

As she steered up the on-ramp and merged with the interstate traffic, she reached into her purse and removed her vial of coke. She held it to the light for a moment, thumped it a time or two with her fingernail, watched the white powder settle a bit, then rolled down her window and tossed it to the highway.

*   *   *

Fifty-eight minutes after pulling out of the driveway of 2719 Centralia Avenue, Detectives Callahan and Mitchum were standing outside the slate gray door of Patricia Simylton's apartment. Callahan bammed on the door, heard a man behind it say "one moment. I'm dressing," and waited with his partner until a woman opened the door.

"Patricia Simylton?"

The look on the woman's face did more for Callahan than anything she could have said to him. What was more than likely a prettier than average face most of the time was drained of color. Her eyes were wide and vacant, her neck red and splotchy, and she was breathing heavier than she should have been.

That look said it all for Callahan. It said their man was either there or he had been. It said Patricia Simylton knew something was wrong and wrong bad.

"Yes?"

She was standing in the doorway, the door cracked open about a foot. Callahan could see a hallway over her shoulder, and the end of a dark blue couch.

His voice was low and steady. All business. "He's here. We saw his car out front. Let us in."

Then a man's voice from behind the door. "It's all right, Patricia. You may let them in."

She backed up and let the two detectives in. Callahan looked at the gentleman standing in the middle of the living room in a suit, his tie hanging loosely around an expensive white shirt, the shock of silver hair on his head disheveled. He was breathing heavy, and holding a glass of something yellow over ice.

"I'd like to know how," the man said. "How you found us out."

Callahan stepped forward, removing his handcuffs from his coat pocket. "John Peterson, you are under arrest for conspiracy to commit fraud, for wire-fraud, for international money laundering, and for violation of multiple federal and state election laws." Mitchum had moved in too, letting Peterson feel his presence.

"No need for those, gentlemen. I have no intention of causing a scene." Callahan ignored him and began cuffing his wrists. "You have the right to remain silent…"

"May I at least use the restroom first? I've had quite a few of these." He raised his scotch glass in the air and jiggled the ice cubes.

"There really isn't much in the world as pleasing to the palate as a good single malt," he said, staring wistfully into the glass, then glancing over at Patricia. "Save perhaps a well-bred woman."

Callahan looked at John Peterson and then over at Patricia.

"Yeah, you can take a piss," Callahan said, taking the cuffs off his wrist. "Make it a quick one."

Peterson turned towards the hall then stopped. He looked over his shoulder at the detectives for a second, his eyes swimming in scotch.

"How, gentlemen?"

"How what?" Callahan said. "How'd we dig you up? Anonymous tip."

Peterson looked confused. "Anonymous?"

Mitchum nodded. "A six page letter. Mentioned you and Mr. J. Fullard Wallace quite a few times. Explained the entire scheme. Complete with account numbers and deposit histories. Very detailed. Very explicit. Someone doesn't like you very much."

"Nonsense. With the exception of perhaps my daughter's boyfriend, everyone likes me."

Neither Callahan nor Mitchum said anything, and Callahan hid almost all of his smile.

Peterson's face went cold.

"The meddling little bastard," he finally said.

He stood there momentarily, hitched as though he were going to say something, then shrugged and turned to walk down the hallway. Callahan watched him go, looking at the back of his silvery head as he walked.

The bathroom was at the very end of the hall, straight ahead. Callahan saw the other door up there on the right, the bedroom, no doubt, and saw it coming before it happened but was still a second too late.

Instead of stepping into the bathroom Peterson dodged to his right and slammed the bedroom door behind him.

Mitchum and Callahan were half-way down the hall when the shot rang out and Patricia screamed, and a sound like a bag of potatoes hit the ground with a thud behind the door.

Chapter 33

The Days After

He was sitting in the corner of the little community library, in his same orange plastic chair, holding the same little mouse in the cup of his right hand. He'd been to this library a thousand times over the years. The smells emanating from the ancient book stacks were pleasantly familiar, and the blessed silence throughout the library was as comforting as a blanket on a Chicago winter's night.

It was some time—almost eight months later—before things had calmed to the point where Miller felt he could safely access Wallace's money and do anything with it. The media ran stories on the trial for weeks after English and Amanda vanished, calling his escape brash, clever, shocking, portraying Miller first as a manipulative, even malevolent influence in his roommate's life. Then, as time passed, a conspirator, and finally, as days became weeks and weeks months, simply another individual in the life of English Mason, the college student who— almost—confessed to murder in open court before scaling the building and disappearing—apparently forever—taking his girlfriend with him.

Miller slipped a diskette into the computer's A drive and clicked "run." When the listing of the disk's files appeared on the screen—term papers mostly: *The Evolving Role of the Secretary of State in a Post-Cold War Community; Gore's Reinvention of the Office of the Vice-Presidency;* one titled "Law School Personal Statements," and another listed as, simply, "Kenilworth"—Miller clicked and waited.

Ten seconds later and a spreadsheet of sorts unfolded before him on the screen, completely blank save for item number one. The Grand Cayman International Bank was listed as having an account—number S090387ZA-25—registered to a male, height of 5'11", brown hair, brown eyes, weighing approximately 175 pounds, with a balance of $4,250,000.00 At the top of the spreadsheet Miller had inserted, shortly after opening the account, a hyperlink to the web address of The Grand Cayman International Bank. Now he clicked on it, and waited.

While the computer made the connection, Miller considered his options. He wasn't sure exactly what it was he would do with the money—there was no emergency now, no dire need to have it, English's little stunt having worked, give or take, as nicely as he could have hoped. The deft Williams had moved successfully for a mistrial the day the court's recess—ordered into effect until the authorities located the missing English Mason, rescinded two weeks later upon their failure to do so—ended, and life slowly returned to normal for Miller Dispenberg. He finished the semester out—graduating near the top of his class, though not as high as he would have liked, the ordeal of the trial having taken its toll and assisted Miller in delivering two A's and three B's, this not as bad as it would seem, Yale Law having accepted him, a vindicated man, back in mid-march—and occupied himself through the summer with his physical therapy. They had—five months ago—removed the wires from his jaw and fitted him with a bridge for the teeth he'd swallowed. That was back in February, and he'd regained most all of the weight the liquid diet had taken off of him. He'd also recovered some of the vision in his right eye—he could see shapes well enough, provided there was ample lighting—and the doctors seemed to think there was a chance for still more, though modest, improvement. He limped a bit, and probably always would, but the pain in his lower back and shoulder had begun to ease, and was becoming more manageable every day. He'd begun seeing a chiropractor a few weeks ago, and once every three weeks he drove himself to an herbal spa for a ninety minute back massage

Tracie had broken things off, something which bothered Miller more than he would have thought. They'd made it through the immediate aftermath of the trial, and had had plans to spend New Year's together, but she'd called him up abruptly the afternoon of the 31st and explained in measured voice to his answering machine that neither she nor her family thought it was a good idea for them to continue seeing one another. Miller had since heard from someone he couldn't remember that she'd gotten engaged to, ironically enough, a third year law student at Chicago.

He spent much of his time alone that summer, unable to shake the feeling that he had, quite unwillingly, forever ended a permanent period in his life prematurely. English was gone. Tracie was gone; not as far, but gone all the same. And for months afterwards, when he walked into a grocery store or a bank or the McDonalds near his place, people stared and whispered and tried to subtly avoid him, though this too, like the physical pain, was finally beginning to subside.

His legal bills had run just under forty grand, and Miller thought it'd be appropriate for Wallace's money to take care of that. No reason his father should have to. Aside from that, though, he wasn't sure what he'd do with the money.

He'd been doing some reading in a few of the finance books that English had left behind—he'd left everything behind, it seemed, save his girlfriend; Mr. and Mrs. Mason coming by and picking up his stuff the week after the trial, leaving Miller alone in their apartment, only English's smells left behind as a semblance of the past—and was thinking about investing a portion of it. It was out there, just sitting. No reason he shouldn't make it grow, get his piece of the Great Global Economy everyone was cooing about these days.

He had noticed, reading through English's textbooks, that several of the passages that dealt with the electronic transferal of funds and offshore accounts were already underlined. A great many of the passages, in fact.

Miller had smiled when he discovered this, for it meant that Amanda's little gambit had worked. She'd been right; English was riding the edge and losing his balance fast. He was looking for a way out, nearly any way at all. Amanda had looked into her boyfriend's eyes and seen the desperation and determination, and she'd no doubt pushed—softly and subtly, to be sure, but pushing just the same—him in the only direction he hadn't thought to look himself. To the brass ring of the whole Wallace affair. To the hard-drive, and the money on it.

When the connection to the Caymans was made, Miller entered his account number, then his password, then his pin, and directed the Cayman bank to wire forty thousand dollars into his father's checking account, the routing number to which he'd acquired from his father's checkbook several weeks ago. He then directed another ten thousand dollars into his own student-checking account at First Chicago, figuring a little extra on-hand cash would be a good idea. You never knew.

He then logged out of the account and off the net, and enlarged his spreadsheet again. He typed two new entries in lines 2 and 3, and recorded the transaction. His 4,250,000.00 was now 4,200,000.00

He saved the data, removed the disk, and slipped it into his shirt pocket.

He then reentered the hard-drive through the "my computer" icon, and began his search. He didn't know exactly what it was he was looking for, only that it was there, and he'd likely know it once he found it.

He typed in his search parameters. Created between October 1 and December 8 of last year.

A minute later and there it was. A tiny little file, created on November 10 of last year. English had labeled it "OFC."

Miller chuckled. Outta Fuckin Control. That pretty well summed up the entire Wallace incident, didn't it?

Hard to believe, Miller thought as he opened the file, English could know for so long and still go through with it.

And now, as he sat in the little community library, in his same orange chair, holding the same little mouse in the cup of his right hand, Miller was staring at English's note displayed on the screen.

Miller,

As you and the rest of Chicago clearly know by now, I'm gone, and have every intention of remaining that way. Don't try to find me because you can't, and I don't want to be found. Since you're reading this, you obviously aren't in jail, and because I'm gone I never have to consider the possibility that my plan didn't work. By the time you read this, I suspect I'll be rather detached from Chicago and her trimmings.

I kept the guns that day in Kenilworth; went out and buried them—covered in my prints—that night after we took the OFC under the bridge. I wrestled more than I could ever tell you with how to play all this, and I came almost simultaneously to two startling and equally troubling conclusions about myself.

The first was that despite it all, I do on some level love you. I love the friendship we forged through the awkward and mysterious years of youth and adolescence. I love the solidity with which I knew you would always be there for me, regardless of the circumstance. It is because of this love that I came to realize that I would do nearly anything it took to prevent your going to jail for what we did that day in Kenilworth.

But the second was, just as plainly, that I would do whatever it took to protect and keep Amanda, even if it meant sending you to jail for what we did that day in Kenilworth. I tried—dear God I tried—to find a way to protect you both, but I made certain that if someone was cheated, it would not be her.

Which brings us to the money. It's gone, as I'm sure you've discovered by now. I found it (ironically enough, it was Amanda who gave me the idea to look; I'd been so wrapped up in horror and self-pity that it hadn't even occurred to me). If things work out the way I hope, we'll spend the rest of our lives spending it. It's nice, but it can't replace the things I've lost. I'll never walk the stage at Chicago, land that first job, or eat another Sunday dinner with my parents. I doubt

I will ever sleep the sleep of the innocent and worry-free again. I expect my nights will be forever filled with fears of shadows and approaching sounds. The money can't change any of that. It will simply get us where we're going and keep us there comfortably. The rest we'll have to take as it comes.

You were right that day on the courts—there is always a back door. Rightly or wrongly, I found mine. I think I've found yours, too. I'm not sure, but I think so, and when it comes round to my turn—when the spotlight's on me and my words have their most weight, when Palto puts me on the stand and starts pulling his truths from me—I'm going to be trying awfully hard to carry you through it.

I hope you're able find peace on the other side, Miller.

Until you do, have a beer and think of me now and again. Have many beers and try to forget all this ever happened. Not much of it was good.

—English

P.S. You may have, somewhere down the line, the desire to look me up. Don't. I did what I did for the sake of our past, and in search of closure to that past. But my future is my own now. And if, by some unfortunate happenstance, my path should happen to cross yours in that future, I won't even know you.

Sitting in the corner of the little community library, in his same orange plastic chair, holding the same little mouse in the cup of his right hand, Miller wept.

Epilogue

Time moves slowly in the absence of structure or schedule. Without parameters—without appointments or classes or even watches and clocks—there's little notice of the minutes and hours at all. In the absence of structure or schedule, time begins to lose its significance, its linear qualities, and assumes the properties of elastic.

Or so it is for the two of them, as they walk alongside one another barefoot over the sand, their hands melted into one another's like clouds on the horizon. The sun is high this time of day, and it hammers down through the thick, damp air, its heat an almost physical weight upon their skin.

But the nights here are cool and temperate, and they are learning to adjust to the days. It's been over four months since they've stopped running, since the last time they checked over their shoulder and noticed a man staring too long or following too closely. They'd been in France the last time, where they'd considered staying, but she'd seen a commercial in a Paris hotel for suntan oil, and that evening they'd decided over glazed duck and champagne to move again.

But they'd been here for over four months now, and each of them felt that the other was comfortable enough to stay this time. She hoped so, but she'd hoped the same months back, in Playa del Carmen.

It was there that Miller had joined them, as she had always known he would somehow. Even as they left, as far back as their first night as fugitives, she'd known that somehow, in some way, they'd be forced to deal with him again.

The first night after they'd left they crossed the Mexican Border in a car they'd rented with cash, driving two hundred miles on a Southeastern course roughly towards Cozumel. From there they'd ridden the trains for three days straight, coming out of their cabin only at night, wearing a different change of clothes each time. He'd grown a beard. She'd cut her hair off at the shoulders and dyed the rest of it brown. They spoke to no one during those days, a little to one another. He suspected she might be regretting her decision to come with him. She worried about his health.

In their Playa del Carmen motel on the evening of their fourth night, she'd unpacked their bags while he slept. They'd spent upwards of eighteen hours at a time lying in bed in their train cabin over the previous three days and nights, but he hadn't slept much. So in the Mexican motel he finally succumbed to sleep, and she quietly busied herself with their bags.

She'd found the note in the bottom of his suitcase, and had almost cried out. It had been folded tightly into a little square, much like they'd done as kids in elementary school, and wedged into a corner. The word "English" was scribbled carelessly across it in black ink.

She hadn't read it immediately, feeling somehow that it wasn't her place. She'd considered destroying it, taking it into the bathroom with her, then shredding it into tiny, unread bits before flushing it all down a Mexican toilet.

She considered it a long while; it would be right for it to end that way. It would be right and just and more than appropriate. The note—whatever it might say, whatever secrets it might reveal—had no place with them now. Not here. Not after all they'd been through to get here. She'd be doing them both a favor by destroying it.

But she hadn't destroyed it. She owed him more than that, particularly now. She'd drawn a hot bath instead, and spent the next hour crying in it.

He'd awakened some time later, and she'd given him the note. He'd taken it with a shaking hand and read it, aloud, slowly, just once.

English,

I had a hunch it might go this way. If you're reading this, then you've cut and run. I can't blame you; as of this writing I'm considering the same course, though I'm reluctant for obvious reasons. But the only thing worse than being a fugitive is being a convict. Neither looks great on resumes.

I thought about what you said on the courts that day, about God and His role in our lives. I thought about it a great deal. I remembered something you said about it; how Amanda believes He's real and present and plays an active role in our lives.

And I wanted to believe that, English. I wanted quite badly to believe it. And I wanted Him on my side.

So I prayed, English. I prayed to God and he answered me with an angel. When I look back on it now it seems like a dream, one of those dreams you wake up from and swear was real. It happened only once (it seems only my nightmares are recurring these days) but once was enough.

In my dream—dream or reality, it doesn't matter much now, as the moment has passed and exists only as memory—this angel comes to me, glowing a pure and delicate gold, and English…she takes me by the hand and she tells me not to worry, that she'll take care of things, that hers is the role of protector. She tells me in a voice made of music that she has a way out of all this. And I started crying—I swear to God I started crying, just like I was a little boy again, but she took me and she held me and she touched her mouth to mine, and she kissed my tears into moonlight.

And my body, English…Dear God but my body caught fire beneath her touch and her kiss, and for those moments everything was all right again…But there was a price, English. There's always a price for redemption and absolution, even when it comes from an angel.

So I agreed. I moved some of the money—over two million dollars, nearly a third of what it took Wallace untold years to quietly acquire—out of Wallace's account and onto my little computer in my little corner of the little library in the hopes that you might find it, in the hopes that you might help her—my angel, if only for the night, if only for those few precious hours—help me.

I did it for me, English. It was selfish and mean and unequivocally necessary. There's no disputing that. But I also did it for you. Because if it works, well, I think you'll likely have most everything you ever wanted, which isn't too bad a trade, is it?

As time passes, try to remember that…that I also did it for you—and your angel.

—Mill

They hadn't discussed it at all afterwards. She'd tried to explain and, in failing, to apologize, but he'd touched his finger to her lips to silence her. They'd made love through the tears that night, and they hadn't discussed the note at all.

Two days later they left Mexico for Argentina, where they stayed for several weeks before deciding Europe was better. Europe or Barbados. She liked the sound of Europe. He liked the banking laws in Barbados. They'd settled on Europe, and agreed to leave Barbados a possibility. But she'd seen the suntan commercial and they'd left the following night, and now they were here, at the place they had already begun calling "our beach," and each of them understood that here they—the two of them, and the child growing within her—would most likely stay.

One day he would ask her, perhaps, what occurred during those days before the end, and what part she might have played in things. One day he would ask her why she'd encouraged him to check Wallace's hard-drive, how she could have known what it appeared she'd known. But not now. Not now.

Now they were here, where the sand was white and the blue of the water was so blue it hurt your eyes, and at night she would hold him, and he'd place his hands on her stomach and feel their baby kick, and with her whisper and kiss she'd turn his tears into moonlight.

And here it was enough.

About the Author

Wade Tabor lives with his wife and cats in Charleston, South Carolina, where he teaches English at Fort Dorchester High School.

He is currently at work on his next novel.